# The Guernsey Girls Go to War

Mary Wood was born in Maidstone, Kent, and brought up in Claybrooke, Leicestershire. Born one of fifteen children to a middle-class mother and an East End barrow boy, Mary's family were poor but rich in love. This encouraged her to develop a natural empathy with the less fortunate and a fascination with social history. In 1989 Mary was inspired to pen her first novel and she is now a full-time novelist.

Mary welcomes interaction with readers and invites you to subscribe to her website where you can contact her, receive regular newsletters and follow links to meet her on Facebook and Twitter: www.authormarywood.com

# The Guernsey Girls Go to War

## Mary Wood

PAN BOOKS

First published 2024 by Pan Books
an imprint of Pan Macmillan
The Smithson, 6 Briset Street, London EC1M 5NR
*EU representative:* Macmillan Publishers Ireland Ltd, 1st Floor,
The Liffey Trust Centre, 117–126 Sheriff Street Upper,
Dublin 1, D01 YC43
Associated companies throughout the world
www.panmacmillan.com

ISBN 978-1-5290-8977-6

1 3 5 7 9 8 6 4 2

A CIP catalogue record for this book is available from the British Library.

Typeset by Palimpsest Book Production Ltd, Falkirk, Stirlingshire
Printed and bound by CPI Group (UK) Ltd, Croydon, CR0 4YY

Visit **www.panmacmillan.com** to read more about all our books
and to buy them. You will also find features, author interviews and
news of any author events, and you can sign up for e-newsletters
so that you're always first to hear about our new releases.

With thanks to a superb editor, who became a dear friend. Wayne Brookes, your faith in me never wavered – you're simply the best.

# PART ONE

Love Will Find a Way

# Chapter One

## Olivia

Guernsey, January 1940

Olivia couldn't focus on her work in her father's bank on the island of Guernsey. War threatening the safety of her loved ones weighed heavily on her mind.

She was never cut out for this type of work anyway, but so many of the bank's employees – mainly men – had gone to war, a war that had separated her from her beloved Hendrick.

She put down her pen and gazed over at his portrait.

Hendrick's beautiful face smiled down on her, making her heart race, his eyes seeming to follow her wherever she went around this small office that used to be his. *Will I ever again feel your gaze on me for real? Will your arms once more encircle me and hold me close?*

She closed her eyes. A shudder trembled through her body as fear of Hendrick's position gripped her.

German by birth, though brought up in St Peter Port, Hendrick had been forced by the threat of death hanging over his dissident father to join Hitler's government. A linguist, he now worked as an interpreter in the German civil service even though he hated the Nazi regime and all it stood for. This had led to him devising a way he

3

could pass information to Olivia that might help the British in their war with Germany. A war that had seemed phoney, but now with her knowledge of troops digging in on the borders of Saarland in readiness for an attempt to halt Hitler's advance into France, the reality of it had hit home.

What if the Germans took France? Normandy was so close to Guernsey. Would they come here?

The telephone ringing interrupted Olivia's thoughts, and as if she'd conjured him up, Hendrick's voice came down the line. 'Hello . . . Olivia?'

'Hendrick! Oh, my darling, I was thinking of you.'

'And I you, my dearest.'

As always, after their initial greeting, she began with a simple everyday phrase to discover if it was safe to talk without using code. 'How are you today, my love?'

'I am well.'

Olivia breathed a sigh of relief. If his answer had been, 'I am quite well,' she would have had to take notes to decipher later as Hendrick would reveal something she was to pass on to the British government through her dearest friend, Annie, who lived in the East End of London.

If either of them wanted to switch to code later, they would make a reference to Rupert, an old toy bear she had.

But this time, Hendrick completely surprised her by saying, 'I've been thinking that your language skills will be waning without practice, darling, so I'm going to speak in Italian this time, maybe French next time, and I might even use Japanese in a few weeks, but will give you time to brush up on that first.'

Olivia relaxed, as her Italian was excellent.

'Firstly, my darling, as you may have guessed, I'm at Mr Meyer's, not at work.'

Following his example, she answered in Italian. 'Yes, oh, it's so good to hear you, but are you really safe? I feel afraid of the circumstances there.'

'Don't worry. Still nothing is known.'

This, Olivia knew, referred to Mrs Meyer's Jewish ancestors. Hendrick had probably said it this way thinking she may stumble on the Italian word for Jewish, which she would have done as it wasn't a word used often until now. But her relief at hearing Mrs Meyer still wasn't under suspicion was tempered with trepidation over what might happen in the future. Hendrick had told of how the Jews were looked upon and treated by Hitler's regime. What if they ever found out about Mr Meyer's wife, and of Hendrick's friendship with them?

Trying not to show her fears in her voice, she lightened her tone. 'That's good. So, begin by telling me if you really are all right, my darling.'

'I am, but . . . Oh, Olivia, I am missing you so much.'

The tears that had trickled at first now flooded Olivia's face as he spoke the words she'd so longed to hear. 'I must see you, darling, and I have a plan.'

'Oh, Hendrick, can it be possible? Can we really find a way?'

'I believe so. I still have my passport stating I am a Guernsey citizen.'

Olivia held her breath, the fingers on her free hand clenching as she waited.

'I know I won't be welcome back in Guernsey, but what about the island of Sark? Doesn't Daphne have relatives there?'

'Yes, but . . .'

'Do you think she would help you, or is she of the same mind as most of the islanders that I am some kind of traitor?'

5

'She has never suggested anything like that, nor have any of my father's household staff, though a lot here do make snide remarks to me showing how angry they are that you're working for Hitler's regime.'

'Well, I don't blame them. It does look bad, but it is the only way I can keep my father safe. He . . . Well, he goes through all the right motions of seeming to be a reformed character and appearing to toe the Hitler line, but he still works away in the background. He, Mr Meyer and a friend of my father's, who lives on the Swiss border, are still helping Jews to escape. I fear every day that they will be caught.'

Olivia's nails dug further into the palms of her hands. 'While I admire him . . . oh, Hendrick, I fear for him and for you.'

'I do too, and yet I will never stop him, and will even help him if I can. Something has to be done! The Jews need help.'

He paused, then changed the subject. 'But we must talk about my plan before we lose the connection, Olivia. I am going to take a trip to Switzerland soon. I have put in for a period of leave and been granted it for next week. Then, using my Guernsey passport, I will drive through to France and charter a boat from there. If the British stop me, my passport will keep me safe. And if the Germans do, I will use my German papers and my leave of absence ticket. It's perfect, darling. You, me and our darling son can spend at least four days together.'

'Oh, Hendrick. Are you sure it's safe?'

'Let's just do it, my darling. I love you and want to hold you.'

'I love you too . . . And yes, I will put everything in motion. I was about to go home now anyway. Try to ring me again so we can finalize everything.'

'I will my love, I'll . . .'

The line crackled and then went dead. Olivia sat back; it was as if a whirlwind had struck her. It took her a moment to let what had just happened sink in. *My God! Hendrick is coming! I'm going to be in his arms!*

This was something that hadn't happened for months!

Wiping her eyes, she gathered everything on her desk and quickly put any private papers away in the filing cabinet before locking it, picking up her bag, and unhooking her coat from the stand in the corner. She was out of her office and running down the corridor to her father's office in a flash.

'Daddy, may I come in?'

'It looks to me that you are in! Is something wrong, my dear?'

Closing the door behind her, she looked at her father and beamed. 'No, everything couldn't be more right.'

As she blurted out her and Hendrick's plan, her father frowned, then cupped his chin with his forefinger and thumb and slid them as if he was stroking an imaginary beard. 'Olivia, my dear, it all sounds very dangerous.'

'I will be fine, no harm can come to me, and no one on the island need know the real reason why I am going to Sark . . . That is, if Daphne will cover me by allowing me to use something to do with her family as an excuse.'

'Olivia . . . Olivia, you get more like your dear mother every day! Impetuous, and with a way of thinking that nothing is impossible.'

Olivia laughed as she looked at the framed photo of her beautiful mother sitting on her father's desk. Having never met her as she'd died at her birth, it seemed she'd always known her as her father had kept her memory alive. And she saw her mother's face in her own reflection every time she looked into the mirror as they were like twins in their looks.

The same dark, glossy hair worn shoulder-length and huge dark eyes. And her father had told her that her mother had been tall like herself.

As she looked back at her father, she understood his concern. Having not married until in his forties, he was now sixty-seven and had experienced the horrors of war. A kind and thoughtful being, well loved by all, he'd fought in the Great War.

'You're not going to put obstacles in my way, are you, Daddy?'

His half-smile showed the sense of humour he could bring to any situation. 'Would there be any point? But no, I can't deny you and Hendrick this . . . If Daphne is willing, she could go with you, we can manage fine at the house. Maybe she could say that she needs to see her cousins and is taking you and Karl with her for a break?'

'Yes, that would work . . . I shouldn't need a reason to travel, but everyone seems so suspicious of me, and I don't blame them. It isn't easy for them to accept that Hendrick, who they thought of as one of them, seemed to go willingly to join the regime in Germany.'

'That could be so very dangerous for Hendrick.'

Brushing this away, not wanting to have any further scary thoughts, Olivia blew her father a kiss. 'Must dash, there is so little time to make arrangements.'

Once home – a three-storey house, four with the cellar space, that stood on the shore of St Peter Port – Olivia sought Daphne out without making any fuss about needing to speak to her.

A local young woman, in her mid-twenties as Olivia was, their lives couldn't be more different, and yet they had always got on well together.

With fingers crossed, she entered the dining room where she guessed she would find Daphne, this being the time she laid the table for the evening meal.

'Miss Olivia! What are you doing home so early?'

'I need to talk to you, Daphne.'

Daphne's eyes widened as she listened.

'I – I . . . well . . .'

Her hesitation struck a fear into Olivia that her plan wouldn't work. 'Please, Daphne, I beg of you. Hendrick cannot come openly. He doesn't have permission to come onto British soil and besides, everyone here would hound him out.'

'But he's a German . . . our enemy, miss . . . Oh, I don't know . . . how can he be that? He's our own Hendrick! I've known him all me life . . . Yes, I'll do it. I'll do it for you, Miss Olivia. And oh, I'd love to see me cousins. I haven't seen them in months and Petra has a new baby too!'

'Thank you so much. Once in Sark, do you know of anywhere we could stay?'

'Yes, Stocks Hotel. It's owned by the Falle family. They keep a nice place and it's only up the road from me family's farm.'

'That sounds ideal. Thanks, Daphne.'

'Well, you make all the arrangements, miss, and I'll put it about that I have leave and I'm off to see family . . . though how I'll appease me mum who'll want to come with me, I don't know.'

'I'm sorry, Daphne, but that can't happen . . . You see, Hendrick shouldn't come onto British soil and could be arrested and imprisoned . . . I – I know it's asking a lot of you . . .'

'Oh? Well, yes, he is the enemy, like I said, and could be thought of as up to no good . . . But I know Hendrick.

9

I know for him to be doing what he is, he must have been left with no choice. Our lads won't have any either, poor things.'

'That's exactly it. So, you can see why I don't want the islanders to know of this visit, or that he has been. I'm desperately trying to think of ways of stopping Karl telling folk when he gets back that he's been with his daddy, but I can't not take him, that would break Hendrick's heart.'

'Hmm, that's a dilemma. I've never met a chatterbox like Karl, even if it is one word at a time! From the moment he could talk, and that was early for most kids, he's never stopped, unless he's asleep as he is now. His nanny's often glad of a break when he nods off.'

'Poor Loes. But she loves Karl with all her heart, so that gives me peace of mind.'

'She does, miss, as we all do. He's adorable.'

Puffed up with pride, Olivia grinned. No one adored her son more than she did, and she couldn't wait to see him and his daddy together again, if only for a short time. And what would it really matter if he did tell everyone he'd seen his daddy? By that time, Hendrick would be well on his way back to Germany and safe from any fallout from his visit.

Five days later, Olivia stood on the edge of the road that looked over the harbour of the beautiful island of Sark, just a short distance from Guernsey and yet seeming to be a different world. Here the pace was slow, and with the main industry being farming, there were no cars, only tractors and bicycles.

Pulling her coat around her against the sting of the bitter wind and hugging Karl to her, she looked out to sea. On the horizon a boat approached. Her heart thudded her anticipation around her body. *Oh, Hendrick, my darling Hendrick*.

'Daddy's coming! Look, Karl!'

'Daddy?'

'Yes, your daddy. The one whose photo you kiss every night and tell him you love him? That daddy.'

'Daddy in boat!'

His little hand pointed out to sea. The fringe of his too-long blond hair, poking out of his bonnet, blew into a peak. Olivia giggled. 'Yes . . . Oh, Karl, he's nearly here . . . Wave, Karl. Wave to your daddy.'

And then it happened. The boat docked, and Hendrick disembarked and ran up the steps of the harbour, around and past the tunnel and down the slope towards her with his arms open, and his face wet with tears.

Her feet lifted off the ground with his hug. He twirled her, lifting her high above him. Her beautiful world spun around her. She gazed into the face she loved with all that she was. When he lowered her, she clung to him, wanted to touch every part of him to know this was real. Cupping his face with her hands, she knew the intensity of his love as his tear-filled eyes looked into hers.

'Daddy?'

Hendrick bent and scooped Karl up. 'Yes, I'm your daddy, my son. May I have a hug?'

To see the two most important people in her life clinging on to one another, and then to hear Karl say, 'Love Daddy. Kiss picture,' completed Olivia's world.

Holding hands, they fought against the wind to reach the horse and cart waiting for them.

'I booked us into Stocks Hotel, darling, but they have a burst pipe, so we have moved into Daphne's aunt's old home that the family keeps ready for visitors. Daphne was using it, but she has moved out to sleep in her cousin's farmhouse instead.'

11

'I don't mind where we stay, darling, as long as we're together.'

Olivia smiled up at him. Her heart had been full of trepidation when she'd moved her and Karl into the croft this morning, as Daphne had apologized profusely for the state of it, saying it only had one room with a bed that could be partitioned off by a curtain and a lean-to with two beds that her uncle had built for his daughters. The toilet was outside and was one that had to be emptied. Daphne had said it had been done and she wasn't to worry about it. Her trepidation had left her when she and Karl had arrived at the croft for as soon as she saw it – a small, one-storey building standing on the edge of the road, prettily declaring itself their home for the next few days as its white walls gleamed in the low winter sun – she loved it.

Seeming to be weighed down by its overhanging roof, the croft had fresh pink gingham curtains hanging at its only window and brambles that promised the flowering of wild roses creeping along its walls. To Olivia, it was a little place of heaven.

'Is this it? It's lovely and that smoke curling from the chimney is a welcome sight. I haven't been warm since I left home . . . I mean, the apartment that I exist in! Oh, Olivia, my dearest, I wish we could stay here for ever!'

She tightened her grip on his hand and swallowed hard. So many tears to shed. Tears she let flow every night in the privacy of her bedroom. But they were sad tears. Now happy tears blurred her vision.

Inside, the fire she'd lit earlier with Daphne's help roared up the chimney and its heaven-sent warmth set about tackling their chilled bodies.

Cosy, and nice-shabby rather than dilapidated, this one main room was furnished with a huge sofa draped with a freshly laundered, beige, loose cover patterned with pink roses. A faded and patchy rose-coloured rug and a table and chairs that shone with many layers of polish were the only other furniture.

A pot sink stood in one corner, and next to that a dresser with white practical china displayed on its shelves. On the other side of this, a door stood ajar showing that it was a larder with shelves and a cold slab for meats and milk.

The fire served as a cooker too, having a warming oven and a hot oven as well as a grate plate that swung over the flames. On this a kettle bubbled away, its lid rattling a greeting.

'I'll make tea. I have it all ready for us.'

This wasn't what Olivia wanted to do. She wanted to be in Hendrick's arms and have him kiss her from the top of her head to the soles of her feet. She caught her breath as this thought zinged a feeling through her that was familiar, longed for, and yet almost a distant memory.

Hendrick's hand clasped hers, staying her progress. His eyes told her he was experiencing the same longings.

She smiled at him and whispered, 'Soon, my love, soon.'

As they sipped their tea Karl played happily with a box of wooden bricks. Those and the wooden train engine were the only toys she'd brought with her for him.

'Darling, I want to talk to you about things that are happening and not all of them are being reported. The situation with the Jews, for one, but they aren't the only ones being persecuted.' Hendrick dropped his head. When he looked up his expression showed his despair. 'They . . . Oh, Olivia, it's anyone who's different. I – I've seen soldiers hitting crippled people . . . and I was asked to translate a document condemning gypsies, and then there's anyone who is homosexual . . . There are camps . . . Extermination is happening . . . They are killing men, women and children because of their creed, sexuality, lack of ability or for being what they describe as vagabonds. It's unbearable . . . These are meant to be my people!'

'Oh, Hendrick! You're not to blame . . . It's all horrific . . . Do you have any involvement . . . I mean, do they directly involve you?'

'In translations of their orders, yes. They're inhuman.'

'But you aren't, and neither is your father. He is who you come from, not these Nazis.'

'Yes, and I have to help him. I can't physically help him, but I can give him information that allows him to make decisions on where to target his help.'

'I'm glad, but so afraid. You're in such danger, my darling, I can't bear it.'

His hand reached out to her. 'We all are. The whole world. Hitler won't stop. I fear that the effort Britain and France are putting in won't be enough to stop him. He is prepared, they are not. They don't have enough to throw at his might.'

'Hendrick, let's forget it all for the few days we have. We can't change anything, but we can make the most of the little time we have together.'

'Yes, you're right, my darling. I so want to hold you.'

Realizing how quiet Karl was, Olivia looked over to where he was playing then smiled. He was fast asleep leaning forward on his knees with his bottom in the air.

Hendrick had looked too, but turned towards her now. They swayed towards each other. His arms encircled her.

Shifting along the sofa to get even closer to her, his lips found hers and she was lost in a world so beautiful, she gave her body free rein to accept, to give and to be fulfilled.

14

It didn't matter that they had to suppress their urge to call out, to release their joy of what they felt in guttural sounds – making love silently was just as pleasurable and all they wanted from each other.

When at last it ended with feelings Olivia knew so well, although she had forgotten their intensity, they clung together, sobbing at their knowledge of having to part again very soon.

Lifting her chin and looking into her eyes, Hendrick said, 'My darling, remember this day for ever. Remember everything about it, even our tears, our anxieties, and our despair at knowing it cannot last for us. For this is a day in our lives that we stole together – an oasis amid all the horror.'

'I will, Hendrick. It's etched on my mind. And I shall think to myself that if we did it once, we can do it again, so this won't be the last time we're together until there is peace.'

Hendrick didn't answer this. He just kissed her hair and then the tip of her nose. 'I love you, my darling. So much that it hurts.'

His body trembled. Olivia clung on to him. Life seemed so unfair. *Please God, let all of this go away. I want my Hendrick back. I want our lives back.*

# Chapter Two

## Annie

The canteen buzzed with police officers, gathered for the latest briefing. All meetings had been held there since the war had begun.

It had been Annie's suggestion as it gave a less formal atmosphere and offered the chance of a cup of tea, something they rarely had time for in such a busy station.

Annie twisted her hankie into a knot as she waited for the sergeant to begin. It seemed every day something came to try them and to bring the reality of war to them.

This was particularly hard on her and the other five women police officers serving here in Stepney in east London as they took on duties they weren't used to. Most of the young male officers had been called up, including her own beloved Ricky.

Besides the female officers, the force now was made up of older coppers who'd been called out of retirement and special constables who only put in part-time hours during time off from their exempt occupations – teachers and railway workers mostly.

The sarge coughed, hushing the room. 'Right. I want a

presence on the street. A reassurance that everything will be all right.'

'But it ain't, Sarge, is it? Women fighting over the last slab of butter and falling out over there being no sugar left.'

Betty Randal always had a gripe, no matter what the sarge said.

In the same position as Annie as her Jack had left the day after Annie had waved Ricky off to war, and both having only been married a few days before, Betty acted like a victim for the most part.

'Well, just calm things down, that's all you have to do.'

'Huh!'

Sarge sighed. But Annie understood. Betty had liked her job more before everything had been turned upside down, back when female officers spent their days typing and only had the occasional youth offender to attend to. For Annie, it was different, she loved being involved in the community, tramping the beat, giving an air of reassurance, and helping to sort out what she could for the people of Stepney, east London, as they battled with fear, loneliness and now food shortages.

It all helped to make the longing for Ricky a little easier to bear.

As the sarge finished giving them their duties for the day, he called to Annie to follow him.

In his office, a square room with just a small window, making the pokey space seem dark and closed in, the sarge gave one of his famous sighs. 'Annie, we need a morale booster of some kind, girl. The few male officers I have are doing okay, most glad to be back and useful, as are the specials. They've got variety in their life and being a part-time copper makes them feel they're contributing. But the women! So much has changed for them and of the six of you, you're the only one coping, and yet you have the same problem of missing your man as they do.'

He scratched the top of his head.

'Sarge, you need to be more aware of how it is out there. We've gone from having an office camaraderie to being part of the community, but not in the way the men were – trusted to help with all situations. We're often mocked and always seeming to be clamping down on our fellow East Enders and acting like custodians, not of the law, but of the war!'

'How do yer mean, Annie?'

'Well, we're sent out to patrol the streets with orders to clamp down on this and that – the sort of things that coppers traditionally let go with a ticking off or sorted out in a friendly manner. For instance, a woman trying to get enough food for her kids and driven to pushing in on a queue is treated like a thief!'

'Well, we have to have some sort of discipline to it all otherwise it'll be chaos.'

'It takes time, Sarge. Most folk are scared. Especially the women. They find themselves without their men, and with all these new rules. I think we should handle everything in a much friendlier way, as we always used to.'

'But they get complacent then. The number of lights showing through blackouts not in place properly as I made me way home last night gave me nightmares.'

Putting her brimmed hat on his desk, Annie leaned forward, steadying herself with her hands.

'That's just it! Most can't afford proper blackouts and have done what they can with spare blankets and velvet tablecloths. But not many fit properly. And yet we're constantly banging on their doors frightening the life out of them instead of helping them.'

'Well, other than fitting the blackouts for them, what can we do? We have to impose the law, Annie. Softly, softly is all right in some situations but this is a breach of security that threatens our city!'

Annie knew he was right, and yet understood the people too. 'I'll go down to the docks and see if I can get a load of cardboard. We could take it around and show how that can be effective.'

'That's a good idea. I'll assign Arthur to go around showing the way to fix it. He's good at that kind of stuff. I've a list of those not getting a good cover up. They've been warned, but yes, helping them is a better solution. Ta, Annie.'

'About that morale booster, Sarge. Me mate as lives in Guernsey started a local choir. It went down really well. We could do something like that – a police choir.'

'Singing yer mean?'

Annie grinned. She wanted to say, *No, telling stories.* But didn't. 'Yes, singing. It's good for the soul.'

The sarge laughed. 'Half of this lot ain't got a soul, luv, but okay. I like to belt a tune out meself. Put feelers out to see if anyone's interested. We needn't do anything with it, just have a bit of a social time together. Yeah, I like that idea, Annie. I knew you'd come up with something. Things have changed but we'll make the best we can of it – lead the way, so to speak.'

From his tone, Annie guessed that as strong as the sarge was, he was feeling the strain as much as any of them.

Her beat took her towards West Quay. Thinking there was no time like the present, Annie made for the dockside. Catcalls set up the moment she was spotted. 'Come to arrest me, darlin'?' 'Yer can put handcuffs on me any day, luv!'

Knowing this wouldn't happen to a male copper and annoyed that it should to her, Annie ignored it.

'Quieten down, you lot, have some respect!' This came from a man as big as Ricky, who at times had seemed like a giant to her – her own protector, the love of her life.

'How can we help yer, Officer?'

Annie told of her idea.

'Cardboard? I tell yer, they collect it by the sackful now. It's good for burning, yer see.'

'Oh? I didn't know that.' As soon as she said this, Annie felt ashamed. She'd have known every trick those who hadn't two halfpennies to rub together got up to when she was one of them. Had she left her roots that far behind?

She still lived in Bethnal Green but more towards the posher end in a huge house that Jimmy, her sister Janey's husband, owned and which was arranged into three flats.

Her days of scrounging for a crust of bread had ended when she'd gone to Cornwall to work as a maid to the Wallingtons. Life had taken many twists since, and she wanted for nothing now.

A pang of conscience made her regret for the umpteenth time leaving her mum and sister to the extreme poverty she'd escaped. Not that life had been easy for her. It had been constant drudgery for twelve hours a day, but she'd been fed well and kept warm. And she'd been able to give every penny she'd earned to her mum and sister to make their lives a little better.

As she thanked him and walked away, she couldn't shake the memories of the poverty she'd known before she'd left the East End – living in a two-up, two-down terraced house. And yet it hadn't all been bad. Neighbours always looked out for one another and shared what they had. One or two of them came to mind. She smiled to herself when she thought of young Harry next door always having his fingers into dodgy goings-on. She wondered what had happened to him. He'd be around eighteen now and most probably with his fingers into all sorts to make the most of the situation the country was in.

Her thoughts were interrupted by a shout of, 'Oi, Copper!' Then a voice singing, '*Knees up Mother Brown . . .*'

Annie stood stock still. The singing went on, but she dared not turn towards it. Her mind told her it was him . . . Ricky! But she couldn't accept it and didn't want it not to be.

'*Knees up, Annie, don't get the breeze up* . . . Annie, Annie, me girl, me love, it's me, Ricky!'

Annie gasped. Her arms instinctively wrapped around her waist, partly to quell the nerves that jumped around inside her threatening to make her faint, but partly from disbelief.

An arm came around her waist. A waft of Brylcreem and that special, fresh smell of Ricky enveloped her. Still, she dared not look.

'Oh, Annie. I'm home.'

He turned her towards him.

'Ricky! How . . . ? When . . . ? Oh, Ricky!'

She was in his arms clinging on to him, trying to make him real to her. Looking up into his beloved face, she lifted her hand and traced her finger along his jagged scar, part of him she loved. She saw his crooked broken nose, and as if these medals to his injuries as a police officer convinced her, she burst into tears. 'Oh, Ricky!'

Tears flowed down Ricky's face as he gazed at her. Holding her tightly, rocking her from side to side, he didn't speak.

Then his lips came onto hers and Annie thought she would drown in happiness.

The catcalling pulled them up. 'Ha, this is what you policewomen get up to, is it? Hey, mate, save some for us!'

Ricky turned towards them, and as if seeing his uniform for the first time, they quietened down. 'Sorry about the show, lads. You know how it is.'

Under his breath he said, 'Or, rather they don't. I should have been a dockworker, luv, I wouldn't have had to leave you then. Come on, let's get out of here.'

A few minutes later, they were sitting in a cafe, a none too clean place where the owner, who Ricky knew as Marg, served them with a fag hanging out of her mouth, dropping ash onto the dirty tablecloth then wiping it off with her hand and leaving a black stain. But none of that mattered to Annie. She couldn't take her eyes off Ricky.

'Why didn't you write and tell me you were coming, luv?'

'Uh-oh, am I in trouble?'

Annie giggled. 'Not yet!'

They both laughed, but it was a nervous laugh, as if the spell could break at any moment and they would be back to being apart.

'It was sudden. A case of pack your kit bag and get on the train, you're going home. A bit of a pick-me-up for us reservists lads who went on the first trains out. None of us had leave like those who had to do training did after they'd been serving six weeks or so. Well, now they're all over there, the powers that be thought to let us come home.'

'Oh, luv, I can't believe it . . . How long?'

Ricky burst out laughing, a hefty sound bellowing from his huge frame. He brushed his fingers through his dark curls and his blue eyes twinkled. 'All the lads say that's the first question, luv. I've got a week.'

A week. So short a time and yet a lifetime when he wasn't by her side.

'I went to the station and Sarge told me where you were

heading. He said to tell you to leave the cardboard duty to him, he'll sort it, you can go back when you're ready and sign off duty for a week! I didn't hang around to ask what he meant by cardboard duty.'

Annie explained, despite not wanting to. Not wanting to talk about anything, but to whip Ricky off somewhere and be alone with him.

'How's things at home, luv? Can you get away? I was thinking as we never had a chance to set up home and I don't want to spend me time at me mum's and you at Janey's, we could go away for a few days – inland, not seaside. Too many reminders of the war on the coast.'

'I can't take all of this in yet. You're here! You're truly here!'

'I am, me darlin', and I want you all to meself for most of me stay, but we ain't got much time. I met a bloke from a place called Market Harborough. It's in Leicestershire. He said it was a small market town with a lot of history, that there's an old coaching inn there called The Swan, and they still let rooms to travellers to this day. He spoke of it in such a way, I thought I'd like to visit.' His hand clutched hers. 'Can we?'

'I – I . . . Oh, Ricky. Janey ain't been too good. She needs me.'

Ricky's face dropped. His expression of eager anticipation turned to a look of devastation. 'Is she hurting herself again, luv?'

'No, not that, but she cries a lot, and her pregnancy gets her down as she's constantly sick. She ain't coping with Jimmy being away. He's been back on leave, like you say, after his training, and she was happy then, but . . . Oh, to hell with it! Yes, Ricky. Yes, me darlin', I will come away with you. Janey'll be all right with Mum and Cissy.'

23

'Are you sure, luv?'

'I am. Cissy can manage Janey. She's been teaching her to sew. You know what a good needlewoman Cissy is, well, Janey is finding she has talent too, and it's given her an interest. She's making an outfit for little Beth at the moment.'

'That's good. It can only help her to know that you'll follow your own life, luv. She's a lot stronger than you think.'

'She still holds on to her guilt about her and Jimmy deceiving me. It doesn't matter how many times I tell her how glad I am that they did as it led to me meeting you – the real, true love of me life.'

'You have to face it, some folk like to be the martyr, luv. It wasn't good what they did to you, you thinking Jimmy was going to marry you, and then having an affair all the time with your sister, but that's in the past and, as you say, it led to me and you meeting and falling in love . . . Anyway, let's not waste time talking about others, except to tell me how your mum is and then we'll make our plans.'

'Mum's doing really well. It was a good day when Cissy came into her life.'

'They're good friends, aren't they? And with Cissy having her own flat in the same house as your mum and Janey, I don't think you ever need to worry, luv.'

Annie began to relax. It was all sinking in. Ricky was here. Right by her side. He was real. How she wished something like this could happen for Olivia – or that one day, Olivia too would just turn up and they could be together again. The thought brought back to her the dilemma she and Olivia were in.

They were spies. Spies for their country, with information fed to them by Hendrick. Their loving friendship was on hold, except for in secrecy, so as not to raise any suspicions.

Then it hit her. If she went away and Olivia needed to pass something on, which always happened in the evening when Annie manned the station switchboard, what would happen?

'Ricky, I can't. I can't get the time off!'

'You can . . . of course you can, it's already been granted.'

'But Olivia!'

'Oh, I never thought . . . Wait a minute, can we contact her? Surely we can think of something. Maybe she could pass messages to Lucy in your absence?'

Lucy was Annie's contact. An agent of the War Office, who had become a best friend. A girl who worked in a newspaper office as a cover, plain to look at and the type of girl who would never stand out in a crowd, though Annie had grown to love her. And to Annie, Lucy's million freckles and her hazel eyes weren't plain, but marked her for who she was, a lovely young woman.

'I'll work tonight in the hope that Olivia rings, then sort something out with her. I'm seeing Lucy on me break this afternoon . . . I'm sorry, luv, but I must put something in place.'

'I know, I was daft to think I could just come home and whisk you off your feet and run away with you.'

'How I've longed for you to. Every day of me life since you left, Ricky.'

'Oh, Annie, Annie, I love you . . . Look, let's at least book into a hotel for tonight, eh?'

Annie's nerves clenched. 'Yes. Oh yes, Ricky. Let's do that.'

Ricky grinned his lovely grin. 'Come on then, I'll walk back to the station with you to sign you out, and then you can tell Sarge you'll be back for switchboard duty. He'll understand as he knows the gist of what's happening with you and Olivia, he had to be informed when it was first set up.'

'I know, and yet he never mentions it, or gives an inkling he knows who I am talking about if I mention Olivia.'

'Sarge is a professional through and through . . . Anyway, after we've done that, we'll go and see your mum, Janey and Cissy. Me mum's going to be over there, as she knew that's where I was heading – either with you or on me own if you couldn't get off. And then, me little darlin', you can pack a bag. I can take it to a hotel and pick you up when you finish work. How does all that sound?'

'Yes. Oh, yes, Ricky, luv. It sounds like heaven.'

'Right. Yer on. Come on . . . you ain't drunk your tea!'

Annie grimaced. Ricky laughed. 'I thought being a copper you'd be used to a cup of Rosie Lee in any old dive. Come on, love. I'm impatient to get the day on the go and get to tonight.'

Annie blushed. She didn't know why as her heart was singing and she wanted nothing more than for tonight to come and to come quickly.

Everyone crowded around Ricky when they reached home. Even Janey showed nothing but sheer joy in seeing him and didn't turn it around into something sorrowful for herself.

Mum glowed at him. 'Well, Ricky, lad, it's good to see you home.'

'Don't ask him how long for, Mum. Haha, he'll only laugh in your face!'

'Ha, Vera, it's all the lads get asked and yet none of them want to keep saying the day they've to return.' Ricky turned this from a sad statement to a funny one as he said, 'So, I ain't telling, except to say, I'll be gone this time next week. Will that do you?'

As Annie joined in the laughter, it seemed for one moment as if Ricky had never been away.

'Eeh, lad, it's good to see you. Me and Vera haven't had any handsome lads to admire, have we, Vera, lass?'

'We ain't, Cissy, and we like to look even though we're both past it!'

The love between her mum and Cissy shone through at that moment as they grinned at one another. As she'd often done, Annie blessed the day that Olivia came into her life, bringing Cissy to them.

Cissy had worked as housekeeper to Olivia's father, taking care of his apartment in the West End. Now it was closed under the pretence that the government had requisitioned it – a ploy to break any traceable connection between herself and Olivia.

And yet, the way Olivia had become her most treasured friend was the stuff of nightmares – a train crash in which Olivia had been badly injured and she had managed to save her life. That moment had bonded them for ever.

Lilly, who hadn't spoken much till then but had just been gazing at her son in wonderment, piped up, 'I don't know what a girl must do to get a cuppa around here, but I think I'll put the bloomin' kettle on meself!'

A huge part of the family that expanded to Rose, mother of Jimmy, too, Lilly was loved by them all.

As they sat chatting, a little voice came from upstairs. 'Mum . . . Mum . . . Mummeee!'

'Uh-oh, Beth's woken from her nap.'

'I'll get her, Janey, luv, you stay where you are.'

'Well, if you're going, I am,' said Rick. 'I ain't letting you out of me sight until I have to, Annie.'

Annie coloured as she caught a knowing look and a nod from her mum.

Upstairs, Beth had settled to happily playing with her many soft toys surrounding her in her cot. Before she spotted them, Ricky grabbed Annie. 'I need another kiss, me darlin'.'

Annie did too. She melted into him to the sound of Beth clapping her hands.

It was a kiss that held passion, love, and Annie's whole world.

# Chapter Three

## Annie

Lucy sat in the cafe along the way from the station – one of their meeting places, though both preferred the canal cafe near to Old Ford Road and to where Annie lived. This, though, was convenient for a quick meeting when Annie was at work.

They ordered tea and a jam tart each and these were delivered to their table the moment Annie sat down after the two girls had hugged.

'So, Ricky's home?'

'You know?'

'We know most things that go on with our agents, Annie. I'm pleased for you both, but you'll have to remain at work.'

Annie could tell this wasn't what Lucy wanted to say. Her face was a picture of regret. 'But I thought if anything came in, Olivia could report it direct to you, Lucy.'

'No, we must not change anything. In doing so we may slip up. We've everything set up, Annie, and these are vital times when we need to know every plan we can possibly know of Hitler's movements.'

'He doesn't seem to be making any towards France or towards us at the moment.'

'But he may, and we are preparing, alongside the French, to defend France. We have to. If they fall, it is just a short hop across the Channel to invade us.'

'Please, Lucy. I've only got one week, mate, surely something can be sorted?'

Lucy closed her eyes and sighed. 'If I'm found out . . . Oh, Annie. Go on then . . . God, what am I saying? We're supposed to be professionals first and friends last, but I do feel for you . . . I'm still writing to Dan and, well, you know how I feel about him, though he has never expressed anything but a need for a friend. But if he was to come home and want to be with me, I'd go like a shot. So, I can't deny you. But only if you can arrange it with Olivia. Any vital information must still be able to get through.'

'She hasn't got your number, luv, so it can only happen if she contacts. Though I could try ringing her from home.'

'Do that. Now, drink your tea, Annie. Let's take a walk to the post office on the corner. I'll get the number of the phone box there and be there at a certain time each evening.'

'Oh, Luce, you're a darlin' and a good mate.'

'No, I'm an idiot and behaving like a woman and a friend instead of a professional. I could get into a lot of trouble for this, but then I love you, Annie, and would do anything for you.'

Annie found her hand under the table and squeezed it. She knew this was costing Lucy dearly and regretted the need to put it onto her.

Ricky was waiting across the street when they emerged from the cafe. She waved to him and indicated she wouldn't be long but then was soon back with him and telling him the good news.

'There! I knew we could fix it. Oh, Annie, I can't wait to

spend a few days alone together. Somewhere where no one knows us and where we shouldn't have too many reminders of the war.'

They walked a while, just happy to be together, never going far enough that someone didn't know Ricky and stopped to have a few words with him, but then they had to say goodbye for Annie to take up her position manning the phones. They parted on promises of the night ahead.

As Annie settled down with her pad next to her to write details of any messages, she still tingled from their parting kiss that had held so many promises. She didn't feel as resigned as usual to her couple of hours' duty but impatient to have the shift over and praying that Olivia called to save her having to go home just to be able to telephone her.

This happening filled her with the usual joy at hearing from Olivia and gave her a peace that topped up her happiness. Olivia was with Hendrick!

'Oh, Olivia, I'm so happy for you! A croft, you say? Haha, that's not what you're used to.'

'No, but it's wonderful. We're so happy. It's a happy home and it has welcomed us. I wish we could stay here for ever.'

Annie knew this feeling. For her to go somewhere like that with her Ricky and be lost to the world would be as it was for Olivia – heaven.

Down the crackling line came what sounded like, 'Ricky, home?'

'Yes . . . yes. He's home.'

Somehow, they managed to convey to each other that they were free of their clandestine work for at least a week as that's how long it would take before Hendrick was back in Germany and at his desk.

'That's smashing. Enjoy being just a wife and mum, me darlin'.'

'I will . . . I am. Oh, Annie, and you enjoy all the time you have with Ricky. I do miss you. Love to everyone, especially Cissy . . . Love you . . . miss . . .'

The line went dead. Annie sat back in her chair and just giggled as relief swept over her. Her next call was to Lucy's office.

'You just caught me! Have you heard?'

'Yes, and we have nothing to worry about . . . Oh, Luce, a bloomin' marvellous coincidence has happened. Olivia is with Hendrick so we won't be missing any messages.'

After she explained, Lucy said, 'Well, there you go, love. It was meant to be. Enjoy your break, and we'll meet up when you're back.'

A few more calls came in before the night duty sergeant came to her. 'Annie, why are you still here, luv?'

'I've another fifteen minutes to do, Sarge.'

'No, you haven't. One thing this war has done has cut the crime rate by getting the men occupied in a different way, and the second thing it's done is separate us from our loved ones. You have a chance to be with yours, so grab your coat and go. I'll manage anything that comes in.'

Annie didn't need telling twice. She jumped up. 'Ta, Sarge. See you in a week.'

'Annie, make the most of it, girl. Have the time of your life with your Ricky – our Ricky, as we miss him too – and just forget everything except each other.'

Annie didn't remark on this, but she didn't miss the tear that seeped out of the corner of the duty sergeant's eye. It was only a few months since he'd lost his beloved Nancy – his wife of twenty years – to a sudden illness.

As she passed him, Annie did something very unconventional – she leaned towards him and kissed his cheek, then scooted out before he could discipline her.

The blush this had caused still reddened her face as she jumped onto the bus outside the station. A nasty voice turned it to an angry flush.

''Ere, Conductor, what yer doin' letting a bleedin' copper on 'ere?'

Someone chipped in, 'I wondered what the sudden smell was!'

Annie got out of her seat and turned to face them.

'What's the problem, missus?'

'You lot. You're worse than Hitler!'

'It's a trying time for us all, and we're all having to adjust, just as you are.'

'That bitch as arrested me sister needs adjusting, that's for sure!'

'Look, I can see you're angry, and I'll try to sort this out for you. Us women cops have been suddenly called on to carry out duties we aren't trained for, but we're doing our best.'

'Yes, Rita, it ain't her fault, yer know your Phyllis didn't act right. She should have queued like the rest of us. Her pushing that old woman to the ground was a rotten thing to do.'

'Yes, well, I agree. But she needed 'elp, not locking up.'

'I agree, Rita, many of you need our help, and more so now than ever. And us at the station are talking about ways we can do just that. We need to take things easier; we recognize that. Though I ain't condoning anyone who shoves an old lady over. That ain't right, no matter what the circumstances. And if a deliberate act, then it deserves punishment.'

A number of voices agreed.

'Well, our Phyllis can be hot-headed, but then her hubby and two sons 'ave gone to war and she's at her wits' end.'

'She'd be that if someone pushed your and her mum over, Rita.'

With this from another passenger, Rita clamped her mouth shut and folded her arms.

Annie took her chance. 'Look, all of you. What's the code for us East Enders, eh? We watch each other's backs. We don't grab for ourselves until we see our neighbour has what she needs. Where's that all gone, eh? No old lady in our streets should even think of having to queue for something, it should be got for her! It ain't us coppers to blame, it's you, forgetting your roots and what you've been taught all your lives. Look after one another and we'll get through this.'

There was a silence. Then someone said, ''Ear, 'ear,' and began to applaud. That spread around the bus, leaving Annie beaming at them all. 'Ta, everybody. I know you can all pull together, and that you will.'

She sat down. Taking a deep breath, she reflected on what a strange day it had been. When she got up this morning, she didn't think she would be facing disenchanted colleagues, thinking of starting a choir when all she had was a decent enough voice, or battling with her own folk from the East End . . . and never in her wildest dreams did she think she would be on a bus going to the arms of her Ricky.

When she reached the Royal Hotel on Bunhill Road, which looked more like a Victorian house than a hotel, Ricky came out of the door. 'I've been looking through the window for this last hour, luv.' He took her into his arms and hugged her. An elderly woman coming towards them hmphed and walked past. They both giggled.

'Oh dear, we'd better get inside, luv. Then I can cuddle you all I want to.'

Annie's heart raced. Her anticipation was such that she could hardly sign the register with her shaking hands. She smiled a nervous smile at the gentleman behind the small reception desk that encircled a corner of the hall they stood in.

'Welcome, Mrs Stanley. Nice to meet you and I hope you enjoy your stay.'

A shyness came over Annie. She nodded and smiled.

Their room on the first floor was surprisingly big with a bay window that housed two comfy chairs. But it was the bed that loomed in the centre that somehow increased Annie's shyness. She couldn't have said why. She'd never experienced this when she and Ricky had made love at every possible chance when they remained a courting couple so that she could achieve her ambition of being a police officer.

Ricky's hand came into hers. 'Oh, Annie, I've dreamed of this moment, me darlin'.'

She turned into his hug and suddenly all barriers were down. They fell onto the bed together and became a rolling, desperate tangle to kiss, undress and become one.

When they did, Annie cried out her joy as she gave herself to the sheer pleasure of giving and taking as she made love to her adored Ricky.

A few days later, having had a wonderful time walking, talking and just being together in and around the historic town of Market Harborough in Leicestershire, they were on their way home. Both had heavy hearts as their time together was almost over.

When they reached London, they booked back into the

Royal Hotel for their last two nights. 'Let's go for pie and mash tonight, luv, and then we can spend the day with family tomorrow, eh? I just want you to meself for our last few hours.'

'They won't be our last, Ricky, luv. Never say that. This war will end and then we can be a normal couple and have them kids we keep talking of.'

Ricky didn't say any more until they were walking towards The Coach and Horses, a pub just down the road that had a sign outside advertising the best pie and mash in the business.

'I wish we could start now, luv.'

'Start what?'

'Well, I'm thinking of what we were talking about before and was wishing we didn't have to wait, that we could set up home and didn't have to avoid having kids, but it's important you keep your job and be a link for Olivia.'

'It is. Olivia has no such worries as in Guernsey no suspicion of her and Hendrick's activities are raised by him telephoning her and her phoning me. He's her husband and his calls are expected, and everyone knows me and how deep our friendship is. But here, we don't know who is listening in to household phones. Operators do it regularly, but at the station Olivia's calls are lost in the crowd of those we handle. It's the safest way.'

'You're an unsung hero, mate. No one knows how you sacrificed having what other women take for granted. You chose to stay single so you could keep your job and be on hand for Olivia's calls. It was a good day when the government changed its mind and decided married women could be officers and work while setting up a home and having children . . . Mind, on the question of a home, would you like to set one up for us, luv? One that I can come back to?'

'More than anything in the world, Ricky. But not yet. I'd be lonely, me darlin', rattling around a flat on me own, and I'm needed at home. We've got our own East End women against the war going. What with Me, Mum, Cissy, Janey, your mum, Jimmy's mum, Rose and, of course, little Beth. In fact, Janey's under strict instructions to have another girl!'

Ricky laughed out loud. The sound broke the undercurrent of sadness she'd detected in him. 'Ha! I'd like to see Hitler try to beat you lot. He'd be bashed to death by handbags!'

They were laughing together as they entered the pub.

'You know, I bless the day I met you, me darlin', as that brought a new family to me, and especially to Lilly.'

Ricky always called his mum Lilly. He hadn't known she was his mum until he was in his teens. Until then she'd been his adored big sister. He'd thought of his gran as his mum. Lilly hadn't known she was pregnant when she waved Ricky's dad off to the Great War. He never returned. His grandparents moved after the baby was born and claimed he was theirs to save Lilly's reputation and give her a second chance, but she never met anyone she loved like Ricky's dad and so never married.

Over the delicious pie and mash and after debating whether they were better than those from Jones's pie shop in Bethnal Green, Annie told Ricky about her idea of a choir. Ricky had a love of musical theatre as his gran had been a star of their local one and he loved to sing.

'That's a smashing idea, Annie. You could put on concerts. That would give us coppers a human face, so to speak. Let the community see us under a different guise and get to know they can approach us and we're there for them.'

Annie felt the sadness of Ricky using the collective 'us'.

She knew at heart that's what he was. A copper through and through, not a fighting man, but one who sorted folk's problems and helped them. His main passion when he was on his beat before all of this had been the kids. To him, it was his duty to guide them and to channel them into doing good for the community.

As if he'd read her thoughts, he said, 'Why not do something for the youngsters as well, Annie, luv? Organize them into groups who help where help is needed, eh?'

'Ricky, luv, we ain't got many kids on our streets. They're living in the countryside and more rural towns. Remember? As soon as Germany invaded Poland, the government started evacuating them. Mind, you were gone a couple of weeks later yourself. Sending the kids away, in some cases dragging them screaming from their mums' grip, was the most heartbreaking operation I've ever been involved in.'

Ricky's arm came around her. He lifted her chin from where it had fallen onto her chest. 'Oh, me darlin', it's never easy being a cop, but it's harder for you girls. Anything to do with kids always falls to you women officers to do. I'm sorry you had that to do, mate. But you know, I ain't noticed many kids missing off the street.'

'No, some have come home. Parents couldn't bear it, or the kids themselves ran away from their charges and made it back to the East End, but it's frightening. They're our future and everyone thinks if Hitler does come, it'll be London as cops it.'

'It will. But don't worry, girl, we'll stop him, we won't even let him into France, and he'd need to be there to stand a chance of getting here.'

His arm hugged her before he took it away. It was then she saw a change come over him. He looked around the room, then down at his hands, which, Annie noticed, he was wringing together.

She put out her hand and stayed his. 'What's up, luv?'

'I – I . . . Oh, Annie, I think we should talk about . . . well, if the worst happens.'

'No! No, Ricky, don't make me.'

'We need to, luv . . . Like everyone, I've written a letter to be delivered if—'

'Stop it, Ricky. Not now.'

His hand clutched her tight fist. 'We have to, luv, I need to.'

Annie's bottom lip quivered as she looked into his pleading eyes. Seeing how much this meant to him, she nodded. If they had to talk of what might be, then here was better than on their own. Here, she'd control her emotions.

'If I'm killed, Annie, I know without asking that you'll look after Lilly, but I need you to know other things. I've a bit of savings. Me dad had saved to wed Lilly, and his mum, when she heard about me, helped me gran along the way, but when she died, she left what was still in the pot to me. It's never been touched, only added to.' He took his hand away and put it into his inside pocket. 'Here's the account book . . . Open it.'

Annie gasped when she saw the total of fifty-two pounds and ten shillings!

'I want us to go to the bank tomorrow, Annie, and put it into your name. If anything happens, it'd be yours anyway, but all of that takes time. I want to know that you're all right for money.'

'Oh, Ricky. I don't know what to say.'

'Don't say anything, luv. Just let me do this, eh? Let me go knowing me affairs are in order. And Annie, there's

39

something I want you to know. I don't want you to live your life in loneliness. Lilly did. There were a few over the years who loved her and would have made her happy, but she had this notion that she should stay faithful to me dad. Don't do that, Annie. Make a new life for yourself, luv.'

'No, Ricky, please stop.' Annie's head shook, not with a side-to-side movement, but with the tension she felt as her whole body tightened.

'It all needs saying, me darlin'. I'll always be by your side, not judging, but walking in the happiness I want you to find. Then and only then I will be able to rest in peace.'

Annie couldn't speak. Ricky rose and took her hand. Outside he pulled her into the shadows. They clung to one another and sobbed.

# Chapter Four

## *Janey*

Janey glanced again at Jimmy's razor, still standing in a mug on the windowsill of their bathroom. A longing to pick it up and cut deeply into her skin consumed her as she thought of how the pain would relieve her of this pent-up feeling of wanting to scream and not stop screaming out the inner agony of wanting Jimmy home.

Her eyes stared at what she saw as her weapon to end this.

Her thoughts were of it slicing her and the almost exquisite feel of the release it would give her.

Her shaking hand reached out towards it but a voice calling out her name froze her movement.

'Janey, Janey, lass, there's two visitors for you. Shall I bring them up? Eeh, lass. They're from Jimmy's regiment.'

Janey's stomach retched. Fear gripped her. Leaning over the toilet, she vomited violently.

'Janey, Janey, me little lass.'

A hand came onto her back and rubbed it in soothing movements. 'Come on, lass, it'll be all right. I'll stay with you.'

41

Wiping her mouth on the towel, Janey stared at Cissy. 'No, Cissy . . . Not me Jimmy . . . No!'

Cissy held her tighter.

As they stood outside her flat Janey looked down the stairs. At the bottom stood two army-uniformed men.

The colour drained from her face. Her legs went to jelly. A little voice calling, 'Mummy!' steadied her.

'I'll see to little Beth once we have you downstairs, lass.'

Each step seemed to take Janey to her doom.

'Mrs Blaine?'

She nodded.

'I'm Captain Jackson and this is Corporal Smith. We're very sorry, but we don't have good news.'

'Eeh, let me get the lass in with her ma, lads. It's only through that door. At least let her be sat down with her ma before you tell her owt bad.'

'I'm sorry. I – I haven't had to do this duty before, and I was ham-fisted. Forgive me. Of course, we'll follow you in.'

Janey didn't want to hear what they had to say. Her mind went to Rose, Jimmy's mum. She'd be working at the market stall in Covent Garden, blissfully unaware that anything had happened to Jimmy, the apple of her eye.

Sitting obediently on the dining chair Cissy had pulled out for her from under the window, where it stood next to the fold-down table, Janey found her mum's eyes. Mum wheeled her wheelchair over and put out her hand. 'Oh, me Janey, luv. I'm here and Cissy is. We'll help you.'

The officer cleared his throat. 'I have to tell you, Mrs Blaine, that Private Jimmy Blaine has been seriously injured in an accident.'

'A what? Not the Germans? . . . How?'

'No, we're not engaged with fighting the Germans as yet,

madam. But our division have been taking part in training manoeuvres in the area we are gearing up to defend.'

'What happened?'

'Private Blaine was accidentally shot . . . I'm so sorry . . . It is not known if he will make a full recovery. He's had an operation to remove the bullet fragments. It seems the bullet passed through his skull . . . He . . . he has brain damage.'

'No! Where is he? . . . Oh, Jimmy, me Jimmy.'

Cissy shot to her side. 'Hold on, me little lass. Jimmy's still alive. Hang on to that, Janey.'

'Private Blaine has been operated on in the field hospital and is being brought back to be transported to the Royal Herbert Hospital in Greenwich. We will inform you of when he arrives and when you can visit, madam . . . Now, is there anything we can do for you?'

It was Mum who answered. 'No, we'll look after her, ta, mate.'

The captain saluted and they left.

'Janey, Janey, luv, you've to be strong. Jimmy's alive, and he'll fight back from this, you'll see.'

'Oh, Mum! Head injury . . . brain damage, and by one of his own? No . . . No . . . How?'

'We don't know. That captain didn't seem to know, but we know Jimmy's hurt and he's going to need you, me darlin'. You've got to stay strong for him and Beth and your unborn. Please, Janey, girl. We'll all help you. Annie's due back today. She'll know what to do. She'll find out visiting times and make sure Rose is informed.'

Hearing this, Janey relaxed a little. With Annie by her side, she could cope. 'I want Annie, Mum. I want Annie.'

Janey didn't miss the look that passed between Cissy and

Mum. Their worry was tangible. She didn't want to be the cause, but if she didn't have a lifeline, she knew she would drown in the dark thoughts and what seemed like clawing fingers trying to pull her under the weight of madness.

'Eeh, I forgot little Beth. She's the patience of a saint that one. I'll go and get her. She'll distract you, Janey, lass.'

Janey didn't want a distraction. Her mind was on that razor. She needed to cut deep into her skin to release this painful knot of agony that had her in its grip.

'Janey, Janey. Listen to me. Call on the strength I know you have, me darlin'.'

'Oh, Mum, hold me.' Janey fell onto her knees and laid her head in her mum's lap.

'You used to be so tough, luv. You cared for me when we had nothing. You worked at the shop and eked out Annie's yearly wage until she returned the next year. It were you and me against the world, luv, and we came through it all. Look at us now. Jimmy'll need you. He's done a lot for us, keeping us together like this. We can all be there for him now that this has happened, eh?'

Janey knew Mum was right. Her hand soothed as it stroked her hair. 'Your hair's like silk, luv. Still a lovely light brown, almost blonde. Mine was similar at your age.'

'I have your hazel eyes, Mum, everyone's always telling me.'

'And Beth looks like us both too. She's going to need you, and your little unborn is. Only three months to go now, luv. I wonder if you'll have a boy this time?'

Janey knew Mum was trying to distract her. She didn't want to be a burden to her lovely mum, she had enough to cope with, not able to walk, and in constant pain, but none of this chit-chat was helping or suppressing the urge – no, the need – for physical pain. *Oh, Annie where are you? Come to me, come to me now!*

As if she'd conjured her up, the front door opened and her beloved sister's voice came to her. 'Anyone at home to greet a returning daughter and sister?'

'In here, Annie.'

Annie opened the door of Mum's living room. Not a big room, and now crowded with them all gathered there.

They all looked at Annie. Mum sighed with relief.

To Janey, it seemed as though God had sent Annie to her.

Annie had a happy grin on her face, but that changed to an expression of concern, as she looked from one to the other of them and asked, 'What's happened?'

Janey hadn't the strength to stand, so crawled over to Annie. Ricky lifted her, his giant frame gentle in his handling of her as he carried her to the sofa, his voice placating her. 'It's all right, Janey, love, we're here now.'

'Mum, what's happened?'

Pain sliced through Janey as Mum answered Annie, seeming to put a truth to what the captain had told them.

'Oh no! Oh, Janey, me darlin'. I'm here now, luv. We'll get through this and help Jimmy too, eh?'

Annie sat down next to her and held her to her as she told her, 'We'll go and see Jimmy the moment they tell us we can, luv. Does Rose know?'

Janey could only shake her head.

'I'll go and tell her, Annie, luv, and if she wants to come, I'll bring her back here,' said Ricky. 'Has she got help with her market stall yet?'

'She's got a woman who is doing the deliveries for her, whose son helps out after school. He could be there now. And Rose was telling us that his mum and him often close and pack up the stall for her, but she has it hard without Jimmy as she has to meet the train early mornings to collect the produce sent up from her farm in Kent.'

'So, she never went and married her manager then? This war has put a lot of folk's happiness on hold . . . Anyway, I'll get off, luv.'

Janey watched Ricky kiss Annie's cheek and felt sorry that she was the cause of them having to part, when she knew they wanted to be together every minute of the time Ricky had and this was his last day before he left for France once more, but there was nothing she could do. Lovely Rose had to be told the awful news, that her Jimmy, her adored son, was badly injured – though, Janey thought, if she could save her from the pain of knowing, she would.

She closed her eyes. *Has this really happened to me? Have I lost me Jimmy as I knew him? A brain injury changes a person, doesn't it?*

She heard an animal-like cry and knew it had come from herself. 'I've lost him, Annie.'

'No, luv, Jimmy has a chance to get better. If he hadn't, I reckon they'd have kept him in that field hospital and nursed him, rather than put him through the journey. That to me says he has a chance, luv. Hang on to that. And as soon as they let you know you can visit, we'll go. You need to keep strong for that. Focus on it, luv. Focus on Jimmy needing you rather than how this is knocking you for six. He's been knocked further than that. You're his wife, the love of his life, he's going to need your strength to get him through this.'

Janey lifted her head from Annie's shoulder and straightened her back. Annie was right, Jimmy did need her, when always it had been the other way around.

Suddenly the longing for that razor had gone. She could

do this with Annie's support. She could be strong for her Jimmy.

'There, you see. You have that look of old on your face, luv, that look you used to have when you were going to tackle the rent man to let you pay half this week and half next.'

Janey felt a grin spreading over her face. Yes, she felt like that girl again. The one who would take on the world to save her mum, back in the days when Mum only had her to care for her. Well, she could do that to save Jimmy.

'That's the spirit, Janey. You've got what it takes, girl.'

'I have, haven't I, Annie? I've been someone to reckon with in the past, and I can be again.'

Annie hugged her. 'Now, luv, where's me Beth, eh?'

'Cissy's with her upstairs. Will you shout her to bring her down, Annie?'

'No, luv, you can do that. You can go and fetch your Beth down so that Cissy doesn't have to lift her. Beth's getting a lump to carry and Cissy ain't that good on the stairs.'

Annie was right. Since becoming frail in her head, she'd let everyone do things for her. But she had to do things for herself and for Beth, and most of all for her Jimmy, as her Jimmy needed her.

Suddenly, it dawned on Janey that she'd given in, and that hadn't been her nature before her breakdown. She looked over at her mum. Guilt shamed her. She hadn't cared for Mum as well as she used to but had left Cissy to do most things. And it was always Cissy who had a hot meal ready for Annie when she came in after a long day at work. Well, that would change.

Standing, Janey walked towards the door. 'I won't be a mo.' Then she giggled to herself as she glanced back. Mum's expression as she looked over at Annie showed that she could hardly believe what was happening.

'Annie's here, Cissy, and Ricky's gone to tell poor Rose the news. I won't be a mo, Beth, me darlin', Mummy just needs the bathroom.'

Once in the bathroom, Janey grabbed the razor from the windowsill and placed it in the cabinet that Jimmy had fixed above the sink, pushing it right to the back. 'You can stay there! I won't be needing you.'

Not understanding how this change had come about, but loving the powerful feeling the action had given her, Janey went through and scooped up her beautiful little twenty-month-old daughter and hugged her to her. The action tore at her heart, to think Jimmy might not be able to do this for her. But she could cuddle Beth for the both of them.

'You're a lump, Beth. Put your legs each side of Mummy's big tummy, that's it. That's your new sister or brover, luv.'

Beth grinned, showing her little pearl teeth. The redness of her cheek told of another coming through. This, Janey had read, would be one of her eye teeth, and would close the gap between her front ones. But the process didn't seem to be bothering Beth as much as some of her teething had, and for that Janey was glad for her.

A placid, loving child, with lovely hazel eyes and light brown hair, she put her chubby arms around Janey's neck and hugged her.

'Hey, you're strangling me, luv. Loosen your grip a bit. That's it. Mummy needs gentle handling.'

Even though she might not have understood, Beth giggled.

Once downstairs, she became the centre of everyone's attention, making Janey feel proud as she watched Beth hugging them all.

'Eeh, lass. Let's hope your next is as good as little Beth.'

Annie piped up, 'It'll probably be a tartar! Beth will spoil it and so will we all, and it'll have us running around doing its bidding.'

Janey's hand went to her mound. She massaged it protectively, and thought how lucky she was to have Jimmy's children, and wondered at Annie not wanting Ricky's just so that she could stay in her career. Annie was made of different stuff to herself and always had been. Stronger and more determined to follow a path she thought the right one and always shoring them all up.

Beth had run to her and was loving the cuddle Annie was giving her. Annie's cuddles always reassured and gave strength. The thought came to Janey that she would be more like Annie, and she prayed her daughter would be too.

Janey had the kettle on by the time Ricky came back with Rose – something she'd have left to Annie or Cissy, but she had the urge to show she had changed. How this had happened, she didn't know, but being needed had given her the strength to be there for others and not always the one who needed shoring up.

She heard Rose before she saw her. 'Where's me Janey . . . ? Oh, girl, 'ow could such a thing 'appen? Come 'ere, me luv.'

Going into Rose's hug almost undid Janey. She clung to her mother-in-law, the rounded, huggable Rose, and swallowed hard to suppress the urge to weep.

'Me Jimmy, I can't take it in. One of his own 'urting him like that. Will he ever be the same again?'

'We don't know, Rose, luv. But we'll take care of him, eh?'

Janey couldn't believe it was her saying this. She saw the surprise in Rose's face. 'We will, luv. Me and you will be a force to be reckoned with when it comes to our Jimmy.'

'It's a bad job all round.' Ricky ran his fingers through his hair. He'd sat next to Annie on the sofa and was holding her hand. 'But the problem is that half the lads asked to handle the weapons we have just ain't skilled and never had the inkling to be soldiers. I blame his sergeant. It's our job to assume they aren't capable and to give them the skills they need. Not all of the sergeants think the same. They take the attitude that the six weeks' training was enough. It is for some, but you take a lad who's been working in a bank, for instance. He's never had to tap into an aggressive feeling in his life. Guns scare him. Such a lad shakes like a leaf if you put a gun in his hand. And on top of that they're worn out from all the physical exertion – the marching for miles, not like the manual labourer, who's fit and used to fending for himself. And yet they treat them all the same and expect the same level from them. To my mind, accidents are waiting to happen.'

There was a silence following this.

Janey hadn't considered that there might be young men who weren't capable of doing what was being asked of them. Ricky had made her look at things differently. If she had to suddenly become a policewoman, she would be so terrified and make mistakes, not like Annie who was strong in mind and body. Her feelings changed with this thought. It wasn't the young soldier's fault.

It was a week later that she stood with Annie outside the ward where Jimmy was, waiting to be told they could go in.

Annie's eyes were red from the many tears she'd shed since Ricky had left to go back to France. At night, the bed they shared – hers and Jimmy's – had shaken with Annie's sobs. Comforting her had drained and yet helped Janey.

Rose was with them, and she too looked worn out as if her shoulders were weighted with cares.

For Janey, the moment held fear. Every now and again, her eye twitched uncontrollably, and her hands ached from twisting them together with fingers entwined, but wringing them gave her a physical release from her anxiety.

A nurse came out of the room where Jimmy was. 'You may come in now, but please be very quiet. Although not fully conscious, sudden noises upset Mr Blaine.'

Janey went in first. The man lying between stark white sheets didn't look like her Jimmy, but a pale, bandaged imitation of him. His cheeks had sunk in and his stubble had grown to a soft down and covered his upper lip and chin. The sockets of his closed eyes were black and swollen. She heard her own gasp, and almost choked on the intensity of it.

Hurrying to his side, she gently stroked his hair – no longer a bush of curls, but half shaven off, leaving just a few strands. 'I'm here, me Jimmy. It's Janey, luv. You're all right.'

But in her heart, she knew he wasn't and she feared losing him. 'You're mum's here as well, and Annie. Oh, Jimmy, I love you. Get well, me darling, come back to me and Beth. We miss you so much.'

Jimmy's lips clamped. The expression this gave him was one of anger. Janey jumped back from it. But then told herself off. Jimmy wouldn't be angry. He rarely got cross, let alone angry. It must be an expression of pain.

'We're here for you, Jimmy, luv. You're going to be all right.'

Once more the lips clamped.

'Jimmy, lad, it's your mum. I need yer better, son. I need yer 'elp on the round. Though we're managing all right. I

51

'ave that Peggy Derby and her lad 'elping me. They work 'ard but it's the mornings. You get well and it'll be me and you again, eh, son?'

Jimmy's face changed. He seemed to be smiling. Janey wanted him to do that when she spoke to him. She took hold of his hand. 'I love you, Jimmy, and Beth is missing you.'

His hand curled into a fist as if resisting her holding it. She turned to look at Annie, bewildered and scared. This man being cold towards her wasn't her Jimmy.

'It's all right, luv. Jimmy's not fully conscious and he can only communicate with gestures. His clamping his lips is him holding in his emotions. He wants to hold you and tell you he loves you, but he can't. He's trying hard to and that makes him look angry.'

'But why tighten his hand so I can't hold it?'

'He's trying to hold yours tightly but missing, that's all.'

Janey could see that what Annie said was right. Her frustration left her and she turned to Jimmy and smiled as she stroked his arm. 'I'm always here for you, me Jimmy. We'll get you better.'

This time he gave the same smile he gave to his mum and this filled Janey with joy. 'Oh, me Jimmy, me Jimmy.'

'There, you see. Jimmy's smiling at you.'

Janey grinned at Annie and then bent and kissed Jimmy's lips. They felt dry and cold. A shudder went through her. She wanted to beg him not to die. But instead, she ran her fingers over his forehead.

Just then, the nurse returned. 'Sorry, but I'll have to ask you to leave now. We don't want to overtax him. It's emotional seeing you all and he cannot let those emotions out yet.'

'I'll come again tomorrow and every day, Jimmy, me darlin'.'

Once more his lips clamped. It was an expression that Janey would rather forget, as for as long as she'd known him, Jimmy had never been angry with her, and despite what Annie said, she had a feeling he was.

Once more she told him she loved him, and this time got the semblance of a smile. This she would take with her and think about, and not the anger, and she would pray hard for God to spare him and to bring him back to her whole again.

Annie put her arm around her when they got outside. 'How will I cope, Annie, luv?'

'You will. You love him and he loves you. Me and Ricky always say that love finds a way.'

'Ah, they're lovely words.'

'And what me and Ricky live by. Love always has found a way for us and for Olivia and Hendrick and it will for you, me darlin'.'

# Chapter Five

## Olivia & Annie

In the month since Hendrick's visit in January, life for Olivia had passed uneventfully but with her heart full of loneliness and longing. She lived for his phone calls, but him making another visit didn't seem as though it would ever happen.

Even the news held little of interest as the talk was of an Australian cricketer called Bradman scoring a record two hundred and nine runs, a wonderful feat, but cricket had never held her attention. War news was that the merchant naval vessels were being armed, which brought into focus that preparations were being made even if most people were still calling it a phoney war.

To Hendrick, it wasn't phoney as he passed on plans that were still being talked of for Germany moving towards Norway and France. The British felt they were ready as their soldiers were on the borders engaged in digging trenches and training manoeuvres.

Olivia tried for the umpteenth time to get her mind back to the accounts she was working on. She was assisting Leonard Preesley, the second young man to take over Hendrick's position managing foreign accounts and investments at her father's bank, the first young man having volunteered to serve in the army. Leonard would never be accepted or conscripted as he had lost a leg in a motorbike accident when in his teens. He'd been training to be an engineer but had to retrain for a sit-down job. Always a square pin in a round hole, he often needed shoring up, though he had a brilliant mind for figures.

'How's it going, Olivia? You look lost in a world no one can enter.'

'I am. A world where I am with Hendrick. But I won't bore you with that. Though I do want to ask you if you've made your mind up to join my choir as I'm going to restart it soon? I'm very short of male singers and I've heard you singing as you walk the corridors here.'

'Walk the corridors! Limp along them, you mean! Anyway, you make me sound like some sort of creep!'

'Ha, sorry. We're a pair together, limping along. But I meant as you go from office to office. Anyway, you may not be a creep, but you do make a play for all the ladies. They all think they're the special one!'

'Ha, that's because I'm the only bloke around! Though I wish I wasn't. This stupid leg prevents me from joining the other lads getting ready to fight Hitler.'

'I know all about stupid legs.'

'Yours was from a train crash, wasn't it . . . ? Sorry, I know from experience that the cause is hard to talk about and brings back unwanted memories. I shouldn't have mentioned it.'

'It's not memories as such as I was knocked out, though I still hear the screeching as the train braked. But, yes, best forgotten. And you're avoiding the subject.'

'Would I be the only male in the choir?'

'No, not the only one. We have a couple of older gentlemen

55

– well, middle-aged. You know Fred Tyler, and we have a farmer who lives on the way to Fermain Bay, Billy Yale.'

'Oh, I know both. Billy's a card. Always keeping everyone laughing. I used to go to his farm to help with the harvest, and I went to school with his son Jack.'

'Has Jack gone to war?'

'No, being a farmer, he's exempt from call-up but he's also a pacifist. He can sing too; he was in the school choir with me.'

'Oh, it would be wonderful if he would come along. It might help you to take the plunge.'

'Ha, you're nothing if not determined, Olivia! All right. I'll do it, I like an adventure.'

'Well, the choir isn't exactly an adventure, but I am hoping we can help morale by raising spirits with a few concerts in the future.'

'Sounds ambitious, but then I've noticed you're a person who always thinks anything is possible, so I'm sure you'll pull it off. I'll make a pact with you: if Jack will, I will.'

'Well, I'd better hope that Jack says yes then. In the meantime, I'll work on a few of the younger girls joining as that will give you both an incentive.'

Olivia cringed when Leon, as Leonard was known, muttered, 'I prefer the mature lady myself.'

A young man of the same height as herself, he had dark hair and blue eyes, features that enhanced his handsome looks and had the girls swooning. But if he thought he could turn his charm on her, he had another thing coming.

'Well, I know what you mean, as I prefer more mature men and have found the perfect one in Hendrick.'

'Oh, I – I didn't mean . . . I meant . . . I'm so sorry, Olivia. It was a throwaway remark that I shouldn't have made. A joke.'

He looked suitably embarrassed and sorry, so she forgave him. 'Well, working so closely to each other, we shouldn't be making throwaway remarks, but I forgive you. Well, I will if you join the choir!'

He laughed out loud, and the moment passed. But Olivia knew that he'd meant it. She'd felt before that he was more than attracted to her, so was glad to nip it in the bud.

'A good time to get our heads back into banking mode, I think, seeing as I'm forgiven.'

Olivia was glad of the distraction and took his cue to begin discussing the account they'd been working on.

Walking home an hour later, the signs of early spring were everywhere with daffodils nodding in the breeze and many-coloured crocuses pushing through the ground in the gardens she passed. It was when she passed Florrie's cafe that Annie, never far from her mind, came rushing into her thoughts. How she missed her and worried about her as she knew from their phone calls that not all was going well.

Jimmy was still in hospital and was sadly a changed man. Annie's description of how he was towards Janey frightened them both. 'He's fine with me, even a bit too much, to be honest,' Annie had told her. 'But nasty with poor Janey and that's not helping her mental state.'

It appeared from what they'd been told that these personality changes could take place and often anger would be directed towards the one the patient loves the most, but still it was so upsetting to hear about, and what it must be like to experience, Olivia couldn't imagine.

She longed to go to the mainland to support Annie, but her father needed her. Since war had broken out, he seemed less able to cope and worried deeply. She knew he had extra information given to him from his many friends in high places in London, but he never spoke about it.

Loes, her son's nanny, greeted her as always, standing on the step holding Karl's hand and then allowing him to run along the promenade of St Peter Port towards her, his little legs going ten to the dozen. She was sure he was far advanced to other twenty-one-month-old children.

Karl's face held such joy that all her feelings of sadness and worry left Olivia as she filled with the same joy when she scooped him up and twirled him around.

'I think we'll drive out to the farmhouse this afternoon, Karl. The sun is warming everywhere and it will be good to see if our daffodils have flowered. Daddy and I planted them the first autumn we bought the house.'

Karl nodded. 'Dills.'

'D-a-ff-o-dills.'

'Daftdills.'

'Haha, that's near enough. Though not a good name as they are beautiful, not daft!'

For some reason, this amused Olivia and she giggled. It felt good and lifted her spirits.

The whitewashed farmhouse looked beautiful in the early spring sunshine as Olivia pulled the car onto the gravel outside the gate.

Being here – the home that was meant to be hers and Hendrick's, and double up as a school teaching languages – brought back the feelings she'd had earlier of loneliness and longing.

Lifting Karl out of the car, memories struck her of going through her pregnancy with Karl here and not having

58

Hendrick by her side. A time made bearable by having Annie with her, taking care of her, and by the laughter and happy times they'd shared together.

'Mummy cry?'

'Mummy always cries a few sad tears here, darling. I think of Daddy and Aunty Annie, and I miss them both.'

'Daddy.'

'Yes, Daddy.'

'Kiss Daddy.'

'You do, darling, you kiss his photo every night and he kisses one of us.'

'Love Daddy.'

Squeezing him tightly, she said, 'I know you do, and so do I . . . Anyway, come on, let's get inside and make some cocoa, shall we? I still have loads left in the big tin I bought ages ago. I'm hoping it will last us through the war as it is like gold dust now.'

Talking to Karl as if he was a grown-up was something that lessened Olivia's loneliness. Though his sentences weren't yet fully formed, they often made sense and amounted to a conversation of sorts.

The schoolroom looked forlorn. A room with no purpose. Olivia used to imagine the pupils here, maybe from foreign lands and boarding in while they took a course in the many languages that she and Hendrick – especially Hendrick – could offer.

Not dwelling on what could not be, she quickly passed through and climbed the stairs to the flat above.

Here was a home. Not the one that was to be their forever home, but a home nonetheless.

With the cocoa made, they sat near to the window. Looking one way, they gazed over the sea, lively today with many birds ducking and diving for food and squawking and seeming to argue with each other as they did.

In the other direction was the field where she and Hendrick intended to build their forever home, a home that was laid out in rocks placed by Hendrick one sunny afternoon to mark out the design as it would one day be. Although the grass had grown almost as tall as the rocks, Olivia could still see where her kitchen was planned to overlook the sea, and their dining room at the back over-looking what would eventually be their garden. And to the side of these the living room. Each room had a stone in the centre stating what would be above it. Where their bedroom was to be had already witnessed them making love in it on a hot sunny day.

A warmth filled her at the memory. But so did it evoke her tears. She turned her face away from Karl. She didn't want his memories of his early years to always feature her sadness.

'Let's go and pick daffodils to take home, shall we, darling?'

As Daphne displayed the daffodils in a vase on top of Hendrick's bureau in Olivia's sitting room, she chatted away.

'How's the dreamboat of the island doing at the bank, Olivia?'

'If you mean Leon, very well. Are all the girls swooning over him?'

'Yes. There's a competition to see who gets him – well, he is about the only eligible man left!'

'If you want to know, why don't you join my choir? I'm always asking you. I've heard you singing around the house.'

'Why, is Leon joining?'

'Possibly.'

'I will then. I thought you only had fuddy-duddies, like that Mrs Green, always busybodying into others' business.'

'She is one of the ladies, but she's all right really. I had a run-in with her over Hendrick being German, but she was easily talked round and has encouraged a lot of folk who were beginning to stay away to come back. I've seen a different side to her, and she has a beautiful soprano voice.'

'What's one of them?'

'She sings very high and very sweetly. It's lovely to listen to.'

'Well, I can't compete with the likes of her.'

'It's not about competing, it's about harmonizing, different voices complementing each other. I wouldn't ask you if I didn't think you would fit in.'

'All right, I will, but I'll only keep coming if Leon does.'

'Ha, you're incorrigible! But honest, always honest. That's why I like you.'

'And I like you, Miss Olivia.'

'Well then, why not drop the "miss" when we're on our own and just be friends, eh?'

'I'll always be your friend. Always loyal to you.'

'I know. You have proven that when you covered for me and Hendrick meeting in Sark . . . Oh, Daphne, that was such a lovely thing to do. I had a wonderful time.'

'Well, you deserve it, Mi . . . I mean, Olivia. And none more so.'

'Thanks, love.'

Daphne almost danced out of the room. Olivia thought her happiness no more than her own. It was lonely without Hendrick and Annie, but even more so as she had no one she could call a friend on the island. Maybe Daphne would be that to her?

*  *  *

Annie tore open Ricky's letter. Always she hoped he would say he was coming home, and yet she knew it wouldn't be that.

'Is the post just for you, Annie, luv?'

Going through to her mum's flat, she told her it was.

'Oh, no one loves me then . . . How did Janey sleep, luv?'

'Fitfully. I feel worn out today as she kept me awake, but I've got to go into work. We've one officer off sick and one on holiday.'

'Poor Janey. How Jimmy is towards her is a massive blow, and with her so fragile. I've thought many a time it'd be easier if Jimmy had been killed . . . There, cut me tongue out, but I've said it.'

'I agree, Mum. This way, we haven't got the bloke we had, but someone hard to cope with who's breaking Janey's heart. The one thing we could all rely on was that Jimmy would keep her happy . . . Now . . . well, I ain't sure he's ever coming back how he was, and they're talking of letting him home!'

'No! Oh, Annie, how will we cope?'

'I don't know but as his family, we've got to. Rose will help, that's for certain. When we've been at the hospital at the same time as her, he's been calm and even civil to Janey.'

'Why has he taken against Janey like this?'

'There's no reason, Mum. His brain is damaged and giving him the wrong signals. The doctor said it could even be that because he loves her so much, he's taking his pain out on her, as he is in pain. He has blinding headaches.'

'Isn't there one of them convalescent homes he could go to? I know they can't do any more for him in a medical hospital, and we know they need the beds, but surely one of these convent places?'

'I'll ask . . . but there's something else, Mum. We didn't

say as it was too upsetting for Janey, but the doctor asked us if Jimmy had ever been out with me.'

'Oh? Why?'

'It seems he asks for me a lot more than for Janey. Anyway, we told him what happened, and he thinks Jimmy's brain may have regressed. That Jimmy is looking on me as the woman he loves and cannot understand how he is married and has a child with Janey.'

'God, no! Not that, Annie. Poor Janey . . . And you, as that's going to be an uncomfortable situation . . . Annie, you won't move out if he returns here, will you, girl?'

'But where could I stay, Mum?'

'There's room in me bedroom for a single bed, luv . . . Oh, Annie, please as I couldn't cope without you.'

'All right, I'll look around the second-hand shops while I'm on me beat this morning, eh? I don't know why we never thought of that before.'

'Ta, luv. That's put me mind at rest. If Jimmy starts . . . or, God forbid, gets violent, you'll know what to do.'

'I do. I can do manoeuvres now that would floor a bloke as big as Jimmy is, or I could stop him with me truncheon. I'd hate doing either and would be afraid of causing further damage to him, but if needs must, I would.'

Mum breathed a sigh of relief. But there was no such relief for Annie. Her shoulders drooped with the weight of her worries. How were they meant to cope with a damaged man the size of Jimmy?

On the bus to the station Annie read Ricky's letter.

*Me darlin' Annie,*
*I miss you every day. Not much to tell as nothing happening.*

Even if there was, Annie knew Ricky wouldn't say. His letters were vetted like every soldier's and in order for it to get to her and not be confiscated, as it would be if it contained information of any kind, he was careful what he said.

*Me and some of the lads have formed a football team and enjoy a kickaround. Others like cricket, but I ain't one for that. I spend me time off either writing to you, me darlin', or thinking about you. Oh, and this'll not surprise you, but I've been entertaining the lads, me and another bloke. We sing duets and, wait for it . . . we dance too!*

Annie felt like bursting out laughing, but crying at the same time as she remembered the times Ricky had danced in the street with her and Olivia, and when he danced her around when they came out of the music hall. Oh, and when he did 'Knees up Mother Brown' with her on Janey's and Jimmy's wedding day.

Silent, lonely tears ran down her face as these memories assailed her. She wiped her face with the back of her hand and read on.

*It's hilarious and a lot of fun and is keeping morale up.*
*I got your letter and remembered when you talked about the choir you thought a good idea. I did too. Have you started it yet, me darlin'? You can be in competition with Olivia. See whose choir is the best, and then when this lot's over all meet up and have a right ole concert.*

The idea sounded fun, though probably impossible. But yes, she had started the choir, and found someone willing to direct them in an old schoolmaster she bumped into. Ted

64

was lovely and was making their practice great fun. She'd write about him to Ricky and tell him how they would get on like a house on fire, them having the same interest in musicals and singing. Her heart warmed at the thought and at her Ricky keeping the lads over there happy. But then he'd keep them happy just being with them and she thought he must be the best sergeant ever.

*Anyway, all this showmanship is making life a little bearable, because at times, me darlin', it's unbearable without you.*

*Write soon, Annie. Let me know how Jimmy is. I hope he makes a good recovery. Poor bloke, no one asks to be injured, but in the way he was, he must feel cheated.*

*Love you with all me heart, me darlin', and you have me arms around you in all you do. Your Ricky x*

Clutching the letter to her, Annie stared out of the window and was glad when at last the bus pulled up at her stop. The short walk to the station gave her time to compose herself.

The banter was as usual among her fellow officers. There was a bit of leg-pulling of Betty, who'd arrested a man she thought was a conchie, but who turned out to be a doctor working at the military hospital! Why she hadn't listened to him and checked his story out was beyond Annie, but always trying to prove herself, Betty had dived in feet first.

When the sarge gave them the beat they were to work, Annie was glad he was sending them out alone. She walked quickly, taking the route over Tower Bridge and stopping for a moment to look down to where she'd met Ricky. A bad day for her, as she'd found out about Jimmy and Janey and had felt like ending her life, but it had turned out to be one of the best days of her life.

'Hey! Annie! Well, luv, it's good to see yer.'

'Just popping in Bert's to get us both a mug of tea, luv, be with you in a mo.'

Aggie, a woman in her sixties, little and bent over as she'd aged before her time, owned a flower stall on the bridge. It had been her who had alerted Ricky to Annie's plight that fateful day and sent him to save her. They'd been friends ever since, and now with Ricky no longer pounding the beat and taking her tea, Annie had willingly taken over the duty.

'Here you are. Sip this, Aggie, it'll warm you up.'

'I need something, luv, the wind's whipping off the Thames today.'

'When are you going to give up, eh, Aggie? It ain't right a woman of your age standing out here in all weathers.'

'Not for a good year or two, mate. What do yer want me to do, sit in a rocking chair twiddling me thumbs? Nah, me customers keep me going and I 'ave some toffs, yer know. I even remind them, when I see them, of their anniversaries. They'd get into all sorts of trouble without knowing that now, wouldn't they?'

Aggie grinned her one-tooth grin. A dribble of tea rolled down her chin. She lifted her hessian apron and wiped it away.

'A good drop of tea this. Always is from Bert's.' She smacked her lips together. 'Now then, missy, what's troubling you besides missing your Ricky, eh?'

Aggie always knew when Annie was feeling low. She told her about Jimmy and her fears.

'That ain't good, luv. Not for you or your poor sister. And yer say they're letting him 'ome?'

'Yes. I'm dreading it, and so are me mum and Cissy, and I'm sure Janey is but she won't admit it. Not that I blame her. I wouldn't if it was Ricky.'

'No, it ain't right, but not a lot yer can do, mate. I don't know, the world's gone mad. I ain't much for loony bins, but they serve their purpose for some poor folk.'

Annie couldn't believe that she agreed. She didn't say so as most of those places were awful. She'd been called upon to take an escaped patient back to an asylum only last year and the smell of the place, not to mention the cries of agony coming from within, stayed with her for a long time. Could she really commit Jimmy to such a place? Would Rose ever forgive them?

'Well, I'll get on me way, Aggie. Ta for the chat, luv.'

'See yer tomorrow, eh?'

Annie knew Aggie looked forward to her visits. 'Yes, I'll be here. You take care, and wrap up warm, you look frozen.' On instinct, Annie bent and kissed Aggie on the cheek. She smelled of fresh air even though she always seemed to have the same long black frock on under her pinny. It smelled freshly washed too. This put Annie's mind at rest that Aggie could still take care of herself and took pride in doing so. She smiled as she waved and walked on, sure that she saw a tear in Aggie's eye. The Aggies of this world were the mainstay of the East End, and while there were women like her – eccentric, and yet talking a lot of sense – Annie somehow felt that the world would always be safe. She prayed it would be so.

# Chapter Six

## Janey

Janey curled up into a ball with the pain in her stomach.

'What the . . . ! Fuck, Janey, the bed's wet! You dirty tyke, you!'

She wanted to scream that her waters had broken and that his thumping of her the night before had probably escalated her labour, but she dared not speak.

Being only mid-March, it was too early by about four weeks for her baby to be born, but the pain she was in and the wetness told her it was happening.

'Call Annie for me, Jimmy.'

'Call her? It's meant to be her in this bed with me, not you, you slag.'

Pain of a different kind sliced through Janey, but she told herself her Jimmy was ill, he didn't know what he was saying or doing. He hadn't meant the blows he'd been giving her since he came home over a week ago. She was glad they were where no one would see the bruising.

'What's up with you anyway?'

'Our baby's coming, Jimmy, luv.'

'Our baby! Ha, more likely Tom, Dick or Harry's baby! I've been away. How can it be mine, eh? You slag!'

A thump landed on her arm. Janey cried out.

'Oh, shut up! I ain't begun to touch you yet. You hood-winked me and got me away from the love of me life. I've loved Annie since I were a nipper! But you couldn't bear that, could you? You wanted me for yourself.' Jimmy pulled his fist back, but as he did a massive pain gripped Janey. Her scream echoed around the house.

Footsteps could be heard running up the stairs. Jimmy jumped back off the bed and went into the bathroom. Mixed emotions made Janey let out a sigh of despair and relief, but her breaking heart gave her questions. *How could me lovely Jimmy change to become this monster who scares the life out of me?*

'I want me Jimmy back.'

This was screamed out of her as another pain clutched her stomach, forcing her to push until she thought her temples would explode. But then the door opened and she heard lovely Cissy's voice telling Annie, 'Eeh, Annie, the babby's coming!'

Relief conquered Janey's despair at Annie's comforting words, 'It's all right . . . Janey, luv, we're here now. . . Cissy, get the kettle on and bring a bowl of cold water and a cloth . . . Oh, and shout down to Mum to keep Beth down there with her.'

Janey couldn't think for a minute why Beth was downstairs, but then remembered her cot had been taken down to be in with Mum and Annie. They all thought it best.

Annie's arms came around her. 'I've got you, me darlin'. Let's get baby into the world, eh?'

'It's too early, Annie!'

'We don't know that for sure, do we? At least, how early. A couple of weeks is nothing. You just do what you know you have to, eh?'

Janey had no choice as the next pain swept over her and she pushed with all her might once more.

'I can see the head. Pant, Janey, while I get it through. Cissy, hold her and mop her brow for her, luv.'

'I've got you, lass. You hold on to me.'

'Oh, Cissy. Annie! Help me!'

No sooner had she said this than she felt Annie's fingers tugging her child. The urge to push came with the feeling. She bore down and was rewarded by a loud baby cry.

'Oh, Annie, Annie, is it all right?'

'She is, me darlin'. She's beautiful . . . Another East End girl! . . . Where's Jimmy, luv?'

'He – he went to the bathroom. Is she really all right? She's gone quiet.'

'She's fine. Cissy, sorry, luv, but can you get me some scissors? And pour some warm water into a jug. I need to clean her eyes once I have the cord cut . . . Now, little one, let's see if I can give you a neat belly button. The midwife who taught us coppers to deliver babies said it's a measure of a good delivery. Well, we want that for you, me little darlin'.'

The baby squirmed, but to Janey, now leaning on her elbows watching her child and all going on, it looked to all the world as if she'd smiled.

'Hello, Angela . . . That's your new name, me little darlin'.'

Annie smiled and Janey knew she was thinking of how when Beth was born, she'd been rejected at first. Janey felt ashamed of that now and no matter what, she'd told herself that wouldn't happen again, even if she did feel the same repulsion. But she didn't feel it! She felt nothing but a deep love for her Angie, as she was going to be known.

Janey gave a big sigh. *Maybe Angie will heal Jimmy. If he*

*feels the love he should for his own flesh and blood, maybe he'll*
*accept her as his and be happy again.*

But despite these brave thoughts, hearing the click of the bathroom door awoke the streak of fear she'd felt whenever she heard him approach.

'What's going on . . . ? Annie, Annie, luv, you're covered in blood!'

'Well, I have just delivered your baby, Jimmy.'

'We have a baby? Oh, Annie!'

'No, Jimmy. Not me and you. Remember? You're married to Janey, and she has just given birth to your second daughter. I think she deserves a kiss and a cuddle for that now I have the little Angela's cord cut.'

'Huh! I doubt it's mine.'

'Jimmy, Janey's never been with anyone else, now stop this. The doctor said you can if you keep telling yourself the truth. You married Janey, you and she have two children now, Beth who is downstairs awaiting reassurance from her daddy, and now Angela, who has just entered this world and is looking to you to love and protect her.'

'It should have been us, Annie, and it will be, I promise.'

Janey's tears tumbled down her face. She didn't try to stop them. She thought she might never stop crying again.

Without looking at her, or their new daughter, Jimmy turned. 'I'm going to me mum's. I can't bear to look at that slut any longer.'

Janey screamed out, 'Jimmy, I love you . . . Please, Jimmy . . . JIMMY!'

Cissy's arms held her this time.

But no matter who held her, they couldn't have stopped her body shaking. Every limb trembled. Sweat stood in beads on her skin, and then ran down her body.

'Wrap the blankets around her, quickly, Cissy, then go and tell Mum what's happening as I ain't seen anything like this.'

When Cissy came back, she was gasping for breath. 'It – it's sommat called the ague. It happens after the birth or if there's a fever. Your ma said to just keep her warm and reassure her, but if you think she's got a fever, then call the doctor.'

Annie had put little Angie down and now stood by the bedside. Janey felt her weight dip the mattress and then Annie's arms take hold of her and cuddle her. It seemed to Janey that everything would come right, her sister would make it so. Gradually the shaking stopped and she flopped her head onto Annie's shoulder. 'I want to hold me Angie now, Annie.'

'Let's get you cleaned up first, eh?'

'No! I'll do that. I'll go to the bathroom. I've some clean nighties in there and some rags for me bleeding.'

'But you ain't meant to get off the bed, luv.'

'I've got to, Annie, I can't pee in the bed!'

Annie agreed and supported her to the bathroom. Sitting on the lav, Janey put her head in her hands. She felt so weak, so hurt and bruised. But she mustn't let Annie see her injuries. She would have Jimmy sectioned. Shaking her head, she thought, *I don't want that. I can help Jimmy get better. I can. He loves me. He does. He can't help his head being all over the place.*

Finding the energy to wash herself, pin the rags in place and then put on a long nightgown that covered all, Janey went back into the room and managed a smile.

'You look lovely, me darlin'. Your little girl can't wait to meet you, and I reckon she's hungry too.'

When she got into bed, Janey undid the buttons that went

down to her waist and took little Angie. Putting her to her breast, she smiled. The feeling was lovely as Angie found her nipple and sucked for all she was worth.

'Shall I bring Beth up, me darlin'?'

'Yes, please . . . Oh, I wish Mum could get up the stairs. If Jimmy was here, he'd lift her up in no time.'

'Well, we'll see when he gets back, eh?'

Janey didn't miss the look that passed between Annie and Cissy. She wanted to cry out her grief for the Jimmy she'd lost, but she also wanted to fight to get him back. 'Will you ring Rose and see if Jimmy got there all right, Annie, and tell her she has another granddaughter? If Jimmy's there, she'll talk to him and make him see that he's wrong about me.'

''Course I will, luv. It's lucky I'm here, only I swapped shifts with Betty.' Annie rolled her eyes. 'She had a hair appointment! She's a one that one. She ain't been wed five minutes, her bloke's gone to war and she's knocking off some dockworker who she met on her beat!'

'And her bloke'll come back to her in one piece, forgive her and they'll live happily ever after, whereas I ain't never been unfaithful to Jimmy and go through hell!'

'By, you're a brave lass, Janey. You hold on to the fact that you've done nowt wrong and never start to blame yourself for any of this. Nor Jimmy for that matter. He don't knaw what he's doing, poor lad.'

'Ta, Cissy. It's hard, but I took him in sickness and in health.'

'You did, luv, but you will tell us if he's hurting you, won't you? Not even brain damage – even though it's the reason for it – excuses that and you need protection. You ain't strong as it is.'

'I will, Annie, I promise . . . I'm tired now and just want me Beth.'

Beth brought a ray of sunshine into the room when she bounded in. 'Baba!' She pointed towards the cot where Angie was now swaddled in a blanket and fast asleep.

'Yes, darlin'. Your sister.'

'Me sister.'

'Clever girl! You'll look after her, won't you, eh? Her name's Angie.'

'An-An.'

'Yes, that will do. An-An. Come and give Mummy a cuddle.'

'Daddy gone.'

'He'll be back, me darlin'.'

'Daddy cwoss.'

'Not really. He had a bad headache. Now, I want my cuddle.'

Annie lifted Beth onto the bed. She snuggled into Janey. The feel of her little chubby arms around her neck soothed some of the pain knotted in Janey's heart.

When she woke later, it was to Angie crying. Cissy was sat in the armchair in the corner of the room, her mouth open and little snores sounding when she breathed out. Angie's louder cry woke Cissy. She looked bemused for a moment, then rose and picked Angie up. 'There, there, your ma's ready for you, me wee lass.'

Cissy had come down to London from the North of England as a maid and eventually got the job with Olivia's dad. Now with the apartment taken by the government for goodness knows what, she had a retainer from the family to keep her going. It had been a good day when she'd moved into the flat downstairs. That had been through the kindness of Jimmy, who'd seen how much Cissy and Mum loved one another.

Jimmy had been such a kind, gentle person. Would she ever see that side of him again?

'Here you are, lass. She wants feeding again, I reckon. Annie had to go to work so she took Beth downstairs to your ma again. I've been keeping me eye on them, and they're all right. But Vera wants to see little 'un when you've done.'

'Poor Mum, she'd love to come up to see me . . . Has there been any word of Jimmy?'

'Annie phoned his ma. He's there . . . Look, lass, it's safer that he stays there. It's not safe him being here, but Rose seems able to get through to him. She said she'd come later to see you when he drops off to sleep. He's had his pill and you knaw he allus sleeps for a good while after it takes effect.'

Janey's mouth quivered. How much more could she take? The immense pain of her body released that of her heart, when only hurting herself had done that in the past. Her thoughts went to the razor in the bathroom cabinet. Knowing it was there was a comfort, but using it wouldn't surpass the pain she had, only give the satisfaction of hurting herself and not being hurt by the man she loved. But did she want to hurt herself? It came to her that she didn't. She was worn out. Broken. Slicing her arms and body would only add to that, not help it.

With these thoughts calming her emotions, she was able to make a decision.

'When Rose comes, I'll get her to help me downstairs, Cissy. Lugging bags of spuds and the like around have made her strong, she'll lift me easily.'

'Aye, she is that, lass. She's muscles as big as any man's. Mind, I feel sorry for her. She were meant to be married to her Alf and living on her farm in Kent by now. It ain't fair. If Jimmy'd been all right, she might've been able to hand the business over to him and gone to her man, but as it is, I can't see that ever happening for her now.'

Janey had always thought it funny that Rose, her mother-in-law, wanted to marry. She seemed too old for that. Though thinking about it, she said she was only seventeen when her dad raped her, and she had Jimmy. So, she'd only be about forty-one now.

'Cissy, do you think Jimmy's inbreeding has contributed to how he is now?'

'I don't knaw, lass. He were all right before the shooting. The brain's a funny thing. It's our main hub, so to speak.'

'Will he ever be well again?'

'Another question I can't answer. What did the doctor say?'

'He said there were little chance, but even a little chance is worth hoping for.'

'To my mind, they should never have let him out.'

Horror gripped Janey. Jimmy wasn't right, she knew that, but to condemn him to some asylum or such wasn't something she thought a wife should do, nor did she think that would be fair on Jimmy. It was down to her to find a way to cope with his moods.

'How is he with Beth when we ain't around, Janey? He don't do nowt to her, does he?'

'No, he adores her and her him. He accepts he's her daddy, but this little one, he just doesn't seem sure of. He's mixed up about how long he was away.'

'Eeh, lass, I fear for you. Think seriously about talking to the doctor about his moods. Be honest with me, lass, is Jimmy hurting you?'

'Yes, but don't tell Annie, or Mum, will you, Cissy? I don't think they've guessed yet.'

'By, lass, you're asking sommat of me there. You need protecting.'

'Please, Cissy. Just give me time. I think I make break-throughs every now and then. It all takes patience.'

'You knaw, you've surprised us all, lass. You've risen to this challenge. We've all been thinking you'd crumble and become ill yourself over it, but you haven't. And that's a good thing . . . so, well, if you're willing to do this, and it's helping you, I won't say owt. But tell me, does he hurt you badly?'

'No. He slaps me if he gets frustrated, but it only stings for a while. And he's always sorry.'

Janey crossed her fingers against the lie, but she didn't want to lose Jimmy. Even this new, frightening Jimmy. She loved him. It was as simple as that.

When Rose arrived, she hugged Janey. 'It'll come right, luv. I keep talking to him, reminding him how he was with Annie, but how he fell in love with you. I've told him he was the one to pursue you and that I know for a fact you ain't been with anyone else. Now, where's me new granddaughter? I've had cuddles with Beth first. She's full of An-An her baby sister! So, that bodes well.'

'You can pick her up if you like, Rose. She needs a nappy change, though. I just heard her let rip and was going to get out to clean her up.'

'I'll do it. Where's your terry towels, me darlin'?'

'In the bathroom, piled on the bathroom stool.'

'Right, I'll fetch one and a towel to lay her on.'

When Rose picked Angie up, she cooed over her. 'You look just like your daddy, little one, and Granny loves you.

He can't disown this one, Janey, she has his hair, black and curly, and his features. It's striking.'

'Yes, I saw that.'

Once Angie was all cleaned up and smelling of talc, Rose said, 'Cissy said you want help getting down the stairs, me darlin'. Are yer sure you'll be all right?'

'Yes, I'll be fine. I need to see me mum, Rose, and show her me baby.'

''Course you do, luv. Right, I'll put Angie down then I'll take you first and come back for her.'

Once they were down and Janey was lying on her mum's bed with her mum holding her the best she could from her wheelchair, Janey couldn't stop the tears.

'There, there, me darlin', it's all over with.'

When Rose handed Angie to Mum, her face lit up like a shining light of love. This spilled Janey's tears again.

'You're like me, luv, I was tearful after giving birth.'

'And me, Vera. When I held Jimmy, I cried all over him. Mind, we were homeless and in the workhouse, and I didn't know if they were going to take him from me, but eventually we got the little house near to you. As yer know, I had to do stuff to earn money, but though I hated it, I'd do it again to feed me son. None of what I went through was his fault, just as what he's going through now ain't.'

This helped Janey. Rose was right, Jimmy wasn't to blame, so like Rose, she would stick by him, and no one would change her mind. She loved him and Annie had said that love always finds a way through troubles. Hers were bad but she'd get through it all.

# PART TWO

A Changing World

# Chapter Seven

## *Olivia*

### June 1940

The war wasn't going well. Germany was making strides in France and the British soldiers had been evacuated from Dunkirk. The operation had been a miracle of courage as every boat available from small family crafts to huge ferries fought valiantly to get the soldiers home.

But this terrible news of Britain's defeat paled in the light of the frightening prospect Guernsey might face after the announcement on the fifteenth of June that had struck fear into every islander.

Britain had ordered that island administrators demilitarize the island. All arms, uniforms and equipment used by the militia and defence volunteers were to be deposited at the town arsenal, and private firearms handed to police.

Churchill had said that he could defend the islands from the sea, but this wasn't being imposed as so many dissented, citing that the islands were of no strategic value and the cost of defending them prohibitive.

Evacuation of the children had begun. Everyone thought they would be so much safer on the mainland.

Olivia's fear deepened with every snippet of news. Her

instinct had been to contact Hendrick and so she'd left messages with Mr Meyer, his father's neighbour.

Every time the telephone rang, she prayed it would be him. At last, it was.

After the initial code intro, she found they could speak freely.

'My darling, I have been increasingly afraid this may happen and now that it has, I fear for our beloved Guernsey and its people, and for you and our son. I cannot believe that the islands are left with no military protection. It has seemed to me that they are a sitting target for Hitler to gain what he desires the most – occupation of British soil.'

'Yes, many feel that way and are leaving the island for the mainland. Oh, Hendrick, the children are being evacuated with their teachers. And many mothers are leaving with babes in arms. But me and little Karl will be all right, won't we? You always said that being married to a German civil servant would protect us if Guernsey was directly caught up in the war. Has that changed?'

'Not really . . . but I fear that as Hitler doesn't know the islands aren't protected by the military, if he decides to take them, he will use his might to do so. That will mean bombing! He won't care that they are of no strategic value. He wants that triumph over the British. Oh, I wish I knew what his plans were on this, but I can't find anything out. For some reason his strategists are being very tight-lipped.'

'They don't suspect you, do they?'

'No, I'm sure they don't . . . Oh, Olivia, my love, I want you to leave. Go to London to Annie. Take Karl and your father, if he will go. Find a place in the country where you will be safe. Though not with your aunt . . . Cornwall, with it being coastal, may also be a dangerous place.'

'But what about the bank? Daddy can't just leave it even though his manager could take over, we are so short-staffed. Our international investors only have me and Leon, who I told you of, and none of us have the skills you had. But we're doing our best to cope, which isn't easy as so many more are looking on us as a safe place for their money and causing us even more work. I fear that if I go, we will let down so many.'

'Well, maybe your father cannot leave. I know you and Leon are looking after these accounts, but he will know every last penny in them and can take over running them at the drop of a hat. You must leave it to him and get out with Karl. Please, Olivia. You and I can carry on our work just as well with you in England – maybe better as you won't need Annie to pass what I give you to the War Office but can do it yourself.'

'This is against all you thought in the beginning, Hendrick. You thought that if in England, I would be used by the Hitler regime to gain information for them. I don't want to be a double agent, Hendrick, I just couldn't do it, and yet, if asked and I refuse, it could be bad for you!'

'I know, I did think that, but only if you were in London, and because of the many contacts your father has there, both business and political. But if you were in the countryside . . . say in the Midlands, or in the North even . . . yes, the North would be ideal. Cissy will tell you how it is up there, and you will settle well as it is so like Guernsey, a lovely, friendly place, where the people all know each other and look out for one another.'

Olivia smiled at the thought of the lovely Cissy, an adored mother figure to herself and her dearest friend, Annie.

'I urge you to act, Olivia . . . no, I'm begging you to.'

'I will, my dear. I promise.'

To Olivia, it was as if Hendrick knew more than he was saying – but no, he would never do that. If he had information that might save any part of Britain and the Channel Isles, he would give it to her. He was acting on a hunch, she was sure of that.

'Go today. Charter a boat to take you. It won't seem strange as you say many are leaving. You could even offer places in your boat to others as I imagine there is a big demand. Oh, and take Nanny. Being from Holland and of Jewish origin, she won't be safe in the event of an invasion.'

'I'm not sure about—'

'Please, Olivia, please do as I say. It is awful here, but I cope . . . Well, just. But to be here and to know that you and little Karl aren't safe would be unbearable for me.'

'All right, darling. I'm sure your fears are unfounded, but if so, it won't be a wasted journey. I'll get to see Annie and Cissy and everyone . . . Yes, I'm beginning to look forward to it.'

Hendrick's sigh of relief could be heard over the crackling of the line.

Olivia dropped her head into her hands the moment she replaced the receiver. Everything Hendrick had asked her to do was so against her basic instincts. Yes, many shared Hendrick's fears, but many more thought it ludicrous that Hitler should bother himself with a few small islands that wouldn't further his cause in any way. But she'd promised, and so drying her eyes and taking a deep breath, she gathered the papers together that she'd been working on and neatly stacked them. She would get her secretary to see that the report on the completed analysis would be given to the company secretary of the firm they belonged to.

Taking a moment to check her in-tray, Olivia took decisions on whom to distribute her remaining work to before calling her secretary in and instructing her. She didn't do this with her international clients as they would be safe in Leon's hands.

A few moments later, she stood in her father's office. His face held shock, and then a look passed over him that spoke of his own vulnerability, and increased the knotting in Olivia's stomach. For a moment she thought she would be sick. It was as if she'd lost the rock that had held her safe all her life as her father's stature diminished. At this moment he was no longer the strong, clever and very rich father whom she had always looked up to.

Not that he was one to flaunt his riches. A kind man who never saw others go without, he lived his life quietly for most of the time, though his wealth had brought him contacts in all walks of life. 'Word has been passed to me of the very real possibility of Hitler glancing this way once he has his regime entrenched in Paris and running France according to his wishes. It's right, too, that you and Karl should go, but I must stay. I must protect what is ours. If an invasion happens, my clients will want to know that I am firmly in place looking after their accounts. Many of those whose investments are in our hands are German, so that will give me a level of protection. But, oh, my dear, for us to be apart while such fear surrounds our lives is unbearable to think about.'

Olivia went over to him. He'd been sitting behind his huge walnut desk but now stood. His arms enclosed her the moment she was by his side. With her head on his strong chest, he stroked her hair.

He wasn't a young man – at least, not as young as her friends' fathers.

'You know, my dear, for the very first time, I'm glad your mother isn't here to suffer this fear and uncertainty. She was a strong person, and would have been at the forefront of any organization set up to help. I can see her getting herself into all sorts of bother with Hitler.' He chuckled. 'Even hitting him with her handbag!'

Olivia smiled up at him.

'Dearest, you take after her in more than looks, and that is making it easier for me to let you go. For you, too, could be getting into bother if an invasion does happen. Not only will you want to fight people's corner, but with the work that you and Hendrick are carrying out – as admirable as it is – it would be very dangerous if it does happen that we have to live right under the Germans' noses. Hendrick is right, you will be safer in the countryside of England.'

'But the mainland could be invaded too!'

'Yes, that's true, but less likely. Look, if you go with Karl, I'll do all I can to follow you, I promise. Anyway, we were talking of my retirement recently, so if I can get enough staff to support the managerial team here, then I will be by your side before you know it.'

'But how? We are short-staffed already!'

'There are still many Guernsey women we could recruit from. We have to find a way to entice more of them and to give them the confidence that they can do this work.'

'I have been thinking about that and concluded that you need to offer flexible working hours that fit in with taking care of their families. And to find a way of overcoming this barrier of banking always having been a male domain.'

'Well, you're a pioneer in that, my dear.'

'Not really. Other women are probably still thinking it isn't a career they would be considered for and that I only got in due to nepotism. Being female, I doubt that anyone credits me with the ability to deserve the post in my own right!'

'Ha, let's not go down the women's rights path today, my dearest. You must get your skates on. There'll be no boatman willing to take you if it gets much later.'

His hug tightened around her. When he released her, he said, 'You'd better go home now and get everything sorted. I'll come home very shortly and spend time with little Karl, but first, I'll arrange your boat for you.'

Bending over the papers he'd been working on, her father shuffled them around. Olivia knew he was near to tears and thought it best to leave him. Speaking in a light tone, she said, 'That would be such a help, thanks, Daddy. I'll see you at home,' and left him to a private moment of coming to terms with this new development.

At the quayside, Bertie, the port master, fussed over Karl. 'It's a rum do, Miss Olivia. One I never thought to see happen again. Bloody Germany, I thought they'd taken such a pasting in the last lot that they'd be peaceful for ever. They seem to have a hunger for power. They ain't ones for earning it but taking it!'

Olivia felt compelled to refute this on Hendrick's behalf. 'They *are* hard-working, Bertie. And fiercely patriotic, believing that lands that did belong to them should still do so. A proud nation who have withstood a lot of oppression since the end of the Great War. Hitler and his distorted view of everything is driving this, not the ordinary people.'

'Huh, so says the woman of a German!'

This cut Olivia as she heard the disgust in Bertie's voice and saw his look of hate.

'I'm the wife of Hendrick, who is one of us! You watched him grow up, you know what a good and kind man he is.'

'Aye, I did, and I watched him run to his fellow countrymen the moment they looked like being powerful as well.'

'It wasn't like that, Bertie. All German nationals were called to duty and not given a choice as to whether they wanted to support Hitler or not. It wasn't . . .' Olivia stopped herself. She was always torn between defending Hendrick and being careful not to betray him by giving a hint of how he was working against the regime. He was in so much danger.

'Well, whatever. We'll have to agree to disagree. Now, if you ladies are ready, it's time to board or you'll miss the tide.'

Olivia couldn't leave it there. 'Bertie, I've always loved and respected you. You all know that there was no talk of war when Hendrick and I fell in love as kids, you watched us grow and helped to nurture us. We are still those people, caught up like you in what is happening in the world around us.'

'Aye, I'm sorry, love. Put it down to fear. If we see an enemy, we group together, that's what's happening. But we're wrong to do that against one of our own and to judge him.'

He hung his head. On an impulse, Olivia put up her hand and touched his shoulder. 'I will always be an islander, shaped by you all. You are my people, and you are Hendrick's too. He misses you all, and while he is doing the duty that he was called to do, he asks after you all the time.'

'That's good, love. I don't wish him ill, just his fellow countrymen. Now off with you and get that little one to safety. No doubt we'll be doing many runs like this – have already. The island will soon be deserted. It's a lot to take in and to deal with.'

As tall as him, Olivia leaned forward and kissed his cheek. Something she'd never done. As he held his lamp up, she saw a tear glistening in his eye. If only she could tell him what extreme danger her darling Hendrick was putting himself in to try to save them all and their beloved island life. But she turned away and walked along the boards, her tread clomping and as heavy as her heart.

Loes had put Karl down while she saw to folding his carriage and he now ran towards Olivia. A sturdy two-year-old, who'd enjoyed his birthday last month and was so like his father with his fair hair and dark eyes, his arms were open and his face full of glee.

Gathering him up, Olivia held him to her.

'Boat. Me going on a boat.'

'Yes, you are, my darling. And you're going to see your lovely Aunty Annie, your godmother and mummy's greatest friend.'

Karl frowned. 'Annie?'

'Aunty Annie. You will love her. She was at your birth, and has always been by my side. She's in my heart and yours too, and though you don't remember her, I know you will love her as I do.'

'Aunty Annie.'

'Yes, a lovely cockney, who is also a Guernsey Girl as that's the nickname we gave ourselves when she lived here with me. She'll look after us, Karl, my darling.'

# Chapter Eight

## Annie

A distraught Annie fumbled with the buttons of her police uniform jacket.

Tired to the bones of her having not slept a wink, she pulled on one shiny button as if she would tear it off and throw it at the wall.

Bending forward with the weight of her anguish, she clutched the kitchen table and stared at the toast she'd made but hadn't touched. *Please let today be the day I hear news of me darlin' Ricky. Please, please don't let him be hurt . . . or . . . !* No, she refused to let the awfulness of that thought into her head. She had to keep believing.

But the BBC news had announced over a week ago that the last of the men had been rescued and still she'd heard nothing. *Please, please let me Ricky have been one of them!* She didn't listen to the voice that kept telling her he couldn't have been or he would be home by now.

The kitchen door opening had her straightening her back and putting on a brave smile for her sister, Janey.

'What're you doing down here, luv? Are you all right?'

'I – I just wanted to be with you, Annie. Is Mum still asleep?'

'She is. She had a good night too. I'll go as soon as Lilly arrives. She's Mum-sitting this morning and will help her to get up. Will you be able to make them their porridge when they're ready, luv?'

'Yes, I'll see to it, Beth will want some then too. She's a sleepyhead that one, but she loves having her breakfast with her granny. I've just fed Angie and she's fast asleep, so I'm free for a while.'

'No word from Jimmy?'

'No. I don't think he's ever coming home for good. He just visits when . . . Anyway, he's happier at his mum's. Rose can handle him. He was even civil to me when I took the kids around there yesterday.'

'Poor Rose, she's supposed to be with her Alf on her farm, but now she's stuck with the business and Jimmy. How she copes, I don't know.'

'Well, she is looking for someone to buy her stall and she'll supply the produce from her farm as she does now, but there's so few men left at home, and even fewer wanting to invest with the way things are.'

'I hope she finds someone soon. I'll keep me nose to the ground. I meet a lot of folk in the day as I walk me beat.'

Janey worried Annie. She had so much to contend with and there was a look about her face that Annie dreaded. It told of her mental health problems weighing her down once more but then, with how Jimmy was, Annie wasn't surprised.

Trying to be cheerful, Annie broadened her smile. 'Well, luv, another day dawns, eh? And here we are all doom and gloom. Come here, mate.'

Holding Janey's frail body increased Annie's anxiety. 'Everything'll be all right, Janey. Grab hold of the East Enders' spirit, luv. You're surrounded by strong women who'll always be there for you, and though he ain't the same, at least your Jimmy's out of danger. There's a lot to be thankful for, eh?'

Janey burst into tears.

Annie's worry increased. Janey looked on the verge of suffering another breakdown. 'Luv, you ain't hurting yourself, are you?'

'No, but the thought keeps coming to me, Annie, I just keep fighting it.'

'Oh, me darlin', I'm here for you.'

'Would you move back upstairs with me, Annie? I miss having you in me bed. I slept well then and felt safe.'

'If I do that, luv, you'll be shutting Jimmy out completely. As it is, he comes home now and again and spends a night with you. You need to keep that door open to him, luv.'

'It's like he's using me for his release and then he's off again. He don't seem to love me, he's always on about you, Annie.'

'Look, you know the doctor said that's something he can't help and that it could, given time, stop happening as his mind catches up with reality. He's never tried anything on with me. I'd tell you if he did, luv . . . Janey, well, to my mind, you've got to decide if you want to carry on . . . I mean, you've grounds for divorce, and you could look to start a new life for you and the kids.'

'No. I couldn't do that. I love Jimmy. I couldn't turn me back on him.'

Annie sighed. She was lost herself and in need of comfort rather than to be giving it.

The sound of the front door opening and Lilly, her mother-in-law's voice calling out, 'It's only me, duckie,' was a welcome distraction.

'The door's open as always, Lilly, luv.' Annie patted Janey's back and stepped away. 'Now, you'll be all right, luv. Lilly'll see to that as I'm on duty in an hour.'

Meeting Lilly at the door, Annie was grateful for the lovely hug she gave her but detected all wasn't well. Lilly looked as though she'd been up all night. 'Is everything all right, luv?'

'Well, if you can bleedin' count me son being at war as all right, girl, it is.'

This wasn't said in a sarcastic or angry way, but in a way that Annie could detect Lilly's sadness and worry.

'He'll be fine. You know Ricky. He's like a tank on his own, no German'll hurt him.' Annie wished she believed this, but with Lilly's worry, her own had increased.

'Yes, he's taken some knocks. Spoiled his looks it did. But then that always 'elped him as no one would tackle him after he had them injuries, he looked too intimidating.'

'Well, Lilly, and if they save him, then we should be grateful for it.' Annie smiled, but inside she felt a longing to run her fingers down the deep scar on her beloved Ricky's face and trace the shape of his crooked nose that Lilly had brought to mind. Lilly was suffering and trying to convince herself her son was all right.

Mum called out at that moment, and they all went in to her. She greeted them with a smile, the kind of smile that tried to hide the pain she was in, but her agony from her chronic arthritis was etched into every line of her face.

'I've brought you a cuppa, Mum. How're you feeling?'

'I'll be better for having a cuppa, luv.'

Both Annie and Janey kissed her. Then Lilly pushed past them. 'Hey, it's me to have a turn now. Hello, Vera, luv.' They hugged. 'I'm going to 'elp you to dress when I've had me tea.'

'Ta. You're a love. How is everyone? I'm worried about the lot of you. You've all got troubles.'

After catching Mum up with how they'd slept, Jimmy not having been to visit, the kids sleeping soundly, and Annie having to go in half an hour, they sat around her bed drinking their tea.

'I expect Jimmy has a lot of sleep to catch up on, Janey, luv. He'll be here tonight, you'll see.'

It seemed to Annie that their mum was trying to avoid any issues as she asked after how Angie had slept, and if Beth was awake, and whether Lilly's bus was crowded for her journey.

It all served to distract Annie and help her to relax, even to be lulled into feeling all was well. A banging on the main door of the house shot her fears back into her. She stood up. 'I'll go.'

The lad who delivered telegrams and the last person Annie wanted to see in all the world stood on the doorstep. 'Two for Mrs Stanley.'

Annie wanted to scream, *No! No!* but she took them and thanked him. Closing the door, she leaned against it. Her body trembled. Her throat dried.

'Who is it, luv? Is it Sister Mary, not that she's due?'

Annie took a minute to remember that Sister Mary was the nun who came in to check on Mum and see if she needed anything. She'd been a godsend during Janey's pregnancy when she'd often taken over and washed and dressed Mum if Lilly hadn't done it.

Staring at the envelopes, one of them screeched out at her, stamped as it was with the word 'priority'.

'Please, no!' Annie's head shook from side to side. Her knees went to jelly, and she sank to the ground.

'Annie! Annie, luv, is everything all right?'

Annie looked up. Lilly stood in the doorway of Mum's flat staring down at her. 'It ain't . . . it can't be . . . not me Ricky?'

Annie couldn't move.

'What's going on? Lilly, luv, is Annie all right?'

Cissy's door opened. 'I heard your mum shouting . . . Eeh, Annie, what is it?'

Cissy hurried over to her and picked up the telegrams she'd dropped. 'Naw, love! Not this.'

A scream sliced through Annie. She knew it was Lilly, but she couldn't react.

'Should I open it, lass?'

Annie found herself nodding.

The sound of the crisp brown envelope being ripped open tore her heart in two. *Not me lovely Ricky, please, please . . .*

This thought had hardly died when Cissy gasped, 'Eeh, Annie, Annie, lass.'

Annie put out her hand and took the paper she knew held pain.

*We regret to inform you that on May 31st 1940 Sergeant Richard Stanley was reported as missing in action in France.*

The number before his name was a blur, but one she knew Ricky had been proud of. It stated he had been a soldier in the Essex Regiment. The words 'proud to die for my country' came to her. Ricky had said those words when they were talking of the dangers. 'I hope I don't,' he'd joked, 'but if it was to happen, you will know that I was proud to die for my country.'

*Proud! How can anyone be proud to die? I don't want you dead . . .* 'I don't want him dead!'

The words spoken aloud triggered a torrent of noise – Cissy crying and begging her to get up off the cold floor. 'It don't say he's dead, love. Eeh, Annie, listen, it says "missing".' At the same time, Lilly was sobbing her pain, and Mum was shouting for help. 'Get me to Annie, someone help me get to Annie!' Janey's distraught voice was screaming down into the telephone handset, 'Jimmy! Jimmy, help us. For God's sake, help us!'

Annie let go of it all and allowed the blackness she could feel beckoning her to swallow her up.

'Annie, Annie, open your eyes, lass. We're all here to help you and Lilly. Eeh, come on now, Annie. Take a sip of this water, lass.'

Through the thick fog that held a veil of agony for her, Annie saw Cissy's lovely round, dimply face looking down at her. Sounds came to her. A painful wail and shocked tones of her mum asking God to help them.

To Annie, there was no God. How could there be? At least not the loving, caring one they were meant to believe in. What caring had He ever shown to them? And now, he'd taken the meaning of her life away.

'By, lass, that's right. Now drink up, it will help you.'

The cold liquid did help. It brought Annie fully round. Though she didn't look on that as altogether helping, as the terrible truth gnawed at her – her lovely Ricky was missing! Everyone said that meant dead, but no body had been found. She might never see him again. Never would she feel his arms around her, or be loved by him, laugh with him, or eagerly await his return – he was never coming back, never!

\* \* \*

It was an hour later that some hope entered Annie.

Exhausted from crying, she didn't stop Jimmy taking hold of her hand as he sat with her on Mum's sofa.

'Annie, I went to see one of me mates who made it back from Dunkirk. He told me that Ricky was leading some of our lot in an attack to deflect the Germans while the boats came in to rescue those stranded on the beach. Me mate was one of them, but they were being overrun when Ricky told him to run for the beach. He got on the last boat, but he said the rumour was that those left were captured. Though the official line was that they were most probably killed. But me mate ain't thinking that, as the shooting stopped. He thinks those of our men that were left surrendered. He says they had no choice, that it was carnage. If they did, then Ricky could be a POW.'

'But how will I know?'

'You'll have to badger the Red Cross to find out, luv.'

'Really? They could find him? He could be safe?'

'I'm not saying safe as from what I've heard of how prisoners are treated, it ain't good. But it is hopeful that he was captured. And if he was, that means he's alive and, knowing Ricky, will do his damnedest to make it home. But in any case, once the Red Cross are allowed, they'll make a list of them as are prisoners, and'll get parcels to them. I should have been with him. We'd made a pact to stay together.'

Jimmy hung his head and fell silent. Annie saw Janey take his hand and squeeze it. Jimmy snatched it away.

She wanted to scream at him to stop his stupid and hurtful campaign against Janey. To open his eyes and see how she loved him and was standing by him. She wanted to tell him that she'd never loved him in that way. That he wasn't a patch on her Ricky. But she couldn't, she felt so weak.

'There's another telegram, lass. Shall I open it?'

Annie didn't answer as she caught sight of Lilly, her lovely ma-in-law, in a heap at the knees of Mum. Getting up, Annie walked on unsteady legs towards them. They both opened their arms. Her mum from her wheelchair, which she must have got herself into, even though she was still in her nightie, and Lilly from her now kneeling position. As she had done with Cissy, Annie felt their love for her.

She stroked Lilly's hair, the action marrying Lilly's pain with her own. A mother and a wife, joined in grief.

Cissy's voice interrupted this thought.

'Eeh, lass, I think I should open the other telegram. Telegrams are always urgent.'

Annie managed to nod at Cissy, then cringed when once again the sound of the envelope crackling as Cissy opened it grated on her nerves.

'It's from Miss Olivia!'

'What? Why? How?'

'I don't knaw, love. Let's see.'

'It says, "Arriving on the 18th at Southend, around midday. Will catch a train and go to your mum's. Explain all when I arrive, love Olivia."'

Annie's heart lifted a little. To be with her adored friend at such a time would help. Suddenly she wanted to be with her the moment she stepped off the boat.

'I want to go to Southampton to meet Olivia . . . Oh, but work! I'm supposed to be on duty!'

'Don't worry, Annie.' Janey came over to them. Her arm came around Annie. 'I phoned the station and you're on compassionate leave for as long as you need . . . Oh, Annie, I wish I had words to comfort you . . . It's awful . . . I – I don't know what to say.'

Feeling Janey's body trembling, Annie looked up into her face. 'Just being with me helps, luv. Be strong for me, that's all I ask.'

'I will, and for you, Lilly, luv. Me and Jimmy'll do all we can, won't we, Jimmy?'

Jimmy didn't look at Janey or acknowledge she'd spoken. Janey's head drooped as, almost as if she wasn't there, Jimmy said, 'I'll do anything I can for you, Annie, luv. I can go to Southend with you, we can take me car. You can drive. You're a good driver. You drive them police wagons around.'

Annie nodded. 'There's no need for you to come, Jimmy. If I could borrow your car . . .'

'But I want to . . . I, well, I can make sure you're all right and you get to the dock safely.'

The sound of a baby crying and then Beth screaming stopped the conversation.

Jimmy looked at Janey with a look that shocked Annie as he uttered, 'For Christ's sake! You left me kid upstairs on her own! What kind of a mother are you?' before turning and hurrying out of the door. Janey didn't follow him but stood looking like a scared rabbit. Before Annie could react, Jimmy reappeared carrying Beth. 'Beth's all right, I didn't look in on your other kid, though. She's screaming her head off! She scared me Beth!'

Tensing, Annie didn't need this. 'Her other kid is your kid too, Jimmy. What the hell have you got in your head, mate? I ain't having you accuse me sister of stuff like that, no matter how damaged you are!'

Jimmy's eyebrows rose. His shock registered in his staring eyes as he looked from her to Janey. 'What have you been saying to Annie, eh?'

'Shut up! Bleedin' shut up, will yer! Me son's missing and

all you lot can talk about is Olivia coming and whose kid belongs to who!'

Lilly broke down afresh.

Annie's pain increased once more – talking about Olivia coming had taken over. She'd let it. Wanted it to. But this awful scene wasn't what any of them wanted or needed.

'Oh, Lilly, Lilly. I – I . . . it helped, I didn't want . . . I'm sorry.'

Lilly put her arm out to her and Annie sank into the comfort.

'I know, girl, but this . . . him talking his filthy talk to Janey who least deserves it, and making up to you, me son's wife. That ain't on no matter how sick he is.' She turned on Jimmy. 'Yer should be in a loony bin! Yer ain't right in yer head.'

Jimmy made for the door.

'No, Jimmy . . . No, Lilly's upset. She don't know what she's saying, she's grieving for Ricky. Don't go. I love you, Jimmy.'

Jimmy stopped in his tracks. He looked back at Janey. Tears ran down his face. Janey went to him. Beth put her arms out to her, her little face pale and terrified. There was a moment when all held their breaths, but then a surprising thing happened. Jimmy put his other arm out to Janey. He held her and Beth in a loving way. His eyes scanned them all. 'I'm sorry . . . I should be the one that didn't come back, not Ricky . . . Janey, can I come home?'

'You are home, me darlin'. Let's go upstairs and see to our Angie, eh? She'll bring the house down with them lungs of hers, as she never gives in till she's got what she's demanding.'

Jimmy went with Janey. Annie didn't feel comfortable

about him doing so. She didn't like how glassy Jimmy's eyes had become.

Closing her eyes against all they had to bear, Annie just wanted to sob and sob. No, more than that, she wanted to wipe today away, take it off the calendar. She didn't want it being marked as the day she heard she'd lost her darling Ricky.

After a restless night crying herself to sleep, then waking and feeling so alone and crying till she fell asleep again, Annie's head was pounding when she finally woke to find it was morning. The sun shining through her window felt like an insult, as if it was a normal day – it wasn't, it was the second day of hell for her. The agony of her loss ground into her.

Her eyes went to the framed photo standing on Mum's dresser but facing her bed. In it, Ricky stood proudly with her on his arm. Their wedding day. Her in Olivia's wedding dress, Ricky in his suit smiling down at her. His profile wasn't from his scarred side. She wanted it to be as that was Ricky, the Ricky she loved. The face she loved.

Getting out of bed, she went to it and picked it up. Holding it to her breast, she felt Ricky's love warm her. He would never leave her.

At that moment she became convinced that he was alive and would be found. This gave her comfort, and she knew that she could hold on, for wherever Ricky was, he would always be in her heart.

Later that morning, Annie stood on the dock at Southend. The dockworkers assured her that no boat had come in from Guernsey that day so far, though loads had been arriving daily with evacuees and they were expecting more.

As she waited, she looked along the coastline and was reminded of her and Ricky coming down to this shore just before they were wed. The huge concrete constructions dotted along it, designed to hinder an invasion, were being built at the time. War had seemed something that wouldn't really happen. Even though Ricky, as a reservist, had been given orders to go to France in a couple of weeks' time.

She remembered how they'd been turned back by the soldiers, and had walked away from the front. Then she blushed as she thought of what happened on their walk. How Ricky had pulled her into a deserted alley and kissed her. How they had forgotten themselves in their love and passion and had made love in broad daylight! Giggling after and imagining what would have happened if they'd been caught – two police officers arrested for lewd behaviour in a public place.

'What you smiling at, Annie?'

She'd forgotten Jimmy was with her. She hadn't been able to stop him coming, especially as Janey had insisted too. He hadn't spoken much on the journey.

'Just a memory.'

'Well, they'll help you, girl. Good memories helped me. Like when you and me were together.'

'Stop that, Jimmy. You fell in love with Janey. And I'm glad as I found a love with Ricky that I'd never experienced. You and me were never meant to be. Me and Ricky were and you and Janey were. She's one in a million, Jimmy, with how she's stood by you.'

He looked to the ground and shuffled his feet. 'I know. But I can't help how I feel. I don't know what came over me when I had that affair with Janey, and I wish it had never happened.'

'Jimmy, please . . . This is why I didn't want you to come

today. What you feel for me ain't love, it's your brain giving you the wrong signals. You've to fight it, luv, as only you can do that . . .'

A shout interrupted them. Turning towards the sea, Annie saw a boat coming through the mist. *Please let me Olivia be on this one, please.*

To Annie, it seemed no time from sending up that prayer until she was in Olivia's arms clinging on to her as if she was a lifeline.

Olivia must have sensed something dreadful had happened and didn't ask questions, just held Annie and patted her back.

'He's gone. Oh, Olivia, me lovely Ricky's missing!'

There was a shocked gasp from Olivia before she burst into tears.

They stood there with people milling around, to the shouts of the workers and calls of passengers asking the way. They didn't speak, just held on to each other, sobbing.

Olivia had loved Ricky.

'Come on, girls. Your nanny is already in me car with your little lad, Olivia. He's beginning to fret. Let's get you back to mine, eh?'

They followed Jimmy, still clinging on to one another as if their lives depended on it.

When they got into the car, Annie in the driving seat and Jimmy next to her with Olivia and Loes in the back, Karl asked, 'Why you crying, Mummy?'

'It's what grown-ups do, darling. Mummy's so happy to see Aunty Annie.'

'Me happy too. Hello, Aunty Annie.'

Annie looked through the mirror at him. Though he looked just like Hendrick, she felt the pity of him not being with his daddy. She dried her tears and blew her nose. 'Hello, Karl. It's nice to see you. You've grown to be a big boy.'

His reply was, 'We've come to stay.'

Four simple words but the very best ones Annie could have heard at this moment – Olivia had come to stay. Though what Lucy would have to say about it she dreaded to think. Lucy had always advocated that her and Olivia's relationship should only be seen as boss and ex-employee, thinking that if their deep friendship was known of, there could be those who became suspicious of them.

Brushing this thought away, Annie turned and put her hand out to Olivia, who took hers, holding it tightly.

# Chapter Nine

## Olivia

Olivia felt cross when she met Lucy a couple of days later as she seemed to have no compassion for Annie, nor did she attempt to understand how they needed to be together.

'This operation that we are all involved in is vital and *must* take precedence over everything else. Already it has helped to minimize casualties and fuelled the rescue of so many men. The information of the second front the Germans had planned allowed us to get more soldiers off Dunkirk than we would have been able to . . . I – I'm sorry . . . Oh, Annie, what am I thinking?'

Lucy taking Annie's hand softened how Olivia thought about her. She was glad that it appeared that she'd made a wrong judgement. She wanted to like Lucy as she knew Annie did. Now, she thought she could.

'How could I have put duty before you, my lovely Annie?'

'You have to, Luce, and you're right. I know Ricky would agree with you. He knew the importance of what me, Hendrick and Olivia are doing.'

'And we can still do it. Hendrick begged me to come here. He thinks Guernsey could be invaded.'

'Oh? Has he any evidence, Olivia?'

'No. This is purely a hunch, otherwise he'd have passed on any concrete information.'

'Sadly, the powers that be won't act on a hunch. It's vital Hendrick keeps his nose to the ground on this one. The island is unprotected. Churchill would change his mind and protect it if he knew there was to be an invasion. He sees no strategic value attached to the islands and therefore feels our soldiers are better engaged elsewhere.'

'I know Hendrick will pass on any information he gets concerning this and I will get it to you immediately, Lucy.'

'Thanks, Olivia. It's nice meeting you, by the way. Sorry about my tetchiness . . . Look, there's a canalside cafe that me and Annie use, let's go there . . . That's if you have time? You have a son, don't you?'

'Yes, I've time. I brought my nanny with me, she has charge of Karl for the morning. And I need a seat for a while . . . my leg.' Olivia pulled her skirt up slightly. 'My medal to the train crash that me and Annie were in. Though it's Annie who should have a medal – she saved my life.'

'I noticed your limp. Poor you. Do you get a lot of pain with it?'

Olivia was warming to Lucy by the minute and was glad that her first impression was wrong. 'Quite a bit. It'll never be right. But like I say, I could have died if Annie hadn't risked her life to get me out. I owe everything to her. A gammy leg is a small price to pay and it rarely hinders me these days, but the long journey and little rest is making it play me up a little.'

Gill, the owner of the cafe, greeted them like old friends, asking who Olivia was.

'Oh, this is just a work colleague. Anyway, don't be a nosy parker, Gill!'

Gill laughed out loud, not a bit offended by Lucy. But then, insults in a posh voice always sounded funny.

When they sat waiting for their tea and biscuits, Olivia thought that it was a measure of Annie's personality that she made friends so easily and with those she wouldn't normally meet. It didn't matter to Annie that Olivia, and obviously Lucy too, had privileged backgrounds when her own had been difficult, fighting poverty in a back street of London's East End.

This was part of what made her so loveable. She accepted everyone as they were, and didn't put them into pigeonholes. Lucy seemed like that too.

As Olivia looked at Lucy, she thought that though she wasn't a beauty with her mousy hair, hazel eyes and freckles by the million covering her face, she somehow drew you to her and became attractive in a cute kind of way. She hadn't wanted to like Lucy after the way she'd greeted them but found she couldn't help herself.

Her eyes went from Lucy to Annie. Beautiful Annie with her dark hair and blue eyes, tarnished today with the heaviness of grief and lack of sleep.

Not talking about their work as Olivia had expected, Lucy grabbed Annie's hand. 'I know you'll want to know, Annie. I had a letter from Dan!' She turned to Olivia. 'I have loved Dan from afar for such a long time, but never thought I stood a chance. He's a journalist and I was his admin – my cover. Anyway, he has been sent to Africa to report on the progress of the war, and he's written to me asking me to write to him. He says it's to keep him up with the gossip of the office, but he could have asked any one of the clericals to do that and he chose me!'

Annie managed a smile. 'I'm pleased for you, luv.'

'Oh, Annie, my heart is breaking for you. What do you plan to do?'

'I can't think. Me head's splitting with pain. I just don't want to do anything but lie on a bed in a quiet room and think about me Ricky.'

Olivia found Annie's hand and held it tightly. But Lucy took a different stance.

'You have to be strong, Annie. Ricky would expect you to be. We have to carry on through it all, otherwise we'll be lost. It will help you too if you get back to work as soon as you can and continue to do your duty. You're needed.'

'Just a minute—'

'No, Olivia, it's all right. Lucy's right, I know that. But, Luce, we have a problem. Is it all right for me to live with Olivia? I so want to. I feel in the way now my sister's husband's home, though I'm welcome there of course, it's just . . .'

'I don't know. My orders in the beginning were to warn you off being seen as friends, but things may have changed. We don't know how good German intelligence is and haven't uncovered any suspicious persons who may be doing what Hendrick is doing, but in reverse. The worry would be that the Germans would want to use you, Olivia, if they find out about you being here and your father's many powerful connections in London.'

'Hendrick had that concern, but he says that if I live in the country, or up in the North of England, then that wouldn't be as likely to happen.'

'That would work, but Annie couldn't go with you. She's my contact, and her job is her perfect cover.'

Annie looked distraught. 'But . . . I – I thought we could live in the apartment together again . . . I need you, Olivia, I can't get through this on me own.'

'No one should live in the apartment. It's supposed to have been requisitioned. If you are staying there, you must move out, Olivia, as it once more connects you with your father's powerful friends and could lead you into being approached by the Germans. Look, if you can't stay with Annie, go to a hotel and I will contact you after I have spoken to O.'

'O?' Olivia looked bemused as she repeated this.

'That's a code name for my coordinator – my boss . . . Olivia, you speak many languages, don't you?'

'I speak French, Italian, German and a little Japanese. Hendrick had to learn that language before he went to Germany, and he taught me what I know. But I am fluent in French and German.'

'Mmm, interesting.'

Olivia couldn't think why but didn't say anything. She did ask, 'Can we go now, Lucy? Annie's all in.'

'Of course. Look, stay together in a hotel for now, but keep a low profile. Let's meet again in a few days. I'll contact you as to when, Annie . . . But before you go, Olivia . . .' Lucy looked around, obviously checking if Gill was in hearing distance as there were no other customers in the cafe. Seemingly satisfied, she asked, 'Have you put arrangements in place to keep receiving messages from your husband?'

'Yes . . . that is, he will ring me at the apartment.'

Lucy stood. 'Find a hotel and contact him. Tell him only to ring you there if he has a message. We don't want you traced . . . Oh, this is a mess. Are you sure Olivia couldn't fit into your flats somewhere, Annie? She'd be less detectable there.'

Olivia hadn't even given this a thought, but Annie piped up, 'I'll see what I can do. I'll sort something.'

'Good . . . Well, I'll go now. I'll be in touch.'

After she'd left, Gill came over under the pretence of clearing the pots. 'Annie, luv, you ain't looking good. It ain't like Lucy to leave you, and with a colleague of hers who you don't know.'

Olivia had alarm bells ringing loudly in her mind. It seemed that Gill was prying, so she thought of an answer quickly to satisfy her nosiness. 'Oh, we've met before on many occasions, but not in here.' Turning to Annie, Olivia said, 'Nice to see you again, Annie. Hope we meet again, next time Lucy calls on you.'

Catching on, Annie said, 'Ta, yes, it was good to see you.'

Olivia waited at the gate that led into the towpath, hoping Annie wouldn't be long. She sighed. She really needed to get home to Karl.

When Annie came out of the cafe, it was obvious that she'd been crying. Gill must have got it out of her about Ricky. Poor Annie. Her heart was broken. How she was going to cope with what had happened, Olivia couldn't think.

A lump came into Olivia's throat. She so wanted to open her arms to Annie but stepped back out of sight in case Gill came out and saw her.

When she voiced her concerns, Annie laughed. 'Gill ain't no spy, luv. Her and her family have owned that cafe for ever. She's just naturally nosy. You've nothing to worry about with her, I promise.'

Olivia laughed, more with relief than anything. Lucy had spooked her and made her suspicious of everyone. It was as if there were eyes on her, belonging to those who would want to lure her into some spy ring or something. Linking arms with Annie, she said, 'So, will we be able to come up with some excuse as to why I'm living with you that might satisfy her then? After all, I'm only supposed to be a colleague.'

'I doubt it. But we'll have to think of something.'

'Mind, I can't see how you can fit us in, there's three of us. Maybe I'd better go to a hotel.'

'Yes. It would be best. Lucy can be overcautious at times. And . . . well, I know I said I'd stay with you, but it'll be hard to leave me mum and especially Janey. I don't trust Jimmy. But besides that, I'm tired, Olivia, so tired. I couldn't face a move . . . and as for getting back to work . . .'

'No, that can't happen. Lucy came over a bit cold-hearted at times and shouldn't have suggested that.'

'It's her professionalism. I suppose we should be more like that. I just can't get me head around some of what she says – us being watched, for instance. Who by, and why are they even in our country, for that matter?'

'There will be spies here, just as we have them over there, love. But in the chaos of evacuees, I doubt anyone has noticed that I am one of them. Lucy's right. I was stupid to go to the apartment. I'll have to go at once and move us out of there . . . God! What was I thinking?'

'Surely . . .'

'Oh, Annie, we must think more like Lucy. We could put Hendrick in danger if we don't. But where can I go?'

'Look, I've had an idea. There's still nothing been done with the basement at our house, but Jimmy once said that he'd turn the rooms down there into a flat for me if I wanted it. I've been down a few times to see how I'd like it doing, and there's a couple of rooms that with a good clean-up could be habitable . . . though there's only the outside lav at the moment. It's accessed by coming out of the basement's back door and up a few steps into the yard.'

'It sounds perfect . . . Well, not perfect, but to be with you, I mean. Let's go back to yours now and have a look. I want to say hello to Cissy anyway.'

Annie became more animated than she'd seen her so far as they walked home. The idea of the basement began to take shape as her enthusiasm for the idea made Olivia feel it was doable.

'I think that could be the answer, Olivia. With all hands on deck we'd soon have it scrubbed out, and with some rugs on the floor and a bit of second-hand furniture, I think it will do you fine . . . Oh, I feel there is something to look forward to when me world had seemed to collapse around me.'

When they arrived at what was once a huge house and still looked impressive as it stood on the kerbside of Old Ford Road, Annie told her, 'I'd love it if it was done up. I could live in it after you've moved to the countryside. It'd be like a home of me own.'

Olivia thought how sad it was that Annie and Ricky had never had the chance to make a home together. For herself, although she now lived with her father, she did have her beloved farmhouse to go to, and now the weather was getting warmer she had been planning to live there with Karl. She sighed an inward sigh. That couldn't happen now. Life was going to change for her. Already she missed her father and her beloved Guernsey. How long would it be before she could go home again?

But she had her memories, especially of when she'd visited the farmhouse, which Annie didn't have. She couldn't go to a place where she could find Ricky. For herself, she'd only had to go to her and Hendrick's bedroom at the farmhouse. There, though he was hundreds of miles away, she could sense Hendrick and still smell him on the clothes he'd left behind. Ricky's clothes would all be at his mother's house. Annie only had memories of him in her workplace, and on dates when they were courting, as they married just before Ricky had to go away to war, leaving no time to set up a home. They'd only ever been together as man and wife in hotel rooms.

As she followed Annie up the steps to the front door, tears prickled Olivia's eyes. It was devastating to think of the lovely Ricky and not know if he was alive or dead. She swallowed hard. 'Are you all right, love?'

'I don't know, I have a strange feeling that seems to be shielding me. It's like it ain't happening to me. I feel so lost, and there's me job to consider . . . And, well, I just don't know how to mark . . . I mean, if Ricky's dead, there should be a funeral but . . . I – I ain't got Ricky to bury.'

With this Annie gasped in a breath. The sound she made was like that of an injured animal. Olivia's heart bled for her.

'We'll mark Ricky's being a hero. I promise you, Annie, love. But not until we've done all there is to try to track him down. Hendrick might be able to help. It's known that a lot of men – thousands of them – have been taken prisoner. He may know where it is planned that they will be shipped to. Then we can make enquiries. Hendrick might be able to help in that too.'

'Jimmy said the Red Cross help with that.'

'Yes, they do. I've read about their work. The main thing is that you stop talking about burials and funerals and start to fuel your heart with hope. Looking for Ricky will do that.'

'Oh, Olivia, ta. I feel better already, and I know Lilly will when I tell her what our plans are.'

When they opened the door, it was to the sound of a piano playing. It sounded inappropriate to Olivia as the old London songs – all jolly, no matter what they were about – echoed around the building.

'That'll be Mum, she'll be playing a tribute to Ricky. He loved the music halls.'

'Are you all right with it, Annie?'

'I am. It's the way of the Londoner and especially East Enders. Whatever the occasion, happy or sad, they have the honkytonk piano blaring. Ricky would have loved this.'

'Will love it . . . not "would have". You must speak of Ricky as though he is still alive, Annie. Feel it in your gut that he is and then you will make it so.'

Annie nodded as she continued on into the house and opened the first door on the right, calling out, 'It's only me and Olivia, Mum, can we come in?'

Vera, as Olivia knew Annie's mum, stopped playing and turned her wheelchair around to face them. 'I was just playing for Ricky.'

Lilly, who sat next to Vera on a dining chair, piped up, 'It were lovely, girl, I enjoyed it. Made me see him. He'd have been singing his heart out as you played . . . 'Ello, you two, I were just going to put the kettle on.'

When Lilly rose, Annie went into her arms. The two grieving women hugged as if they would never part.

'I were just saying me goodbye through the music he loved, Annie, luv.'

'Not goodbye, Lilly. Olivia's made me see that we ain't to think of Ricky as dead, but do all we can to find out where he is. She's going to help us.' Annie held Lilly at arm's length as she told her all they'd been talking about.

'And so, with an estimate of thirty to forty thousand men

114

taken as prisoners of war, it's more than likely that Ricky was one of them.'

Lilly had visible signs of hope entering her as a smile came on her face. She looked from one to the other. 'So, me Ricky could be alive?'

'Yes, Lilly. From now on, he is to us, eh?'

'Oh, Annie, girl. We'll find him, won't we?' The tears rolled down her face. She tried to brush them away but Annie stopped her. 'It's all right to cry, luv. And to scream and wail against the injustice of it and our grief at this having befallen our lovely Ricky. We can share tears and laughter, we can live our lives the way Ricky would want us to, but we'll never give up on him. He's alive, Lilly. Hang on to that, girl.'

Olivia made her way over to Vera who was quietly sobbing. She held her in her arms. 'It's going to be all right, Vera. I promise . . . Now, what does a girl returning to the fold have to do around here to get a cup of tea, eh?'

Annie and Lilly both scooted into the kitchen giving a little giggle. This lightened Olivia's heart.

Vera wheeled over to be next to her where she sat on the sofa. 'I luv me wheelchair, Olivia. Ta for giving me yours, luv.'

'And I'm glad to see it is still serving you well.'

'It is, luv. It's given me freedom. I go out quite a bit in it. Jimmy made a ramp for the steps, so one of them puts that down for me and off I go. I'm known all round here so I ain't stuck for someone to talk to.'

'That's nice to hear. I've not forgotten how it felt not to be able to walk – my leg gives me plenty of reminders of that time.'

'Does Cissy know you're 'ere, luv?'

'Not yet, nor Janey. I can't wait to meet baby Angie. I'll pop through to Cissy's and call up the stairs as I go. By that time, those two might just have organized themselves into making the tea I was promised.'

From the kitchen Annie called through, 'We're on it, luv. You go and get the others as no doubt Cissy'll want one and Janey. They can smell tea brewing a mile away!'

This made Lilly giggle. For the moment, bereavement had been put on the back shelf.

'Good work, Olivia, girl. Poor souls are lost and while they do have to cry it out, they need a bit of light relief too.'

'They do, Vera. Hopefully the other plans that Annie and I have come up with will go down well with Jimmy and then I'll be here all the time.'

'Oh?'

'We talked of us making another flat in the basement. But we'll tell you all about it later. I'll just pop and knock on Cissy's door.'

Before she could, an impatient knock and then the door opening hailed Cissy looking most put out. 'Eeh, I heard you come in, Miss Olivia, and I've been waiting, but I couldn't contain meself naw longer.'

To hear Cissy's lovely northern accent again brought a lump to Olivia's throat. She swallowed hard and soon found herself encased in Cissy's chubby arms.

'By, lass, I've waited for this moment from when Jimmy and Annie went to meet you yesterday. I didn't knaw whether to go to the apartment to get it ready for you or not. The government have released it back to you then?'

Feeling ashamed of the lie she'd been forced to tell Cissy by the War Office, she didn't enlighten her. 'No, I went as an emergency but have already been told off. It's madness, they've done nothing with it. Anyway, I'll tell you all about my plans, Cissy, when we're all together, love.'

With this, Olivia called out Janey's name and was rewarded with the door at the top of the stairs opening and Janey standing there with a huge grin on her face. 'Olivia! I wondered when we'd see you. I'll be down in a mo, only Jimmy's out, so I'll need to bring the kids down with me.'

'You better had, Janey. I've only come to see them, you know.'

Janey laughed, then turned away, but stopped and turned back again. 'How's Annie, luv? Is she all right?'

'Delicate is how I would describe her. Delicate and lost, poor darling. Anyway, see you in a few minutes. Annie and Lilly have the kettle on.'

Olivia turned back to Cissy and squeezed her arm. 'It's good to see you, Cissy, love.'

'Aye, that's how I feel about seeing you, me lovely lass. Where's Karl? Is he in with Vera?'

'No, he . . . He was tired after the journey and Loes, my nanny, is caring for him. I was desperate to come to see you, so left them both behind.'

Another lie, but then she couldn't tell the truth about meeting Lucy. Once more shame washed over her, though it helped her to think that her, Annie's and Hendrick's work was to save them all and had to be secret.

'You'll like Loes. She's Dutch and a lovely girl. She adores Karl and he her.'

'By, that's good to hear, lass. And I'm too old to have charge of a toddler. I help out sometimes with Beth, but that's only to support Vera, so she can have Granny time with her. Mind, now there's the young 'un arrived, I'm not

117

so sure. Janey'll have to be there all the time for Vera to enjoy the babby.'

Olivia was glad that Cissy had taken everything in a matter-of-fact way and hadn't questioned her too much.

The next hour was full of laughter, which Olivia thought lovely to hear, as she held the gorgeous Angie, though she only had a moment with Beth, who'd come over all shy.

Stories were recounted, and memories exchanged. Though Olivia could feel that some were causing Annie pain, and so admired her lovely brave friend for joining in with the banter. She even had them all in stitches when she told of a time when she and Ricky stayed in a boarding house and the landlord wanted to see their marriage certificate. Ricky, not knowing if the man had ever committed a crime, had told him that if he continued with this line, then he would make sure he paid for an old misdemeanour. The man shook in his shoes and let them stay for half price.

But then Ricky, always a copper, looked him up in their old files and found that he had been investigated for handling stolen goods – the case was reopened, and the man went to prison! The way Annie told it was hilarious and it was made even more so as Vera coughed loudly while they were all laughing and in a stern voice said, 'So, you slept with Ricky before you married him, then?'

Annie looked confused for a moment, until Vera burst out laughing and said, 'Good on you, luv, you take after me in that. Me and your dad were at it like rabbits from the moment we met!'

This had them all laughing again.

Olivia was surprised at how all this near-the-mark talk never fazed her, when before she'd married Hendrick, she'd have died with embarrassment at such openness.

But it all went to show her that giving Annie another way of looking at Ricky's possible plight was the best thing she could have done. For though she knew she would still grieve, it would be a grief that held hope.

# Chapter Ten

## Olivia & Annie

After they all settled down from the laughter, they discussed the basement in earnest, and all except Vera took a trip down the stairs to take a look.

Though it needed a lot doing to it, Olivia thought it perfect – huge, as it was the size of the whole house, and it was a lot lighter than she thought it would be with its windows all looking out on walls. 'Oh, we can make a lovely home here, Annie. I can't wait.'

Annie looked pleased.

The space which had obviously been used as the kitchens, stores, laundry and offices for staff when the house had been a home to someone wealthy would easily convert to a kitchen, living room, bathroom and two bedrooms – one being for her and Annie and the other for Loes, as well as a small room that would make a nursery.

'Well, I think I have found my home. Though I still think we may have to move to the country at some point. Anyway, now, I must call a cab to get back to the apartment and arrange for us to go into a hotel. I'll ring you when we're settled, Annie.'

They went into a lovely hug. Olivia didn't want to leave her but knew that Lucy was right. They must think of safety first as unwittingly they could put Hendrick into more danger than he was already.

When she arrived home and stepped out of the apartment's lift, everything changed for Olivia.

Loes was distressed as a telegram had arrived. 'It is for you, Olivia.' Her hand shook as she handed it over. Everyone had a fear of the brown-coloured envelopes.

Tearing it open, Olivia asked, 'Where's Karl?'

'He is still asleep; he has had an hour already, but then we did go for a walk to the park, and he exhausted himself playing and chasing ducks.'

Olivia smiled at the picture this conjured up, but her fear over the contents of the telegram didn't let the feeling last. Tearing it open, she read:

*Dearest Olivia, need you home for a couple of weeks. Can you come immediately? Sending Joe to pick you up. Will be in Southend on 18th. I'm in hospital, nothing serious, but Vernon expressing concerns over balances. Needs looking into. Your loving father x*

Almost laughing with relief, Olivia told a tense Loes, 'I'll have to go . . . But what can be wrong with Father, I can't imagine! I wish he'd said, as not knowing makes me worry even more!'

'But he's not saying come home because he's ill, just that he's concerned over the bank's business, so don't worry too much, Miss Olivia.'

'Yes, there was some concern at the last reconciliation. It was sorted out, but I had my suspicions. Father pooh-poohed them. But if someone is embezzling us in some way, it could not only bankrupt Father, but discredit him and even lead to prosecution!'

'Oh no, that cannot happen. Your poor father!'

'I know. It's scary. I'm sorry this has happened, Loes. Will you be all right staying here? Only I think it will be too much for Karl to travel back and forwards again and I am sure I will be back within a couple of weeks . . . I mean, I will, no matter what is happening.'

'Of course, we will be fine.'

'The only thing is that I must move you to a hotel with Karl. I can't explain, but we cannot stay here . . . though I could check. Hold on a moment, I'll make a call.'

A call to Annie caused a little upset, but she understood.

'I'll contact Lucy. I can't see that a young woman and her child living in the apartment can cause a stir. No one knows who they are.'

It was a nerve-racking twenty minutes before Annie called back. Olivia felt tied into a knot with worry. She knew she was right to leave Karl here but hated the idea of them being in a hotel and not having home comforts.

When Annie rang back it was with good news. Lucy didn't see any reason why Loes and Karl couldn't stay in the apartment, as the fear of Olivia and Annie being seen to be more than maid and mistress had now passed. But Lucy did say she thought it best Olivia take them both with her back to Guernsey so that all could continue as it had done.

That wasn't an option for Olivia. Now she'd been back with Annie, she knew that's where she wanted to be. And it was where Annie needed her to be too.

With the urgency to get to Southampton on time to catch

Joe, Olivia and Annie found themselves at the train station later that evening. They stood close holding hands, then as the train drew in they hugged, clinging on to one another as if this was the last time that they would be together.

'It don't seem a minute since we stood here and said goodbye to Ricky, Olivia. I never dreamed it would end like this . . . Oh, Olivia, me heart hurts.'

'Mine does too, Annie. I want to make it all right again, but I can't.'

'No one can. Still, this isn't about me. Here you are going across the water without your little Karl. Your own heart must be wrenched.'

'It is. It'll be unbearable to be without him. I'll come back as soon as I can, and I hope to bring my father back with me. We'll sort everything out then. We'll all go and live in the country together.'

'Olivia, I can't leave London, luv. I have me duty to do. I'm going to get back to work as soon as I can now. It's for the best and what Ricky would want for me. Life must go on and if ever Hitler starts to attack us here, then it'll be all hands on deck – police hands as much as any other of the services.'

This was a blow to Olivia. She imagined them safely tucked away in the countryside where no aggression could reach them, but the reality was very different. She had to realize that.

She had to latch on to Annie's bravery. But as she waved for as long as she could to the disappearing, lonely figure on the platform, for all the world she thought she could get off at the next station and travel back to Annie.

A feeling had taken her that leaving would mean not seeing Karl and Annie for a long time. But then she shook herself.

Yes, two weeks was a long time to be away from Karl and Annie, now they'd finally got together again, but she was being silly. It would soon pass.

Annie didn't go straight home. Instead, she decided to go to the Thames, to the spot where she'd first met Ricky.

When she stepped out of the cab having paid the driver, she made for the steps and ran down to the towpath. It was as if Ricky was there waiting for her. But he wasn't, and yet she had the weirdest notion he was close.

She stared out at Tower Bridge. Its edges blurred against the blue sky as her mind gave her the scene of yesteryear.

She saw herself teetering on the edge of the lapping water, her heart broken at the deceit of Janey and Jimmy.

A voice had seemed to come from nowhere and had broken the spell that had held her.

'Hey!'

She'd turned to see a huge policeman striding at a pace along the path towards her.

It was Ricky.

'Now then, miss. Nothing's that bad that we can't fix it,' he'd said and he had then coaxed her away from the water's edge.

Looking down, Annie realized that she was in the same position now. Her feet were over the edge.

'Come on now, come back from the water's edge, luv.'

This time the voice wasn't Ricky's but Aggie's, the flower seller who had alerted Ricky that fateful day.

Annie looked around, then felt herself falling. Two arms grabbed her. Old arms and yet strong.

With the support they gave, Annie found she could step back.

'Oh, Annie, luv.'

Shaking from the fright she'd had, she held on to Aggie. 'I – I didn't mean, I wasn't going to . . . I sort of got me head into the past, Aggie.'

'I know. I heard what 'appened, luv. It were in the paper. Come and sit down a mo.'

Annie let Aggie guide her to the bench, the same one Ricky had sat her down on that day.

'Now then, Annie, me darlin', your Ricky were a lovely man and he adored you, but he ain't gone. I know that. I ain't saying I can see into the future as I don't hold with that, but I had gypsy ancestors that could. They told me I had the gift if I nurtured it. I didn't want anything to do with all that poppycock, so found meself standing 'ere selling flowers.' She smacked her lips together and smiled her one-tooth smile.

'In them days, some of me flowers were real, some were what me relatives had fashioned out of wood and painted. They used to go down well with me customers. But the last of the tribe 'ave gone now. Anyway, luv, I do see things now and again, and I know your Ricky ain't gone.' Aggie shuddered from head to toe. 'Though he ain't in good 'ands and I wish that wasn't the case, luv.'

'Oh, Aggie, really? Is it possible for you to know?'

'Oh, yes. I know that much about me visions. Whenever I've let them in, they've been shown to be right.'

Annie's heart leapt. But then fell again. Aggie had said that Ricky was in a bad place. A prison camp? Would he survive and come home eventually?'

'Aggie, will he . . . ?'

Aggie shook her head. 'I don't know. I fear for him.'

This tore at Annie. What was happening to her Ricky? Then it came to her and once more she felt a trickle of hope

– maybe Hendrick would find something out as to where Ricky had been taken and help him in some way.

'Annie, girl, the last time Ricky came to see me when he'd just come home on leave, he told me he were taking you away for a week. I didn't see him again. But did you have a good week away together, eh?'

'We did. Oh, Aggie, I love him. How am I to live knowing he could be a prisoner of war and in a labour camp under the cruel German regime?'

'You will, luv, 'cause of who he is. You'll do him proud, 'cause he don't deserve no less, girl. He was so 'appy that you became a policewoman.' Aggie's head was nodding. It was as if she was all-knowing and all-seeing, instead of just being Aggie, the woman who sold flowers and loved a mug of tea.

'What you've got to do, Annie, luv, is to go home, get your uniform on and report for duty. We need you coppers, and I think we're going to need you more than we've ever done.'

Aggie was right. She nodded her head.

'Ricky has a mum, doesn't he? He told me he called her Lilly. 'Ow that woman must be suffering, bless her. 'Ere, I tell you what, will you take some flowers to her, eh? On her birthday, Ricky used to take her a bunch of roses, with a lily in among them. He told me once that he'd say to her, "'Ere you are, Mum, you've come up smelling of roses!"'

Annie didn't know why but she found this funny. She giggled, then laughed out loud.

'That's the way, girl. Ha! Ricky is one for joking, and he showed kindness too. And that's how you're to remember him and keep him in your heart. I remember once he saw a lad nicking a bunch of flowers from me stall. He ran after him and, holding his ear, brought him back to me. The lad was snivelling, saying it were his mum's birthday, and he was sorry, he just wanted a present for her. Your Ricky told him, "You earn what you want, lad, you don't take it from others. Now, ask Aggie if she has any jobs she wants doing." I couldn't resist the snotty-nosed little rascal, so I had him take me bucket to the river to top up the water for me flowers, then run an errand to the shop for me, and after that I gave him the flowers. Ricky told him he had a good deal, but only if he'd learned a lesson. Not many weeks after that, the lad came to see me. He brought me a stool that he'd made. He said he loved woodwork and had found a broken chair. His dad had been a carpenter, but had passed away, and the lad had all his tools. I still sit on that stool now, and until the war, the lad came to see me every week. I know he went to France, but I don't know if he got back as he ain't come to see me yet.'

Aggie bowed her head. Annie reached out and took her hand. 'That's a lovely story and a measure of the difference that me Ricky made to people's lives. Ta for sharing it, Aggie.'

'Well, I want you to see that his work can be carried on through you, luv, while he's away. You can keep him close to us and all the other snotty-nosed kids who need guidance, not punishment. That was always Ricky's motto.'

'I will. I feel different to what I did when I came down to the river. I feel like I can tackle life.'

'You'll 'ave many moments of despair, luv. I still do and it's been twenty-five years since I lost me Alfie in the last war, only I know that he was killed. In a way, I find that helped as I knew and could tackle it. A lot were left with the same hanging thread you 'ave.'

'Did any of those come back? I mean, those missing in action?'

'Yes, they did, droves of them. They were in a poor state and some of their wives and girlfriends hadn't waited for them, which led to a lot topping themselves, poor buggers.'

Annie gasped in horror at this appalling story. She'd never give up on her Ricky. Especially now after talking to Aggie. She felt convinced Ricky was out there somewhere. And now, she had a purpose – to carry on Ricky's good work.

'Ta, Aggie. You've made such a difference to me. I'll come and see you as normal with your mug of tea when I'm on this beat . . . Oh, and I'll come and get those flowers for Lilly. That's so kind of you. I'll do as you say, and I'll always be there for Lilly as much as she needs me to be and share me feelings and let her give vent to hers and help her through them.'

'Yes, and in doing so, you'll help your own, luv.'

'You're a wise lady, Aggie. Can I give you a hug?'

'That'd make me day, girl. I ain't been hugged for as long as I can remember.'

As Annie hugged Aggie's thin body, she said, 'So, you've no family now, Aggie?'

'No. There's just me. They're all gone.'

'Ahh, that's sad. But I'll always be here for yer, Aggie, luv. I know what loneliness feels like, even though me family are with me at home – well, the womenfolk, that is. Though we do have me sister's husband, Jimmy back from the war.' She told Aggie how Jimmy had been injured. 'He just ain't the same, though we think he's improving.'

They'd come out of the hug, but still held hands. Once again, Aggie trembled. 'Just be careful of Jimmy, luv. I ain't never met him, but I 'ave me feelings just 'earing his name.'

This was a new side to Aggie. She'd never expressed anything about seeing the future before.

They walked together to Aggie's stall and Annie waited while Aggie put the flowers together for her.

'There you are, luv, they're on me. You tell Lilly they're a gift from her lovely Ricky even though it ain't her birthday. Tell her what I told you as well as that'll bring her comfort.'

'Ta, I will. And can I have three more bunches, please, Aggie? Any flowers that you have bunched up ready will do. I want to take me own mum some, and me sister, and me friend, Cissy. They've all supported me.'

With her arms full of flowers, Annie hailed a cab, and asked the driver to take her to Old Ford Road.

Once back with her family, there were tears, hugs and smiles. They all loved their flowers, as apart from Lilly who had received them every year, none of them had been given flowers until now. Annie made her mind up that she would put that right from now on.

They were all shocked about Olivia having to go home.

'You tell her nanny that she's welcome here whenever she wants to come.'

'I will, Mum.'

'And tell her that little Karl can come and play with Beth, Annie. Poor girl in a strange place on her own, she'll need company.'

'Ta, Janey, luv. Perhaps you can take the kids up west to meet her in the park?'

'Oh, I ain't one for that end of town, luv. But if she can't get here, I'll see.'

Helping her mum to put her flowers in a vase, Annie felt a tug on her cardigan.

'I could do with a hug, luv. I've been so worried about

you, but you seem to have turned a corner. There's something different about you.'

Annie told her about Aggie. 'I ain't saying I ain't grieving any more, I am, but more for what me Ricky might be going through and fear of whether he'll make it back, but I'm convinced now that he is still alive, Mum.'

'That's good. It gives us all something to hang on to and has lifted me grief a little. You should bring this Aggie for tea one day, luv. She sounds right up our street.'

Bending and hugging her mum, who sat in her wheelchair, Annie felt how frail she was. As she did, she realized that it was hard to remember a time before her mum had suffered with a progressive form of arthritis. She'd watched her deteriorate over the years, until now she couldn't walk.

Annie kissed her mum's hair. 'I promise and I know Aggie will love you. And I'll bring Loes and Karl here to meet you all as well. After all, they'll be living here when we get the basement sorted once Olivia's back. You can be a granny to Karl then, and Cissy can too. He ain't got a granny, only two granddads, Olivia's dad, and Hendrick's.'

'Doesn't Hendrick ever tell you what we're to expect from that Hitler bloke? He should know a thing or two with working over there.'

Fear clutched Annie. Could their secret be sussed out this easily? Would others in official capacities start to ask questions? Now she understood why Lucy hadn't wanted her and Olivia to seem to be close friends. Why had they been so stupid, putting their own needs before that of their country?

Going down on her haunches, she knew she would have to put Hendrick in a bad light and hated doing so. 'Hendrick is German, Mum. He ain't one of us. I know Olivia likes to think he is, but she's torn between her love for him and her love for her mother country and her beloved Guernsey. At this moment, Hendrick is our enemy, and we must remember that, but not show that we feel this way to Olivia.'

'I won't, luv. Poor Olivia, I feel sorry for her. But I could never feel sorry for a bastard German. They took your dad's life and millions of others in the last lot, and now they're at it again and have taken your lovely Ricky from you, luv. I hope I never meet Hendrick again or I'll be tempted to kick him where it hurts!'

This hurt Annie, but she knew it was the safest way if Mum and all of her family felt like this.

Her mum's hand took hold of hers. Annie held it gently as anything else would cause pain, but inside she had an urge to squeeze it to convey her anguish and have her mum put things right for her. But no one could do that as she knew they wouldn't be right for a long, long time.

Once she got to her mum's bedroom where her clothes hung in the wardrobe, Annie decided that instead of telephoning the sergeant, she'd put her uniform on and hail a cab to take her to her police station in Stepney.

A silence fell when she walked through the door. 'I – I shouldn't have come . . . I just thought . . . I – I needed to be here.'

The scraping of the sergeant's chair as he rose from his desk behind the counter grated on Annie. Her eyes travelled to where Ricky would most likely be if he was here.

A copper who walked the beat, he'd have sat to one side of the sarge as he told him of any incidents that he'd logged in his notebook. She'd have been sitting at the desk behind the sarge, typing away, grinning every time Ricky sneaked a peek at her.

The sarge cleared his throat, but still didn't speak. Then

something Annie hadn't expected happened – the sound of hesitant clapping. This soon became a loud enthusiastic applause.

Annie's cheeks burned. Tears prickled her eyes, her throat tightened, but she swallowed hard and kept in control.

'Well, luv, we didn't expect to see you, but it's good to.' Sarge came towards her. Annie wanted to run, but her legs wouldn't work. He held out his hand in a manly handshake. Relief flooded Annie. She couldn't have taken him hugging her.

'I won't ask you how you are, Annie, luv, as I've an idea. But just to say, Ricky would've been proud of you for taking this step.'

'Not would have, Sarge. Ricky ain't dead. He's missing. I believe he was one of the thousands taken prisoner. His life will be hell, as mine will be, but he'll come back, you'll see.'

'Oh? Right . . . well . . . Betty, put the kettle on, girl. I think Annie could do with one of your pea-soup cups of tea!'

Soon she was huddled in the midst of them: hers and Ricky's colleagues, with a few he hadn't worked with for a long time – coppers who'd been retired and called back to work.

Their laughter helped as they told little stories of Ricky, but she did detect that to them Ricky was dead. Killed.

'Please. It ain't a whim, or a fantasy. Me brother-in-law knows a lad that was fighting alongside Ricky, and he said that Ricky didn't fall, that he made him and others run for the last boat and stayed and warded off the Germans for a few moments. He said that then all those remaining surrendered. I have to go on believing that. Don't make a mockery of it by trying to appease me. Ricky is alive!'

A few embarrassed coughs could be heard, but then the

sergeant said, 'My God, he could very well be. That sounds exactly like our Ricky. He wouldn't want to quit, but he'd also see the sense in doing so to save any further loss of life if he's got all the men off that he could. Right. The new line is that Ricky is alive. I will make what enquiries I can and try to find out where he would have been taken, and then, if the Red Cross can get parcels through to him and other inmates, we'll do all we can to raise money and to collect things to be sent to the camp for our Ricky and our lads.'

A cheer went up. More hugs followed but these weren't saying they were sorry. They were full of joy at her news.

# Chapter Eleven

## Olivia

The heartache that was her constant companion at being separated from Hendrick was now twofold as Olivia pined for her little Karl too.

But her job was done, the anomaly in the balances sorted out, which had thankfully been down to one of the new women clerks making a simple, and yet almost disastrous error, on the comptometer – an amazing machine that added figures up even quicker than Hendrick could, which was really going some!

Olivia smiled as she packed the last of her clothes and wondered if Father had done the same yet.

It was such a relief that at last her father had consented to go to the mainland with her. There was more and more of an unsettled feeling on the island, and it was a sad place with the majority of the children and hundreds of young mothers and teachers having been evacuated.

It had been his heart scare that had made Father's mind up. Doctors were unsure if his racing heartbeat was a permanent condition or brought on by anxiety but had advised a complete rest for a few weeks – if there was such a thing to be had in the awful atmosphere of an almost world war!

Olivia glanced at the clock. Almost six p.m. Dinner would be ready soon and then an early night as tomorrow, the twenty-ninth of June, they had an early sailing.

Her heart had been in her mouth when the harbour master had announced that sailings must be limited and very few boats would get a pass to leave the island. Those that were scheduled were oversold to people desperate to leave.

With her case clicked closed, Olivia sat on the bed for a moment as a feeling overwhelmed her that the fear felt by everyone could so easily be rooted in reality.

Hendrick had warned that Hitler could turn his sights on the Channel Isles. He'd look on having taken some British soil as being a massive victory.

Taking small islands that had armed forces surrounding them and on land would be a very difficult task for him and might make him think that the losses involved wouldn't be worth it. The huge thing was for him to never find out the truth – Guernsey, Jersey and all the islands were on their own. Not a single soldier or sailor looked out for them.

A shudder trembled through Olivia. A feeling of fear knotted her stomach. Standing, she shook the thoughts from her and went in search of her father.

'Daddy, may I come in? How are you getting along with your packing?'

'Yes, come in, dear. Nearly done. Just can't decide whether to take two or three pairs of shoes.'

Olivia laughed. 'You have at least six pairs at the apartment in London already. I'm sure you'll be able to go there to get what you need and will be fine with the pair you decide to wear!'

'I suppose so . . . Oh, Olivia, I don't want to go, you

135

know. I'm convinced that we're safer here than we will be in London!'

'I told you, we aren't going to stay in London, but find a country property to buy and live there for the duration of the war. Hendrick suggested the North of England. He said Cissy would help us with where is the best place.'

'But Guernsey isn't of any use to anyone! I think this scaremongering is a lot of poppycock!'

'Ha, Daddy, stop being awkward. You won't do your heart any good . . . Look, if you're proved right, we can come back. But you have nothing to worry about by leaving here. The bank will be perfectly managed – putting a team in charge was an excellent idea as all have a say in any decision-making and then have to pass it by you. And with the blip in the system now sorted out and with the team knowing what to watch out for, we're all set. You need never work in the bank again!'

'Hmph, yes, it all sounds good but . . . my golf! And my social life . . . and, well, it feels like I'm leaving your mother behind.'

'No *buts*! Let's go down to dinner, eh? It's six thirty already!'

Olivia linked arms with her father and was rewarded with a pat on her hand and a lovely smile.

The smile went into a look of puzzlement as a droning sound filled the space around them, and then horror, as a massive boom deafened them.

Within seconds it seemed hell had come to earth as shattered glass splintered them, and screams pierced the air. Before they had time to recover, another blast, the force of which blew in the downstairs hall window and door, pinned them both to the wall.

Clinging on to one another, the next blast lit the sky and knocked them off their feet. They huddled in a ball on the landing floor listening to blast after blast and to gunfire hack-hacking close by, putting them in a strange world of echoing crashes. Father's words seemed to elongate as if someone had put him into slow motion as he said, 'Stay down.'

Dust filled Olivia's mouth and rasped her throat. Her mind spiralled back to when the train she and Annie had been travelling on crashed. But she and her father weren't on a train, they were safely in their own home – no, not safe. Something or someone had violated that safety and left them terrified for their lives. *The Germans!* Fear struck Olivia's heart. *No! No! Please God, no!*

With the plea came the realization that her fellow countrymen were out there in the thick of what was happening. Making a huge effort, she stood and went to the window. Beneath her, boards that hadn't creaked now protested their weakness at her every step.

Looking through the window laid bare the dread she'd felt. The tomato lorries awaiting the cargo ship lay in ruins. Most were on fire. Bodies lay around them. People were pulling drivers out of cabs; others were crawling under the lorry carriages. And all to the drone of aircraft receding then swooping and the crashing of bombs, which blinded her with their flashes of fire and further assaulted her ears.

'I'm going to help those caught up in this, Daddy . . . Daddy, are you all right?'

Her father lay in a funny, twisted position, his eyes closed, his mouth clamped with his lips protruding. 'DADDY!' His name was a scream of terror mixed with hysteria.

Going to him, Olivia shook him. 'Daddy, please wake up.

It's the Germans, they've attacked us! Our people need our help!'

'Are you all right, Miss Olivia?'

Daphne's shaky voice coming through all the chaos made Olivia feel as though an angel had appeared at her side. 'Oh, Daphne, it's Father! Help me!'

As she stepped towards them Daphne tripped and fell on top of Father. He opened his eyes. 'What the . . . ?'

'I'm sorry, sir, so sorry, I . . .'

'Oh, Daddy, are you all right?'

'What's happening, dear? Why is Daphne sitting on me?'

Even though the situation was dire, and Olivia couldn't keep a limb still, she felt herself smiling. Daphne gave a nervous little giggle as she rolled off her boss and got to her feet. 'Hitler did that, sir. He caused damage to the floor, and I tripped.'

'Well, no harm done, but . . . Ooh, my head hurts.' And then as if the noise going on around him penetrated, he said, 'Good God, it's the Germans. They've come, Olivia!'

His near hysterical voice had the effect of giving Olivia a sense of having to calm them all. 'They have, Daddy, and so far we're all right. But our neighbours need help. Can you get yourself up and go and lie on the bed for a while?'

'The bed! We all need to be in the cellar! Order the staff down there at once. Bloody Germans! They weren't satisfied with the pasting we gave them in '18, they've come back for more!'

This was typical of her father – taking charge helped him to cope.

They made their way down the stairs, treading carefully over the splinters of wood.

'Did we take a direct hit, Daphne, is everyone all right?'

'No, sir, not hit.' Even Daphne sounded less afraid now. 'But things have cracked and blown in, windows and doors. It's the force of the explosions that's caused the damage . . . Will . . . will we all die, sir?'

'No. If this is an invasion, bloody Hitler will want us alive and subservient . . . Look, let's not think the worst, eh? The bombing may have been a mistake. They've claimed a lot of errors saying the victims weren't their target.'

Feeling sick, Olivia didn't think this could be true of what was happening to them. The attack wasn't a stray incident, but a prolonged bombardment. From what she'd seen from the window, St Peter Port was the prime target and for some reason, the tomato wagons were being focused on.

'I'm going to help! I'll take our first-aid kit.'

Grabbing the box of bandages, plasters, iodine and scissors from the bathroom, Olivia scrabbled through the hole that used to be the door and ran for all she was worth towards the scene. Smoke and sulphur choked her and stung her eyes, but she carried on.

When she arrived at the carnage it took her breath away. Lorries were a heap of mangled scrap metal, with flames licking them. Tomatoes carpeted the road. Moans and screams of agony filled the air.

'Oh, Miss Olivia!'

Ruby, the woman who came to help in the kitchen some-times, ran towards her, her face blackened by smoke, her eyes red raw. 'It's . . .'

Her words went into the drone of aircraft.

Ruby dived under a lorry that was still intact.

'No! Ruby! It's too dangerous! RUBY!' But Ruby didn't respond. Dashing over to the weighbridge, Olivia crouched against the wall. The droning deafened her. There was a flash, then a boom and the lorry Ruby had gone under erupted into a ball of flames that seared Olivia's legs.

Screaming in agony, Olivia rolled over and crawled towards the sea. But then a bomb hit the weighbridge. Something cracked her head and all sound left her as she sank into nothingness.

'Olivia! Olivia, my darling girl. You're all right, my dear, wake up!'

'D – Daddy?'

'Yes, I'm here.'

'My leg . . .'

'You've been burned, my dear, but not badly, though it looks very sore.'

'Ruby?'

'I'm sorry, we lost Ruby . . . and so many. Over thirty, with others left critically injured. They hit Jersey too. They must have thought we had a military presence.'

'Are they here?'

'They will be today . . . Hendrick telephoned. He's morti-fied. He told me . . . we are to be occupied. The Germans are full of the news that their beloved Hitler has made yet another gain. His heart is breaking to hear you are here and injured . . . He says . . . Oh, my dear, I'm sorry, but we cannot get you off the island.'

'What?' Olivia sat up, all physical pain forgotten. 'No, not that!' Her head shook from side to side. 'No, Daddy! I must go . . . Karl . . . Oh, God! No!'

A tear trickled down her father's face. He sat down on the edge of her bed and put his head in his hands. 'I'm sorry. So very sorry . . . I shouldn't have called you back . . . Hendrick is upset with me . . . I just felt so vulnerable in

140

the hospital . . . and not able to sort things at the bank myself.'

Olivia placed her hand on his back. 'Don't, Daddy. Don't blame yourself. None of us could predict this happening . . . At least, not when it did. We were just going to dinner! But, God, why? Why? What use are we to bloody Hitler, eh? Just a cameo that he can use against the mainland, that's all.'

'We do have a lot of land that could produce food. I have said all along that we should have been producing more for the mainland . . . But that's by the by now. We have to deal with what we are facing.'

As her father looked at her his expression was one of despair. 'Hendrick said that we must be compliant in every way, work with the Germans, socialize with them . . . invite them to our home . . . Oh, God!'

Once more, Father lowered his head.

'No! No, Daddy, I can never do that! Why is Hendrick asking this of us?'

'So that you will still be able to come and go freely, receive his telephone calls and pass his information to Annie.'

Olivia sank back onto her pillow. The trickle of tears turned into a torrent as she sobbed out the injustice of it all. She was being asked to fraternize to help Britain, and yet they'd done nothing to save her beloved Guernsey and her people, At this moment, she hated the British as much as she hated the Germans. But her darling Karl was on the mainland, and so were Annie and Cissy and Annie's family, all of whom she loved. She had to do what she could to save them all and if that meant fraternizing to eventually bring the Germans down, then she would. Even though it would break her heart to do so.

\* \* \*

The next day the droning was heard again. As Olivia and her father stood outside looking up at the passenger planes bearing the swastika, she knew they were sealing her fate – she might never see her son again.

'Don't worry, my dear, they won't be able to land. Some of the farmers have herded their cattle onto the runway.'

Olivia leaned her head on her father's shoulder, knowing the animals would run in fright and for sure, the planes would land, but part of her felt a sense of pride at the gesture which showed the spirit of the islanders.

'We should go down to the street and stand with our fellow countrymen, Daddy.'

As they stood side by side with their neighbours, the sound of the Germans approaching – hundreds of feet pounding the concrete – caused Olivia's throat to tighten and her heart to become heavy. For her, the beat of their march emulated a clock ticking down towards doomsday.

But the reality wasn't like she thought it would be. These men didn't frighten, they were young, handsome, and yes, had the look of Hendrick, with similar shaped faces and the same fairness of skin and hair. They were smart, upright and proud.

Around her, Olivia could feel the people begin to relax and chatter. A group of young girls giggled, giving a feel of it being an occasion.

That changed when Mr Goldman, owner of a small grocery stall, suddenly spat on the ground then stepped forward, shouting, 'You have no right to be here!'

A silence fell.

Olivia held her breath. But the soldiers marched on as if he hadn't spoken. Mr Goldman slumped against the wall. Running to him, Olivia took his hand. 'That was very brave and something we all wanted to do, but from now on, it's about survival. Better to keep a low profile.' These weren't the words she wanted to say. She wanted to hug him and hail him a hero.

'Miss Olivia, I can no longer contact my family – my brother and his wife and children, who lived in Berlin. When I could, they told of having to wear a yellow star, of their businesses being taken, of not being allowed to walk on the same side of the street as others and of friends herded into trucks and taken away.'

Olivia couldn't say that she knew. 'Rumours have circulated about the Nazis' behaviour towards the Jewish people and if they are to be believed, then it is better for you and your family that you live quietly and don't make a fuss.'

'You're right, I know, but I couldn't help myself.' He straightened up and looked down at her. 'You won't know such pain, though, will you, Miss Olivia?'

His tone held a disgust of her. 'You've got German protection afforded to you by that traitor, Hendrick!'

He turned away and left her standing there, staring after him. Her heart dropped as with Hendrick's instructions to be welcoming to his countrymen, all of her own people would soon be treating her in just such a way.

Going back to her father, she linked arms with him. 'We must find a way of helping the Jewish people who live here, Daddy.'

He patted her hand. 'We will. But how at this moment, I do not know.'

Olivia didn't either, but she couldn't bear to think of their fate being that of the others Hendrick had told her of.

Holding on tightly to her father, Olivia suddenly felt that the bottom had dropped out of the world as she'd known it.

More and more soldiers marched by. None of them looked their way or any way other than straight ahead. She tried to hate them, for they had taken her life away from her. But she couldn't. At the end of the day, they were just boys doing what they were ordered to do.

'We'll have to make the best of it, my dear. Why don't you carry on with your choir and music lessons again? You'll need something. We all will.'

Olivia didn't answer. She didn't need the choir, or the band, she just needed Hendrick and Karl. Her heart broke to think that couldn't happen. Her beloved Guernsey was now under German occupation.

# Chapter Twelve

## Annie

On Monday morning, the first of July, those in the main office of the police station stood in shocked silence at the news that was filtering through. Annie looked around them, frantic for one of them to reassure her.

'Doesn't your mate come from Guernsey, Annie? Is she over there, or back here?'

Annie's voice shook. 'She was supposed to have left to come here the day after the bombing happened. I've been worried sick about her, and now this! Oh, God! I can't take it all in.'

'Well, it doesn't sound good, luv. Bloody Germans taking some of our land as their own! Let's hope you hear from her, eh? At least if you know she's safe that'll be something.'

'Yes, but . . .' Annie told them of Karl, before turning to the sarge. 'Sarge, can you do without me for a couple of hours or so? Me mate's little boy has a nanny with him, but she'll be frantic if she's heard this.'

'Yes, you get off, but be back to man the phones at five o'clock. I've got no one else. Blimey, it's a state of affairs this. I knew married women would be a problem in this job and you bloomin' well are half the time! Having to go early for this or that, I can't run a proper ship with all your demands.'

Everyone laughed. Sarge was a good bloke but old-fashioned. He hated how things were – having to send women out on foot patrol when that had always been done by the men. And yet he loved it too, as the women were doing a splendid job.

'I'll be back, I promise.'

As she grabbed her coat, Annie knew this was one promise she had to keep. Olivia might ring during her shift later. She prayed she would. *Please don't let her be one of the dead*.

As soon as she opened the door to the apartment, Karl flung himself at her. 'Nanny crying.'

'Oh? She ain't, is she, mate? Now, what's upset her, do you know?'

'That!'

Annie followed his finger as he pointed at the wireless set. 'Oh, I see. Well, there's always something to cry about these days. Go and tell her Aunty Annie's here, luv.'

Karl ran off in the direction of the bedroom that Loes occupied.

Before Annie had time to hang up her lightweight uniform coat on one of the hooks in the hallway, Loes came hurrying out of her room.

'Have you heard from Olivia, Annie?'

'No, nothing. But try not to show your distress in front of Karl!' Annie couldn't help but snap this out as she felt really cross at Loes for going to pieces in this way. Wasn't a nanny meant to be strong and reassuring?

As if Annie's tone alone had reminded Loes of this, she pulled herself together. 'Karl, Nanny is all right. It is a summer

146

cold that I have. Let's tidy your things away now and then it is time for your milk.'

'And biccy.'

'Biscuit. Yes, if there are any left, you can have a biscuit. Now take those bricks into your bedroom before Aunty Annie trips over them.'

Karl, always obedient, did as he was told, and looked much happier than when Annie arrived.

'I'm sorry I snapped, Loes, but at all times you should be putting Karl first. He has a lot to face, and we must be strong for him.'

'You are right. It was the thought of the devastation and danger . . . Did Miss Olivia get off the island?'

'We don't know, but it doesn't look likely at all, mate. And that's probably best as being at sea in a small boat could mean she isn't going to make it.'

Annie couldn't believe how calmly she said this.

'But the Germans . . .'

'I know. It's hard to take it in. I only know the same as you if you heard the news.'

Loes nodded. 'I am glad that I'm not there. Being Jewish . . .'

'Oh, Loes. Come here, mate. We could do with a hug. If Olivia doesn't make it home, then we have to take care of Karl for her. She'd expect that of us, luv.'

'I know, Annie. And we will. But it is so sad. Poor, poor Miss Olivia. Already she suffers greatly from being parted from her husband. How is she to bear it?'

'I don't know. But I do know she is the bravest person I've ever met and that she will find a way. It is surprising what we can bear when called upon to do so. I know from experience. I long every day for news of my Ricky.'

'Oh, Annie. I wish you would hear . . . It's all so sad.'

'The best way is to deal with everything as it comes up. We must deal with how you and Karl will manage now as it's possible Olivia won't be able to get funds to you.'

Loes looked shocked.

'Don't worry, we'll look after you. As it happens, I got the builders in to do the little work needed on the basement. Jimmy's been supervising them. You met Jimmy when you brought Karl over. Well, they've got on really well in the past seven days. The basement has been painted and oilcloth has been laid throughout. So, I'm moving you both there, with me. We won't have a lav but'll have to use the outside one, and go back to using a tin bath and piddle pots, but it'll be warm and comfortable, and you'll have company and food, et cetera.'

'What's this, piddle pots?'

Despite everything, Annie burst out laughing. 'You'll soon find out, luv. I have to go now. You pack everything up, and strip the beds and pack the linen. Then grab all you can of the household stuff and put it into the trunks you'll find in the box room, as Olivia calls it, though what it has to do with boxes I have no idea. Pack all the food too. I'll get a truck to come tonight. I'll talk to Fred, the caretaker, on me way out. He'll help strip a couple of beds down and help you with any furniture we'll need to take. I can't afford to buy any, so we'll take what we need from here. Olivia and her father would want us to do that.' She didn't say that there were powers that be that might object as that wasn't for Loes's ears. But she didn't care about any objections Lucy might have. It would be done and dusted before she knew what was going on.

\* \* \*

148

It was just on six that a call came through from Olivia. Annie caught her breath, bracing herself for awful news, and yet she was so happy to know that her dear friend was alive and well. And she was happy, too, that Olivia hadn't started the conversation with their codewords 'The Guernsey Girls', so Annie knew that this wasn't a call to give her a message to pass on to Lucy.

Trying to keep her anguish out of her voice, she asked, 'How are you, luv? It's so good to hear from you.'

'Physically, I'm all right, Annie. Though I was burned badly and stayed a night in hospital, but mentally, I'm going out of my mind.'

'Oh, Olivia, luv. My heart is breaking for you. I just want to be with you. Have you no chance of getting off the island and getting here?'

'None, Annie. The coastal road is guarded, and all fishing is banned, let alone boats used for ferrying. I – I feel devastated . . . lost. Already I was a figure of suspicion with my own people, for being married to a German. That I fear will worsen. I feel I'm going to be isolated.'

'No! How can they think badly of you, luv? They all knew Hendrick. Knew him as a lad growing up and as a young man working with your father. They even lined the streets on your wedding day!'

'But all that's changed. You saw it for yourself when you were over. I try to tell them that Hendrick was forced to go, citing the way Britain conscripted its young men, but I can't change their minds from thinking he went willingly. We know he had to go to save his father's life. But I cannot tell them that as I might put him in danger.'

With Olivia saying this, Annie felt a streak of terror pass

through her. Any number of people could be listening in. She hated what she said next.

'Olivia, we do know he went willingly. As much as we love him, he is a German, and we do have to be wary of him. He thinks like a German, and he put his country before you and his son. He used his father as an excuse!'

There was a shocked gasp from Olivia, but she recovered quickly. 'What I meant was . . . well, Hendrick wouldn't do anything to deliberately hurt me, his son, or the islanders.'

'Well, we must understand them mistrusting him in the circumstances, and though I am cross with them for taking it out on you, I am more cross with him. I'm sorry, so sorry, but that's how I feel.'

Annie so wanted to say something kind but had to think of Olivia's and Hendrick's safety. Olivia had slipped up badly. They could only pray that no one had picked up on it.

Hitting on an idea, she brought in their codeword, hoping that Olivia would know that she didn't mean what she'd said about Hendrick but was just trying to cover Olivia's gaffe.

'Oh, Olivia, how I wish the days were simple like they were when we first called ourselves "The Guernsey Girls".'

'Me too, my lovely friend. Life was simple then, as was everything with Hendrick. I know you're right in what you say about him.'

Sighing with relief, Annie felt sure they would have fooled anyone that was listening in. Hopefully they would take Olivia's first outburst concerning Hendrick's father as emotional wishful thinking on Olivia's part. It was vital that they didn't compromise Hendrick's position. Changing the subject, Annie told Olivia, 'Karl's doing fine. He's asking for you all the time, but Loes manages him and keeps him happy and distracted and he loves coming to play with Beth. But

I've changed things this end to make it easier to look after them.' She told Olivia about the move. 'Oh, and tell your father I am requisitioning the furniture from his apartment but will look after it.'

Now they were on safe ground, talking of the kind of things that any listener would expect them to.

'Oh, Annie, thank you. That will be fine and something I was going to suggest. Will you manage to get it out without problems?'

'Yes. It's happening tonight.'

'That's good news. I'll try to ring your home to talk to Karl but whether I will get through, or even if we will be allowed to use our telephones freely, I don't know. But it's all made me think of how we did things as kids: we used cocoa tins with a knotted string between them, but then things moved to code between the Guernsey boys, but not so much the Guernsey Girls . . .'

Annie grabbed a pen. Olivia had mentioned the Guernsey Girls, which meant she was going to tell her something in code.

'I remember, we were nine when Hendrick taught me Morse code. We tapped a pencil on a table to communicate. When you were here, it was me who was top dog and when we were bored, I should've taken time to teach you it. Ha, these days, though, top dogs have access to transmitters. Anyway, back to my darling Karl, hug him every night and tell him it's me with my arms around him as I fear I won't be able to make contact.'

This signalled the message was over. 'I will, me darling,' and then to show she had the gist of the code, Annie added, 'I understand, and will do all I can to make sure that happens. And Olivia . . . stay strong. We all love you.'

There was a sob, and then, 'I love you too, Annie.'

When the phone went dead, Annie wiped her eyes. She dared not cry or she would never stop. She got quickly down to the message.

The number nine meant there would be nine words between the important words. Quickly crossing these out, she was left with:

Morse code – communicate – top dog – to teach you – transmitters.

Top dog meant Lucy, though the second time Olivia had used it, Annie felt sure she was referring to herself . . . *Olivia has a transmitter! And she wants Lucy to know and to teach me Morse code and how to use a transmitter in case the people of Guernsey aren't allowed to use the telephone.* 'Oh my God!'

Annie looked around. The office was empty. At least no operator could listen in at her end of any conversation as they had their own switchboard. It was Olivia's end that she worried about.

*Please God nothing about Hendrick not being willing to work for Hitler had been heard.* Screwing up the note, she put it safely in her handbag to burn when she got home, then glanced up at the clock, glad to see it was near the end of her shift. The night duty staff would be here soon. She couldn't wait to get home.

She'd asked Jimmy to arrange a van and had instructed Fred on all that had to come, adding a sofa to the list, two chests of drawers and a wardrobe.

Mentally going through everything she'd organized, it occurred to Annie that the bare oilcloth might feel cold to little Karl, so she dialled the apartment. Loes answered.

'It's Annie, Loes. I've heard from Olivia. I will tell you all about it when you come. Is the van there yet . . . ? Oh good.

Look, roll up a few rugs and get those put onto it as well. Olivia knows all about what we are doing and is fine with it all.'

'Oh, that is good news that you have heard from her. And yes, I can do that with the rugs. I've managed to pack such a lot of things for the kitchen and linen for the beds, even Olivia's warm clothing and her father's too. It may be needed, we don't know. Fred is helping the driver to load as Jimmy has not arrived.'

'Oh? Well, as long as they are managing. Well done, luv. You're a proper Girl Guide.'

'What is this Girl Guide?'

'Ha, that's two things you'll learn! I have three piddle pots so you'll see what they are, but I think when I explain you'll understand what Girl Guides are. I'm sure they have them in your country too . . . Look, I must go, someone is coming to take over from me.'

When at last she stepped outside the station and walked towards the bus that would take her to Old Ford Road, she was surprised when Jimmy drew up beside her.

'You must have read me mind, Jimmy. I was dreading waiting for a bus as I need to get home. Oh, and ta for arranging a van, but I thought you'd have gone with it.'

Jimmy leaned across to open the door and as Annie slid into the passenger seat, he said, 'No. I want to talk to you, Annie. I can't at home.'

Jimmy looked strange. His cheeks were red, and sweat beads stood out on his forehead. A feeling of anguish streaked through Annie. 'Why, what's up, mate?'

'It's Janey. She's harming herself again. She's bruised on her arms and body, where you can't see.'

'Oh no. I've been worrying this might happen. She needs help, Jimmy.'

'Not just help, but putting away. She might hurt the little ones.'

Annie gasped in horror. 'No! How can you think that?'

'I don't want to. And I don't feel towards her how I did when I first came home. But I have to think of the kids, and I want your help in this, Annie.'

'Well, you ain't getting it! That will never happen. We need to get help for her, not make things worse for her, which is what you're doing with how you treat her.'

'So, on your head be it if one of the little ones gets hurt. But I tell you something, if things don't improve, I'm taking my kid to me mum. She's giving up the stall, she's found a buyer and she's going to Kent to be with her Alf. I'll go as well and take me Beth.'

Annie was shocked to the core. How could things have deteriorated for Janey in such a short time?

She thought about Rose, Jimmy's mum. Such a lovely woman who worked on her market stall every day and was always cheerful, though she'd been to hell and back in her younger days at the hands of her dad, then struggling to bring Jimmy up. She was glad that now she had a chance at happiness. She'd meant to have gone to Alf before and leave the business to Jimmy, but with war and now Jimmy's mental health, she'd stayed.

Annie knew she would care for the kids, and her home would be a safe haven for them, but not without Janey! And it sounded as though Jimmy only meant to take Beth!

'Sending both kids and Janey is a better idea, Jimmy. There could be another wave of evacuations anyway, and Janey could go with them if they're forced to go, but she'd be better off settled with your mum. And then you could visit her too. Rose would soon help Janey get her health back.'

'I suppose. Yes, that'd work. But she has to go somewhere, things can't go on!'

'I'll talk to her.'

A shudder went through Annie then as Jimmy put his hand on her knee. It wasn't an awakening of the old feelings she'd had for him before he went off with Janey, but a horror at the intimacy of the gesture. This increased with his words.

'Oh, Annie, it should have been you and me, girl. We were good together . . . I mean, I know we never . . . but, well . . . just as we were going to, Janey wormed her way into me affections and distracted me.'

Annie shifted her knees. 'Don't do that, Jimmy, and don't twist things either. You fell in love with Janey and left me for her. As it turned out, it was the best thing you could have done. I found true happiness with a good and faithful . . . man.'

She hadn't meant to sob. She'd lived with her anguish over no news of her darling Ricky.

But more than that, she didn't want what happened next. Jimmy pulled up on the side of the road and turned to her. 'Oh, Annie, I'm here for you. Ricky were a good bloke. But if he hadn't come on the scene, I reckon you and me would have weathered the fling I had with Janey and be together now.'

'What! What are you talking about? Have you gone mad? Stop saying these things, Jimmy. You fell in love with Janey, she didn't lure you away. You went to the shop where she worked and lured her back to the flats when you were building them! You instigated it all, Jimmy. And you took her down before you wed her! You wanted her, not me! And where all this is coming from, mate, I just don't know and don't want to. I'm grieving me heart out for me lovely Ricky, and you insult him like this, even talking about him as if he were dead, when we all said we wouldn't!'

'I can't help how I feel. I've been an idiot. Janey was young, pretty, she turned me head. You know I loved you, Annie, from when I were a ragged-arsed lad.'

'STOP IT! SHUT YOUR MOUTH!'

Turning to get out of the van, Annie fumbled with the catch. Jimmy caught hold of her waist. 'Please, Annie. We can get rid of Janey. We'd be happy, I know we would.'

Annie hit out at him. 'You bastard! You bleedin' bastard!'

Jimmy's head shot back; blood poured from his nose, but Annie didn't care. She jumped from the van and ran for all she was worth.

When she could run no further, she stepped into the doorway of a shop on Roman Road. Being after seven, all the shops were closed and there were very few people about. Slumping against the door, Annie allowed the tears to stream down her cheeks. *How could this happen to me? To us? To poor, poor Janey?*

Jimmy was a monster. And yet, he hadn't always been. This was a different Jimmy. His brain damage was the worst thing she could ever remember dealing with in her life. He was deranged! Was Janey safe with him? Were the children?

With this last thought, she straightened her back, pulled her uniform jacket down and marched out of the doorway towards Janey's and her mum's flats.

She hadn't gone far when Jimmy's van came along the kerbside. He had his window down and slowly followed her.

'I'm sorry, Annie, I should have thought on. It's too soon for you. But I'm sincere. I'm going to do as you said and send Janey and the kids to me mum. Then the coast'll be clear for us.'

'What part of "No" don't you understand, Jimmy? I don't love you. I don't even like you. And the way I'm feeling at this moment, I hate you! You've turned into someone I don't know. You'll break me Janey's heart!'

'She don't care about me, and I've no feeling for her.'

'Go away! Just go away and leave me alone!'

He continued to crawl along the kerbside, but Annie strode on ignoring him. When they neared Old Ford Road, Jimmy suddenly said, 'I'll be back later. I'll go and see how the van bloke's doing. But think about things, Annie, luv.' With this he roared away.

Feeling as if she was the one who had betrayed Janey, Annie's insides churned as she went inside the building and knocked on her mum's door and opened it.

'Is that you, Cissy?'

'It's me, Mum. Are you in bed?'

'I am, me darlin'. Sister Mary came tonight and helped me to bath and get to bed. I'm comfier when it gets to this time . . . But, oh, Annie, the news. They've gone and done it. First the bombing and now this . . .'

'I know. It's dreadful. I've spoken to Olivia. And as you can imagine, she's distraught.'

Talking about what had happened and what Olivia had said, and then repeating it as Cissy came into mum's flat, steadied Annie's nerves and quietened the impact of the shock she'd received through Jimmy's actions. Still, she couldn't take in all that had hit her from the moment the wireless had made the announcement of Germany having invaded Guernsey.

'Eeh, lass, ain't there nowt that we can do? Can't we rescue Miss Olivia? I can't bear it!'

Annie put her arm around Cissy, who loved Olivia as much as she did herself. 'There's nothing, luv, other than look after Karl and Loes.' She told them what was happening. 'So, me and Loes will need your help, and Janey's. Other than that, we must all make sure Karl has all he needs and that we keep Olivia alive in his memory. Phone calls from her will help with that – that's if the bloody Nazis allow them to make calls. That's me main worry, that communication will be shut off. But with Olivia having access to the phones in the bank, that might give her a chance to ring us.'

Both Mum and Cissy had tears running down their faces. Annie could do nothing to comfort them as she held the same fears as they did.

'Look, the van will be here soon. I'll just nip upstairs and see if Janey can help.'

'Eeh, it's going to be a long night.'

'I know, but don't worry, Cissy, we'll get done what we have to, eh?'

Annie turned to her mum. 'Have you noticed anything about Janey, Mum? I haven't, but then I ain't noticed much at all lately, everything's gone over me head.'

The look on her mum's face told it all. 'I don't like saying, Annie, luv, but if anything, I think her depression is worsening. And . . . well, it ain't none of me business, but I think it's getting Jimmy down. I heard them raising their voices the other night. It was frightening.'

Annie's heart dropped to her stomach. And for some reason guilt clothed her, though she'd done nothing wrong.

'I never hear anything, but then I've slept heavily since . . . But why didn't you say, Mum? . . . I'm sorry, I shouldn't have said that. You've been protecting me. I understand. Look. I'll pop upstairs and judge for meself how Janey is.

It may be that she needs counselling. We come across a lot of those that do in me job. More so now with the men having left.'

'Yes, I can understand that. And with Janey just having had a baby and having to put up with Jimmy's moods and worried over you . . . Poor girl's having it rough.'

'Aye, having a baby can cause a lass to feel down on its own.'

'It can. It's called post-natal depression, Cissy. Janey suffered from it after Beth too, but we'll get her sorted between us.'

Taking the stairs two at a time, Annie knocked, then opened the door of Janey's flat. 'Hiya, sis, it's me.'

The stench that met her made her wriggle her nose and close her eyes tightly for a second.

Janey sat in the chair next to the fireplace, staring into space. Her hair was matted and a bruise on her cheek had a crusted, dried blood streak running from its centre. 'Crikey, luv. Has Angie filled her nappy? Where's the kids?'

Without looking at her, Janey said, 'They're in the bedroom. Jimmy put them to bed and got them to sleep. I – I can't keep up with it all, Annie.' She turned to face Annie for the first time. 'It's the nappies, they're piled up.'

As there wasn't a sound coming from the bedroom, Annie crossed the room and took Janey in her arms. 'Don't worry, luv, I'll help you. What happened to your face?'

'I – it were me being clumsy. I . . . the door swung back at me.'

'Oh, Janey. Janey, luv!' Anguish and fear vied for prominence in Annie. It looked as if her beloved sister was having another mental breakdown and she didn't know how to best help her. She couldn't call on Jimmy. But what was she going to do? How could she look after Janey and her kids, their

mum and Loes and Karl, as well as continue to work? Even
with Cissy's and Loes's help it was going to be difficult. And
then there was the problem of Jimmy. She couldn't see him
giving up his pursuit of her and that disgusted her.

She was dreading seeing him later.

Annie lowered her head onto Janey's as the thought
came to her, *But most of all, how am I going to get through
not knowing what's happened to me Ricky and to come to
terms with maybe never seeing him again? . . . Dear God,
help me!*

'Look, Janey, luv, I've a lot on me plate and I was counting
on you to help me. I've got Loes and Karl coming to live
with me. The van with the furniture'll be here soon. Jimmy's
going to help the driver to get it down the stairs for me,
but I thought you'd be giving me a hand to set it all up.'

'I can't, Annie, luv, I'm sorry.'

'Right, at least get to the bathroom and clean yourself up,
eh?'

She went to lift Janey, but her moan of pain stopped her.
'Oh, Janey, you've been hurting yourself again. Oh, me
darling. Look, I'll fetch Cissy and we'll get you into the bath,
eh?'

'No. Just leave me, luv. I'll be all right.'

Annie stood up straight. For a moment she felt helpless.
Looking around, she decided to pop her head in on the girls
and then deal with the nappies.

Opening the door, she creased her nose as the air in here
was stale, with a fusty smell. A quick glance showed her both
little ones tucked up and not moving. They were facing away
from her. She smiled as she went between the cot and the
bed. For all the world she could have lifted them both, but
she crept by and opened the window and crept out again.

The stench that hit her when she opened the bathroom door knocked her for six and made her heave. 'Oh, Janey, Janey, why didn't you ask for help, me darlin'?'

The next ten minutes were spent frantically running around opening windows, calling down to Cissy to get her boiler on the go and then heaving as she dunked the heavily soiled nappies in the toilet to get the excrement off them, swilled them in the bath and took them downstairs to Cissy.

'I've done me best with them, Cissy. I just need to run up and clean the bathroom. Janey's in a state, but I can't do anything for now. At least the kids are asleep, bless them.'

'Eeh, lass. I'll see to these. By, that van'll be here soon. How we're going to do it all, I don't knaw.'

As Annie ran back up the stairs, despair entered her. She didn't know herself, but somehow, they had to.

Finding Janey bent over, everything else paled. She went to her sister and took her in her arms. 'Oh, Janey. Me Janey.'

# Chapter Thirteen

## Janey

Janey felt no comfort from having Annie hold her. To her, her world was a black hole. All she needed to do was take a step forward and she'd fall into it. She'd tumble and tumble in blissful oblivion of this life and all the pain it held for her.

She'd be away from Jimmy's blows to her body, and him spitting hate at her, telling her how he should have had Annie! That she'd lured him away by flaunting herself in his face and showing she would be an easy lay. That she'd been with other men and Angie wasn't his. Then as she lay crying, he'd taken her brutally, telling her that's all she wanted off him, so she'd get it, but not how she wanted it – all lovey-dovey. Not any more. She was such a miserable sod, who did nothing but mope around. With this, he'd turned her over and forced himself into her, stretching her and ripping her insides. All the while, he mocked her body, saying that he couldn't stand the sight of it or her haggard-looking face.

She'd just wanted to die. She was useless as a wife, useless as a mother, and ugly. Her face was ugly, her body was too, with its stretch marks zigzagging her stomach and her breasts empty and sagging.

Jimmy hated her. But then, he wasn't Jimmy any more.

'What is it, Janey? What's making you feel how you do, eh?'

Janey wanted to scream out all the heartache she was suffering but Annie didn't deserve that. She had a broken heart herself.

'Look, luv, I'll fetch a flannel and a hairbrush, eh? You see to yourself, and I'll make you a cup of tea. Then I'll be busy for a while, but I'll get us all pie and mash in for supper. How would that be?'

'I need the lav, Annie. I'll go to the bathroom to wash me face.'

Annie went to help her again. Trying not to, but not able to help herself, Janey winced as Annie pulled on her arm.

'Are you hurt badly, Janey?'

The time had come for the truth. She sat down and lifted her blouse.

'God, Janey! Oh, me darlin'.'

Annie's tears mingled with her own as they clung to one another.

'It's Jimmy. I ain't hurting meself, Annie, I ain't ill, just . . . I just don't know what to do. I can't function normally. The pain. Not just me body, but . . . I've lost me Jimmy, Annie. I've lost him.'

Suddenly, the urge to scream was too much for Janey. She opened her mouth and let it come out, giving vent to it, releasing her inner pain. Untying the knot of agony that had held her heart. She wanted her Jimmy back. The kind, loving man that had gone off to war, breaking his heart at leaving her. 'I want him back . . .' A huge sob racked her body. 'I – I've lost him, Annie.'

Annie clung on to her and sobbed with her. After a

163

moment, Janey felt Annie stroke her hair and in a gentle voice she said, 'This can't go on, Janey. Jimmy needs help. We'll talk to his doctors, tell them what's happening.'

'But they'll put him in a loony bin. We can't do that to him.'

'Well, he'll have to go with Rose. Look, I ain't said . . . but he gave me a lift and he told me Rose has sold her stall and her greengrocery round and is moving to her farm in Kent . . . He said he wanted to go with her.'

Janey could tell that Annie wasn't telling her everything. Before she could say anything, the door opened.

'Eeh, is everything all right, me lasses? We heard a scream.'

Annie answered. 'Well, things ain't good, Cissy, but we're sorting everything, luv.'

Cissy accepted this. And Janey thought her doing so was a measure of how they all made allowances for her, thinking she could easily be tipped over the edge.

'That's good . . . The van's here, Annie, and so is Jimmy. He's helping the driver and they're getting everything downstairs. The nappies are boiling away, and me and Loes are just going to rinse them and hang them out, then we'll make a start on making up the beds in your flat. Your mum's watching Karl, so you've nowt to worry over. You see to Janey, eh?'

'Ta, Cissy. And there's no need to think about cooking supper.' Annie told Cissy her plans. 'I'll go out for them later.'

Cissy nodded and left.

'Oh, Janey, I thank God for Cissy every day. There're times when I wouldn't know what to do without her.'

Janey couldn't answer this. She had to say now what she knew had to happen.

'I have to get away from Jimmy, Annie . . . I fear he'll kill me.'

'Oh, Janey, luv. I'm sorry, but I believe that too. I'll help you all I can. Loes, me and you will look after all three kids, then we'll get you and Loes to the countryside with them. Somewhere of your own choosing, before the kids are evacuated under orders.'

Janey could only nod. It all sounded so wonderful, and she liked Loes. She'd been over to visit with Karl when Loes had been at the apartment, and they'd had a nice time together.

'But what about Jimmy? What if he won't go to his mum's and he makes a nuisance of himself to Mum, Cissy and you?'

'I'll give him an ultimatum: he either goes, or I have him sectioned. I can do that in me police role . . . Well, one of me colleagues can. But if it gets to that, you'll have to be with me on it, Janey. You'll have to be examined by our police doctor and tell him everything.'

'I will, Annie. But we'll try telling Jimmy he has to go to Rose first, eh?'

'Yes, luv, we will. Now, let's help you to the bathroom and I'll check on the girls and then go and see how they're getting on downstairs. If the driver's gone, I'll tell Jimmy he's to come up here as we need to talk to him.'

A moment later, a strangled, anguished cry came from Annie. 'No . . . No! Oh God! No!'

Janey dashed out of the bathroom and then stood stock still staring towards the children's bedroom door as Annie came through it and slumped against the wall.

'Annie, what's wrong? Me babies? What's happened?'

Annie took a deep gasp of breath. 'Angie . . . Oh, God, Angie . . .'

Janey's head shook from side to side. She didn't want Annie to tell her and yet she felt compelled to ask. 'Annie, what . . . what's happened?'

'Oh, Janey.' Annie staggered to the sofa and collapsed on it.

Janey could barely whisper, 'Me babies.' She went towards the door.

'No! No, Janey, don't go in.' Annie was crying, and yet not crying. Her mouth was stretched, her eyes staring out of their sockets.

Janey could hear herself rambling, but she didn't know why. 'Jimmy put the kids to bed, he said he'd put them to sleep . . . I ain't been in since . . . He stormed out then . . . Annie . . . what's he done? Me babies, not me babies!'

'Angie . . . she's dead . . . Janey, Angie's gone!'

Annie's mouth went slack as she drew in a screeching sob. 'Why, Janey? Why? She's innocent in all of this. Why didn't you ask for help?'

'Dead! Me Angie? How? Why? No! No, no, no, Annie. Don't say that! Stop it! Jimmy put them both to bed . . . She can't be. No! No!'

Annie grabbed her arm. 'I'm sorry. Oh, me Janey, I'm sorry.'

'I've got to go to her . . . and me Beth . . . Oh, me Beth . . . is she . . . ?'

'No, but she's sleeping heavily. Too heavily . . . Oh, God, Janey, has he done something to her too?'

They collided as they went through the door. Annie got to Beth first; she picked her up. 'She's still breathing, but unconscious. What's the bastard done to her? Shout down for help, Janey.'

But Janey couldn't move. She'd picked up the still form of her beautiful Angie.

166

'We need help, Janey, we must save Beth!'

Annie put Beth down and ran through the door; her scream splintered the air.

Janey's eyes fixed on Angie. Her little face was blue and yet perfect in every way. It was then that Annie's voice came to her. Annie must have run down the stairs as she was talking down the phone now. 'Ambulance and police, quickly.' Janey heard Annie give the address.

Then Cissy's voice. 'What happened, Annie . . . ?'

Annie didn't answer that question, she just said, 'Where's Jimmy?'

'He ran out the door and jumped into his van when he heard your scream. Eeh, what's to do?'

It seemed no time at all until Cissy and Annie were by her side and Janey felt Cissy's eyes on her. All she could say to Cissy was, 'Jimmy put them to bed. They never cried. I left them, glad of the peace.' Her world began to spin . . . 'Help me, Annie, help me!'

Her legs gave way and she slumped to the ground.

Everything around her was quiet, then she heard a sob, and Annie's voice saying, 'Cissy, luv. Go down to let the ambulance in, I can hear its bells. The police will be here soon too.'

Annie didn't sound like Annie; she sounded all official. 'Tell Loes to put Karl to bed in my bed in Mum's room and to sit with Mum. You stay with them, Cissy. I'll help Janey.'

Then arms came around her, the strong arms of Annie that had always held her. Annie was crying. Her body was heaving.

'Get up onto the chair, Janey, luv. Come on. Let me take Angie.'

'I – I didn't do it, Annie. I didn't. Jimmy put them to bed.'

'I believe you, luv. Get up now . . . Oh, God, what a mess. The smell. I should have known.'

Janey couldn't think what smell she meant.

'Jimmy put Angie to sleep . . . He hated her, Annie. What's he done to Beth . . . ? Not Beth too . . . Please say not Beth.'

'No, sit down, luv. Beth's all right, but I think he's given her something. She ain't responding. She's laid on the sofa.'

Janey wanted to close her eyes. Let everything drift from her. All the pain. The silly notion that her Angie was dead when she was only sleeping – Jimmy had put her to sleep. Jimmy loved her, didn't he?

All went on around her. People in uniform examining Angie and Beth. One was doing something to Beth. Then she spoke. 'We need to make her sick – I think she's been given an overdose of something. I can't wake her, so I'll have to make her retch by inserting a pipe into her throat. I've a pump that I can use to suck out the contents of her stomach, but that's a bit violent. When was she put down to sleep?'

'It must be almost two hours. I came in about half an hour ago, and I checked on them, they just looked asleep. Jimmy had picked me up from work, so he'd put them to bed before he left here.'

Janey couldn't think how Annie could talk in this precise way.

The nurse continued working on Beth. But a policeman stood in front of Janey now. 'You say you never checked on them, Mrs Blaine?'

Janey shook her head.

'I need you to answer me, Mrs Blaine, what's been going on, eh?'

Janey turned her head to look at Annie. Annie looked wretched. 'Annie . . . Annie?'

Annie moved towards her and knelt beside her. 'Tell the sergeant exactly what's happened this afternoon, Janey, what went on before I arrived. He's here to help you, luv.'

Janey wondered if she should tell him what Jimmy had done to her. Would he be mad at her if she did?

'Come on, luv. It will be all right. We just need to know what happened.'

The policeman sounded kindly. She could tell him, couldn't she?

'Jimmy came in, he were mad at me because everywhere was a mess . . . He . . . he hit me . . . he said . . . he said he didn't love me, that he loved Annie.'

There was a gasp from the officer. He looked at Annie, but she didn't say or do anything. The policeman scribbled in his book.

'The kids began to cry, so he said he would put them to bed. I had bathed them ready. They looked nice, they smelled nice . . . I cared for them . . . It was just the washing, me pain, I couldn't keep up with the nappies.'

'We can see they're both lovely and clean, luv, don't worry, just keep telling me your story.'

Janey couldn't believe how it all tumbled out. She told it all. The beating, the insults, the rape. 'He . . . hurt me. He put me on me stomach and . . . the pain was so bad . . . When he'd gone, I got to me chair . . . the kids were quiet . . . I was glad . . . Oh, God, I was glad! I didn't know . . . I didn't know.'

'Janey, it's all right, luv. Hold it together for Beth. She's waking up, but she must go to hospital where they can care for her. We don't know what was given to her. Have you any ideas, luv?'

'No . . . Jimmy has stuff for his headache . . . aspirin . . .

It's in the cupboard in the bathroom. He . . . he had a new bottle from the chemist yesterday.'

Annie jumped up and ran to the bathroom. When she came back, she said, 'The bottle's nearly full. Did he have any others, Janey?'

'No, he'd run out . . . I want me Angie, Annie. Where is she?'

To the sound of tablets being emptied onto the table and counted, Annie told her, 'The children are in the ambulance, me darling. Oh, Janey, they will take care of them. They think Beth was given something that is making her sleep. They are just checking how many aspirin have gone from the bottle, but it doesn't look like many, so if he only gave a couple to Beth, she'll be all right, I promise.'

Annie's tears flooded her face as she said this. Her distress tore at Janey's heart. But this time Janey knew she mustn't give way to crying. She had to make sense of it if it would help save her little Beth.

'Beth was shouting at Jimmy to stop hurting me. He grabbed her and cuddled her. Angie was on the blanket on the floor, she was all clean . . . I'd bathed her. I was on the floor near to the sofa. Jimmy had flung me there. Jimmy took Beth into her room. He was talking to her in a gentle voice, then . . . I . . . I don't know how long it was, but he fetched Angie . . . When he came out . . . he dragged me by me hair to our bed . . .'

'Oh, me darlin'.'

'Angie wouldn't settle, she was crying. Jimmy got out of bed calling her names. I – I couldn't move. When he came back, he said he'd put them to sleep. Then he did those things before dressing and leaving . . . He – he said he was going to the one he should have had. I know he meant you,

Annie, but I know you don't want him . . . Are my babies still asleep, Annie?'

Annie sat next to her holding her hand. She squeezed it hard. Janey's shoulders relaxed. Annie made her feel safe.

Annie spoke to her sergeant. 'Janey said the same as soon as we found out, Sarge. She said that Jimmy had put the children to bed, and that he'd told her he'd said he'd put them to sleep.'

Janey could feel Annie shaking.

When the sergeant spoke, he didn't sound as though he believed them.

'Well, it's looking like Jimmy did it . . . But I'm not convinced. Jimmy! I mean, well, your sister . . . Look, I'm sorry to say it, but she's obviously mentally ill . . . maybe delusional?'

'Yes, she has been ill in the past, but she got better. She managed well when Jimmy was away. The birth set her back – it can some women. But, Sarge, Jimmy has been brain damaged, I told you all that. Look, when I discovered the bodies, Janey didn't know they had gone, I'm certain of that. She kept saying that Jimmy had put them to bed. And her other story of him hurting her stacks up. Look at her. Have her examined. She's in agony.'

A different fear took hold of Janey. Would the policeman take her Jimmy away from her?

Did she want him to? No. She wanted to shout out that Jimmy didn't hurt her, that she'd made it up . . . But he had. And she couldn't take much more of it, so she kept quiet.

'The doctor is going to examine your sister now as he's finished his work with the children.'

Annie asked, 'Is Beth going to be all right?'

'Yes, he said she should make a full recovery. They've taken them both to the hospital now. You can take Janey along there once the doctor is finished with her.'

'Thanks, Sarge . . . Janey, luv, the doctor is going to examine you. Don't be afraid, I'll stay with you.'

When a man Janey didn't know came over to her, Annie helped her to stand. 'We're going into your bedroom, luv. Hold on to me. This is the doctor. Don't be afraid.'

'I want Mum, Annie.'

'Soon, me darlin'.'

'I'm in a mess, Annie. Will the doctor mind? I did put a rag on, but I think it's wet. Jimmy hurt me bottom.'

'Oh, Janey, luv.' Annie looked up at the sergeant.

'We'll get a full report as you know, Annie . . . And, Annie, remember, these things are never pleasant, but when it's your own sister and your nieces . . . But we want you to know we are all here for you.' Janey saw him shake his head. 'That you have so much on your plate at this moment beggars belief, but try to stay strong for your sister, eh?'

'I will, Sarge, and ta.'

But for all that, Janey could see Annie's tears hadn't stopped running their silent path down her cheeks.

As she turned over onto her back a few minutes later, feeling even sorer than before, Janey saw the doctor shake his head from side to side.

'I've never seen such brutality, Annie. I'd say Jimmy Blaine was a dangerous man . . . See what you can do for your sister to clean her and comfort her while I send for another ambulance. She needs some attention by a surgeon . . . From there, well, she may go to the asylum.'

'No, Doctor, not that! I won't allow that. Janey's upset

172

and in shock and that's causing her to be confused, but she isn't ill . . . This may trigger that, but we'll care for her. We'll get her the help she needs, if she needs it . . . Please, Doctor, please stipulate that she is to come home. She needs to be with her family.'

'That's all very well, Annie, but if she shows the signs she is displaying now, which will worsen when she realizes fully that she has lost one child and what has happened to her other child, it may well tip her over the edge, and then she may be sectioned. I'm sorry, but as much as your heart wants to, you cannot save her if that happens, and neither can I.'

'I can, and I will!'

Janey didn't like the doctor's words, but Annie wouldn't let anything bad happen to her. *But where are me Angie and Beth? . . . Jimmy has put them to bed, hasn't he? I haven't lost them. Annie will make sure that they're all right too.*

With this thought settling her fear, Janey's eyes closed. She dreamed of floating away, of her girls holding her hands and floating with her. She felt happy, as if her cares had gone. Something told her that Jimmy was never coming back, and strangely, that added to her peace.

# PART THREE

Losing Freedoms

# *Chapter Fourteen*

## *Olivia*

### July 1940

It had been days since Olivia had spoken to Annie, and still Hendrick hadn't rung her.

As she paced up and down, she ran her fingers through her hair, unable to come to terms with all that had happened and how everything was changed and yet was the same.

They'd been ordered to carry on their daily life as normal. *Ha! Normal? How can one be expected to do that? Nothing is normal. A mother without her child isn't normal, or a wife without her husband!* Even though it was a shared plight with most of the young women on the island, it didn't help any of them.

And then there were the notices that the Germans posted daily.

Added to those she'd told Annie of – no fishing and no other boats to leave the shore – the islanders had now been ordered to keep to a strict curfew of eleven p.m. And no alcohol could be bought or sold, only what they already had in their homes could be consumed. Father, who'd managed to get the house repaired, had put his fingers up at this one as he had practically a cellar full of his favourite tipples and red wine.

He worried her, though, as he said he would see that his friends had enough and would share if they hadn't. If he got caught doing this, he could be in serious trouble.

But apart from this, two of the other notices had really upset her. One being that all British soldiers on leave on the island had to report to the police by nine o'clock this morning. What their fate would be as enemies of Germany and having been engaged in active combat with them, Olivia shuddered to think.

And the other: that only those providing essential services could buy petrol – doctors and medical staff, as well as farmers and traders needing to transport produce. This would mean that she wouldn't be able to go to her and Hendrick's farmhouse, and she desperately needed to. She had to get the transmitter that Hendrick had insisted he'd wanted to keep when they'd cleared his aunt's house.

When she'd first seen it, she'd thought it was a boy's suitcase, but had then been amazed to see what it contained and what it was capable of.

Hendrick had told her that his father had bought it for him and had taught him to use it on one of his visits to Germany. He'd been twenty-two at the time and had thought it was a toy but soon found that his father was fascinated by these machines and had become hooked himself.

He'd made her laugh then as he'd related how he and his father began to send messages to each other. Hendrick had got the code wrong on one occasion and had sent that he'd had a nice winner instead of dinner. His father had rung to ask his aunt if he was gambling and if it was getting out of hand!

Despite everything, Olivia smiled at how they had giggled and begun to make up sentences that could be misconstrued.

She'd become really interested in the transmitter and had asked Hendrick to teach her. Her first message had been picked up by a ship's radio and she was told not to use that frequency again. This had made them laugh even more and had led to them experimenting with different crystals to find out what frequencies they had. One of their messages was picked up by a British enthusiast who had chatted with them through Morse code for a few nights running.

They'd wrapped the crystals as they'd identified them and had marked which was which and kept them with the machine.

These thoughts convinced Olivia that the transmitter would be her best and only option for keeping in contact with the mainland. But how to get it safely here so that she could try it?

With these concerns weighing heavily on her shoulders, Olivia sat down at Hendrick's desk that stood under the window of her living room, not yet having been moved to the farmhouse, and looked up. She could see how the sun made the sea appear to be a bed of diamonds. Such a peaceful scene in the turmoil of all that was happening.

The telephone ringing made her jump.

'Hendrick! How are you, my love?'

'I am well.'

With this reply, Olivia closed her eyes and released her breath as relief flooded her that there was to be no code, as she needed his attention. 'Oh, Hendrick, it's good to hear your voice, darling. I – I'm so afraid.'

'Please don't be, my love. The officers know who you are and will treat you with the respect a high-ranking civil servant's wife deserves and warrants. This will give us the freedom to telephone each other at their temporary headquarters in the Royal Hotel, as they will still have connections to Germany and France from there.'

'Oh, that's wonderful. I have been worried that we wouldn't be able to communicate.'

'No, that won't happen, though we will have to have a time that I can ring you and you will be there. They will afford you privacy, which will make it easier for us.'

Hendrick then shocked her as he told her how he'd also arranged that they could live out at the farmhouse and that her father should offer his house to the officers. 'This will put you both in their favour.'

Not sure about all of this, Olivia didn't object but just listened and made the right replies when needed, while busying herself scribbling out a quick code. She needed to tell him about the transmitter and how she was trying to sort out a way to contact Annie.

When he told her that she would be allowed a ration of petrol each week and given a permit which would allow her to drive freely around the island she thought that while the ration of petrol would be wonderful, she worried how all he'd told her would go down with her fellow islanders, and even why he was telling her knowing someone might be listening! But then, maybe he needed her to look as though she was collaborating with the Germans.

Olivia hated the thought of this, but reminded herself that she would need to do things the islanders disapproved of to help the war effort and ultimately them.

'I hope all of that makes you feel better, though I know, my dear, that your heart must be breaking because you're missing our darling little Karl. But be happy that he is safe, and in the loving care of Annie and Loes. Think, my dear, if they were with you, you would have to protect Loes, and that would mean your own certain execution and hers if they found out she is a Jewess.'

Then, as if he realized what he'd said, he told her, 'Not that I like that situation. A Jew caring for our son. But we can't do anything about it now.'

Olivia gasped at the horror of this and for the first time let herself accept that Karl was better in Britain, especially if Annie had been able to get him to the countryside. But she knew that what Hendrick had just said cost him dearly as he had no such feelings towards the Jews. He just needed to convince listeners-in that he was what he wasn't. Danger lurked everywhere for him.

Thinking it best to change the subject, Olivia seized on the lull in the conversation as a chance to allow her to get her coded message in.

'You're so right, Hendrick, and even though we can't change the situation of who is looking after our son, the thought of him being safe will help me to bear it all . . . Oh, talking of bearing it, Rupert is doing well.'

'Oh, that's good. Haha, that scruffy old bear will keep you company, dear.'

As best she could she told him in code what her thoughts were around the transmitter.

It was so difficult to do in a hurry as most often she had to really think a code through for a while and work on it to make sure she'd got it right.

She could only hope that he got the gist as she prattled on about a quiz that they listened to on the wireless – her only way of bringing in key words.

'You teased me about cuddling Rupert and playing with his ear while we listened and, oh, do you remember that code question? It was about signalling an SOS message.'

She knew he'd understood as he laughed and said, 'Oh yes, I got the answer first and it was a good answer.'

Not only did this tell her he knew what she was telling him, but that he agreed, as the question was completely made up, as was the quiz itself.

'Well, darling, I need to go. They're working on switching the island's communication off at this very minute and I was lucky to catch you. Go to the farmhouse soon, my dear. And don't worry about the concessions you have. You'll be contacted and told all the arrangements, but you will need to go along to register for your petrol allowance today.'

'I will. I love you, my darling.'

'And I love you with all my heart, Olivia.'

'We'll speak soon . . . Oh, Hendrick, I miss you.'

His line went dead.

But just as Olivia went to put the telephone down, she heard a voice say, 'It's all right for some!'

She lifted the receiver to her ear again. 'Who is this?'

'It's Maggie at the exchange. I heard all of that. Special privileges for a Nazi wife! You should be ashamed. And him! I thought he was one of us, but he obviously isn't. He spoke of Loes as if she were a bit of dirt. I'm glad she's not here.'

The phone clicked and the disengaged sound buzzed in Olivia's ear. For a moment she stared at the handset. Then gingerly, and with a shaking hand, hung up. Her heart pounded against her chest.

The antagonism had begun.

Standing, she caught sight of herself in the oval, ornate mirror that hung on the wall near to the door. Her ashen-white face stared back. 'Can I do this?' she asked her reflection. 'Can I take the wrath of my dear islanders – be an outcast?' Then it came to her that she could – that she had to. She had a job to do, and she would do it to the best of her ability.

Gathering herself, she went in search of her father and found him in his sitting room staring out to sea as she had been. Going to him, she went on her haunches beside him. 'Daddy, I've had a call from Hendrick.' She told him all that had happened.

'Do we have to do it, darling?'

'Hendrick thinks it best.'

'We'll be like traitors to our own people.'

'It will seem like that, but really we will be helping them as we're helping Britain to fight this war, and that will mean the island's liberation.'

'Well, bloody Britain are not doing a very good job of it, are they? You told them about the second front, they should have been ready.'

'That's the problem, everyone backed Chamberlain and his appeasement strategies for so long that now Britain is ill equipped. Churchill advocated building our forces and their resources long ago, but Chamberlain wouldn't listen. Now they are spread too thinly, dealing with different conflicts, and have suffered great losses they could ill afford. But Churchill will come up with something.'

'He already has in leaving us unprotected. Now he does nothing to help us . . . Oh, I don't know. I suppose someone had to be the sacrificial lamb. Us being invaded may just satisfy Hitler for a while and give Churchill time to regroup. I certainly hope it accomplishes something! Anyway, as much as I loathe to do it, I will obey Hendrick. I know he loves us and is working for the good of us and all British people. If he is willing to put himself in such danger, then we can do our bit.'

'Thanks, Daddy. I'm to go along to the Royal Hotel to register the car for its permit which will allow us to use it and to get fuel for it, then I'm going to instruct Daphne to pack for us. Can you make a list of everything you want to take with you?'

'We'll need a cart. I'll telephone Jack Daunter and get him to bring his horse and cart over tomorrow. We'll need to have him do several trips as I'm not leaving my cellar full for them, and there's a few of your mother's things I need to take.'

'Oh, Daddy, I wish we hadn't to do this. I wish we could be in the same boat as our fellow islanders, but more than anything, I wish we'd made it to the mainland. It's as if I've been sliced in two.'

Her father stroked her hair. 'Stay strong for me, my dear. I will need your strength. I just can't think straight or sort out what I must do. I'm worried about the bank. And our clients who are from all over the world. The investments that we have made on their behalf.'

'Don't, Daddy, as there is nothing you can do. They each have their own portfolios and can move their accounts.'

'I know. And that will bankrupt us . . . Oh, my dear. I don't know what will happen to our staff!'

This shocked Olivia. She hadn't thought this far. But the truth of her father's words hit her. They stood to lose the bank, their main source of income besides investments and savings. But would they be able to draw on those?

'We'll still have my allowance from Hendrick. That's paid into my general account held by the Midland Bank.'

'But they can't access funds from their central bank!'

She told him what she'd read about concessions being made for the Midland Bank, and then tried to comfort him

184

by saying, 'We don't know yet if we can trade or not, Daddy. The Germans have said banks and shops must continue to do so.'

'Yes, but we don't trade on the high street, we are an investment bank.'

'I can only suggest we wait and see, or maybe you could ring the manager of the Midland Bank and chat it through with him?'

'Yes, that's a good idea. I'll ring Jack first. Then we'll know if we have transport for our things, and then I'll have a chat with Jeremy at the Midland. I'm letting my fears run ahead of my logic. I'm sorry, darling, you must have umpteen things to do. You go and get on.'

'If you're sure you have a clear plan now?'

'I am.'

Back in her own living room, Olivia rang for Daphne to come to see her.

As soon as she walked into the room, Daphne showed her concern.

'Are you all right, Olivia? You don't look too good to me . . . Mind, with all that's going on it ain't a wonder. We've been warned, no more international telephone calls. The lines are being disconnected as we speak. Only local lines are being left open, but all calls will be listened into. It's a flipping cheek! Well, here's one who won't cower down to them.'

'Sit down, Daphne, I have something to talk to you about.'

When Daphne sat, her expression showed she'd become very nervous. She suddenly blurted out, 'You know?'

This shocked Olivia. She couldn't think what it was she was meant to know, but decided she needed to find out as

Daphne's nerves had suddenly turned to fear. Telling a small fib, she said, 'A bit. But not all.'

'We had to do it. We couldn't see him taken prisoner, or maybe . . . shot!'

Still being very careful but feeling her own fear deepen, Olivia asked, 'Can you tell me from the beginning how it came about?' She hoped this would mean she would be enlightened as to what was on Daphne's mind.

'Henry didn't make it to a boat . . . we had to shelter him . . . I'm sorry, Miss Olivia, but we had nowhere else.'

Henry, Olivia knew, was Cook's son. *My God, I forgot about him. He was one of the soldiers on leave when the invasion happened! They were all meant to report to the police and then to the Royal Hotel this morning!*

Keeping herself calm, Olivia took a deep breath. 'He's in the house?'

'Yes, the cellar . . . Oh, Miss Olivia, what shall we do?'

Daphne reverting to calling her 'miss' showed her distress.

Olivia frantically thought about the situation she was in. This could go very badly wrong for her if Henry was discovered in her home just when Hendrick had identified her as his wife to the German occupying force. It could even have repercussions for him!

'We have to get him away from here.'

'But how? And surely we could keep him safe here?'

'We can't, Daphne. I sent for you as I had something to tell you . . . My father and I . . . Look, there are things I cannot explain, but I have come to look on you as a friend and I hope you will trust me and the decisions I make. But my father and I are going to have to live at the farmhouse.' As she gave the next bit of news as to the use of the house from now on, and for as long as it might be needed, Daphne gasped. 'No . . . No, you wouldn't do that to us. Not the Germans!'

'Please, Daphne, I know how bad it sounds, but believe me when I tell you that I have to do this. I can't tell you why, but there is a very good reason . . . And, well, I wondered if you would come and work at the farmhouse for us?'

'But it's a way out of town!'

'I know, but I have permission to use my car. I'm to be given special privileges as the wife of a high-ranking German civil servant.'

A horrified look crossed Daphne's face, which evoked shame in Olivia, but then defiance. She had to stay focused on her mission. Hendrick had no other means of getting information out of Germany. If he resorted to telephoning Annie, he would come under suspicion for contacting someone in Britain. It would have been different if she was there – his wife. *Oh, if only I was.* For the first time, she had a feeling of being cross with her father. Why hadn't he just left her in England and found someone here who could sort the problem he'd had at the bank?

Suddenly, the enormity of her position washed over her. She bent her head. An unshed tear ran down her face, followed by more she couldn't control.

'Oh, Olivia, I didn't mean to look at you like that. I'll do it. I don't know why you're taking the actions you are, but I know you must have a good reason and that it won't be a selfish one.'

'It isn't, Daphne.'

Olivia so wanted to confide in Daphne, but she dared not put her in the position of maybe unintentionally slipping up and exposing the 'Guernsey Girls' operation. It would only be for her own comfort, to ease the loneliness her mission had brought her. She must stay strong.

'What about Cook? She lives in, we can't leave her in a houseful of Germans.'

Olivia had wrestled with this idea, but could she keep her transmitter secret with two staff in the farmhouse? Frantically, she thought through the logistics of it. There were plenty of bedrooms – five in all, and the attic space that had its own stairs leading to it, which Hendrick had said would be their office. That was it! The attic was where she would keep her transmitter. It was up there anyway with stuff they'd stored. She could do as Hendrick had planned and turn it into her office. A place where no one was allowed to go but her and her father. That would work. And she would turn the schoolroom into a flat for Cook and Daphne. There was already a kitchen they could use that was accessed through the schoolroom.

'Olivia?'

'Sorry, I was working it all out. And, yes, we could offer Cook a position. But as for the rest of the staff who come in daily, we won't need them, and they can keep their jobs here. So far, the Germans have proved to be very polite and respectful, and I am sure it will be one of the officers who takes this house and who will be used to having staff and know how to treat them. If any don't want to continue, then my father will pay them a year's salary and we will have to let them go.' Inwardly she thought this would be another disastrous blow to their finances, but she knew Father always kept plenty of cash in a safe in his office and he, like her, wouldn't see his staff in the lurch.

'Well, under the circumstances I think that's fair. I would have taken it . . . But, well, as it happens, me mum's gone to Sark to be with our family there, so I would have joined her. She went as others went to the mainland. She wanted me to go as she said she'd rather be with family and face anything we have to with them . . . Well, now we know what we're facing, I think she was right.'

'Maybe you will be allowed to visit her. Our invaders will have to allow some coming and going, as we all need to share our food supplies. We'll need potatoes from Jersey, for instance, and they'll need tomatoes from us, as I imagine all trading of supplies with the mainland will cease. But does this mean you will live in with us, too?'

'Yes. And be glad to. It could have been awkward coming and going – not just the transport, but, well, folk are already calling you bad things, Olivia, and that will get worse with these privileges you're going to have. I could find myself in a few skirmishes!'

'I know. I'm sorry. Being at the brunt of this hurts me badly, but . . . well, just believe me when I say I have no choice . . . Now, we must decide what we can do about Henry. We have to get him away from here . . . Look, I think the best thing is once I have registered my car, we hide him in it, and I take him out to the farm. He'll be safe there while we think what we can do . . . Oh, and Father must not know. He is under a tremendous amount of stress, and I am worried about him. We will tell him once Henry is safely hidden at the farm, as then it is accomplished and won't be as bad.'

'Ta ever so much, Olivia. I knew you'd do something. I didn't think for one moment that telling you was the wrong thing to do.'

'Daphne, keep that faith in me alive, no matter what I have to do in the future. Remember, I won't want to do it, but that I am compelled to for reasons I cannot tell you.'

189

'I will. We're friends, and friends don't betray each other.'

'Oh, Daphne, that means so much to me . . . May I have a hug?'

Hugging Daphne spilled the tears once more. Daphne patting her back soothed her a little, but she wondered if anything could ever really soothe her, as she felt so alone. She was cut off from her Hendrick and Karl, who were her soul, and from her dear friend Annie. How was she to bear not even being able to hear Annie's or Karl's voice? Somehow, she knew she had to.

# Chapter Fifteen

## Janey

When Janey woke, it was as if a thick fog encased her mind. She looked around her. The walls of the room she was in were exposed brick, painted cream, and they weren't very far apart. Her eyes went to the door. It had a grid inserted in it – a prison cell!

She tried to move but couldn't. Neither could she use her arms as they were wrapped across her body and held there by something tightly strapped around her. She tried to scream, but something held her mouth clamped shut. Whatever it was held her head too.

Panic gripped her as the memory of where she was flooded into her.

Pain seared that memory as the cruelty of blows and kicks to her body came back to her, as did an awareness of how bruised and injured she was.

In her panic, breathing through her stuffed-up nose became difficult. She writhed from side to side and growled through her sore throat.

The door clanged open. 'You're awake, are yer? Well, yer can't get up to your antics now, can yer? Spitting and biting like an animal. That straitjacket and helmet have stopped you in your tracks, girl! And they ain't coming off!'

*Straitjacket! They use those in loony bins, don't they! No! No, I'm not in a loony bin, am I? Annie wouldn't let that happen to me!*

A voice she loved came to her. 'I demand to see me sister, now!'

'Don't come 'ere in yer fancy copper's uniform and think yer can lord it over us. Yer can't. Yer sister's a madwoman. If we release her, she'll attack us.'

'That's because she's afraid and distraught, not mad! She lost her baby, for Christ's sake, and in circumstances you can't begin to imagine. She needs loving care, not this!'

'Well, the powers that be think differently. They sectioned her, and now it's our job to contain her. If we don't, she'll hurt someone, not least herself!'

'If you cause her harm, there will be more trouble for you than you can imagine. Now, let me see her at once!'

Janey lay still, praying that they would let Annie in.

'Very well. But I have to warn you, she ain't a pretty sight, nor smell. She stinks because she won't let us near her to clean her up and the dirty mare has shit herself!'

'My God! Just let me in, mate. It's me sister you're talking about. I need to see her. She's been through so much.'

The other voice softened. 'Well, all right, and if you can do something to help her, we'd be grateful. We ain't hard-hearted, we just have a difficult job to do with these folk who are mad. There's no being kind to them, they just want to lash out at us.'

'I'll do all I can. Will you come with me so you can make a judgement after I've calmed her?'

'Yes. And if she's compliant and stays so, we'll get her out of that contraption. We don't like them, but like I say, they protect us.'

When Janey opened her eyes again, Annie was there. 'Janey, me little darlin'. Oh, Janey . . .' Annie broke down. All Janey could do was growl in her throat.

'Watch her! She makes that noise before she strikes. Watch her feet!'

Janey shook her head.

Annie touched her cheek.

'Of course she makes that noise, you have her mouth clamped, what else can she do? Take it off and let her speak . . . Please, please take it off.'

Annie sounded distraught now.

'All right, but just the mouth brace for now. Let me see what yer can do with her.'

With her mouth released, Janey could only manage to say, 'Oh, Annie, help me.'

'I will, me darling, but you're not to lash out at anyone. Why are you doing that, Janey? And you have to let me bath you. Oh, Janey you're in such a disgusting mess.'

'Annie . . . I didn't know what was happening. I were terrified. You weren't there and they brought me here. Oh, Annie . . . Annie, me little Angie's d – dead.'

'I know, me darlin'. I asked them to let me be the one to tell you – to convince you – as you did know but you couldn't take it in. But they wouldn't let me near you till now and they tell me that when you did accept Angie had gone you went mad. I'm not surprised, me darling, I've been going mad over it all. But with your history, well, they judged you needed sectioning, when it's that bastard Jimmy who needs that.'

'What's happened to Jimmy?'

'We haven't found him yet. There's a police hunt for him and a warrant for his arrest for murdering Angie and causing harm to you and to Beth.'

'Me little Beth . . . Oh, Annie, I want to be with her.'

'I know, and she asks for you all the time. You have to work at getting back to us, Janey. Whatever happens, you must keep calm and, above all, rational. Now, we're going to clean you up, me luv.'

'Are you taking me out of here, Annie?'

'I can't, luv, I don't have the authority to. But you have the means of working your way out. You can behave yourself. No more violence, cooperate with all they want you to do, eh? And I'll work hard towards your release too. But it will mean assessments by psychiatrists when you must prove that you're sane. It'll take time but it's the only way, luv. Will you do it? Will you do it for Beth, me and mum, and Cissy and Rose and Lilly? Everyone wants you home with us.'

'I will, Annie. Just help me and I will.'

'I'll try to get a pass to see you every day, but it took me a while to get this concession to come today as they had judged you too violent. That ain't the way to do things, Janey.'

'I'm sorry. I don't know what came over me – grief, fear, missing you all. I just wanted to fight me way out. Will you tell them all that I'm sorry?'

'We can hear yer, Janey. And on the basis of it, I'm going to order a bath run for yer, and take yer jacket off, but mark me words, the minute yer upset the apple cart it'll go on again. But if you really are compliant and show us yer ain't mad, I'll put in good reports about yer and recommend yer release to a convalescent home. Yer little girl can visit yer then, as yer story's cut me in two.'

Janey couldn't believe this woman was the same one who'd bullied her and taunted her. Something told her not to trust her, but no matter what she did in future, she made her mind up not to react in any way except to smile.

Janey stood and held on to the edge of the sink. Humiliation clothed her as Annie helped one of the wardens to wipe her down with paper and then wash her bottom clean.

With this done, they helped her into a hot bath.

There was a moment of bliss as she closed her eyes and, despite the stinging of her many wounds, allowed herself to relax. Once she did, she thought she was halfway to heaven. To truly feel she was in heaven, she would need to be holding her Beth. The thought came that she would never hold Angie again and that brought a sob to her throat.

'Try not to get upset, me darling. How's it feeling to be in the bath, luv?'

'Oh, Annie, it's lovely . . . I'm sorry I was in such a mess. I – I couldn't even ask to go to the lav, and in the end, it just all came from me.'

They were on their own now and Annie said, 'You look so thin, and your mouth's all cracked. How have they fed you, luv, and given you a drink?'

Fearing someone might be listening, she didn't say that she'd not been fed every day, or even had a drink on some days, so she just said, 'It's me own fault. I refused everything, though I did drink a little water each day. I – I've not been good, Annie. If they tried to feed me, I bit them.' She didn't say it was in retaliation for them pinching her and laughing at her, as well as pouring freezing cold water over her.

'Oh, Janey. Please don't behave like that again. I know you can stop it. I know you're not ill, just caught in a trap.'

'That's just it, Annie. I was trussed up like an animal. I was scared and it made me react.'

'I know. Oh, me Janey, I can't believe what's happened to us and to Olivia.'

Annie washed her gently. It seemed to Janey that Annie never stopped crying. She wanted to cry like that, to feel the release. She didn't get that from screaming.

'Where is me Angie now?'

'We had to have a funeral for her, me darlin'. We had no choice. We tried to get you released for it, but they wouldn't hear of it. But when you're better, we're going to have a service for her that you can attend.'

'Oh, Annie, I can't bear it.' The animal-like sound that came from her seemed to trigger the door being flung open.

'Stand back, Mrs Stanley!'

Annie stood and placed herself between the bath and the wardens.

'No! Don't! I've just told her that her baby has been buried without her being there, and she reacted like any of us would. You stand back!'

Annie put her hand on her truncheon.

The head warden held up her hands. 'All right. All right. We were only trying to protect yer. It sounded like she was about to kick off.'

'Please leave us. Janey needs this time with me.'

The head warden hmphed as they left.

Annie lowered her voice the moment they were gone. 'I don't like this set-up. They weren't ready to protect you, which is what they should do. I'm going to get you out of here, luv. Let's dry you and dress you. I'm going to need you to hurry as much as you can and obey everything I say.

I've got Ricky's car outside; I fetched it from Lilly's and have been using it. Just follow all I say to the letter.'

Janey knew she was staring at Annie. Her heart thumped in her breast. Could Annie really get her away?

As Annie dressed her, she chatted away about Beth and how every week they'd gone to Angie's grave and taken flowers and how Beth talked to her baby sister in her own little way. Janey knew she was covering what she was doing and just went along with it all.

She'd quietly got her out of the bath and dried her, while saying, 'I'll wash your feet now, luv. Ha, that'll make you giggle – you have the most ticklish feet I've ever known.'

Janey caught on. 'No, Annie, luv, they'll be all right now they've had a soak.'

By this time, she was dressed.

Annie spoke more about Beth and Mum while she got her notebook out. On a blank page, she wrote, *Giggle and tell me to stop.*

Janey started to giggle the moment Annie began to write. 'No, stop it, Annie. Ooh, no, they're clean enough.' She bent down and splashed the water. Annie laughed too as she scribbled ten to the dozen.

Janey read as Annie wrote: *They're scared of me. I'm going to open the door with me truncheon in me hand and threaten to arrest them for grievous bodily harm. You're going to dash to the end of the corridor as fast as you can. Do a left, and go through a door, then you will see the outside door. Ricky's car is there. It is open, get inside, lock the doors and wait. Open them as soon as you see me coming.*

Janey dashed through the door as soon as Annie was through it. Fear gave her wings as she ran as if she was running for her life down the musty-smelling passageway. Her heartbeat drummed in her ears as the walls seemed to close in on her as if they would stop her. But as she rounded the corner that would lead her to the door to safety, she glanced back. Relief flooded her as she saw that Annie had her truncheon and handcuffs in her hands and was issuing a warning to the wardens.

'You don't have to say anything, but anything you do say will be taken down and used in evidence against you.'

The shocked and terrified faces would live with Janey for ever as a testament to Annie, her beautiful, brave sister.

The outside world felt a strange place. Beyond the small, tarmacked area where Annie had parked Ricky's car, there was a busy road, with cars, vans and horse-driven vehicles. Everyone seemed to have somewhere to go and drove by not even noticing this building of hell or giving it a second glance.

Janey wanted to scream out to them what was happening behind the innocent-looking walls, but she remembered she was to keep calm and get into Ricky's car.

Once in, she clicked the locks into place. The passenger seat offered no comfort as she leaned back and breathed in the scent of the leather. A normal smell for a car, and yet one that spoke of freedom to her and added to her list of things that would stay in her memory.

Sitting with her fists clenched and her body tense, a shudder went through her, reminding her that her own behaviour had got her here. That she must work on being able to cope in a different way. Could she get help with that? She had to, as never again did she want to feel that feeling of helplessness. And never did she ever want to think of inflicting harm to herself. Her body and mind had suffered enough.

As she waited, she reflected on how Annie coped. Maybe it was because she'd done something with her life. Gained a responsibility. She was one who took charge, and didn't cower under pressure. Once she knew what she wanted, she went all out for it, and didn't let anything get in her way. Look how she and Ricky didn't marry for a long time as married women couldn't carry on their career in the police force.

*I should be like that, instead of giving up at the first hurdle. I should have carried on with the Red Cross training and not taken notice that the others were from wealthy families and better educated. They hadn't seemed to mind me, but had tried to be friendly. I used them as an excuse to give up!*

Janey sat up straight, her eyes staring ahead as she saw clearly – not what was through the window but her own weaknesses. Her nails dug into the palms of her hands as a newfound determination clenched them into fists.

She would face them and she would conquer them.

# Chapter Sixteen

## Annie

As she confronted the women, Annie's body trembled. Sweat ran down her back, but she stood firm, motivated by knowing that the bruising Janey had suffered as a result of Jimmy's attack had faded to a yellow colour when she'd last seen her. Now her bruises were fresh and angry again and consistent with her having been kicked.

On top of this, Annie couldn't get the other poor souls who must be languishing in padded cells out of her mind. Their muted cries were those of women terrorized and hurt.

'We ain't done nothing but our job. Yer ain't got a case against us. The inmates hurt themselves, don't they, Rene?'

'Yes, they do. They punch themselves, and scratch and bite themselves. We try to stop them.'

Then the head warden: 'You ain't got no right to take your sister out of here without the court saying so.'

'I have as I suspect she is being harmed. As the boss of this place, you are culpable. I am taking me sister to the police station to get a full statement.' Thinking quickly about tales she'd heard in her job, Annie assumed they had happened to Janey and brought them into her accusation as if they were a truth. 'She's already told me about the cold-water treatment and the beatings. That isn't how you treat sick people.'

'They ain't sick, they're mad.'

Annie put her truncheon under her arm and got her notebook out. In it she wrote the statement the warden had just made.

'That will be used if I'm called on to give evidence of what promoted me actions. You're in charge of the welfare of these people confined in here and yet you call them mad and don't recognize their minds are sick.'

'Well, I mean . . . 'course they're sick, but you don't know what it's like.'

Annie knew. She'd seen enough of it. Men who'd fought in the last war, damaged like Jimmy was. In her job they were always dealing with them.

'I know you've a hard job to do here, but you can approach it with kindness. From what I've seen of me sister's injuries, she's been bullied. I can't take you in now as I am taking me sister out of here under section 136, which gives me the power to remove a person to safety if I deem them unsafe where they are. I will file a report and it will be up to me sergeant if further action is taken.'

Annie turned on her heel. As she marched to the end of the corridor, she wanted to be sick, but she swallowed the bile that threatened to undo her and kept going.

Once outside, she dashed to the car. 'Right, let's go, but I daren't take you home, luv. So, I'll take you to Olivia's apartment. You'll be safe there and I've got a key in me bag to get us in.'

'Will you stay with me, Annie?'

'I'm not sure. I'm on duty at five and I've to see someone before that.' Janey didn't ask who. Annie was glad of this as she couldn't have told her the truth. It would seem that she was giving seeing a friend more importance than being with Janey.

Already she was late to meet up with Lucy and to get to work on time too.

'I'll ring the station and report what I've done and then I'll have to leave you. No one will find you, luv. In any case, I don't think them two will do anything, they're scared to death. I'll come back later and get you something to eat.'

'Why there, Annie, why not home?'

'Because I'm not sure until I speak to me sarge if I've done right. But I ain't letting them take you, luv. If I ain't done right, I'll have consequences to face, but whatever happens, I'll get you to safety where no one can find you while I fight your case.'

'Oh, Annie, I don't want you in trouble, luv.'

'Better that than you spend another night in that place.'

Annie stopped at a shop on the way and bought a few essentials for Janey.

'There you go. At least you'll be able to make yourself a cup of tea and if you get hungry, a sandwich, as I don't think I'll be back before eight. And Janey, if I don't come back at all, it's because it ain't safe to do so. I'll phone you, so don't worry. Just look after yourself and be very brave until I can sort everything out.'

When she met up with Lucy, Annie had taken her police jacket and tie off and left them in the car, replacing them with a pale blue jacket from a suit Olivia had given her.

'Annie, are you all right?'

'Yes, luv. Give me a hug, will you?'

'Gladly, dear. Oh, Annie, you look full of troubles. Can you share them?'

'You might be mad at me.'

'I promise I won't.'

They'd met in a cafe not far from the station where they had met many times and yet had never had a friendly word from Marg, the owner, a middle-aged woman who looked as though she could fall out with herself. But this suited them as Gill from the canalside cafe was a little hard to handle sometimes, thinking she could join in all conversations. Mostly they managed to get through to her without hurting her that they wanted to be alone and loved to go there despite this trait she had.

Annie told Lucy what had happened.

'Oh, Annie, have you passed this by your sergeant?'

'Yes. He bawled at me, but said he'd get me out of it as he understood. But in any case, the place needs looking at . . . It's not just Janey being treated badly. Anyway, the sergeant told me that she needs to be examined and passed as fit. I'm scared, Lucy. These people don't like to think they are wrong. I'd like someone independent of it all, but I don't know how to find a doctor other than my own and he'd be biased, having dealt with her when she did have a breakdown.'

'I can sort that out. I know a few. I don't know if I told you, but my brother's a doctor and some of his friends have taken psychiatry as their main specialism. But I can't ask as a favour. This will have to be done on a proper footing. A consultation that is all above board.'

'I can pay . . . Ricky . . . Ricky left me some money.'

'It could be about three to five pounds.'

'As much as that! Not that it matters, I can cover that. Will you fix it up for me, Lucy?'

'I will.'

'And will his report stand up in court?'

'I should say so. I'm thinking of a man at the top of his field.'

'You're a whiz. Ta, luv.'

'Now, to get to the question of communication. Olivia's suggestion sounds good, but we can't contact her now to set it up as they cut all means of communication weeks ago!'

'Oh no! So we've lost the means of even letting her know how Karl is. No wonder I haven't heard from her . . . Oh, Lucy. I can't take that in. Poor Olivia. And how awful that there'll be no more help from Hendrick for our country.'

'I know. HQ are very upset by it. The only thing they have suggested is that someone there keeps trying to contact her on a transmitter. They think hers must be one of the first ones that some rich kids were given for presents. And as it was Hendrick's father's, probably a German model. But that won't matter, they still might make contact by working out the frequency she will need to use.'

'Oh, I hope so, but it will all take time . . . I miss our chats so much.'

'I know . . . I'm here for you, Annie. We can meet up socially if you like? I would love that.'

'Oh, so would I, but would "they" accept that?'

'Yes, the more we look like normal friends, the better.'

'Let me get Janey sorted, then we will. I want to get her, Beth and Karl and his nanny to the country. I don't know where yet, but I'll find somewhere.'

They hugged again and parted. Annie made her way to the station. Her whole demeanour told of how the world weighed on her shoulders.

\* \* \*

'Well, I wondered when you'd show up, girl. Cutting it near to the wire, ain't you?'

'Sorry, Sarge, it's been a busy day.'

'You can say that again. Come into me office.'

Annie's shoulders drooped even more. She didn't think she could take a roasting off Sarge.

'Right, Annie. I've been giving it all some thought and I've concluded that you have right on your side. You removed a person who you thought to be in danger, using the correct act, and you left the perpetrators with a warning. Nothing wrong so far. But more must be done. I've got Betty to stand in for you on the switchboard as it will be impossible for your usual arrangement to be in place.'

Annie knew he referred to Olivia not being able to ring. The sarge was party to the arrangement and had been from the beginning, though he never interfered with it, just allowed her the time to do it by assigning her to the switchboard in the evenings.

'So, you and I are going along to the asylum to carry on your investigation. I think now's a good time as they wouldn't expect you back so soon and, in any case, may think it was a bluff to get Janey away. If they do think that, we don't want to give them time to hatch a plan to cover themselves.'

'Ta, Sarge, I really do think the place wants looking into. Me sister was lying in her own excrement when I eventually got in. She's badly bruised again as if she's been kicked, though I ain't formally interviewed her.'

'That needs doing too, Annie, as does a medical examination of her wounds. And of her mental state.'

'I'm arranging a mental health examination with someone who knows nothing about her, but a man at the top of his field. As for her injuries, shall I bring her here to see the station duty doctor?'

The sergeant raised his eyebrows. 'Well, that all sounds good as it will have to be a formal court hearing that releases her from the section. And yes, bring her tomorrow at ten. The doc is here for another case then. Now, what about you, Annie? How are you coping with Ricky being on the missing in action list?'

Annie closed her eyes against the pain this question caused her. 'I – I just keep functioning. There's been so much to see to. Little Angie's funeral. Settling Karl and his nanny in. Me mum's care, comforting Lilly, Ricky's mum, and phone calls from Rose, Jimmy's mum . . . Though . . . well, Sarge, I know Rose and there's something not quite ringing true in her constant calls to see if we've caught Jimmy. I don't like to say it as she's family . . . well, you know . . . but I think she knows where Jimmy is.'

'The Kent police think the same, but they ain't managed to pick up a clue to his exact whereabouts. Nor can they break Rose and get her to confess. Look, let's get the question of Janey settled first.'

When they arrived at the asylum, the same head warden was on duty, as was Rene, her sidekick.

They learned that the warden was called Joan Banks. The sergeant immediately put her under caution and demanded to see the rest of the patients.

What met them was pitiful.

'It ain't nothing we can help. You should try working here sometimes. We need armed guards, and the straitjackets are what keep us and them safe. They can't harm themselves if they can't move.'

It was all too much for Annie. 'I need to go outside for a bit, Sarge.'

'Righto, I'll come with you.'

Outside, the sergeant had tears in his eyes. 'I've never witnessed anything like that, Annie, and is that how you found your Janey?'

'Yes. It cut me in two.'

'We'll make a full report and submit it to the governing body of this place, but that's all we can do. I ain't sure I can even prosecute, but I'll give out warnings about the cleanliness of the inmates. The problem we have is their insistence that the patients harm themselves.'

Annie knew he was right.

'I'll go back in and have a word about our conclusions; you get in the car. And Annie, if I was you, I'd concentrate on getting Janey a report that says she isn't warranting this kind of detention and get her away to the countryside as soon as you can. We've yet to nail Jimmy, and while she's still around here, we've to be careful he doesn't come after her. She's a key witness against him.'

This was a fear that Anne hadn't considered. Now she did, she felt an increased urgency to get Janey to safety.

Making a quick visit home to check on her mum and Cissy, Annie was faced with another shock.

'Eeh, lass, I'm glad I've caught you. Trouble is well and truly at our door and I ain't sure as there's owt we can do about it.'

'What is it, Cissy? What's happened?'

'A solicitor came around to see us today . . . Eeh, Annie, we've all got to get out of our flats. Jimmy's put the house up for sale and wants to offer vacant possession.'

'What? The bleedin' bastard! And sneaky! We can't nail his whereabouts and yet he has the cheek to contact a local solicitor. Sorry about the swearing, but it made me feel better, Cissy. Did this solicitor say how long we've got?'

'A month . . . Eeh, Annie, love, what are we going to do?'

Annie put her arm around the quivering Cissy. Suddenly, she seemed to have aged, and Annie felt the guilt of this. Until she'd met all of them, she'd had a quiet, if lonely, life as live-in housekeeper at Olivia's father's apartment. Now she was mixed up in many troubles, not least the murder of a tiny, beautiful baby who they'd all adored.

'I'll sort it, Cissy. We could all go to the apartment up west. Janey's there at the moment.'

'But I thought the government had requisitioned that, lass. And you say Janey's there? How? I mean, have you got her out of that asylum? Eeh, lass, are we in for more trouble?'

Annie hated having to perpetuate the lie they'd had to tell Cissy about her former home being requisitioned by the government for purposes of war. The real reason, which she couldn't reveal, had been to minimize the possibility of anyone in the world of espionage making a connection between herself and Olivia. With moving out of the apartment there was no evidence that they were anything other than a mistress and her former maid. Now, with Guernsey cut off from them, she couldn't see that it mattered. Though she would have to speak to Lucy.

'No. We're not in trouble, luv, though we've to sort out getting Janey classed as legally sane . . . And the apartment is free once more and not needed by the government. The only problem we have is whether Olivia's father will be able to continue maintaining the building, and paying Fred's wages, and whatever other costs he has in owning such a place.'

'Well, I ain't sure, but working closely as I did with the family, I knaw the rents of the other apartments were paid into an English bank.'

'Well, that might mean that the costs come from that too. I hope so as you rely on your retention money. But anyway, luv, even if it's a temporary solution to move into the apartment, we'll take it, so stop worrying. Everything can be sorted.'

'Eeh, Annie, lass, how you're standing up to all of this, I don't knaw . . . It's all so sad.'

Cissy sobbed. Annie held her closer. 'I shed many tears, Cissy, luv. But that ain't a bad thing as tears give us a release. Janey hasn't hardly cried, only her heart bleeds, and that ain't good. I ain't brave, just coping on a day-to-day basis. Keeping me hope alive for Ricky, and looking after you all as best I can.'

'Eeh, Annie, I love you, lass.'

'I know you do and that's part of what helps me. Now, let's go and see me mum, she must be worried sick.'

Holding her mum gently, Annie told her Janey was safe, without telling the details. 'She's going to see a doctor who can get her released from the sectioning order. It was her reaction to her grief that caused her not to think rationally. She isn't hurting herself, though she is hurt as she flailed out at the staff, and they were heavy-handed in restraining her. But I cleaned her up and she's comfortable. I'm going to her now, Mum, and might stay the night. Will you be all right, eh? You have Cissy, and I'll ask Loes to keep checking on you once she has Karl and Beth in bed.'

'I'm fine, me darlin'. More than I was as now I know you've got Janey. But can't you bring her home now the sergeant's involved? She'd be better here.'

'I don't think she will, Mum, too many memories, and I don't think Beth should see her how she is. Let's get her stronger, and us moved in with her. I think that would be the best solution to all our predicaments.'

'So, you really mean to move us up west, luv . . . It won't be for long, will it?'

'We ain't got many options, I'm afraid. But you know me plans for Janey and Loes and the children, so if you like, you and Cissy could go with them when the time comes.'

'I don't know, luv. I've lived around here all me life. I don't know as I'll settle in the country.'

Annie sighed. She understood but had so few options. Even her dream of getting Janey and Loes safe was a daunting prospect to achieve. She'd always thought it would be near to Rose in Kent, and she would have her help in sorting it, but now, with her suspicion that Rose was helping Jimmy, she wasn't so sure. She couldn't even blame Rose if she was doing what they suspected. Mums were like that, they'd protect their kids no matter what.

As if her mum had read her thoughts, she asked, 'Can't we go to Rose?'

Not wanting to touch on her theory, Annie just said, 'We'll see. But don't worry too much, we've got a month, so we can mull over our choices for a week. But then we need to get a move on. There's a lot of us to house – five of us and two children! But I will sort it, I promise.'

Back at the apartment Janey surprised her as she told her she'd found some bedding and had made up two of the beds that were left there. 'Why are the rooms all so empty, Annie? It weren't like this when we all came to stay with Olivia.'

Annie reminded her that she'd taken Loes and Karl to live

in the flat she'd made in the basement. 'I thought it would be easier for me to look out for them there as Loes has no income coming in.' She explained about how Guernsey was now cut off. 'Olivia would have been able to put arrangements in place for Loes and Karl, but she never knew she would have to, she was to come back here to live the day after it all happened . . . Anyway, something else has happened, but I'm starving. I'll pop out and get us something.'

'How about that pie and mash that you promised me . . . well, on the day it all happened?'

For Janey to mention this seemed like a massive step forward for her.

'Oh, yes, I did, didn't I? That's a great idea and easily sorted as even up here in the posh West End you can find pie and mash.'

When she was back and they sat eating their meal, Janey asked, 'You said there was something else?'

Annie's heart dropped. How would Janey take the news of what Jimmy had done? But she had to know.

Another surprise followed. An even bigger one than Annie ever expected to happen.

'He can't do that. I own that house and all of the flats in it.'

'What?'

'Jimmy put the deeds into my name. He said it would give me security if anything happened to him. He did it just before he left for France, when he came home on leave that time.'

'But, Janey, this is massive. You never said!'

'I wasn't meself and didn't take it all in. But I had letters from the solicitor about it and one saying it was finalized and the property now belonged to me.'

'Where is the letter, luv?' Annie had a sinking feeling that with Jimmy having taken the action he had, he'd made sure to destroy any evidence of what Janey had told her.

'It's in a drawer in the kitchen table back in our flat. I put all papers there and bills.'

'Janey, we have to think that maybe Jimmy's destroyed the letter, otherwise he wouldn't be able to take this action. Or that he's done something to mean he has all rights over the property again. If he has, can you remember the name of the solicitor that wrote to you?'

'Yes, because it made me giggle. Potter and Gardener!'

Annie laughed out loud. Janey joined her. This warmed her heart. 'Oh, Janey, they sound like landscapers rather than solicitors! Did you ever meet them?'

'No, but one telephoned me. He said that he had papers for me to sign and asked if it was all right to send them with Jimmy and have him deliver them back. He sounded so posh, and old. Then Jimmy said that him and his partner were old as their sons had signed up and they'd had to come out of retirement. He said they were very efficient, though.'

'That's good as they will have kept copies of the trans-action. Also, they won't have gone to war, so we have a good chance of speaking to them, not to someone who's taken over . . . I think we're saved, Janey, love, though why Jimmy thinks he can sell over your head, I don't know. I wonder if he's conned these solicitors in some way.'

Annie sighed. 'I know I should hate Jimmy. He's done something unforgiveable and shattered me heart but, as we promised we would, I still think of the Jimmy that went off to war, smiling and waving. The loving Jimmy, who was the best husband I could wish for . . . And that's the Jimmy I'm grieving for, Annie.'

'I know, luv. I can't imagine what it would be like if Ricky did make it home, only to be damaged in the same way and not be my Ricky again. It's right that you grieve the Jimmy you married and loved, me darlin', and if you feel like crying and wailing in the way I've done many a time, then you should.'

'That's the thing, though, Annie. You can, and then you bring it back under control. If I let meself go, I'm scared that I'll never stop and be taken away.'

'That won't happen, not here, not where there's just you and me, luv. I'll just hold you and cry with you.'

# Chapter Seventeen

## Olivia

Olivia stared out of the window of the attic of her farmhouse. She'd tried all morning to get some response using the frequency that she knew, but nothing. And yet she was sure that the person she and Hendrick had contacted all those years ago lived in London.

She sat back in her chair. Just to contact him, or one of his relatives, would help her situation. She'd have to trust him to deliver a message to the War Office, but then surely any citizen of London would do that? If only she could get an answer!

Even though her efforts had proved to be futile, she'd focused on trying – she had to. The uncertainty was driving her mad. The loneliness crowded her.

Hendrick had managed to telephone three times in the past three weeks. Always on a Tuesday as that was his half day. But taking his calls with German soldiers within earshot made them very stilted.

Hendrick had shown his frustration in code when he'd told her he had some vital information of plans that were being talked about and she'd had to report to him that she still hadn't been able to get through. She had a code all ready for that information as she had to repeat it so often to him.

She'd longed to have some intimacy in their conversation and so had tried talking to him in Italian telling him she loved him so much, but a soldier had eyed her suspiciously and made her feel afraid. When she told Hendrick this, he'd told her to put him on the phone. Afterwards the soldier had apologized to her.

'I told him that with them not allowing you privacy, darling, you'd resorted to telling me in Italian that you loved me, but please don't do that again. Don't do anything that may warrant them asking to have me looked into.'

Olivia had been mortified.

But the information he had given her played on her mind. She'd checked and double checked, but couldn't make his code say anything other than that there were plans to bomb London!

Frantic, she'd wracked her brains as to how she could get a message to Annie, even thinking of homing pigeons, and then laughing as she hadn't got any and didn't know anyone who had. She'd watched the few that flew around the farmhouse and wondered whether if she caught one, she could train it but had laughed this off too.

Suddenly, a shadow caught her eye. As she watched from behind her curtain, a curl of smoke became a cloud just above a bush in the garden that she had been meaning to have cut down.

'Henry!'

Her fists clenched. Her anger was such that she wanted to bang on the window. How dare he even venture out of the house during the day! He knew it was only safe for him to walk around the garden at night.

As she hurried downstairs, it came to her what Daphne had told her just a couple of days ago, and suddenly it seemed like the answer to her prayers.

It appeared that some boats were leaving the island in the dead of night from remote coves. They were charging massive fees, but they were getting people to the mainland.

Outside, she nipped behind the bush, making Henry jump. 'Bugger! Caught red-handed!'

'Not much of a soldier, are you, Henry? Your smoke gave you away. Come inside, I want to talk to you.'

Once inside, Henry looked suitably ashamed. A tall young man who she knew was a year younger than herself, he was of a quiet and gentle nature. Good-looking with chiselled features, his hazel eyes always seemed to be smiling. He liked to read and was working his way through the mountain of books she and Hendrick had collected for that day they could relax together – a day that never came.

'I'm sorry, Olivia, I didn't mean to cause you concern, but I'm going out of my mind. I need to find a way to get to the mainland. Then to rejoin my regiment, wherever they are. I *am* a soldier, Miss Olivia, through and through. I did a thorough recce of the garden and road without being seen. Mostly on my stomach. Then when the coast was clear I allowed myself the luxury of being in the peace and quiet and having a fag.'

'Let's forget it now. You scared me, that's all. You just never know when the Germans are going to patrol.'

'How does all this sit with you? I mean, being married to a serving officer of the enemy?'

Olivia knew she had to trust someone as she needed help. And if she could get Henry to the mainland, he could be the link to Annie, and then Annie to Lucy.

'Hendrick isn't the enemy . . . You say you are a soldier, how loyal are you? I mean, if you were told a secret that is vital to your country's defence and future strategies, would you keep it to your death?'

'Hey, that's a bit strong, isn't it? . . . My God, you're serious, aren't you?'

'I am. I need your help. I'll do everything I can to get you to the mainland – that takes a lot of money which you don't have, and I can pay for you – but I need your absolute commitment. As a soldier of the King.'

He stared at her. His lips moved, but whatever he was going to say, he changed his mind, clipped his heels and saluted her. 'You have my word that whatever this is, if it is something that will help our island to be free and our mother country be protected and further its cause in the war, I will be loyal to my death.'

'Thank you.' Olivia looked around. 'Walk with me to the end of the garden. There's a gate there. It leads to the field behind the house which is ours and will one day be where we build our house. We'll be out of sight of the road, and it will look to Daphne and Cook as if I am pointing out the design, while I tell you what this is all about.'

'I did wonder what those stones were. They did look like they mapped out a house . . . After you.'

When they were by the gate, Olivia looked longingly at the small rocks marking her future home. Her heart ached as it always did when she thought of what should have been but she brushed these thoughts away. 'Firstly, Hendrick isn't our enemy. He's actually spying for the British government. He is party to things as an interpreter that are vital to Britain. Secondly, I need your help. Hendrick passed me messages in code. I passed them on to my friend – you remember Annie?'

Henry nodded. He looked shocked and yet very interested and didn't interrupt her.

'Some of the information has already helped shape decisions and in a huge way. But we're stumped now as I have no communication with the mainland.'

'How can I help?'

Olivia told him about the transmitter.

'Oh, my God, Miss Olivia . . .'

'Olivia. We have left the old life behind us, Henry.'

'Yes. We have, but this is all astounding. Everyone hates Hendrick and yet he is putting himself in grave danger to try to help them. If only they knew!'

'They must never know – at least, not until victory for Britain and our liberation.'

'Of course. No. Never. But may I say, I owe you an apology, and a thanks. I did think badly of Hendrick, and though I have had to put all my trust in you to keep me safe, I have had bad thoughts about you too. You seemed like the enemy and yet I knew you weren't. I'll do anything, anything at all to help, and no one, not even if they held a gun to my head, will ever find a scrap of information out from me. I give you my solemn pledge on that.'

'Thank you. And I understand how you felt.'

'So, what exactly can I do?'

'I will help arrange for you to escape the island. Once you have, we can only pray that you make it to the mainland, but reports are good, especially for Joe, the harbour master's son, who is one of those helping people to leave – at a price! Anyway, so far he has been successful and returned triumphant. I only know this because Joe was originally funded by my father and is one of the few people on the island who trusts me and still shares island information with me.'

'But why haven't you gone yourself?'

'Believe me, I have so wanted to. My heart would have me leaping off the cliff into the boat, but now that Hendrick has made arrangements for me to have special privileges, I am on the radar so to speak and me escaping would throw suspicion onto him. He had the best intentions, not knowing there was an escape route and thinking it would be the only way he could contact me – even visit me in the future – but I am now trapped here in order to protect him. You see, they must know that they have a traitor in their midst – or if not, when they do come to realize, then me having escaped from under the rule of his countrymen will not look good for him.'

'Oh dear. From what I am hearing, you and Hendrick are the bravest people I know and yet you are being vilified. And unless we win this war, will be for ever . . . I'm so sorry. Looking at this layout, you had such dreams for your future . . . Rest assured I will do all I can. Even if I have to lay down my life, I'll get the message to Annie. But will you do something for me?'

'If I can.'

'Look after my mother . . . I know you do and have always treated her well. But despite this she is lonely in her soul since my father died, and now she faces losing me. I didn't want her to give up our house and be a live-in member of your staff as it left me having to rent a flat, but I have seen how it has been the best thing for her. She put all the money she had from the sale into an account in your father's bank, and in my name. She fears now that it may be lost as she sees how worried your father is.'

'Oh, Henry. Things aren't good because of lack of communication with our investors and investment projects abroad, not to mention an unsettled world affecting dividends. But I will look into your account and whatever it stands at, we will give you a cheque to take with you to put into a British bank . . . In the event . . . well, there is a risk, but if you don't make it and the cheque is never processed, then I will put the amount into the Midland Bank here. We understand they are to have special arrangements put into place to help them to continue to trade. They are financially secure being part of a large chain of banks and your money will be safe for your mother to live off for the rest of her life.'

'Thank you. I have made a will to that effect, explaining what I would like to happen to the money in the event Mum doesn't outlive me.'

'That's good. Now, before Daphne comes to ask if we're all right, or her suspicions are raised that we're up to something, we must talk about what I need you to do. I will give you a message in code. It is vital you memorize it and pass it to Annie. And, as well as this, I want you to tell her that Ricky is most likely on a very long march to Germany, which is what is happening with those taken prisoner at Dunkirk. When he arrives, he could be taken to Poland to work on a farm, or to a labour camp elsewhere, but tell her we love her and are praying for Ricky to be safe.'

'But that's shocking!'

'Don't. I can't bear to think of it. I just want Annie to know that there is hope, that thousands are alive and being taken prisoner. Will you put it like that to her?'

'I will. I liked Annie. We often chatted when she was working in the sweet shop. My mum likes her too, and that's always something to go by. But I didn't know she was married. Mum said that when she asked you, you told her Annie was in the police force.'

Olivia explained how everything happened. The more they talked, the more she liked Henry. Her mind was at rest, and she felt she could trust him. Not that she had any choice. He was her only chance to get information to Annie and with Hendrick's vital message. Not only that, but she needed to give information about her transmitter and frequency.

It was two days later when Olivia spoke to Joe. She'd gone along to the town on the pretence of doing some shopping and had seen him talking to his dad.

Taking a walk along the promenade path, she stood gazing at her old home, praying he would come over to her. When he did, he asked her if she was taking a trip down memory lane.

'I can't understand it. They say you gave your house to the Germans, and you've got special favours.'

'We did, and I do. I just need you to remember, Joe, how we've always got along and ask you not to judge me. And I need a favour from you.'

'I've never done that, Miss Olivia. I've always helped you.'

'I know . . . Look, my favour is a big one. I've got a soldier in hiding; I need you to help him to escape.'

'A soldier! A British soldier?'

She nodded, not prepared to tell him more yet. As it was, her body was trembling with fear as she hoped she could still trust Joe. But he was her only hope.

'You've been sheltering a soldier! God! If you're caught, you'll be shot!'

'I know. Keep your voice down and smile a bit as if you're having a joke with me, we don't want to attract attention. Anyway, what else can I do but shelter him – hand him in? No, we have to get him off the island, Joe. Please say you'll help.'

She put her head back and laughed. Joe took her cue and laughed with her, then carried on smiling as he said, 'The thing is, I ain't planning any more trips. It's getting too risky. The Germans are getting more organized by the day. They have more patrols, searchlights, the lot. They fired shots at a boat the other day and no one has seen the owner since, but the boat's bobbing up and down out there as a warning . . . I'm sorry, but I can't help . . . I've not enough petrol anyway.'

Making her mind up that the only way was to tell him who it was, Olivia said, 'It's Henry Coombs. And I can get petrol.'

'What? I thought he'd surrendered as I hadn't seen him . . . Well, that puts a different light on it. But, like I say, it's risky. I'll be putting me life on the line for him. Not that he ain't worth it.' Joe shuffled his feet. 'I should've signed up, but I was underage when they were all leaving. Mind, I went to Dunkirk to get a lot of the soldiers off and got them back home. I did three trips in all.'

'I know you did, you've nothing to feel guilty about . . . How much fuel will you need?'

'I've about half a tankful. That'll only take me halfway, though if it's a windy night, I can put the sail up and that'll take us in.'

'My car's full, we can cypher that off . . . Laugh, Joe, we're being watched. Actually, laugh and go, as remember the notice about groups talking together. Meet me in half an hour near to the garage. I'll get some cans of fuel, I'll make some excuse.'

Joe didn't hesitate. He waved in a friendly manner as he went in the direction of his father, who was also watching them intently.

As Olivia walked towards the now wrecked weighbridge, dear Ruby and the ball of flames that took her came into her mind. As if on cue, an aching pain started up in her leg. She stopped to rub it. As she did a pair of German boots came into her vision. She straightened and looked into the startling blue eyes of a German soldier. She greeted him in German.

His look changed. His eyes veiled as he frowned. His German was easy to interpret. He wanted to know her name, what she was up to with the young man and how she came to speak German.

Continuing in German, Olivia told him who she was and who her husband was. 'The boy is a friend of many years – since his birth. We always have a joke together.'

He clipped his heels and saluted.

Smiling a smile she didn't feel, Olivia nodded and walked on, trying not to limp. She hadn't gone far when spit sprayed her face before running down her cheek.

'German whore!'

Through eyes misted with tears, Olivia saw the young woman who'd made the error at the bank and been the cause of her having to return home.

Her expression held hate as she spat out, 'You don't have to sack me, I walked out!' before hurrying away.

Olivia sat down on the remains of a wall and wiped her face, wanting to heave at such a disgusting act.

The soldier seemed to come from nowhere to help her up, when she'd thought he'd marched away.

'Are you all right? That woman will be apprehended for insulting the wife of one of our civil servants. She will give you no more problems. We will make an example of her so that you can walk the streets with dignity.'

'No, please! Please don't do that. The people of the island are afraid. They need to lash out at someone. They will be fine once they get used to this new way of living. They've never had rules. Our way of life was very easy-going. They're missing their children too, as they were evacuated and they can't get news or speak to them now that you have cut communication. I understand their feelings when I can still talk to my husband, and he might even visit.'

'These things are unfortunate, but we are at war. We want the people here to carry on their normal lives. I will see that on this occasion the woman is reprimanded but nothing more. That may give more confidence in us.'

'Thank you . . . I'm sorry, I must go. I have to call into my father's bank and the garage.'

Once again, he saluted. Olivia hurried away as fast as her leg would let her go.

When she got to the bank she opened the door, taking the opportunity to look back to see if the soldier had gone. He had, so she gave the staff a quick wave and hurried on towards the garage.

Joe was waiting for her.

'We haven't much time. Did you see what happened?'

'I did. I'm sorry, Miss Olivia, but I fear you'll get a lot of that. Maybe staying out at your farm would be the best idea.'

'I think you're right. I had to fight to keep Bessie from being arrested. But the soldier promised me he would only reprimand her on this occasion . . . Joe, I've been thinking. Why don't you stay over on the mainland, eh? Henry will have Annie's address, she'll help you with a job, or if they will accept you, you could join up.'

'I've thought about it on other trips . . . You mean, Annie would give me a home till I could join up?'

'Yes, she'll sort you out. If you stay here, you just don't know what is planned for lads of your age. It's all very scary.'

'When you put it like that, it is . . . I'll do it! But I won't tell me dad, he'd stop me. I'll just leave him a note on the table. I go out to these jobs after he's asleep. He doesn't know about them.'

Olivia thought this unlikely as a lot of people did know and there wasn't much that passed by Bertie, Joe's dad, who'd been harbour master for many years.

'Just don't put in your note that it was my idea. I'm vilified enough as it is.'

'I know. That was terrible to see. I'm disgusted with Bessie . . . Not that I'm . . . well . . . to be honest, I ain't keen on having Hendrick on the other side, but it don't stop me liking him, and you said he works in an office and is not engaged in battle, so that makes it all right.'

'Thank you, Joe. You don't know what that means to me.'

Joe grinned. 'Right. Arrangements. I'll come into your bay at two a.m. Tell Henry to be on the beach with as much fuel as you can get. And to wear black clothing. I'll give owl-like hoots. On hearing them he's to wade into the water as soon as it's safe, and head to the rock to the left of him. I'll be behind the rock. We'll bide our time and at the right moment, we'll set off. I won't fire the engine up until we're well away and I daren't put the sails up, so tell him to be prepared to help me row the boat out to sea. Tell him to bring nothing with him. We want no weight at all other than ourselves and fuel.'

Olivia's nerves clenched. 'How safe is it, Joe?'

'It isn't. But I've done a few trips and on most of them, getting back here's been the worst bit. I'm not doing that, so don't worry. Oh, and me payment. Would you be able to pay me in British pounds? I want a tenner . . . I know it's a lot, but I've to set meself up when I get there with clothes and stuff while I go through the process of joining up.'

'It's not too much at all. Worth every penny. And British pounds is fine. Just be careful, I'd be mortified if you came to any harm.'

As Olivia waved and drove away, her heart was in her mouth. What she proposed could, if discovered, mean not only her being shot, but Henry and Joe too.

Sweat ran from her forehead down her nose and into her eyes. She blinked, but then tears joined the torrent and she had to pull up. Leaning her head on the steering wheel, she wept out her desperation, heaved at the thought of spittle running down her face, and screamed out her loneliness, beating the wheel with her fists.

When a calmness came to her, she felt stronger. She would do whatever it took to beat the bloody Germans. And the day they were beaten, she would cheer louder than anyone.

# Chapter Eighteen

## Olivia

Olivia saw every hour ticking away on her bedside clock. By one, she was up and dressed.

She found Henry in the garden with two cans in his hands. He whispered, 'You shouldn't have got up. I'm fine. I've taken two cans of fuel to the rock already.'

Olivia squinted through the darkness. 'You must be soaked!'

'No, I have waders on. Don't forget I was a fisherman, so I have the right gear. I'm enjoying it all in a strange, scary kind of way. My heart's going ten to the dozen, but that's good, it's keeping my adrenaline going.'

Olivia thought him so brave, and Joe more so, as he was just a youngster. But then, he'd love the adventure and have the mindset that nothing could harm him.

'Have you remembered all I told you, Henry?'

'It's engraved on my mind. And I will deliver it, even if I have to swim most of the way . . . Olivia, I'm very proud of you. You could so easily get into the boat with us and get back to your child and safety, but you've chosen to stay, despite the way those who were once your friends treat you.

And all so that you can continue to help the war effort. What you and Hendrick are doing is commendable. Although if he is found out, I cannot think what will happen, but one consequence is that you will be too, and—'

'Don't say it! I know, but don't want to hear it.'

'Oh, Olivia, I want to beg you to come, but you have your mission . . . I will always be thinking of you both and praying you get through this safely.'

Olivia felt the tears prickling her eyes. She could so easily run to the sea, hide behind the rock, and then jump into the boat with them. Her heart tugged at her to do so. Her little Karl's face swam before her, and her arms ached to hold him. But he was safe. She had to remember that. Hendrick wasn't. She couldn't put more danger onto him by betraying him. Nor could she let her fellow islanders down. Her work with Hendrick might one day save them all if they managed to solve the problem of contacting Annie. And she had every faith that her message sent with Henry would do that.

'Thank you. And I will be praying for you and Joe. Look out for him as much as you can. His youth makes him take risks for the thrill of it . . . I didn't tell you, but he isn't coming back. I encouraged him not to. I'm afraid what will happen to his age group – the young men anyway. I can't see this regime letting them just live their lives here. I think they may eventually be sent to Germany, to work in the labour camps.'

'However his life pans out, it isn't going to be easy for him. That's the pity of the bloody war!'

'I know that of course he will be in danger if he joins up, but better to be so fighting for your country than forced to help the country that caused all this.'

'Yes, you're right . . . I presume his dad doesn't know?'

Olivia shook her head.

'Anyway, good for Joe. I'll encourage him and point him in the right direction for joining up. But I doubt I'll be around long.'

Olivia told him how she was sure Annie would care for Joe and this seemed to put his mind at rest. 'Ha, she's going to wonder what's hit her with us both landing on her doorstep! But it'll be good to see her.'

'Don't forget to give her my love . . . Oh, God! What was that?'

The sound of tramping feet froze them both. They crouched down. Olivia's heartbeat increased wildly. As she seemed always to be doing lately, she clenched her fists and prayed they hadn't been heard, or, if Joe was out there, he hadn't been seen.

The sound receded.

When it was hardly discernible, Henry told her, 'They patrol every night. I lie awake listening for them, always fearful they may stop and hammer on the door. It's good that they have passed. We only have the searchlights to contend with now.'

'Good luck, Henry. I'll pray you make it.'

'We will, but, Olivia, if not, don't live your life feeling regret. Remember that you shielded me at great danger to yourself and possibly to Hendrick. That you provided me with the means of escape. There is nothing more you could have done for me, except to look after my mother. If the worst happens, it is on my head for disobeying the regime's orders and not surrendering. Joe's fate lies with me too. If I hadn't done what I did, you wouldn't have had to ask him to do what he is doing. So let it all go and no matter what, know you did your best for us.'

'Thank you, Henry. God speed.'

With that, he was gone. Olivia bowed her head and prayed for their safe passage.

Not able to rest, she went back to her room and grabbed a pillow. Imagining it was Hendrick and Karl, she hugged it as she stood in the darkened room and gazed through the window at the sea shimmering in the moonlight.

After an hour, stiff and cold, she presumed they had gone and were in safe waters, but then, suddenly, the night sky lit with a powerful light that turned blackened night into daylight.

Jumping back and peeping from a safe place next to the window where she couldn't be seen, Olivia scanned the sea. A black shape bobbing up and down could clearly be seen on the horizon, picked out by the strong beam of light scanning the water.

Gunfire awoke the household. Daphne came running and banged on Olivia's bedroom door. 'Olivia, what's happening?'

Olivia let her in. 'It's Henry and Joe, they're escaping. Go to Cook's room and stay there, both of you, even if the Germans knock on our door. Tell Cook that no matter how she feels, she must not show it or make a sound. If we are found to have harboured Henry, we'll all be shot!'

Daphne stared at her in horror, but turned and ran towards Cook's bedroom without protesting. With this, Olivia hurried to her father's room. He met her at the door. 'Oh, my dear, they've been rumbled.'

Into the other sounds came the roar of the boat engine. Olivia wanted to cheer. 'They'll make it, Daddy, they will. But we must be so careful . . .' A banging on the door interrupted her.

'I'll go, Olivia, you hurry and undress and get your house-coat on. Try to look as if you've just been woken up!'

Olivia gasped.

In no time she'd stripped, donned her nightdress, ruffled her hair, and then grabbing her housecoat, she ran downstairs. Two German officers stood in the kitchen. Father stood with them, looking confident, when she knew he was afraid. *Oh, why had she put them all in this danger?*

'Daddy, what's happening? I heard gunfire . . . Oh . . .' Her arms shot up. One soldier had swung around. Startled by her appearance, he aimed a gun at her. Olivia thought quickly. In German she demanded, 'What on earth are you doing? Do you know who I am? I am Frau Kraus! Wife of Hendrick Kraus, senior German civil servant, serving officer and interpreter to Herr Hitler himself!'

Under his breath the German uttered, 'Yes, and son of a known dissident!'

The colour drained from Olivia's face. Her body shook, but she lifted her head high and kept her voice steady as she told him, 'We are not our father's image. Hendrick has proved where his loyalty lies. He left his wife and son long before he had to. He volunteered his services and has served the Führer very well . . . I am sure if he was to tell the Führer what you have said and how you are treating his family, you would be severely taken to task. Please stop pointing your gun at me and leave my house at once!'

'I apologize. I should not have made the remark. We were trying to apprehend escapees. It is vital to the law and order we are trying to maintain, as well as to us building confidence in our rule, that we stop all such activity. Yours is the nearest house, and we wish to know if you have seen or heard anything.'

'No, we haven't. If we had, we would have reported it, but surely that was the engine of a boat we heard when you woke us? Have they not already escaped?'

'Yes, it is unfortunate, but they have. But all who do this need assistance to achieve it. We must stop them getting this help now!'

'The young men of this island have been brought up with the sea being their main source of living. They fish it for food and export, they work on unloading ships of supplies or loading our own produce for shipping, they swim in the sea, they play on the beaches from being born, they are all excellent sailors. They do not need help to escape. They know everything about boats and navigation. What your job should be is to create a fear-free environment whereby they can continue their way of life. That would be beneficial to yourselves and to the prosperity of Guernsey.'

Taking a breath, Olivia felt more like a politician than a scared to death, guilty woman. This must have come across as the German soldier clipped his heels.

'We will do our best, but always we must keep security uppermost in our minds. Goodnight, Frau Kraus.' He turned to her father and bowed, then beckoned to the second soldier to follow him and left.

Olivia bent with the weight of her fear. Her hands landed on the table, supporting her. Sweat ran down her body. She had to gasp for air.

Her father steadied her as he touched her shoulder. 'I don't know what you said but your demeanour so reminded me of your mother. While she resides in you, my dear, you will win all your battles.'

She couldn't answer him. It was all she could do to stop herself from sobbing her heart out, but she straightened her back. 'Let's go back to bed, Daddy.'

'Well, I was going to have a cup of tea first.'

She smiled. A cup of tea is just what Annie would have in this situation.

As she filled the kettle, Olivia heard footsteps on the stairs so topped it up to make enough for four. *Annie, my darling, you've made a cockney out of me, and I've passed that on, but oh, how I wish it was you I was making a cup of tea for. Will that ever happen again?*

'Darling, I'm worried about you, all this espionage and intrigue.'

'Shush, Daddy.'

Her father grimaced.

How easy it was to forget and let things slip when you lived as they were doing, so close to others, while trying to carry out secret activity.

The door opened. 'You aren't the only one feeling fatigue. I'm that tired, my bones hurt almost as badly as my heart, sir.'

Olivia sighed with relief at Cook mishearing her father. She opened her arms to Cook, something she'd never done, but she could see it was what Cook needed more than anything in the world.

As she held Cook to her, Olivia was reminded of holding dear Cissy – both had a lovely scent of baking clinging to them and both were soft and squidgy to cuddle – but she brushed the thought away before it undid her.

'Henry and Joe are going to be fine. They got away. Be pleased for them, Cook, and look forward to the day this war ends, and we can all be together again.'

Then as the thought occurred to her that Cook had never challenged her, or even made a sly remark over Hendrick, she gave her an extra squeeze. 'I'll always be here for you, Cook.'

'I know that, Olivia. I'll even let you call me by my name if you like, being as you let us drop the miss.'

'Oh dear, I don't know what that is . . . Well, I know you are called Mrs Combes, but not your Christian name.'

'Jean. It'll be nice to be called by it. I'll feel part of the family then.'

'You are, Jean. A very important part. Cook is a term of respect, but Jean is a term of love. We're all one big family in this. And together, we will get through.'

Jean surprised Olivia then as she looked up and said, 'I can sing, you know. I wanted to join the choir you started before but felt as a member of staff it wouldn't be fitting, but if you start it up again, you can count me in now that I'm family.'

For some reason, they all giggled.

'Well, my family, it's time we all went back to bed, and yes, Olivia, my dear, you can count me in too. So, you have no excuse now. There's four of us here, and I know Mrs Green and Leonard from the bank are keen. Once it begins, you may find more and more joining.'

'Well, we'll have to get permission. The German authorities have said no meetings of two or more are to take place unless authorized by them.'

'That should be easy for you to do, Olivia. They trust you.' Olivia stiffened for a moment as Jean said this. But then she added, 'You want to use having the Germans' fellow countryman for your husband as much as you can. Hendrick can be an asset to you. Nice young man. Always was and always will be. I don't think he'd have gone unless he was forced. Well, he's still the Hendrick I knew and liked, so you won't hear anything bad about him from me. But if he can get you favours, you take them and use them for the good of the islanders. They'll soon come around to realizing the way of things.'

'Thank you so much, Jean. That means a lot to me.'

'Well, you have proved yourself by shielding and saving me son. I was always in your corner, but now, no one will get me out of it!'

Father intervened. 'Right, bed! We may be a family, but I am the head of it and I demand you do as I say this time as I am about dead on my feet!'

They giggled like schoolgirls as they went towards the stairs, and then as they parted she, Jean and Daphne hugged and kissed goodnight.

To Olivia, it was as if they truly were a family and they filled part of her lonely heart with hope and love.

# Chapter Nineteen

## Annie

Two days after they had spoken about the deeds to their family home, Annie and Janey had an appointment with Mr Potter, the solicitor involved.

Annie had collected clothes for them both and taken them to the apartment – for Janey a red costume that was light enough for summer wear, teamed with a black blouse, and for Annie another of the costumes Olivia had given her – navy coloured, with a black velvet collar. This she paired with a pink blouse, not wanting to wear the white one that had come with it, thinking it too like her uniform.

But being dressed fashionably and smartly didn't help their nerves as they followed Mr Potter of Potter and Gardener's solicitors into his office – a dark room with only one small window and shelves filled with huge leather-bound books lining three of its walls.

Annie's first thought on entering was that it could do with a good clean as the sun found the small pane of glass to shine through and picked up a layer of dust on the top of the imposing mahogany desk.

Mr Potter sat down with a flourish on his rickety green leather chair, causing it to groan.

Wanting to brush the chairs he indicated they sat on – grubby beige leather ones – Annie's nosed crinkled at the musty smell of the room.

She wished she was anywhere but here. And yet she was desperate for Mr Potter, an old gentleman wearing half-moon glasses, to give them good news.

He did.

'Well now, the file pertaining to why you are making this visit is right here in front of me. It was on hand because we received a request from your husband, Mrs Blaine, to revert the deeds to his name. His reason for doing so was that he is home from war and has sustained injuries that will mean he won't be called on to fight again. Therefore, he can resume being the head of the household. He also produced evidence of you being sectioned as a madwoman. He was told that his case would have to be heard in court in this area, and we are in the throes of arranging that.'

'But it ain't true.'

'No, Mrs Blaine, I can see that. Though you do appear to be a nervous young woman, and you have no need to be. We solicitors can be intimidating in our tweed and sitting in musty old offices, but we are human, and I can smell a rat when I see one . . . I take it your husband is acting underhand?'

Annie felt proud of Janey as she answered confidently, 'Yes, he is. He is wanted by the police. He . . . he murdered our baby . . .'

'Good God! When? How? I mean . . . Oh, I am so dreadfully sorry, Mrs Blaine. If there is anything we can do for you, we will.'

'Ta, that's good of you . . . You see, Jimmy . . . Mr Blaine . . . is a changed man. It isn't his fault.'

Janey showed clarity Annie hadn't seen in weeks as she told what had happened to Jimmy, herself and the children and finished by saying, 'I'm not excusing what he has done, but me heart can forgive him as he ain't the Jimmy I married and that ain't his fault.'

'Well! That's quite a story. Now, I have two copies of the original deeds as I had them done ready for what Mr Blaine had asked us to do. I will hand one over to you, so you have your proof of ownership. Also, a signed statement by Mr Blaine that states you were in an asylum, which I now think is lies and should be ripped up.'

Before Janey could answer this, the policewoman in Annie came to the fore. 'Jimmy has been here, in person? Did he give an address? . . . Sorry, I am not only Janey's sister, but a serving police officer too. I'm not on the murder case, but my colleagues are searching for Mr Blaine. He has not been formally charged yet and there is a warrant out for his arrest. He's a very dangerous man.'

'In that case, I can help you. Mr Blaine hasn't been here. He went into our partners' office in Kent. They have set a further appointment with him to keep him up to date with how everything is proceeding at our end. But, Mrs Slater, before I give you further details, I would like to see your warrant card.'

As Annie handed over her warrant card, she wanted to jump for joy. She'd been afraid for Janey since the moment she'd brought her out of the asylum. If at last they caught Jimmy and brought him to justice, her sister would be safe!

After examining her warrant card, Mr Potter nodded. 'Very well, Officer. Mr Blaine's appointment is in two days' time, at two p.m. Just a moment . . .' He opened a drawer of his desk. 'Ah, something in this office is in the place it should be.' He handed over a card with the address of his Kent partnership.

'May I use your phone, sir? I need to inform me sarge so he can put things in motion.'

With this done, Annie glanced at Janey. She saw her tremble, heard her swallow, and then she clamped her lips tightly together. A tear trickled slowly down her cheek. This new development could hail the end of Jimmy, and though Janey had grieved for the Jimmy that he used to be, she would know that this would mean she had lost him for ever.

Annie took hold of Janey's cold hand. 'It's nearly over, luv.'

'Are you all right, Mrs Blaine? Can I get my secretary to get you a cup of tea?'

Janey nodded, and then surprised Annie by saying, 'But I do have to correct something you're thinking that ain't true.'

'Oh? Well, let me order tea and then you can do that.'

After the secretary had asked what they wanted and how they liked it, Mr Potter turned back to them. 'Now then, what is it that I have got wrong, Mrs Blaine?'

Annie clasped Janey's hand tighter. Janey looked straight at Mr Potter and told him how she had been in an asylum. 'But Annie rescued me, as I was only distraught, not mad.'

'Understandably so, my dear, with what you have told me happened. Don't distress yourself. Making one part of what Mr Blaine told us true doesn't mean that your house is in jeopardy or that Mr Blaine is innocent of wrongdoing.'

Janey relaxed, but seemed intent on making sure Mr Potter knew this wasn't the Jimmy she'd known.

'Me Jimmy signing the house over to me in the first place shows that he was a good man.'

'It does, and the man I met when he did that was a gentleman and very much in love with you. He showed that by his action of wanting to protect you and his children – well, his child and unborn at the time. But we must accept, my dear, that the tragic shooting accident you have told me of took that man away and left a man capable of wicked acts. That doesn't mean you should not grieve for the man you lost.'

Janey dropped her head. A tear plopped onto Annie's hand. On a deep sob, Janey said, 'Oh, Annie, I've lost me Jimmy and me Angie.'

Annie put her arm around Janey's thin body. She wanted to weep with her, for the deep loss they'd both suffered, but she held it together. This wasn't the place. Maybe, though, for Janey, this acceptance might give her release.

Mr Potter handed Janey a huge white hankie. 'Ah, here's the tea. I always think a nice hot cup of tea makes everyone feel better and able to cope.'

Janey made a huge effort as she wiped her tears and handed the hankie back.

'You keep it, my dear. I have a feeling you may need it. A hankie is a comfort when we have the moments that give us temporary relief . . . I know, as I have cried over my son going to war and pray hard that he returns to me.' His voice filled with pride as he added, 'He's training to be a pilot, and like everything he does, he's excelling in his training and passing every grade with flying colours . . . Ha, they are appropriate words, "flying colours!"'

Janey giggled and the moment lightened.

'Well, that was nice to hear. Now, drink up your tea while it's hot.'

240

'Ta, it's a lovely cup of tea. It tastes different out of this china cup.'

'Do you know, Mrs Blaine, I always say that myself. Mrs Potter has what she calls her "everyday china", hardy stuff that saves her best china, but my tea doesn't taste the same in those cups at all.'

'Mine's everyday stuff, but I'm going to treat meself to some nice cups like this one . . . Oh, but what will I do for money now? Jimmy has always looked after me!'

'Everything can be worked out, Mrs Blaine. There will be a way.'

'I'll take care of you, Janey. We'll move back into the house and me wages will cover us both.'

'There, you see, a solution is found.'

'There's a lot of us, though. Me little girl, me mum, and we've a friend's child and his nanny.'

'Don't worry Mr Potter with all of that, Janey. We'll cope, luv.'

'You're not worrying me, I'm here to help, but I am intrigued how you come to have another woman's child and nanny living with you.'

Annie explained, leaving out anything about how she and Olivia were helping the war effort.

'Oh dear, that is sad for your friend . . . It's an altogether sad world now, and none of us know if we're on our head or our heels, as everything we knew has changed. I was quite happy in my retirement and me and Mrs Potter were talking of going on a world cruise. Now, here I am working again, and my son is preparing to fight a war! Everything can change so very quickly for us all. My advice would be that you should deal with what you have to on a day-to-day basis until you are stronger and a lot of what is going on is resolved. Then have

241

a look at your options. If there is ever anything I can help you with, I will. You only have to drop in to see me.'

'Ta, that's good to know. Annie's the one for sorting things usually, so I'll be all right . . . Only, well, I am still sectioned and . . .'

Annie took over explaining what had gone on and how they were going to sort this out. Then had a sudden thought. 'Mr Potter, would you be able to act for us in this matter, if we get solid proof from the doctor we're going to see?'

'Of course. I'm not a criminal lawyer, but we do deal with family matters. I would very much like to help you further. Let me have the doctor's report when you have it. But how will you keep from being forced back into the asylum?'

'Me sergeant has the matter in hand. He is filing complaints about the state of the place Janey was in. They have agreed not to report her missing until that is sorted if he gives them time to change their ways. It's precarious, we know, and everything will have to move at a pace.'

'Well, as old and decrepit as I might look, I can move quickly too. And, I won't be charging you, Mrs Slater, so don't worry about that extra expense. Your sister has been dealt many awful blows and I want to help her.'

'Ta, that's kind of you. Me and Janey ain't ever had to deal with a solicitor before – well, I've dealt with them as I see in court, but this were different, and we were nervous, but you've been very kind and helped us a lot. Ta ever so much.'

'You're welcome, I will enjoy the challenge . . . You know, I once thought of going into criminal law . . . But don't get me started. Mrs Potter's always saying I could talk the hind leg off a donkey!'

They all laughed as Annie and Janey stood up.

Once in the street, Janey linked arms with Annie. 'I feel strange, Annie. It seems a lot of our troubles are going to be sorted, and yet part of me wants to curl up somewhere and weep me heart out. But a bigger part wants to get to me Beth and hold her and hold her and never let her go.'

'I think you can do both, luv. Like me, you can weep at night for your loss, and in the daytime, you can be a proper mum to Beth . . . But something occurred to me when we were in there with Mr Potter, and you suddenly realized that you wouldn't have Jimmy's money coming in. Maybe you could go out to work.'

Janey stopped in her tracks. 'How?'

'Well, not if you don't want to, but we've a house full of women to feed and clothe and get medical help for when needed, and I ain't able to keep all the bills going on me own. But we have Loes. Being Dutch, Loes hasn't got papers allowing her to work here, so she could look after both Karl and Beth, and Cissy and the nuns take care of mum. And with all this talk of women having to do the men's jobs, it seems there's going to be plenty of work about. Besides, I think it will do you good, luv. It won't give you so much time to think about stuff. I know that's helped me. When I'm at work everyone keeps me going and me mind's occupied.'

Janey's expression changed from one of shock to one of a light dawning. 'I had thought again recently about nursing, Annie.'

'Well, there you go. I read in the paper at work that the Red Cross have joined forces with the St John Ambulance Brigade and are running a recruitment drive. They offer training and are accepting married women for some of the jobs.'

'And I did most of me training. Oh, Annie, do you think I could really do it?'

'Well, we could look into it all. There must be something you can do connected to nursing, luv.'

'Whatever work there is for me, I'll do it, and if I can't do anything to do with nursing, I'll look at other things. I'd just love to go out to work, Annie. Even if it's back at Mr Sutherland's shop! Me and you'll make sure there's food on the table for our gang of East End women and one little boy!'

'Ha, we'll adopt Loes as an East Ender, but she'll have to learn to drop her aitches!'

They were laughing together in a way that Annie never thought they would again.

Annie thought that it had helped them to know they still had a home where their heart lay and that they had others relying on them.

'As you've got the day off, Annie, I feel ready to visit me little Angie and take her some flowers, then let's go home . . . Only, Annie . . . Well, will you come back and live with me in me flat as I don't think I could do this without you by me side, especially at night?'

'I will, luv. I need you, too. Night-time's the worst time of all. Loes will be fine taking the basement flat over with Karl. She's settling down well, and we're all there for her. She spends a lot of time with Mum. They get on together like a house on fire.'

'Ooh, this could really work out for us all, Annie. I feel different. Like I can cope.'

'You can, luv. Though you will have moments when you can't but that's all right. I'll be there for you when it happens, and you'll be there for me when it all hits me.'

'Oh, Annie, do you remember a long time ago you told me that you and Olivia had called yourselves the Guernsey Girls?

I was a bit jealous at the time as I thought, no, you're my sister, not Olivia's, but I soon got over it. Well, me and you can be the East End Sisters!'

Annie was shocked at first to hear of how Janey had felt. And alarm bells rang – did Janey know about their secret code name? But then, she and Olivia calling themselves the Guernsey Girls had started a long time ago, and wasn't something they'd invented for the sharing of secrets, and she relaxed once more.

'I love that, Janey. And we're proper sisters. Nothing or no one can come between that.'

And with this, they didn't care that they were in a busy street with shops all around them, brightly displaying all manner of goods and attracting well-to-do women who gave the feeling of there being no shortages or a war with their brown paper bags full of purchases, and turned to each other and hugged.

Having bought a bunch of sweet williams of many colours, they came to the bus stop.

It was only a short bus ride to the Tower Hamlets Cemetery, but to Annie it was an agonizing one as she saw Janey's demeanour change. She was no longer the giggling young woman, but the grieving one, who, from the moment they'd sat down on the hard bench seat of the bus, clung on to Annie's arm as if it was her saviour.

When they arrived, Annie's heart weighed heavy as she guided Janey to the little mound that held their precious Angie.

Janey fell to her knees. 'Angie, me little Angie.' Her hands clawed at the earth.

'No. Oh, Janey, don't do that, me darlin'.'

'I want her back, Annie.'

Her sobs triggered Annie's. She sank to her knees beside Janey and sobbed with her.

'She – she was beautiful, Annie. Warm and cuddly. She loved to suckle on me and was always looking for me breast.'

Annie couldn't speak. She just held on to Janey and let her own grief for Angie, Ricky and what had happened to the lovely Jimmy they used to know flow from her.

After a time, Janey asked, 'What . . . what happened? . . . I mean, how . . . how did Jimmy do it?'

Not wanting to say, but knowing Janey would find out, Annie told her, 'He strangled her . . . Oh, Janey!'

Janey let out a scream of, 'No, no! . . . Not that! . . . Me baby, me baby!'

'Oh, Janey. I'm sorry. I had to tell you. You'll see the death certificate at home. It's a document that belongs to you. I couldn't not let you see it.'

A deep-throated growl came from Janey. 'I want him to hang! I want him strangled to death! I hate him, I hate him . . .'

But the sobbing that came after this didn't tell of Janey's hate for Jimmy but her deep love of the man he'd been and who they had lost.

Annie allowed Janey this time. She'd promised she would and now it was time to honour that promise. She just held her tightly and cried with her.

At last, Janey pulled the hankie that Mr Potter had given her from her pocket and blew her nose. 'I need to go home, Annie. I need Mum and Cissy, but most of all I need to cuddle me little Beth.'

'Yes, let's do that. We can collect the things we have at the apartment another time . . . You know, I'd thought that I was going to have to move us all there if Jimmy had been

246

allowed to sell it. Mum wasn't at all happy about that. But she'll be pleased now that we can stay . . . And to see you, Janey. She's been pining for you.'

'And me for her, and all of them, but mostly for me little Beth.'

Home welcomed them like never before.

Annie was shocked to realize that this house had become home to her and that she loved it even more than the house they'd grown up in.

The reunion between Janey and Beth brought tears to everyone's eyes.

When it all settled down, with Janey taking Beth upstairs, Mum said, 'There was a phone message for you, Annie, luv. Your friend, Lucy. She'd like to meet you for a cup of tea in Gill's cafe around four-ish.'

Annie glanced at the clock. 'Eek, that's now. I'll be back soon.'

Blowing them all kisses, Annie hurried out of the door.

Lucy stood and hugged her as Annie entered the cafe. 'I've good news, love.'

As soon as they sat down, Lucy handed her a card. 'There, that's the doctor and he will see Janey as soon as you like as he recognizes the urgency of acting very quickly. He even said you can ring him tonight and he will fit Janey in tomorrow.'

'Oh, ta, Lucy. This is amazing. I'll ring him as soon as I get home.' Annie relaxed back and released a huge sigh.

'You looked whacked out, love.'

'I am. Totally.'

'Right, you need some light relief. Now, no objections. Take your glad rags to work with you tomorrow and change into them after your afternoon shift. I'll make it right that you don't do the evening, and I'll pick you up. I'll get tickets for the theatre for us both and then we'll have supper afterwards . . . no buts!'

'My only but was that I'm off work tomorrow. It's me two days off, but oh, Lucy, I've so much to see to.'

'Nothing that can't wait. Get Janey to see the doctor, then home, rest, bath, and I'll pick you up . . . It's happening, Annie, no matter what you say.'

Annie thought quickly. 'Okay, I'll get a casserole on the go. I managed to get a little meat from the butcher, I can make dumplings and I've plenty of root veg in – that'll do nicely as a supper for the gang. They'll be all right together . . . Only, if Janey needs me, it will be difficult not to call it off.'

'Janey will always need you, Annie. But you both have to learn that it cannot always be that way. Janey must stand on her own two feet.'

'I think she will gradually. I'll take her to the Red Cross headquarters after her assessment. It's not far from the solicitor's . . . Oh, I didn't tell you . . .'

Annie caught Lucy up with everything that had been happening.

'That's good, I hope Janey will have a good report and this solicitor can help her to get the sectioning lifted. But a job? Well, maybe it will be a good thing for her. I hope so.'

Gill came over to them then. 'You two always have your heads together like some secret society or something. I try to earwig, but I can never hear what you're getting up to.'

Lucy handled this well. 'Nosy parker! If you must know, we're planning a theatre trip and like all women when we get a moment, we like a good gossip.'

'Well, I do meself, but I don't get time.'

Lucy retorted, 'Ha, you don't do badly, Gill, you're always nattering with the customers.'

'Well, they like it.'

Annie laughed out loud. If only Gill knew. But then, she was a harmless soul and Annie would never disillusion her.

'Well, as much as we do too, we'll have to go. See you next time, Gill.'

Once outside, Lucy said, 'We'll have to be more careful. It's an ideal place to meet as being long and narrow, we can get to the back and see Gill coming, but what she said gave me the willies.'

'The secret society bit . . . Oh, I wish we still did talk about those things. I hate being out of touch with Olivia.'

'We will. Our experts are still working on it. They'll make contact, just you see.'

They parted then and as Annie walked back, she hoped with all her heart that they would. She knew she wouldn't hear Olivia's voice and they wouldn't be able to chat, just send very quick messages so that Olivia wasn't put in danger of being caught, but just to be in touch would mean the world.

As they left the Prince of Wales Theatre the next evening, having seen *Present Arms*, Annie and Lucy were in good voice as they made their way through the blacked-out streets of London.

By the time they reached the taxi rank, they'd got to the second verse of 'You Took Advantage of Me'.

As she listened and watched Lucy dance, Annie remembered such nights with Ricky. It was his voice she heard, and him dancing. For this was one of the songs from the music hall they'd attended, and he loved it.

*'I'm a sentimental sap, that's all.*
*What's the use of trying not to fall?*
*I have no will,*
*You've made your kill*
*'Cause you took advantage of me!'*

When she got to the lines:

*'So what's the use,*
*You've cooked my goose*
*'Cause you took advantage of me!'*

Annie clutched herself and held on tightly.

'Annie, love, what is it?'

'Oh, you know. Memories.'

'Oh, my dear, I haven't said, but we are working on trying to establish what happened to the men left behind in Dunkirk. Well, my department aren't doing it, but it is happening. I was talking to a colleague and they and the Red Cross are making progress . . . I just didn't want to give you false hope. But I have asked to be informed the moment any news comes through concerning Ricky.'

'Ta, Lucy. It's good to know. I thought no one cared and I hadn't a chance of finding out.'

'There's every chance, love. I just hope and pray it is good news – not that being a prisoner is good news, but it is the better of what could come out.'

'It would be the best news, as knowing my Ricky and the strength he has, if he has a chance to survive, he will!'

'That's the spirit. And with that hopeful thought, let's go and have supper, shall we?'

They linked arms and strolled along Old Compton Street to a pub Lucy knew.

Standing on a corner, The Three Greyhounds looked like everywhere, darkened and unwelcoming, but when they stepped inside, they entered a different world of honkytonk piano and loud singing voices. The joy of it entered Annie, and soon, along with Lucy, she was singing the songs Ricky loved.

As '*Daisy, Daisy, give me your answer do,*' was belted out, Annie lifted her sherry. 'To you, Ricky, me luv. Always and for ever, to you.'

A week later, with Janey getting a good report on her mental health, Annie had her fingers crossed as they stood waiting for Mr Potter to come out of the magistrate's court.

She and Janey hadn't been required to attend the hearing but couldn't just wait at home.

When he appeared at the top of the steps, he was all smiles and waving a document. 'You are free, Mrs Blaine.'

Annie's relief ran into the thought, *Truly free, both of us, as Jimmy is in custody and not likely to see the light of day again*.

As this thought died, Janey put out her arms. 'Oh, Annie, thanks, mate, for everything. For helping me to get me job working in the Red Cross headquarters' stores and supplies department and for saving our home and rescuing me from horror. A new day starts – a new life . . . Not that I'll forget me old one, but I will try to forget the bad things, and get on with me new life.'

These words were all Annie needed to hear.

# Chapter Twenty

## Annie

Aggie had a crowd around her as Annie approached the flower stall on Tower Bridge. It was good to see her doing a good trade even though times were hard for everyone, and rationing was beginning to bite. Maybe the cheer of a bunch of flowers was just what was needed.

Waiting a few moments with two steaming mugs of tea in her hands, Annie looked over the bridge. Always when here she could see Ricky and herself sitting on the bench when they first met.

The thought came to her that they would do that again. There was no doubt in her mind about that.

As the crowd cleared, Annie took the tea over to Aggie.

When she looked up, Aggie had a vacant stare. 'You'll hear news today, luv.'

'Oh?'

'Yes, later today visitors will bring you news.'

'Honestly, Aggie, you've gone from saying you don't hold with all the nonsense of seeing into the future and calling it poppycock to telling me something every time you see me!'

'I know, it's as if I opened up a can of worms when I

shared me vision on Ricky, luv. I ain't 'appy about it, but it just 'appens.'

'Well, drink your tea and I'll let you know if your prediction's right or not . . . Anyway, how are you, luv?'

'Feeling me bones, as they say. I think I'm getting too old for this lark, luv. I were counting me savings the other day and looking at retiring. I'd need parish relief now and then, but I ain't too proud for that.'

'I've never asked, but where do you live, Aggie?'

'I've got a couple of rooms in Mile End. They ain't much, and some of the tenants are a bit of a nuisance as we all share the one lav, but I do all right.'

Annie felt the pity of lovely Aggie being bothered by the other tenants and having to share a lav with goodness knows how many residents, as some of those houses could have up to a dozen boarding in them. But there was so little she could do.

'Never go without, Aggie. You'll always find me at the police station, or you can get on a bus to me address. I'll write it down for you.'

Handing her a bit of paper she'd ripped out of her notebook and written her address on, Annie said, 'Well, I'm to get off. I've me paperwork to do back at the station before I head home.'

'Ta, luv, it's good to 'ave this. By the way, do you still work the evening shift as well, Annie, luv?'

'No. Not every night, though I do take me turn.'

'I'm glad. That gives you a chance of getting out a bit.'

Taking a last slurp of her tea, Aggie took Annie's mug. 'I'll take these back to Marg, luv. You get on your way . . . Though can I have one of your hugs before you do? . . . Or ain't it proper for a copper to be seen doing such things with Jo public?'

'Ha, not all of them, but I reckon you'll be all right.'

Hugging Aggie, Annie just wanted to take her home with her, but they were full to the rafters. But then an idea occurred to her.

'Why not come on Sunday, to me house, Aggie? You'd be very welcome. We all try to get together for dinner on a Sunday if I'm off, and I am this week. I'd love you to meet me mum, Cissy, Lilly, Janey and Loes, as well as the youngsters.'

'All right, I will. Ta, Annie, luv. I'll look forward to that.'

This really brightened Annie. She'd wanted to ask Aggie for a long time to come over. She'd even thought of asking Janey if they could take her in. There was a spare bedroom in Janey's flat as she and Janey shared a bedroom, and Beth had the small room that she'd always slept in.

Thinking of Beth, Annie was glad that little children didn't seem to remember things that happened weeks ago. Beth, now a bright two-year-old, never asked after her daddy.

An hour later when she drove into Old Ford Road and pulled up outside her home, Annie had the shock of her life. There, standing on the corner, were Henry and Joe.

Jumping out of the car, she called over to them. 'What on earth? Joe? Henry? . . . How . . . ? What . . . ? I mean, are you all right?'

Jo laughed. 'We are now we've seen you, Annie.'

Henry smiled a smile of relief. 'We thought we'd never get here. It's good to see you, Annie.'

'But what are you doing here? How did you get here? . . . I mean, oh, it's good to see you too.'

With this, she slammed her car door closed and ran towards them with her arms open. Both came to meet her and she found herself in a huddle with them.

Joe was nearest and she felt a wet patch on her cheek. Joe was crying.

Patting his back, she told them, 'Come inside. I'm baffled as to how you came to be here. Cissy – that's a lady who used to be housekeeper in Olivia's dad's apartment up west – will have the kettle on. I expect you could do with a cuppa.'

'Yes, and a crust, Annie. We ain't eaten for days . . . Well, only scraps and stuff out of fields.'

'Oh, Joe, really? What on earth has happened to you both? No, don't answer that. Come on, let's get inside.'

As she opened the door, Mum called out, 'Is that you, Annie?'

And Cissy called, 'I've kettle on, lass, in your mum's flat.'

'I've two visitors, so I hope it's full, Cissy, luv.'

Going into her mum's flat with Joe and Henry following her, her mum took one look at them and said, 'You picked up some waifs and strays, luv? Come in, young men, you're very welcome. I'm Vera and this is Cissy.'

Cissy grinned. 'By, we ain't had any lads here for a few weeks. You're very welcome. Come and sit down.'

'Ha, don't mind these two, they're man mad!'

Everyone laughed at this from Annie.

'Mum, Cissy, meet Joe and Henry, from Guernsey, only don't ask me how they got here as I haven't had a chance yet to find out. Shock of me life seeing them on the corner, though a good one as I hope you've brought me news of Olivia.'

Cissy handed them a mug each of steaming hot tea. 'Eeh, Annie, lass, let them have a drink first, they look all in.'

'It's all right, Cissy. And nice to meet you both. We escaped . . . Well, thanks to Olivia and Joe here we did. But that was almost two weeks ago now. We've had quite a journey, running out of fuel for the boat, rowing, and losing an oar and finally swimming and landing miles away from Southampton, soaked and hungry. We're exhausted.'

'You're here now, Henry, and we'll take care of you, luv. Ooh, it's so good to see you and I've a million questions, but I'll let you drink your tea.'

Henry took another sip. Joe sat with his head bowed. But Henry seemed more able to cope.

'Well, firstly, Olivia's all right.' Annie sat listening in amazement as Henry told them of Olivia living in the farmhouse and having privileges the other islanders didn't have. 'She sends her love to you all and is suffering badly with loneliness.'

Annie's heart dropped. She took a deep breath to stop herself from crying. She wanted to ask so many things but knew she couldn't. Even if Henry did know, he couldn't tell her here.

'And I've left for good, Annie,' said Joe. 'Well, until the war's over. That is, if we win. Henry's going back to his army base, but I need a home till I get meself settled.'

'You'll have one here, Joe, luv, don't you worry about that.'

'Thanks, Annie, only before that, I could do with the lavatory, please.'

Annie smiled. She'd never heard it asked for in such a polite way.

'This way. There's one out in the backyard. You'll be more comfortable using that one as Mum's is only just through that door.'

'Ha, I'd have to ask you all to sing if I used that one!'

They all laughed and some of the tension broke. Annie was glad to see the old Joe back. It meant he was relaxing and feeling safe.

'Annie, can I see you outside for a moment?'

'Of course, Henry, as long as you haven't got bad news. We've had a bellyful of that!'

'Oh, I'm sorry to hear that. No, not bad news, but . . . well . . .'

Then, as if he'd had inspiration, Henry quickly said, 'It's about Joe, only I don't want him coming back and I'm halfway through telling you.'

Realizing that she'd put Henry on the spot, Annie got up. 'Yes, of course. Let's take our tea outside.'

Once they were sitting on the step, Henry quickly told her, 'I know about the Guernsey Girls and Hendrick. I find it all amazing and think Olivia and him so very brave.'

Knowing from this that Olivia had trusted him, Annie began to feel a twinge of excitement as she hoped what he had to say meant he had information about how to contact Olivia.

As he told her what he knew about the transmitter and frequency, he promised to write it all down for her.

'I have another message too. It's all in code and I have had to memorize it. Do you want me to write that down too?'

'Tell me it first, Henry. I'm used to deciphering them.'

Annie listened in growing horror.

'What is it, Annie? . . . Oh no, of course, don't answer that. It's obviously not for my ears or Olivia wouldn't have given it in code.'

'It's best you don't know, then you can't slip up. We have to be so careful. We just don't know who is genuine and who isn't, so don't mention the transmitter to anyone, Henry.'

'You have my word.'

'Thank you . . . I still can't believe you're here. It's like a dream.'

'For me too.' Once more Annie listened with a feeling of sadness mixed with horror as Henry told her how things were on the island and how they were for Olivia. 'If only these people who spit at her and have a go at her knew how courageous she really is and how she is putting her life on the line for them.'

'I know. It used to incense me, but Olivia copes with it . . . Oh, it's good to know she's all right and has Daphne and Cook with her as well as her father.'

'Yes, she copes, though often there is many a tell-tale sign that she's spent the night crying.'

'Poor darlin' . . . Oh, it's all so unfair!'

Though she said this, Annie's heart was thumping as she knew from the message that soon they too would feel some of that unfairness and be in the thick of the war . . . She just couldn't imagine it. London! Her home was to be bombed. She had to tell Lucy as soon as possible. Though the city had prepared, with sandbags everywhere, blackouts, shelters and sirens going off at odd times to give the people a chance to practice, it was still going to come as a shock. Fear trembled through her. *Will we all be killed?*

'Annie, it's good that you can care for Joe. He's had a shock. He always took everything in his stride, but leaving the island and not going back is massive for him, as was our horrendous journey, because everything's always gone smoothly for him before. He's lost his boat and doesn't know when he will see his home or his dad again – if ever! He's eager to join up and I think that would be a good thing, but if you could hang on to him and dissuade him from joining until he's eighteen, that would be good.'

'I will. But what of your plans?'

'If I could use your phone to contact my regiment, and then have a bath, food – though I should have said food first as I'm starving – and then if you could beg, borrow or steal some clothes for me, I hope to be out from under your hair by tomorrow . . . That's if you could put me up for one night?'

'Of course we can. The house is divided into four flats. Me and Janey have the top one, Cissy lives in the one to the left of the hall, you've already been into Mum's, and then there is a basement flat that Loes occupies . . . You remember her, Olivia's nanny?'

'Oh yes, of course. She's here with you?'

'She is. And as it happens, she has a load of Olivia's dad's clothes in a wardrobe in her flat, which she brought with her from Olivia's dad's apartment up the West End of London. So, we can easily kit you out. And I'm sure she won't mind you and Joe sleeping in her spare room tonight . . . Though when it comes to facilities, there is only the outside loo, or piddle pots.'

Henry laughed. 'I'm used to them with the army, or even none at all! So that won't bother me. And Joe, once he lays his head down, for all he's troubled by being away from home and his dad, he's out like a light!'

Janey's voice interrupted them at that moment. 'Annie! Annie!'

'Oh, here's me sister coming in from work.' Annie waved towards Janey. 'We have visitors, luv. All the way from Guernsey.'

'Olivia!'

'No, sadly.'

Janey had reached them now.

'Meet Henry, Janey. He and the porter of the docks and sometime taxi driver, come all sorts, whose name is Joe, escaped the island and have landed up here. Olivia gave them my address. They need somewhere to stay.'

'Pleased to meet you, Henry. As a mate of Olivia's, you're very welcome.'

Henry didn't seem to want to take his eyes off Janey. Janey held his gaze. To Annie, it was as if something had happened to them both.

'Have you hurt yourself, Janey? . . . Forgive me, that was a bit forward, only . . . well, you have what looks like old bruising.'

Annie jumped in. 'She's a clumsy one, this one, mate. Always dropping things and running into things.'

Janey laughed a nervous laugh and shrugged. 'I'm the daft sister, Annie's the sensible one.'

'You don't look daft to me. Hurt, very hurt, and not just the bruising, but inside, but not daft.'

Janey coloured. Her bottom lip quivered. Annie jumped in once more. 'You're tired, I expect, luv. You've done a long shift. Let's get inside, eh?'

When they entered the hall, they heard squeals of delight from Beth and Karl. They opened the door to Mum's flat to find Joe on his knees chasing the little ones.

Loes stood up as they entered. 'Henry, it is good to see you and Joe. How is Olivia and her father and everyone? The children took Joe's attention, and I haven't been told yet.'

After Henry answered this by saying they were bearing up, Annie told Loes about them wanting a bed for the night.

'You are very welcome to my spare bedroom for as long as you need it, both of you.'

'Thank you, Loes. It's good to see you're safe and well.' Henry turned to Annie once more. 'Is it possible I could have that bath?'

'Yes. Janey, it's best in our flat, luv, Henry will get more privacy. Is that all right with you?'

'It is. Just let me cuddle the kids, if I can catch them, and I'll show you upstairs.'

'I'll come with you, Loes, and pick out some suitable clothing for them both. Then I'll have to fix tea. I left a casserole in on low, but I can add more veg and onions to it and we've plenty of bread that you baked, Cissy . . . Only, I need to make a phone call first.'

With Henry, Joe and Beth going upstairs with Janey and Cissy volunteering to cook more potatoes and veg to add to the meal, Annie found she had privacy in the hall.

Taking out her notebook, she quickly changed the message about the transmitter into code and luckily she remembered Olivia's very short one about the possibility of the Germans staging a raid that would destroy the RAF and leave the way clear for them to invade by the means of boats.

Lucy was surprised to hear about Joe and Henry, and was worried about the bombing message, but was over the moon about the transmitter information.

'I'll be in touch, Annie.'

With this the phone went dead.

With the men bathed and changed and Henry having made his call to his regiment and been told to report back in forty-eight hours, they settled down to eat the delicious dinner made plentiful by Cissy's extra potatoes, vegetables and dumplings.

The chatter went from Annie's memories of her time in Guernsey to the war and how different the island was today, such a short time after the invasion.

Annie couldn't think how people who had known nothing but freedom and being able to gather for a natter when they wanted to would fare under such a strict regime.

'It is bad, Annie, and I think it'll get worse,' said Joe. 'When Olivia wanted to talk to me about getting Henry out, she pretended she was gazing at her old house. Then, even though we were talking about serious stuff, we had to keep laughing as this German had his eye on us.'

'Oh, Joe, I can't believe it. And I feel guilty somehow, as it was Churchill's action in leaving you unprotected that led to this.'

Henry answered, 'He had no choice, Annie. It was vital he got all the troops he could to defend France. I know it didn't work anyway, but we all understood why it had to be done. Guernsey just didn't seem to be a likely target. It offers nothing other than an ego trip for blasted Hitler!'

Janey changed the subject. 'Anyway, I have news.'

'Mummy, nooos?'

Beth's interruption made them all laugh, and Karl got in on the act with an even longer version of the word, 'Noooooos!'

The laughter became louder, and the little ones giggled along, puffing their chests out with pride at being the cause of the merriment.

'Well, if you all shut up, I'll be able to tell you!'

This brought them to order.

'I've been offered a job to work as a nursing assistant in a clinic not far away. It's for pregnant women and babies. It's run by the Red Cross, and it don't matter that I'm married as it's only assisting. I won't be classed as a nurse, but will feel like one as I'm to have a uniform and be involved in the care of those needing the clinic.'

'Oh, I'm glad for you, Janey. All you ever wanted was to be a nurse.'

'Ta, Annie, luv.'

'Eeh, I nearly forgot. An official-looking letter came for you, Janey.'

Annie's eyebrows shot up. Was this the dreaded notification that Jimmy would finally be facing trial?

Cissy was out of the door and scooting over to her flat before Annie could gather her wits to stop her and suggest it was left till later. When she came back with the brown envelope, Annie felt the dreaded moment was on them.

Janey took the letter and ran out of the door with it.

Annie followed.

Once in their flat, Janey ripped open the envelope, cast her eyes over the letter, then threw it onto the settee and ran for the bathroom. Annie heard her retching.

Picking up the letter, she read:

*The trial of James Blaine, accused of the murder of one Angela Blaine, is due to begin at 10 a.m. on 19th August at the Old Bailey courthouse. As a witness for the prosecution, you are required to attend.*

Annie felt her stomach churn as Janey's had. She went to the bathroom.

'Can I come in, Janey, luv?'

'It's not locked.'

The strength in Janey's voice surprised Annie, when she'd thought she would be sobbing. Opening the door, she found

Janey sitting on the lav, her body slumped forward, her elbows on her knees and holding her head in her hands.

'Oh, Janey, luv.'

When she looked up she seemed to have aged and her expression was one of despair. But her answer showed the strength she'd gained recently.

'I'm all right, Annie. It was a shock, even though I've been expecting it.'

'Yes, I'm dreading my letter now. But this is the last hurdle, luv. How do you feel?'

'Mixed feelings. Part of me feels like a traitor to the Jimmy I loved, but part of me wants the bastard to hang.'

'I understand, luv, but will you cope?'

'Seeing him will be the worst thing, Annie, but I can do this for me Angie, and Beth, as he could have killed her too. He had no way of knowing how much aspirin would just make her sleep and how much would kill her, but he gave them to her anyway.'

'Stand up and let me give you a hug.' Taking her hand, Annie walked Janey back through to the living room to hold her and try to reassure her. 'I'll be with you as much as I can. I'm due leave, so I'll ask if I can take a week, as the trial will probably last that long. We'll do this together, luv.'

She'd hardly stopped speaking when a knock came on the door, and it opened. 'May I come in? I wondered if there's anything I can do. Your mum told us what this is all about. I'm so sorry.'

'Yes, come in, Henry.'

'I – I wondered if you'd like to go for a walk, Janey? . . . I . . . well, sometimes it can help to talk to someone who isn't involved.'

Janey didn't hesitate. 'Yes, I'd like that, Henry, but I may chew your ear off.'

Henry looked taken aback. Janey giggled. 'Not literally! Ha, it means I'll talk a lot.'

'Oh? Well, that's fine. You can tell me everything and anything. I just want to help in some way. I can't imagine what you're going through.'

Annie was shocked at this turn in events. Henry even asking such a thing only hours after meeting Janey and even more so at Janey agreeing! It seemed a massive step for her to talk to anyone about her problems, let alone a virtual stranger. But looking at the two of them smiling at one another, she had the strange feeling that they weren't strangers but had known one another the moment they set eyes on each other.

With this knowledge, her shoulders relaxed, even though she hadn't realized the tension she'd been holding in them.

'Well, you go ahead, it'll do you good, Janey, and it's a nice night. It'd be lovely walking along by the canal.'

When they went downstairs, they found that Joe and Loes were sitting on the wall outside, and Mum and Cissy were playing with the children in Mum's flat.

To Annie, it was as if there was a contentment about the whole situation. Yes, they had bad things to face, probably in a lot more ways than with the murder trial. But still, human nature was such that friendships could be forged from out of the blue, and ones that could bring great comfort.

She hoped that would happen for Janey, and for Loes and Joe. And she hoped that the trial would progress in a way that wasn't too distressing and bring closure to them all.

As she sat down, she thought of how good it would be to be back in touch with Olivia. Sadly, they wouldn't be able to communicate much more than what was necessary, but just to know it was her tapping out the Morse code would be like a dream come true, even though she was hundreds of miles away.

Two days later, Annie's dream was shattered when Lucy told her that to minimize the risk to Olivia, they had made contact and she was to communicate directly with the special unit at the War Office.

'I'm sorry, Annie, I truly am, but the danger is that as friends you will want to chat about anything and everything, and that would mean longer airtime, and increase the chances of Olivia's set being discovered. If that happened, it could mean her and Hendrick being shot. And besides this, there's the time it would take to teach you how to use a transmitter and to understand Morse code. Olivia's messages are vital, and we cannot jeopardize her safety, or risk not receiving them.'

Though devastated, Annie understood and forced herself to accept this decision. 'But you will tell her how Karl is?'

'We will tell her that she won't receive bulletins on his progress but is to assume he is all right as the only time we will mention him, or you, or any of your family unit, is if it is necessary to.'

Annie's heart bled at this news. Not just for herself and Karl, but for dear Olivia. She just couldn't imagine her pain and wanted to reach out and hug her. How long would it be before she could do this?

# PART FOUR

A Shattered World

# Chapter Twenty-One

## Olivia

### Mid-August 1940

Olivia sometimes thought that if it wasn't for the choir, and her twice-weekly calls with Hendrick, she would go mad.

Having been given permission to run the choir once a week and maybe put on a concert in the future, Olivia looked around the small group gathered in the church hall on this lovely sunny afternoon – her father, Daphne, Mrs Green, and a portly lady from St Peter Port, who disapproved of Hendrick, but was a lonely soul and had decided to put her feelings aside to enjoy some company. Then there was Jean who Olivia still wanted to call 'Cook' but was gradually getting used to referring to by her rightful name, and lastly Leonard Preesley, the young man she worked with in her father's bank – not that there was anything much for them to do these days. Mostly they transferred locals' funds to the Midland Bank and wrote letters to their clients asking them to move their portfolios to another investment bank as soon as possible. A heartbreaking task as they watched their assets dwindle and knew the inevitable would happen.

How her father coped with this prospect was by hoping

that his own investments would yield funds when this was all over. He still had a sizeable amount of personal funds but the investment bank facing bankruptcy weighed heavily on his shoulders. Olivia sighed as she knew this would mean a foreclosure on his property holdings in London, which included the apartment block in St James's Street, as they were tied to the investment bank business.

Lifting her head, she made herself focus. 'Right! Shall we begin our warm-up exercises? Hands on diaphragm and hum.'

This was cut short by the doors of the church being flung open. Two German soldiers stood in the doorway.

Immediately defensive, Olivia pulled herself to her full height, ignoring the butterflies in her stomach. In German, she said, 'We have permission to gather for choir practice.'

The taller of the two, who she'd spoken to before and who'd made the remark about Hendrick's father being a dissident, fixed his piercing blue eyes on her and in perfect English answered her. 'Quite so. And we wish to join you.'

Olivia could have screamed, *No!* as she envisaged what they had all looked upon as their safe place to chat turning into a stilted, tension-filled gathering, which would peter out through sheer fear.

Instead, she said, 'Well, if you can sing, you are welcome.'

Ignoring the horrified glances, especially from Jean and Mrs Green, she invited the soldiers to get in line and to begin warming up with them. 'But first, introductions. May we know your names?'

The same soldier answered, 'Gunter, and this is Stefan. Stefan cannot speak English, but can sing in English. I have been teaching him many of the songs I have heard you sing. It has only been twice that I have stood outside listening, but I have picked them up.'

Wishing to humiliate them, Olivia said, 'Well, I do have to hear you before I can consider you as members.'

She sat at the piano. 'What would you like to sing?'

'"Greensleeves". It is a favourite of us both.'

'Very well, just the first verse will do.'

As soon as Olivia had played the intro, she was astounded as two beautiful tenors sang in harmony:

> *'Alas, my love, you do me wrong*
> *To cast me off discourteously;*
> *And I have loved you oh so long*
> *Delighting in your company.*
> *Greensleeves was my delight,*
> *Greensleeves my heart of gold*
> *Greensleeves was my heart of joy*
> *And who but my Lady Greensleeves.'*

There was a silence as they hung on to the last note, and for a few seconds after they finished too. Then an impulsive cheer went up, which Olivia joined in with.

Father stepped forward. 'Bravo, that was beautiful.' He offered his hand. 'William Renouf, sir, owner of Renouf Bank.'

'Oh? Hendrick invested some money for my father with you, but we moved it before the invasion.'

'As many of your countrymen did. You had the good fortune of knowing plans we knew nothing of . . . You know Hendrick?'

Olivia held her breath.

'We grew up together. We were once friends – that is, until Hendrick was sent here to his aunt. Though it is good to know he retained the principles of his mother country, even though his father became a dissident!'

Father coughed uncomfortably.

'But it is of no importance.' He turned to Olivia. 'Well, madam, are we good enough?'

Knowing that all were willing her to say 'no', Olivia couldn't think of a reason that was plausible to do so. She couldn't very well tell them they would turn a safe space into one where all were on edge, so she nodded her head.

'This is good.'

He spoke in German to Stefan. Olivia understood as he said, 'The answer is yes . . . Frau Kraus will give you any instructions in German.'

Once more Olivia nodded.

She was fearful that she would never be able to speak freely again.

Once the practice began, it turned out to be a very pleasant session as Mrs Green's soprano voice complemented the tenor voices of Gunter, Stefan and Leonard. As did her father's deeper baritone and the sweet, clear voices of Jean and Daphne. The sound they produced together was wonderful and brought tears to Olivia's eyes. So much so that she clapped her hands as they came to the end of the whole choir's rendition of 'Greensleeves'.

All were smiles and seemed to forget their differences as they congratulated each other.

'We are good enough to do a concert for our Kommandant, Major Albrecht Lanz. He is very fond of music and will appreciate this effort on your behalf. So, please arrange a show and we will arrange a date.'

Olivia said she would.

Stefan then spoke to Gunter. Gunter nodded.

'Frau Kraus, Stefan would like to know if you would teach

him to speak English? I have tried, but my time and my patience is limited.'

'Yes, Hendrick and I were to start a language school before he did his duty and left for Germany. I could hire this hall and teach a few of you if there's anyone else interested.'

'There may well be. Leave it with me.'

They both clipped their heels and left. The room fell silent. Mrs Green was the first to speak. 'Don't worry yourself, Olivia. Though you agreed with everything, you didn't have a choice. I think we're all best to toe the line in the same way as they're here now, so we have to get on with it.'

'Thank you.'

They all gestured their consent except for Leonard.

'I'm not so sure. We should be putting up some kind of resistance, not cowing down to them.'

Father quelled this.

'What can we do? We're only allowed to gather in small groups and then only if we have permission and can prove we are legitimate. Why do you think they came here today? I doubt it was to join us, but even so, doing that, they now have us under surveillance every time.'

Leonard shuffled his good leg. 'I suppose.'

Olivia spoke up then. 'Mrs Green is right, better we have a good relationship.' She lowered her voice. 'But I also agree that if an opportunity presents itself, we will do what we can, but nothing that will put the islanders in danger.'

'I'll come up with something.'

'Just be careful, Leonard.'

Olivia brought the meeting to a close. 'Well, everyone, well done for today, but I must get back now. So, till Friday, when I'll have a score for a concert worked out. All of you take care.'

With this, she picked up her bundle of music, gestured to Jean and Daphne to follow her and made for the door. When she opened it Gunter and Stefan stood outside.

Olivia gasped.

'Is there anything wrong, Frau Kraus?'

'No . . . no, you just startled me.'

Hurrying past them, she bid them good evening. Her heart seemed to be in her throat as she walked away. But then she stopped as she heard a cry. Turning, she saw Leonard on the floor. Gunter had a gun pointed at the back of his head.

'Your voice carries. We heard what you said. We make examples of those who will plot behind our back.'

Olivia cried, 'No! It wasn't what you think.'

'I understood what it was. This man tried to incite you all to cause disruption for us.'

Mrs Green ran at them. 'Don't you dare hurt him!' She landed on her back. No one moved to help her as a deafening crack froze them to the spot.

Olivia stared at the ever-widening pool of blood that ran from the still body of Leonard. Gasping in a deep and painful breath, she put out her hand, hoping to grab hold of anything that would steady her. Her father grabbed it.

'Shush, please, Olivia, don't say anything.' His hand trembled.

Letting go, she walked steadily back towards where Mrs Green lay. 'Let me help you, dear.'

But there was no response.

'Mrs Green, come on. Let's get you up. Help me, Daphne.'

As Daphne approached, she sobbed. 'She's dead, Olivia . . . She's dead.'

Olivia seemed to see for the first time then. Mrs Green, too, had blood making a pool around her head.

'It looks like she cracked her head on the kerb . . . Oh, Olivia . . . Oh, God!'

Stefan stepped forward and took hold of Daphne. In German, he said, 'I'm sorry. It is the fault of the young man. We heard him plotting.'

Daphne burst into tears. 'We're trying to please you all. But everything has changed for us. We fear you. Yes, Leonard said things, but he agreed with us that we are better to get on with you. Wouldn't you as a young man have these thoughts if your country had been overrun?'

Stefan looked at Olivia. She translated word for word as she thought Daphne so brave and Stefan obviously cared something for her.

'Please tell Daphne . . . is that the correct pronunciation?'

'Yes . . . *Ja*.'

'Please tell her that it is better to be compliant, but . . .' He looked around to where Gunter was supervising some soldiers to remove poor Leonard's body, then back to her and lowered his voice. 'But I understand and yes, I would be the same as Leonard . . . I – I'm sorry.'

'*Danke schön*.'

Thank you very much seemed an almost insulting thing to say for Leonard's life when really Olivia wanted to spit at Stefan, and yet she detected that he was different and just maybe they would have a true friend in him.

Gunter came over. 'Why isn't this woman getting up?'

Olivia wanted to shout that the reason was because he had murdered her just as surely as he had Leonard. But she could not speak, only stare at what she saw as a monster.

Shock held her still and quiet as she knew it did her father, Jean and Daphne as the reality kicked in. Mrs Green was dead too. How would the islanders take it all?

'Well, you had better hold auditions for replacements. I want that concert to go ahead, and I want it to sound as we did. That was perfect.' He turned and issued orders to remove Mrs Green's body, and then marched away.

Stefan looked towards Daphne. He shrugged his shoulders in an apologetic way and followed Gunter.

The four of them just stood there staring as the soldiers, none too gently, lifted Mrs Green. Olivia saw the struggle they had, and the thought flitted through her mind that Mrs Green was a fighter to the last.

She remembered how months ago Mrs Green had taken her to task over Hendrick and how she'd listened and had retracted her awful comments with an apology. She was a good woman and would be missed.

When they reached the car, Olivia was the first to crumble and give way to tears. Daphne and Jean joined her, and her father sniffed loudly but didn't stop them as they sobbed their hearts out.

Guernsey had truly changed. Their lovely island had witnessed two murders of two of its nicest people. How was she to stand much more?

Eventually, Father took charge.

'I'll drive. I don't care that I don't have a permit. Give me the keys, Olivia.'

'No, Daddy. We have seen an example of what can happen. I'll be all right. Let's just get home.'

Home offered no comfort. To Olivia, even though it housed four of them, it was a lonely place where her love had been caged. She wanted to scream out against the world. But instead, she agreed to them having a mug of cocoa, which Jean and Daphne prepared.

They sat out in the garden and drank it in silence to the sounds of the sea lapping the shore and a breeze rustling the trees – gentle sounds that didn't intrude but helped them.

Olivia knew that each of them, like herself, was seeing the scene over and over, but each dealt with it alone.

She lay back and thought of Karl and Annie and prayed that Annie had been able to keep her promise to get Janey, Loes and the precious little ones to the country by now. Hendrick was certain that the raid on London, to clear the way for an invasion, would happen soon.

*Please God, let it be so. Protect my dear friends and my darling son.*

# Chapter Twenty-Two

## Janey

Janey stood at the top of what should have been the fire escape of her flat but was used as stairs to the garden. She sipped her tea as she watched the workmen finishing off installing an Anderson shelter in the centre of her garden.

Her mind was in turmoil. Torn between getting Beth and Karl to safety with Loes and herself or just sending Loes with the children. She sighed.

The talk was of London being bombed, in retaliation for the night raids the British air force had carried out in Berlin. It seemed now that it wasn't 'if', but 'when'. They could happen at any time.

She nervously scanned the skies.

'Don't worry, girl. If they come, it'll be at night, but they'll have a job to get by our RAF. They're all crack pilots and'll ditch the bloody lot of them.'

Janey smiled at the workman. 'I hope so.'

'Well, if they don't, this shelter will take most of the street – at least your bit of it – so you'll all be safe. Nothing will get through it.'

'Ta, that's reassuring.' Turning, she went inside, wishing

that Annie was home. Her glance took in the telephone. Should she ring Rose? Since the trial, they'd only spoken once. Rose had been prosecuted for harbouring a known criminal but had been let off with a warning. She'd only done what every East End mother would do.

With Jimmy locked away in Broadmoor for life, Rose must be going through hell. But how would Rose react if she called?

Making her mind up, she lifted the receiver and asked for Rose's number. Her nerves made her tremble, but she waited, listening to it ringing out and then being answered and the operator saying, 'I have a call for you. Putting it through now.'

'Rose?'

'Janey, is that you?'

'Yes, Rose.'

'Oh, Janey! How are you, girl?'

'I'm all right . . .'

The conversation went along like this for a few seconds, and then Rose said, 'Can you forgive me, Janey? I – I didn't know . . . not all of it. I'm so sorry . . . Oh, Janey.'

'Don't cry, Rose. There's nothing to forgive. You did what we would all do.'

'Ta, luv, ta for that . . . Is everyone all right with me?'

'They are, Rose. They understand. But Rose, that weren't our Jimmy that did that terrible thing. We lost our Jimmy in France.'

'Oh, Janey, ta, luv. I've been so alone. How's Beth?'

'She's all right. Doing fine. Only, well, we're going to have a service for Angie. I – I missed the funeral, and I need something . . . I think Annie's idea of a service is best. We can remember her and finally put her to rest.'

'Oh, I'd love to come, and me Alfie.'

'It's this Sunday, the first of September. It's at St John's in Cambridge Heath Road.'

'We'll be there, luv. Can yer put us up?'

'If you don't mind having single beds. Only we have a young man from Guernsey staying with us in our flat . . . It's all changed. We've got Olivia's nanny too, and her little boy. They have a basement flat, so you'll be in with her in her spare room.'

'That'll do us, luv. We'll see you on Saturday . . . And, Janey, why don't yer come back with me, eh? You and Beth. It'll be safer here.'

'Have you room for Olivia's nanny and her little boy too?'

'We have. There's a cottage on our land. We could let you have that.'

'Ta, though I ain't sure I'll come as I have a job and it's one that is needed badly, but I'll see as I can't bear to be away from me Beth either . . . How big is the cottage, Rose? Could we have a bedroom downstairs?'

'Are yer thinking of your mum, luv?'

'Yes. I'd like to get her to safety, though whether she'd go . . .'

'You'll be asking for Cissy and Lilly next . . . But, well, there's not enough room, girl, I'm sorry. It's a two-up, two-down. And it's a tin bath and an outside lav, but cosy and warm. It'd do you and this nanny and the two little ones.'

'I'll think about it, but ta, Rose . . . And Rose, ta for talking to me and being the same with me.'

'It ain't you as needs to thank me, but me you, girl. Yer've made me day!'

'I love you, Rose. See you on Saturday.'

'Ta, luv. And I love you too.'

Just before the phone clicked, Janey heard a sob. She hoped it was a happy sob, as her own tears were. She did love Rose and couldn't wait to see her. How she wished she could turn the clock back to before this war.

But she hardly had time to dwell on the phone call and how happy it had made her as Joe burst through the door.

'I'm in! I can join up!'

'What? . . . You mean, you've been to sign up?'

'I have, Janey, and all's looking good. I know I ain't eighteen till next month, but the recruiting officer said by the time they processed my application and got me started on me training, I will be . . . Oh, and I had a letter from Henry.'

Janey didn't know why, but her heart skipped a beat at hearing Henry's name, and an image of his caring smile and lovely dark eyes came to her.

'He says he hasn't yet received any of mine, though he knows I must have written to him as promised. He says morale is low because of the problem of getting letters to them and that he still wants me to write all about my news as one day it will all arrive at once and he will have the pleasure of reading a sackful of letters then.'

'Well, that ain't a good state of affairs, luv. I feel sorry for our lads as receiving letters keeps them going.'

'Poor Henry, he must feel abandoned. And from what you read, the fighting there is intense . . . Anyway, Janey, he asked if you'd write to him too.'

Janey raised her eyebrows as the surprise of this request caught her off guard, but then she thought again of how lovely Henry was and it hurt her heart to think of him longing for a letter from his mum – well, anyone it seemed.

'Of course I will, luv. I like Henry very much. He showed

me kindness when I most needed it, as did you, Joe. We're going to miss you, luv.'

'I'm worried about you all. I know you've got your shelter going in, but . . . well, all this talk of air raids on London . . .'

'It might never happen, but yes, it is scary. I've just been talking to Beth's granny . . .'

'What, her as shielded Jimmy?'

'Yes. She's a lovely woman, Joe, and only did what any mum would do.'

'I can't remember my mum. Me dad brought me up. He was a good dad, and he must be worried sick about me.'

'Olivia would have told him that you escaped, but then he don't know if you made it or not. And we don't know how she is. Annie's worried about her and misses her.'

'Bloody Germans. I can't wait to get me hand on a gun, I'm going to kill as many as I can.'

'Don't forget that they are being forced to fight, just like you are, Joe . . . Oh, I mean, of course you're willing, but it ain't what you'd choose to do. You loved your life, and by the sounds of it, it was ideal, but so did the German soldiers. So, don't hate them.'

'If I don't, Janey, I'll not be able to fight them. No, I hate them with me gut, and I daren't think of them as just young lads forced to fight. That would make me a conchie and I ain't one of them!'

Janey thought how sad it was that a whole generation felt this hate of others, though she knew the feeling herself as this past year her own hate had burned inside her, even for those she'd once loved with all her heart.

One of the workmen calling up, 'We're done, come and see what you think!' had them both going down the steps to the garden.

With her attention being taken by Joe, Janey hadn't noticed how the construction had progressed. Now she was surprised to see what looked like a mound of grass in her garden as the shelter had been covered in soil and then the turf cut from the lawn relaid over the top of it.

When she got down to ground level she saw a slope leading to a door.

Cissy stood outside her flat with Mum in the wheelchair. Suddenly it occurred to Janey the difficulty they would have in getting Mum inside as through the shelter's open door, she saw there were steps leading down into it.

'Eeh, lass, we'll all be safe in that.' Cissy had come over to her and stood with Janey looking into the darkened interior.

To Janey, it looked cold and uninviting. She didn't like the idea of it at all.

'We can make it cosy, love. We've still got them oil lamps that you brought from your old house. They'll light it up and give a little warmth. And we can put blankets inside to cosy up in and take some food and a billy can of tea with us. By, I'm looking forward to it!'

Janey shuddered.

'Why don't yer go inside and have a proper look, luv?'

Janey nodded at the workman who'd said this, then tentatively walked towards the door of the shelter.

'I'm with you, Janey. It's not going to be so bad. You'll always have folk with you.'

'Ta, Joe.'

Once inside, the space was bigger than she'd thought, but still she didn't like it and turned to get out as soon as she could.

'We'll get used to it darlin'.'

'Oh, Mum, how are we going to get you down into it?'

'There'll be a way, luv. Once Annie gets in from her shift,

283

we'll have a practice. She has to do so much stuff in her training she'll probably have a solution right away.'

'Aye, I'm sure she will. Me mum used to say, "There's nowt that can't be sorted, and best not to meet trouble halfway."'

'Where you from, missus?'

Janey left Cissy nattering to the workmen and turned back to where Mum still sat in her wheelchair next to Cissy's door.

Mum put her hand out and Janey took it. 'Try not to worry, luv. Like Cissy says, everything can be sorted.'

'I – I rang Rose, Mum.'

'Oh, that's good news, me darlin'. How is she?'

After hearing how the conversation between herself and Rose went, Mum smiled her lovely smile. 'There, you see, that's a huge thing you've sorted, girl. And I'm so pleased. So, Rose is coming for the service. Well, that gladdens me heart, luv. I can't wait to see her. Especially after the way you said she was broken at the trial. Poor luv.'

'Yes. And I was meself and so was Annie, so we couldn't help her. We were distraught, but all that's been put right . . . and, Mum, well, I'm thinking that it might be best if Loes and the children went to stay with her. She has a cottage they can have.'

'And what about you, darlin'?'

'I could visit, but I think it best I stay here . . . I mean, if you could go, I would, but you wouldn't manage in the cottage and with Annie's shifts and all we might face, I think it's best I'm on hand. Me job's vital too. There's talk of us extending care to those soldiers who are injured and have returned home. I'd like to do that, Mum.'

'Yes. There was nothing to help Jimmy, poor lad.'

'Have you forgiven him then, Mum?'

'I have, and you should too, then you'll find life easier. Hate destroys us, luv.'

'I don't hate him, but forgiving . . . well, I'll try. Though I don't want to stay married to him.'

'No, I don't think you should, nor do I think you should have anything to do with him for the sake of your own peace of mind. He's where he isn't a danger to others now and we just have to hope he's being cared for.'

Flashes of the asylum she was in invaded Janey's mind, but she took a deep breath. All she could hope was that Jimmy was being treated better than that. But always she reminded herself that he put his hands on Angie's neck and squeezed the life from her. She didn't deserve that. And he'd never recognized that he was her dad. This, and what he did to Beth, and to herself, reassured her that he was where he should be.

She didn't know why, but she told her mum then about Henry asking her to write to him.

'That's lovely! You do that, luv. It will help you both as Henry's out there going through hell, I imagine, and he hooked on to you and your plight. I liked him and his letters'll give you something else to look forward to as well as your visits to Rose to see Beth.'

Cissy came over then. 'Eeh, we need to get busy to turn that shelter into a home. Me and Joe have had some ideas. Joe here was telling me he can turn his hand to owt, so he's going to make a ramp for your wheelchair and build some bunk beds, so it'll sleep four of us, and one on a shake-me-down on the floor in the middle. The young 'uns can get in with who they choose. I think we'd be right cosy if them Germans do come!'

'There will only be the four of us, Cissy.' Janey told Cissy of her plans.

'By, that's grand! It'll be good to see Rose, but, eeh, we'll miss Loes and the children. Have you told her yet?'

'No. I didn't know till just now when I spoke to Rose.'

Mum squeezed her hand. 'No time like the present, luv. Loes was getting ready to take the children to the park as we came out.'

'Oh, I'll see if I can catch her.' Turning to the workmen, she thanked them and them hurried into the house. Loes was in the hallway.

'Oh, I caught you, luv. I need a word.'

'I wouldn't have gone without telling you, Janey. But I thought to get the children ready first.'

'Ta, luv, and ta for having Beth this morning for me.' Bending down and hugging Karl and Beth, Janey said, 'I'll come with you. I need to talk to you.'

As they walked, each holding Beth's hand and Karl pushing the empty pushchair by the back of its seat, Janey had a pang of guilt at what she proposed. Loes and Karl had never met Rose.

'You say you won't be coming? But I will feel lonely and not know where I am.'

'You won't, luv, not with Rose. But, well, it's more than likely the Germans will bomb London at some point. It's been said on the radio and there's all these preparations. I just feel we have to keep the kids safe and not have them see and hear stuff that will terrify them . . . Look, I'll take a week off work and come and help you all to settle in, eh? Then if you hate it, we'll think of another way. But I know Olivia wanted Karl in the countryside out of danger, and I do Beth too. This seems the best way as you'll be with someone we all know and love and know will look out for you.'

\* \* \*

Three days later, Rose arrived. Janey and Annie had been busy cooking all day – not just a dinner for all of them, but cakes and buns for when they came back from church the next day.

Rose looked different, as if the light had gone out of her life. How changed things were for her from shouting out her wares in Covent Garden and being part of that community and a regular visitor to see them all, to living miles away and having to contend with what had happened.

Her hug settled Janey's mind. She hugged her back and both shed tears. 'It's good to see you, Rose.'

'And you, luv. Now, where's me Beth?'

Beth came running over to Rose saying, 'Gan-gan Rose.'

All smiled teary smiles.

Karl, not to be outdone, came up behind Beth. A much better speaker, he said, 'Hello, Granny Rose,' very clearly.

Rose dabbed at her eyes as she bent down and scooped them both into her arms.

'Well, me darlin's, that's a lovely welcome. And this is Granddad Alfie.'

Without a trace of shyness, both children went into the group hug with Alfie and Rose. Everyone dabbed at their eyes as Beth put up her finger to Rose's face and said, 'Gan-gan crying?'

'No, me little luv, not sad tears. These are happy tears because I love you and now I can cuddle you.'

The service gave a kind of closure to Janey. She cried buckets and her heart was heavy with more unshed tears, but she also felt uplifted and as if she'd let her little Angie go to heaven, and that gave her peace.

It surprised her too how jolly she felt when they arrived home. 'Mum, play the piano, eh? Let's give me Angie a proper cockney send-off.'

All hugged her and said how brave she was, but to Janey, it was as if Angie was letting her live her life again.

Annie came over to her. 'Are you sure, Janey?'

'I am. I've never been surer about anything. Me little Angie was a happy and contented soul during her little life and she wouldn't want her mum to be sad. Besides, it's better for Beth. I don't want her sad when we talk about Angie. I know she won't remember her, but she does know there was something in her life. I want that something to be special, not surrounded in misery.'

'Oh, Janey. You're so brave and I love you.'

'Ta, Annie. I love you too. You're the best sister anyone could have. And allowing Angie to rest in peace ain't the only thing I'm going to do. I'm going to see Mr Potter about divorcing Jimmy.'

There was a gasp from Rose and Janey wished she could take the words back. 'Oh, Rose, I'll never be divorced from the Jimmy we all knew. But I can't be married to the Jimmy we've been left with.'

'I understand, luv . . . Now, I agree, let's have some music and tuck into this lovely spread. I won't ask how yer got it all, but that soup looks delicious, and the bread and ham too.'

Annie laughed. 'Nothing underhand. We all pooled our rations for a week, and Cissy baked all the bread. We've only got margarine to put on it but tuck in, everyone.'

Two days later, Janey and Loes and the children stood on the platform saying goodbye to Annie and Joe, who himself was to leave for Aldershot the next day.

Rose and Alfie had set off the day before with their van full to the rafters with all that Loes and the children would need.

As she hugged Annie, Janey told her, 'I might stay the week, Annie, I'll see how it goes. I haven't had a chance to see you with you being on early shift, but I rang work this morning and they have said I can take as much of the week as I need as long as I'm back by next Monday.'

'That's good then, Janey. Now you can really see that Loes and the kids are settled.'

Loes turned from where she was talking to Joe. 'I keep telling Janey that we will be fine. I wasn't sure but after meeting Rose and Alfie, I know I will be all right. I loved them both and they say I will be like a daughter to them.'

'I know, luv, but I need to see where me Beth's going to be so I can picture her there. And I will come every couple of weeks or so. I can't bear to be away from her for longer than that.'

Once they arrived, it seemed to Janey that being in this part of Kent was like landing in heaven. All she could see for miles were green and cultured fields dotted with what Rose told her were hop dryers – dome-shaped buildings which filled the air with a lovely scent of warmed hops.

'All you can see is land that belongs to me, Janey. And one day, it'll be yours and Beth's. One day we'll talk about Beth's future. I want her to have a good chance in life and to that end, I've started a fund for her. For her schooling and such.'

'Ta, Rose.' Janey didn't know what else to say. It all overwhelmed her. She couldn't imagine owning something like this beautiful part of the world. For Rose, it was where she grew up, though it must hold painful memories for her.

The cottage was lovely. Just a few yards away from Rose's rambling farmhouse, its thatched roof and white painted exterior gave it a fairy-tale look.

Inside, it had a low, beamed ceiling and a huge brick fireplace, and was furnished with a comfy red sofa and a table and chairs. The shiny stone floor was covered by a huge rag rug of many colours. Out in the backyard a tin bath hung, and there was a lav. But besides these there were pot plants and an old settee, and in the corner, a sandpit for the children.

Both of them ran for it the moment they spotted it. Loes stopped them jumping in, telling them that she would get them out of their best clothes and into their playsuits first.

Janey could imagine them playing for hours with the jars and tin cans that lay in it, filling them up and using them to help to build whatever their imagination gave them.

Upstairs they found three bedrooms, all with tiny windows which were too high for the children to come to harm.

'It's so lovely, Loes. Do you like it?'

'I do. It reminds me of home, though there the hop dryers would be windmills.'

Loes let out a sigh. Janey took her hand. She couldn't imagine what it must be like for Loes. Leaving Holland, her home country, then knowing it had been invaded and not knowing what might have happened to her Jewish parents. And now finding herself in Britain away from the island she'd made her home in.

Loes looked at Janey and smiled. 'We know what it is to suffer and us so young too.'

'Have you ever been in love, Loes?'

Loes giggled. 'I tell you a secret. I have a look for Joe.'

'Oh, you mean you fancy him?'

'What is fancy?'

'You like him more than anyone else.'

'Yes, I do, and when you go back, you're to give him the address here, and when he has leave he will visit.'

290

Janey didn't know why but this made her feel very happy, as if everyone's life was slotting back into place, as she intended to write to Henry while she was here, and Annie had seemed to come to terms with not knowing where Ricky was.

She'd said it to herself many times, but now she thought it again: Annie was a wonderful person and if it wasn't for her, she knew she'd be living a very different life.

# Chapter Twenty-Three

## Annie

'Look, we need to give this our attention, everyone.'

'We're trying, Annie, but without music, and without Ted being here, it's difficult to keep everyone together.'

Annie looked around at her fellow officers. All had lovely voices, but their collective sound needed some attention. She was so out of her depth but with Ted having a heavy cold she'd done her best to keep the choir practice on schedule.

'I mean, we're great on the old London songs, we really put our hearts into them, but I thought we should try some of the songs Ted introduced for different tastes.'

'Will anyone come to listen to us, Annie?'

'I don't know, but you all agreed and wanted this choir, Betty.'

'And I love it. An afternoon, like today, or an evening with you all, singing our hearts out and then nipping over to the pub for a drink together, or up to Marg's for a cuppa and a laugh, but I think we should leave it at that.'

A few voices agreed with this, and Annie had to admit that would take the pressure off them all. 'All right, let's run it like that then. Last one up at Marg's buys the cakes!'

There was a rush for the door. Annie looked after them and sighed. *My treat then!*

She looked at the clock. Three thirty. She should be home by five with Lilly and the pie and mash she'd promised to pick up on the way, and then her weekend would start. Janey was due into the station at four and she couldn't wait to see her.

She, Mum and Cissy had planned a sing-song of their own with this being Saturday. *And I might run to a jug of ale too. They all like a glass of ale with their pie and mash.*

Giggling to herself, she called out her goodbyes to those still on duty and made her way to Marg's.

When she got there, the tea and cakes were all paid for, and everyone gave her a mocking cheer.

'To our choirmaster!'

'Ha, stop it, Peggy.'

'More like our knees-up officer!'

Betty laughed at her own joke and Annie joined her, thinking how strange it was that since Ricky went missing, her and Betty got on so well.

As she lifted her mug to say cheers, a whining noise began. Its volume increased till it drowned out everything anyone said.

The only words that got through were from the sergeant as he bellowed, 'Quick, to the Underground! And knock on doors as you go and tell anyone you see to get into a shelter. This could be for real with all the talk there's been.'

Outside a group of kids kicked a ball.

Putting on her best police voice, Annie shouted, 'You kids, get home. NOW!'

'Nah, it's always 'appening, miss. No need to worry.'

Grabbing the hand of one young man she knew, Annie shouted to the others to follow.

Not waiting to knock, she opened the door of the child's house and almost threw him in. 'Get to the shelters, and quick!'

Thank goodness everyone seemed to take note and the street was empty now.

Frantically praying that Cissy managed to get Mum into the shelter, and wishing that they still had Joe with them, Annie ran for all she was worth as a droning sound filled the air.

The first bomb split the atmosphere, leaving her deaf to all sound. Her body hit the ground. Debris fell around her – bricks and shards of glass – cutting her legs and arms. Fear gripped her chest. Turning her head, she cried out a strangled, 'No-o-o-o!'

The house where she'd shoved the little boy into was just a gaping hole.

Crawling along towards the Underground, it seemed hell was visiting earth as wave after wave of explosions ripped through the houses around her. Something hit her head and took her into oblivion.

When she awoke, she looked around her. The world came alive with cries of, 'Help me!' and voices calling, 'This one's a gonna. Get a porter!' and, 'We must stem the bleeding!'

For London, the war had started in earnest.

The next day, still feeling shaky, Annie was discharged with minor cuts and bruising. She made her way to the station through ruined streets and with the smell of burning buildings hanging in the air. It seemed to her when she looked in the direction of the docks that they were encased in flames.

Many families passed her, pushing prams with what possessions they'd managed to salvage. Where they were going, she just couldn't think.

When she opened the door of the station, Betty jumped up. 'Annie, oh, Annie, luv!'

Her arms were around Annie, tears running down her face. 'We thought we'd lost you, luv . . . Oh, Annie, I couldn't bear that.'

Annie clung on to her. 'Ta, Betty. How bad was it?'

'Bad. A lot of factories have been hit, and houses, and, well, I'm sorry, luv, but Bethnal Green took a pasting. Have you been home?'

'No, I was taken to hospital. I just got out and came for me car.'

The sergeant came out of his office then. 'Are you all right to drive, Annie?'

'I am, Sarge, and I have to get home. I doubt there'll be any buses and you know what I'm like on trains.'

'Yes, well, just go steady, and I hope you find everything all right at home. We'll see you Monday morning. I'm going to be working out strategies for us to cope with this lot.'

Annie thought it a bit late but didn't say so. The sarge did have a plan, she knew that, but he'd never really believed it would happen.

At home, having passed broken houses and driven through smoke-filled air, Annie was greeted with tears of fear mixed with relief.

'The three of us slept in the shelter, Annie. It wasn't bad, but we were all so worried about you . . . Oh, and the noise!'

'I know, Mum. I was caught in the thick of it.'

The little boy came to mind, but she didn't tell them about him. She couldn't bear to make it a truth by giving voice to it.

Cissy made them laugh and brought some cheer back to them as she said, 'Eeh, and you ain't even got our pie and mash!'

When the laughter died, Annie realized that this was what

would get them through, laughing in the face of whatever Hitler could throw at them. With this, the shock left her and she began to think like a police officer once more.

'I'll get some tonight and we'll have that sing-song, even if we have to have it in the shelter. But I just need a cuppa now and to get a wash. I'm going to put a clean uniform on and go back to work to see what I can do.'

'And I'm going to the clinic, Mum,' said Janey. 'They may need extra hands as I imagine many wounded turned up there, but we'll all be together tonight, don't worry.'

When they got outside, having both changed and with Annie feeling more like her old self, she asked Janey, 'Want a lift, luv?'

'Yes, please, Annie . . . Oh, Annie, I can't believe it really happened.'

'And I think it will again tonight. Hitler's trying to break us. But he won't. Look . . . look, Janey. The folk who must have lost their homes are walking to find shelter. And not one of them is crying. They're all smiling and calling out to one another. That's the spirit of the East End, and no one'll break that.'

Back at the station, the sergeant was briefing everyone. He acknowledged her with a nod of his head.

Annie looked around. Almost every officer was in attendance. Even those she knew would be on night duty that night.

'Right, listen up, everyone. What we dreaded has begun. We must be even more vigilant where blackouts are concerned. We must steer people caught out in the street to safety. We have to assist all other emergency services. And I want four of you in each car. This will mean that as many of you as possible will be able to quickly get to an area where you're needed and be ready to assist.'

'Sarge, can I make a suggestion?'

'What is it, Annie?'

'I reckon most raids – if there are any more – will be at night. So, I think we need most officers on then. I don't mind volunteering for permanent night shift. That way I think we'll get into a routine of how to best help.'

'Good idea. Anyone else willing to do the same?'

Everyone put their hand up.

'Right, I'll work out a different rota to normal whereby most officers are on during the night from around four o'clock until we get a pattern of what is likely to happen. Dismissed for now, and those who can start the new rota tonight, put your names down and turn up in around two hours from now.'

Annie made a detour on the way home, calling into the clinic to see Janey. She was directed to St John's church hall which was being used for an overspill.

The hall was bursting with the walking wounded, and in the thick of it applying dressings was Janey.

Annie stood waiting and watching. Pride filled her at the skill Janey showed and how kind and reassuring she was. At last she caught her eye.

'Can you take a few minutes, Janey?'

'Be with you in a mo, luv, and I've a message for you from HQ.'

'For me?'

Janey finished applying a sling to an elderly gentleman and then came over.

'Yes. I've been asking about Ricky, every time I went there or saw someone from the office, and oh, Annie, they have news!'

'What? . . Oh, my God! Really? . . . Have they found him?'

Janey nodded her head vigorously, while grinning wider than Annie had ever seen her.

'Where? Oh me darlin', is he . . . ?'

'All they would say was that he's alive! You have to go to see them with identification, and proof of you being married to him, then they will tell you the full story.'

Annie knew her mouth was open and her eyes were staring, while she could feel tears running down her face, but she couldn't do anything else. It was the shock, and the sheer joy, mixed with hope and also despair as unasked questions popped in and out of her head. *How is he? Is he wounded? Will he survive the horror of it?*

'Oh, Annie, luv, you should be overjoyed!'

'I am . . . I just can't take it in!'

'Well, tell me what you came for, then get home to collect your marriage certificate and go and find out, me darlin'.'

'Oh . . . I – I just came to tell you about my new working hours – I'll be on almost permanent night shift – and to ask you if you would pick the pie and mash up for everyone's supper?'

'That's not a problem, now go! And, Annie, I'm so pleased for you.'

'Ta, luv. See you in the morning. I'll leave all the information with Mum and Cissy. I'm going to have a busy couple of hours, though, as I'll have to call in on Lilly, bless her.'

Arriving at Lilly's an hour later, Annie almost fell into her arms.

'What is it, Annie? I expected you last night, luv. I'd have starved but for next door. We all went into their shelter and shared a pan of stew. But none of that matters. What happened to you is more to the point? You look like you took a battering.'

'I was hit by debris and ended up in hospital, but I'm all right now . . . Oh, Lilly, I have news.'

'Come and sit down and I'll put the kettle on. I've managed to get a bit of tea, but I've no sugar, luv.'

'I'm used to it without now, and Lilly, only put one spoon of tea leaves in – I've got used to it being weak too.'

Once they were sitting with their tea, Annie felt she would burst if Lilly didn't let her tell her, so instead of explaining anything, she just blurted out, 'They've found Ricky! He's alive, Lilly, he's a prisoner of war in –' Annie consulted the paper the Red Cross had written the name of the camp on and read out – '"Stalag XX1-D, Poznań, Poland". The Red Cross told me he is healthy and working on a farm . . . And, best of all . . . Oh, Lilly, they've received letters from the Polish Red Cross . . . They say they will sort them all out, as they are on scraps of paper. I will know tomorrow and will bring anything round to you.'

Lilly was sobbing. Annie held her, but in doing so, broke down too.

Stroking Lilly's hair, which had been a lovely brown when they met but had turned white since Ricky went missing, she told her, 'I love you, Lilly, and we'll get through this together, eh?'

'Ta, Annie. I'm sort of happy and yet sad, as I don't trust them Germans. They're cruel bleeders.'

'Don't even think of that, Lilly. Ricky will take care. He won't be a troublemaker and is most likely respected by the other prisoners. They'll all take care of one another. Just think that he's alive and will one day come back to us.'

'Please God, Annie. Only for us, this lot seems to be just starting.'

Annie looked around the small front room of this two-up, two-down terraced house. It showed the pride Ricky had in looking after Lilly, who he'd thought was his sister until his gran died.

The room was furnished with a highly polished table and chairs and two armchairs with wooden arms and green cushions, which sat each side of the fireplace. On the mantel shelf there was a picture of her beloved Ricky and one of his gran and Lilly. In the centre was hers and Ricky's wedding photo.

The green and red rug that lay in front of the fireplace held many memories for her as she and Ricky had made love there so often when Lilly had gone to bed. That was during the time when they couldn't wed, or she would have lost her job, which meant so much to her. Now, she couldn't think why she held out. She could have had a home like this with Ricky, and children too, but they'd always been careful not to get her pregnant. They married a couple of days before Ricky left to go to war.

Her longing must have shown on her face as Lilly said, 'Oh, luv, I know what you're going through.'

Annie knew she did as the young man Lilly was going to marry had gone off to the Great War, not knowing he'd left her pregnant. He never returned.

They hugged again.

'I wish you'd come and live here with me, Annie. I get lonely, and now I'm scared to death. Last night was terrible.'

'I know, luv, and I would, but so many need me at home. And in any case, things are changing at work.' She told Lilly of the new arrangement. 'But I'll try to call in every morning and check you're all right. And I'll bring you some tea – we can get more than we need as we have so many living in the one house.'

'Ta, luv. Yer know what a tea belly I am and me two ounces don't last a week.'

'Well, I'll get off. I need to see Mum and Cissy before I leave again for work. Make sure you get into the shelter if the sirens go, Lilly. See you tomorrow. And hang on to the good news that Ricky's alive!'

Annie could have skipped along the pavement to get to her car, if it had been clear, but still so much debris lay around making it so she had to pick her way along. It was shocking to see the damage done and she wondered about the families.

A voice called to her, 'Oi, can yer come over 'ere, Officer? You'll know first aid, won't yer?'

Annie ran over to a house where rescuers were trying to shift the rubble.

'Did it take a direct hit? Is anyone trapped?'

'No, the bomb fell in the garden, and as you can see it's mainly broken windows. We're only just getting around these to check them, and we found this young pregnant woman. We think she's in labour.'

'Right, run round to the church hall and ask for Janey. She's me sister and a nurse, she'll sort her.'

'Well, we could carry the young lady to her if that's where she is.'

With this, they loaded the young woman onto a fallen door.

Annie took hold of her hand. 'Breathe deeply, darlin', it helps. I've been at a couple of deliveries and seen it work . . .

Good luck. And don't forget to ask for Janey and tell her Annie sent yer.'

With this, the rescuers carried her off.

The excitement that met her news about Ricky cheered Annie. She'd not stopped feeling full of joy, but Lilly's reaction and how frail she seemed to be had dampened the feeling a little.

'Eeh, that's grand news! And knowing Ricky, he'll get out of there afore they even knaw he's gone.'

'Oh, Cissy, I hope he doesn't try. That could be so dangerous for him.'

As Annie set off back to the station, she was amazed by the resilience of her fellow East Enders.

The fires still raging along the docks sent billows of smoke everywhere, but this was Sunday, and Sunday meant Sunday roast. All along her route women had small bonfires going and were cooking dinner. She saw more than one youngster scavenging among the rubble of those houses that had been destroyed and coming out with pots and pans, and even one with a salt cellar, which he waved high in triumph.

At the station, the sarge gave them the news that a squadron of German bombers had been turned back over the Channel by the efforts of the RAF.

'You mean, they were going to bomb us during the day?'

'Yes, it looks that way. But they will be back under cover of darkness, no doubt, so let's be ready. I've noticed a few of you going out without your gas masks. I don't want to see that again. We need to set an example.'

Annie blushed as she'd been guilty of leaving the cumbersome thing behind, but now she dutifully put it over her shoulder as she announced, 'I've news of me own everyone . . . Ricky's been found!'

A massive cheer went up, then questions ten to the dozen.

When all knew what she knew, the sarge packed them off to start their beat.

Betty was teamed with Annie. A couple of weeks ago, Annie would have hated this, but with them being on a better footing she was happy to link arms with Betty on the way to the pound where the police cars were kept.

'I'll drive, Betty. Only, I need to check on a friend. It's on our beat. It's Aggie, the flower lady who stands on the wharf near to Tower Bridge.'

'Ah, yes, I know Aggie. I think we all do. A lovely lady.'

As they neared the Thames, the air hung thick with smoke and the smell of sulphur. Aggie was nowhere in sight.

Worried, Annie decided to head towards Mile End Road hoping to find Aggie at home.

When she reached the house that Aggie had told her was made into flats, and in which she had a couple of rooms, Annie knocked on the door, relieved to see there hadn't been much damage around the area.

A young woman answered.

To Annie's enquiry, she shook her head. 'She went out to the shops just before the bombing happened and ain't returned, luv. We're all worried about her, as though she don't do much more than moan about us, we do care about her.'

'Ta, I'll go along there and see if I can find out what happened.'

A shock awaited Annie when she reached the shops as here was a different story. There was destruction and debris and even one building still on fire. Annie's heart fell as she saw the small newsagent's shop that also sold a few groceries was completely destroyed. Firefighters were working on shifting the debris.

Enquiries gave no information on Aggie. But one man told her that if she was in the newsagent's at the time it was hit, then there wasn't much chance for her. Rescuers had already pulled the shopkeeper's body out and were working on finding anyone else.

At that moment, one of the rescuers called out, 'I've got another one – at least, an arm!'

Climbing over the rubble, Annie and Betty joined in the desperate shifting of bricks and broken window frames. At last, the rest of the body was uncovered.

'Oh, Aggie, Aggie!'

'Do you know her, luv?'

Annie nodded. 'It's Aggie Brown. The flower seller.'

'Ah, yes, I know. Well, we have a van on standby collecting the bodies. Will you inform any relatives?'

'She hasn't any as far as we know. But I'll let her landlady know.'

It didn't seem right talking in this businesslike way when all Annie wanted to do was cry. The thought came to her, *Just how big a supply of tears do I have? I seem to do nothing but shed them lately.*

Betty's hand came into hers. 'We can't do any more here, luv. Let's get back to our patch and have a cuppa in Marg's, eh? I think we've earned it.'

They didn't make it to Marg's cafe. All hell let loose as the sirens sounded. People scattered, running in panic towards the Underground, or into shelters.

Annie felt fear gnawing in the pit of her stomach. She didn't give into it, but helped others as she saw Betty was doing.

With the street cleared of panic, only the van carrying bodies remained. Annie watched as the men loaded Aggie onto it.

'Goodbye, lovely lady. Rest in peace.'

'Amen to that. We've lost a good person there. It'll never be the same now as we'll never be able to take her a mug of tea again.'

Annie didn't have a chance to reply as the same droning they'd heard yesterday filled the air around them. Looking across in the direction of the Thames, Annie saw row after row of aeroplanes in formation.

The crashing of explosions began at that moment and her fear left her. She would do her duty in the face of it. And if one of the bombs had her name on it, it would be known that she didn't leave her post.

'Well, we can do no more,' Betty shouted above the din. 'Time to get into the Underground and then we can resume our work once it's over, Annie.'

It didn't end till morning and left even worse destruction in its wake. To Annie, it was as if their lovely city was bleeding as water from burst pipes ran down its streets – pink as it mixed with the blood of their people.

# Chapter Twenty-Four

## Olivia

Olivia waited anxiously for a response to her attempts to contact London. News had filtered through to the islanders that the bombing of the mainland had begun. But that was five days ago.

Desperate for news, and not having heard from London, or Hendrick, Olivia made the decision that she would tune into the BBC.

The Germans hardly ever came along this stretch of coastal road during the day, though she had seen what seemed to be architects measuring and pointing before scribbling on pads.

When she got into her office, she looked through the window that faced the sea. All was clear and she'd told Daphne that she didn't want to be disturbed.

Luckily they had swallowed the story that she was busy translating books from German so that they would be an aid to her teaching Stefan.

Only, it wasn't just Stefan. Over time, others had begun to join him, until now she had six soldiers who all wanted to learn English.

Three of them had asked to also join the choir, but so far,

she'd made the excuse that what had happened had upset them all too much for practice to continue. Gunter was being very patient about it, but she didn't know for how long.

Muffling the sound of the wireless by placing cushions either side of it, Olivia hardly dared turn the volume above an almost whisper. If she was caught, she would be sent to a German camp. A fate she didn't think even being Hendrick's wife could save her from, such was the strictness of the order banning them from listening to the wireless.

What she heard struck horror into her. London was under constant bombardment and had suffered many losses to life and damage to its buildings and infrastructure.

Switching the set off, Olivia stared at it. What if Annie hadn't got Karl and Beth to the countryside? *Oh, my God!*

Hiding the set under a floorboard she'd loosened for the purpose of storing it, her eyes fell on her transmitter, deciding she could no longer wait for news from London, even though they'd forbidden her to use it to contact anyone.

Pulling out the case containing the transmitter, Olivia set it up ready and began to Morse code her question.

'Are my son, Annie and her family safe?'

Nothing.

She tried again. But nothing.

Had she lost her connection to London? What was happening? No Hendrick and no London. The world seemed to suddenly be an empty void that she filled with worrying.

Daphne called up the stairs, and Olivia froze for a second.

'We have visitors. A German officer. He wants to speak to you, Olivia. Shall I bring him up, or will you come down?'

Jumping up made her chair scrape on the wooden floor. She put out her hand to steady it, then gathered her wits.

'I'm coming down.'

Faster than she'd ever done, Olivia packed away the transmitter, returned it under the boards and replaced the carpet, before unhurriedly walking out of her study and down the two sets of stairs. Making an extreme effort, she calmly greeted who she'd guessed was an architect and offered him a coffee.

'No, thank you. I am Offizier Hans Schmidt. I have been informed that you speak excellent German, Frau Kraus.'

'Thank you. I studied languages for years, as did my husband.'

'Ah, yes, you were to start a language school, I believe? Well, from what I hear you are not letting that talent go to waste. But I fear you will have many problems as English is a very difficult language to learn.'

'Not for your countrymen as it is a west Germanic language that we speak. There are many words that are very similar.'

'Yes, that is interesting. But I cannot tarry to discuss it. I am here with an order.'

Olivia tensed.

'We need this house – well, not need it, but need to demolish it.'

'What?' She knew her eyes had opened wide, and her mouth hung open in surprise.

'Yes. There will eventually be a wall around the whole of the island. Guernsey will be impregnable. Your house stands in the way of that. And though it will be some time before this work commences, we are preparing for it and marking out the land we need. Have you somewhere you can live?'

'No! . . . I mean, this is our only home. We handed over our family home to your Kommandant when you first arrived.'

'I believe you own the building of your investment bank?'

'Yes, that's true, but it isn't suitable.'

'You will make it so. Your husband, Officer Kraus, has been consulted and it is his suggestion that you move into the bank.'

Olivia couldn't believe what she was hearing. Hendrick would never do such a thing without consulting her! *Oh, why hasn't he rung?* She'd been made to look a fool the last time she'd been to the German headquarters to receive his call, leaving with her tail between her legs as the telephone hadn't rung for her.

She wanted to scream that she wasn't going to do it, that they weren't going to knock her beloved farmhouse down, that it held all her hopes and dreams, but she remained dignified.

'When is this to happen?'

'As soon as possible. We want to know that when we are ready, we have all the land cleared that we will need.'

Knowing she had no choice, and swallowing the lump in her throat, Olivia lifted her head. 'Very well, but there will be extensive work needed on the bank. I will require at the very least two months.'

'You have four weeks. Good day, Frau Kraus . . . Oh, by the way, you are to resume choir practice immediately. Our Kommandant has a birthday coming up and has been promised a recital. And it has come to our notice that you are something of a musician and ran music lessons here on the island before we arrived. I want this to resume too as we want a full concert for our Kommandant!'

He clipped his boots, bowed slightly, and left.

Footsteps on the stairs told her that her father was coming down.

'My God, Olivia, I heard that! And Hendrick agreed! What is going on? Why has Hendrick stopped contacting you?'

Not answering but taking all her courage in her hands,

309

Olivia opened the door and hurried out, calling, 'Offizier Schmidt, wait a moment, please.'

'Madam, is there something you wish to discuss? As my order is not up for discussion.'

'Yes, there is, and it isn't your order. You say you have spoken to my husband. I want to know if you know why he hasn't rung me when we have an arrangement with your Kommandant?'

'I am not party to such information, madam, but I do know that there is intense work going on at the moment and our Führer needs all of his staff on hand every moment of the day, especially his interpreters. I myself had difficulty in talking to your husband, but wanted to as a common courtesy before I tackled you.'

'So, he is well?'

'Yes, very well. Please be patient, Frau Kraus.'

Going back inside, Olivia was met with a barrage of questions.

'I just don't know. All I know is that we have four weeks to get part of the bank ready for us all to use as a home. And . . . and another piece of my dream has gone . . .'

'Oh, Olivia, my dear.'

Father's arm came around her but didn't give her comfort. She glanced over at Daphne and Jean. 'I'm sorry, so sorry. I know you're very happy here.'

Jean answered, 'We'll be happy anywhere with you, Olivia, and you, William.'

It sounded strange to hear Jean call her father by his Christian name and Olivia wondered when that had begun but she didn't question it.

Daphne echoed Jean. 'But you have your work cut out, Olivia. You've to get the music lessons and the choir up and running, besides teaching more and more Germans to speak

English . . . and, well, I don't want to be in the choir now . . . not after . . . Oh, I'm sorry.' Daphne ran out of the hallway towards the kitchen.

'I'll see to her, Olivia. I don't know if you noticed but she had a crush on poor Leonard.'

'Oh, no . . . well, yes, I had noticed they got on well. But I do know how you all feel. I feel the same. Poor Mrs Green, and Leonard, losing their lives in that way. And it was horrific to watch.' Without thinking, she blurted out, 'I hate the bloody Germans! . . . I mean, well, not Hendrick.'

'They're all the same if you ask me. I mean, I don't wish to be rude, but can we be sure that Hendrick holds the same ideals as when he left?'

Father intervened. 'Jean, I am shocked you have such thoughts, but as you do, kindly keep them to yourself in this household.'

He turned and began to climb the stairs. Jean stared after him, her bottom lip quivering.

'I'm so sorry, Olivia. I don't know where that came from. I honestly haven't felt badly about Hendrick until just then when we were talking about Leonard and Mrs Green. That was horrendous and has unnerved me. And with that Schmidt bloke being how he was with you. And . . . well, he said that Hendrick had approved!'

'I understand. I had a moment myself too. But I know Hendrick, he was probably in such a position that he felt forced to agree and in desperation came up with a solution for us, that's all. I am sure he will explain all when he contacts.'

Thinking she'd said enough, Olivia changed the subject. 'I think we could all do with a hot drink. Coffee for me, please, as it will steady my nerves.'

\* \* \*

Olivia spent the evening drawing up plans for the bank and though her heart was breaking and she found it unbearable that her home was to be flattened, she managed to find some enthusiasm for the task. It was a pleasant surprise to discover that they would have a lot of room and end up with a very nice and spacious apartment.

There was even room for her to have a music room on the first floor as all business was in the process of winding up, and at the very top of the building, she intended to have her own hideaway and store her wireless and transmitter.

Thinking of that, she decided as it was almost four in the afternoon she would have one more try to reach London.

Draining her cup, she told her father, 'Daddy, I'm going to take this upstairs. It will be easier to lay it out.'

When she turned on the transmitter, Olivia was shocked to find someone was trying to get through. Then even further shocked to realize it was Hendrick!

She acknowledged him and then wrote down his Morse code message.

'Have moved to Bad Münstereifel bunker. Have Father's transmitter as now in range. Will use from now on for code. Feeling insecure. Will telephone general chat only. I love you. And am sorry. Had no choice.'

Through her tears, Olivia tapped out, 'Understood. Love you too. Stay strong. Everyone all right here.'

Not expecting anything further, Hendrick surprised her by continuing. She'd thought they had used the set for long enough now.

'Worried about Karl and everyone in London.'

'Me too, but sure Annie would have got them safe. Will find out.'

There was no more. But that was enough to increase

Olivia's worry. What was going on? Why did Hendrick feel insecure and need to communicate this way? Once more she felt gripped by fear.

Switching the frequency, she took her mind off this by trying again to contact London.

At last a 'Go ahead'.

'No code, just worried about son and Annie and family.'

'Agent reported son in country. All others well.'

Communication was cut. But it didn't matter as the tension had left her, and as it did, Olivia wanted to laugh and cry all at once. Karl was safe. Annie and her family were safe!

By the time the four weeks were up Olivia had come to terms with all that was happening. She'd been so busy and that had helped.

The apartment was lovely, bright and airy, and all their furniture fitted in well. The choir was up to full strength. With so many feeling lost and afraid, and needing to be part of something that brought their community together, the auditions were very oversubscribed. But in the end, the balance was almost the same, with a male baritone added.

Stefan was proving to be an excellent pupil, and a kind man who Olivia liked very much and didn't feel a bit wary of. He was a gentleman as she had to admit the majority of the invaders were.

And now, she knew they had all got it wrong and it wasn't poor Leonard that Daphne had a crush on, but Stefan. And he was drawn to her too, though the situation was worrying, as girls taking up with the Germans were ostracized by many.

It had been easy, too, to get her musicians back on track. Even those in the early stages had improved as they'd carried on practising even though the classes had ceased.

For herself, Olivia could sense that she had their respect back and found that now, it was rare to hear insults levelled against her.

As Olivia sat in her office, working on the scores for the coming concert in three weeks, she reflected that for her, life had settled into a manageable pattern. And though her heart ached for her own little family to be reunited, she found that she could cope.

# Chapter Twenty-Five

## Janey

Janey ran upstairs with her post. One bundle she knew was from Henry, the brown envelope she hoped contained her final divorce papers, and thirdly, there was one in Loes's handwriting that would have news of Beth.

She hadn't got long, as since the colder weather had hit and with the Blitz, as it was now called, still relentless, her work schedule was more chaotic with her volunteering to help run the soup kitchen three evenings a week.

Christmas was nearly on them, but what it would be like, or if they would all still be alive, she didn't know.

Funny, but like so many, she'd got used to the nightly and sometimes daily bombing. Now, they never attempted to sleep in their beds, but bedded down in the shelter and, like everyone, they just got on with life the best they could.

Sitting on her sofa, she tore open Beth's letter, and then allowed her tears to fall as she gazed at the lovely drawing – well, it was lovely to her, though just scribbles to anyone else.

Promising herself she would go to Rose for Christmas and be with Beth, Janey put the picture on the mantel shelf and opened the brown envelope.

*Dear Mrs Blaine,*

*Your application to annul your marriage to Mr James Blaine has been looked upon favourably by the magistrates.*

*This is the first step. The finalizing of the procedure will take approximately six months. This is viewed as a 'cooling off period', then if circumstances remain and the marriage has irretrievably broken down, a decree nisi is granted.*

*I will keep you informed every step of the way.*

*Sincerely, Mr Potter. LLB SC*

What the letters after Mr Potter's name stood for Janey didn't know, she only knew that she had every faith in him and blessed the day she'd met him. He seemed able to sort out all of her problems, when to her they felt insurmountable at times. And he understood her financial position and allowed her to settle his bills by making small weekly payments, which really helped.

For a moment, she hesitated before opening Henry's bundle, almost as if she wasn't truly ready. And yet, just to hold them thrilled her.

It was difficult for her to understand the feelings they evoked. She'd thought she would never love again but knew in her heart of hearts that was what was happening to her. But this wasn't the same all-or-nothing feeling that she'd had for Jimmy, which had made her give in to him as soon as he showed interest, but one that came from Henry's kindness to her, and something else she couldn't put her finger on.

Reading the letters was almost like reading a diary that only she had permission to read. As each one was dated, she could see they'd been written within a couple of weeks and told of general things happening in his life – what they had to eat, how they played football in quieter moments, which really wasn't his game, but he joined in with them and, to his amazement, had scored a goal!

*And so, I'm a hero now, and thought of as a good player, when really, all I do is run after the chap who's got the ball and try to get it off him! It just happened that on one occasion when I did, I found myself facing the net with nothing in my path, so I closed my eyes and kicked the blasted ball as hard as I could. Then all hell let loose as it seemed as though the whole team jumped on me!*

Janey laughed. It was as if she was allowed into Henry's secrets. And not just how he complied with what the others wanted to do, but how he missed things, like books to read and having a good shave.

*It's a small comfort, but out here it is so hot that as soon as I get any stubble it feels itchy and uncomfortable. Please get the Red Cross to send more razor blades if they can. Mine, and most of the chaps', are Gillette razors.*

Somehow, to Janey, snippets like this were intimate – the kind of thing you would talk to a girlfriend about. But was that what she was, or just a pen-pal? She read on.

*Oh, and tell them that though it is hot in the day, the nights can be cold, so nice thick socks are still welcome.*

In later letters, this intimacy became stronger.

*My dear Janey, I know we only met for such a short time and during it, you were very distressed, but I haven't been able to get you out of my mind. Please write more about yourself and how you're feeling. Though it is nice to hear you are loving your job and you have managed to get the children to safety, as it is to hear all about your family. I've had no news about my mother, or anyone on Guernsey. It seems they are cut off from the world and I can only imagine what life is like for them.*

Janey clutched the letter to her breast. Henry cared about her.

Tying the bundle of letters up, she quickly changed out of her nurse's uniform and into some warm clothing, before going downstairs to the delicious smell of dinner cooking. *I wonder what genius dish Cissy has conjured up this time.*

'What delight do we have tonight, Cissy, luv? . . . Oh, Lilly! How lovely to see you . . . Are you all right?'

Lilly shook her head. 'It's all getting me down, Janey, girl. The 'ouse two doors away copped it last night and they hadn't come to the shelter. They're all gone!'

Janey went over to where she was sitting on Mum's sofa. Mum sat next to her in her wheelchair holding her hand.

'I've asked Lilly to stay with us tonight, luv. There's room in the shelter with Annie working nights.'

'Yes, of course, you'll be all right with us, Lilly. We have a good time, playing cards or dominoes, or just reading if I can get hold of some magazines. And we've flasks that we fill with hot cocoa, and even biscuits that Cissy somehow manages to make. Mind, you have to get to sleep before Mum starts to snore!'

'Ha! Cheeky! I don't snore.'

Both Janey and Cissy raised their eyebrows and then giggled.

Lilly's face lit up. 'Ta, luv. I can't say how that's made me feel better.'

'You can come every night – you can even move in if you like. We've a whole apartment empty downstairs.'

'Ta, that's good of you, but I don't want to leave all me stuff behind. But to come to the shelter every night would be something I'd like if that's all right.'

''Course it is, and me offer stands, but not for long, Lilly, as there's so many homeless I'm thinking of turning it into temporary accommodation for those who are desperate. Some folk are sleeping in pubs, and school halls, churches – just anywhere – but they've no family life and have lost everything.'

'You do that, Janey. That's a better use of it than me leaving me 'ouse empty, but would there still be room in the shelter for me?'

'Yes. I'll buy another shelter. I often see the blokes who fitted ours and they say they're still fitting them, and we've plenty of room for another.'

'Eeh, lass, you've a kind heart. Now, come and help me dish the meal out. Is Annie up yet?'

'I don't know, Cissy, I didn't hear her. She sleeps like a log that one, but oh, I do miss having her with us at night. I long for her nights off.'

'We all do, luv, and not least because of the danger she's in out there during the raids.'

'I know, Mum. But like she says, there's no good worrying,

someone's got to do it . . . Ah, I can hear her on the stairs. She must have smelled your hash, Cissy.'

Annie came through the door, bleary-eyed and dishevelled. 'What time is it? I smelled dinner and got a shock. Am I late?'

'Ha, we knew the thought of food would get you up, luv. You're all right, it's just on six.'

Annie rubbed her eyes before greeting them all.

'We've someone to take your place in the shelter, Annie. Lilly's going to come every night.'

Annie kissed and hugged Lilly. 'Oh, I am glad. I've been worried about you, luv.'

Dinner was a lively affair with them all laughing over Henry being a reluctant champion footballer.

But their laughter was cut short as the sirens resounded around them.

Annie took charge. 'Oh bugger, they're early tonight! Grab your dinners, you three, and get into the shelter. You can finish it in there. Me and Janey'll make the cocoa, and I can grab me uniform and get changed. If we hurry, we'll have time.'

As she and Annie worked, Janey told her about her idea for the basement apartment and how Lilly had refused the offer of it.

'Good idea, I could fill it ten times over every night . . . Oh, Janey, when will it stop?'

'Someone should tell them that they won't win! Our RAF boys'll have them beaten in time.'

'I don't even feel afraid any more, do you?'

'No. Just determined, like most folk, though I can under-stand Lilly, being on her own.'

'I've called in a lot, and she seemed all right, but then, when it hits on your own street it unnerves you.'

'I was thinking about Christmas earlier and how we're usually all together, and I wondered if we could take Lilly?'

'Oh, Janey, that'd be wonderful. Ring Rose and see how many of us she can put up, and I'll ask for a week's leave. I could take us in the car, as three can easily sit on the bench seat at the front and we could tie Mum's wheelchair to the roof.'

'Ooh, Annie, it seems a possibility now, as the trains are hit and miss with a lot of the lines closed.'

'Right, let's work towards that. Now, hurry with the cocoa. I might see you later. Where are you delivering soup to tonight?'

'I'm assigned to Mile End Underground, and I'd better make me way there the minute I've finished me dinner. Though I hate being out during a raid, it sometimes feels safer than being under the lawn!'

'I know. You can at least see the Luftwaffe and what they're up to and take action. Not being able to see has you tensing every time you hear them swooping. And another thing, you don't know if it's one of ours or theirs when you can't see.'

Singing even though she couldn't hear herself and London looked like a giant bonfire with bombs exploding around her, Janey's happiness at what Henry had said in his letter and at the thought of seeing Beth for Christmas couldn't be diminished. *At least they're lighting me way!* She giggled and then wobbled as a nearby explosion caused a whoosh of wind.

Deafened by the noise and bending down against flying debris, it felt to her that she was in another world, where all went on around her but she wasn't part of it and she thanked God that she had arrived within five minutes of leaving home.

Dumping her bike out of the way of anyone, she ran inside and down the steps. The huddle of dozens of people cheered her.

'We're all right now, food'll soon be on its way!' one shouted.

'Give me a chance, luv. I've to get the stove lit!'

Another Red Cross worker arrived and two WVS women, who carried the huge can of soup.

'I've got the bread, Mabel . . . Oh, 'ello, Janey. All right, girl?' This was shouted from Hattie, a WVS who was a marvel and could produce enough bread for an army every single night. Janey thought she must be kneading, proving the dough, or baking it twenty-four hours a day!

'Yes, all's on the go, Mabel, and we've a hoard of hungry bellies to fill!'

'Let's make them sing for their supper, eh?' Mabel turned as she said this and hollered, 'Cam on then, let's 'ear yer. *My old man said follow the van and . . .*'

All joined in and to Janey, it was as if every spirit lifted as they sang. She thought of Annie and her choir and how she said it really cheered them up, though now they were mostly working the night shift, they didn't meet often.

Janey loved to sing and belted out the words as she waited to serve up the soup.

> *'We had to move away*
> *'cause the rent*
> *we couldn't pay*
> *the moving van came round*
> *just after dark*
> *My old man said follow the van*
> *And don't dilly-dally on the way . . .'*

322

The atmosphere after the first verse was more like a carnival than an air-raid shelter, which should terrify them all but hardly ruffled a feather.

For Janey, the words to the song conjured up worrying times when Annie worked for Olivia's aunt as a live-in maid down in Cornwall, and she and Mum lived in their two-up, two-down that was falling down around them, not far from where they lived now. And how she would eke out what Annie brought home on her yearly visit, but often not be able to pay the rent. She could see her and Mum now, Mum lying on the sofa and her crouching down under the window willing the rent man to think they were out.

Jimmy changed all of that.

A sad feeling clogged her heart. But she brushed it away and sang all the louder. There was a time and place for grieving, and this wasn't it.

Annie came down around one a.m.

'What's it like, luv?'

Annie raised her brows. 'Carnage as usual, but we're getting through it.' A tear appeared in the corner of her eye. Annie brushed it away.

'That bad?'

'Oh, Janey. I've just been trying to comfort an old man who took his dog out for a walk as things had calmed. Then the second wave came and flattened his house and killed his wife. He was devastated. He said he could never get her to go into a shelter. She'd always say, "If it's me time, it's me time." Poor darlin' was sobbing, and asking, "Why couldn't they take us both together? What am I going to do without me Ivy?"'

'Oh, Annie. I'm sorry. Is Betty coming down?'

'Yes. She just had to speak to a young lad walking the street, she'll probably bring him down. But I need a hug.'

Janey took Annie into her arms. Her thoughts were of how often she'd had to be strong for her sister when it had always been the other way around. But she loved being there for her and knew that being needed was helping her to cope.

When Betty came down with the young lad who she said was called Ian, his blackened face was streaked with where tears had run down his cheeks.

'He thinks he's lost his family. He went out to the lav and an incendiary streaked through his house, setting it on fire.'

'I couldn't get near to it, the flames were that hot. There – there was no one around to 'elp me.'

Mildred reacted how she always did. 'Let's get you a hot drink, eh? I've already got the kettle on for the coppers, mate.'

'Ta, Mildred. This is me sister Annie, and her mate Betty.'

'Pleased to meet yer. Yer should come and see us more often, luv.'

'I ain't always in the area where you are, Mildred, but pleased to meet you too. You look like you've a full house tonight.'

'Yes, it's calming down now as a lot are asleep, and some have gone. Poor sods, now's the time yer start to wonder if yer 'ouse is still standing.'

'It's bad out there. They seem to be targeting the houses more now, when before it was the docks and the factories.'

'I wish they'd bugger off! They won't break us, so they'd be best to give up now!'

'That's the spirit, Mildred. Now, is that kettle boiling?'

'Coming up, Annie.'

As Ian sat down and sipped his tea, Janey asked, 'Should I take him home with me, Annie?'

'That's a good idea. He ain't injured as far as we can make

324

out. But if he's safe, me and Betty can make enquiries about his family. Some of them might have survived, there's many a miracle happens. But in any case, he says he has a gran. Why some people don't go to the shelters, I don't know, but Ian said his mum always got him and his two brothers under the table. He never mentioned a dad.'

As Janey pushed her bike and walked with Ian, she told him her name and then gently quizzed him. Once she got him talking, he didn't stop.

She found out that he was ten years old – the eldest of the three.

'But we've all got different dads. Me dad were killed in an accident, then Mum was hurt by a bloke who disappeared. Not long after, she had our Jerry, he's seven. She . . . well, after that she went with men to get money . . . but she ain't a prozzie, not a proper one. It were only to pay the rent and get us some food. But our Charlie were born last year, and since then she just gets parish relief and whatever I can earn doing errands and helping around the market . . . They ain't dead, are they?'

Taken aback by his bluntness, Janey hesitated. 'We don't know yet, luv . . . Look, don't worry, Ian. If the worst has happened, you can live with us, we'll care for you and help you, luv.' Swallowing a lump in her throat, Janey stopped and looked down at him – a little East Ender, doing his best in a rotten world. She wanted to make everything right for him, but she couldn't. 'Look, me little mate, when we get home me and you will say a prayer, eh?'

She heard a snivel. 'I don't want them to be dead, Janey.'

'I know, luv. Do yer want a hug?'

'Yes.'

Putting her bike down on the pavement, she took Ian's thin body into her arms and held him while he sobbed. After a while, she said, 'Let's get you home, eh?'

'Is me home going to be with you then, Janey?'

'It can be for as long as you like, and if any of your family have made it, we'll bring them to us too.'

Janey didn't hold out much hope of that happening from what Ian had said, but she prayed it would be so.

Ian went to bed without protest, after having a good wash and a mug of cocoa with some of Cissy's biscuits.

Janey had given him a pair of her pyjamas. He didn't seem to mind as they were blue, and he even managed a smile as she rolled the bottoms and the sleeves up.

She put him into the small bedroom that had been used by Annie at one time. But she hadn't been in bed long herself before he came in and she felt him get into her bed and snuggle up to her. As he did this, Janey felt a surge of love for him and cradled him in her arms.

Mum, Cissy and Lilly had come inside for breakfast by the time Janey came down.

She was glad Ian hadn't been disturbed by her rising as she was able to tell them about him and what had happened.

They all stopped eating their toast with dripping when Annie came in and all looked expectantly at her, but she shook her head and mouthed, 'Where is he?'

'He was curled up in me bed fast asleep when I came down . . . So, his family didn't survive?'

'No. The house is burned to the ground. Has he told you anything, Janey?'

Janey told what she knew.

'Well, we'll have to find this granny. I'll telephone in as soon as he wakes and tells us where she lives.'

Janey looked down at her hands. She almost didn't want Ian's granny to be found as she had the thought that she wanted to keep him with her for ever. But then she thought, he'd suffered enough loss, it would be awful if they didn't find his granny as she was probably the only relative he had in the world.

# Chapter Twenty-Six

## Annie

When Ian surfaced, Annie dreaded telling him the sad and devastating news. He stood next to Janey, who sat on Mum's sofa, and held on to her hand the whole time. When she finished, he put his head on Janey's shoulder and his arms around her neck and sobbed.

Janey clung on to him and manoeuvred him so that he sat on her knee.

He was small for his age, which made it easier for Janey.

To Annie, it was a pitiful sight and one she couldn't offer any comfort for, other than to say, 'We need to find your granny, Ian, and then we can bring her here to you and let her decide what she wants to do.'

'She fell out with me mum. But I still went to see her. Me mum didn't know.'

From what Janey had said his mum did for money, Annie thought it was probably the cause of the fallout.

'And she's only granny to me as she were me dad's mum.'

'Oh, did you know any of your brothers' grannies?'

'No, Mum never knew them and me Granny Marion died last year.'

'Was that your mum's mum?'

'Yes. She was good to us. When she died . . . that's when me mum . . .'

'I see. Now, what's your granny's name?'

'Granny Mansell. I'm Ian Mansell.'

'And where does Granny Mansell live?'

'I don't know the name of the road as I ain't good at reading, but I used to come out of me 'ouse and walk to the shop at the end, then turn left and then turn right. She was in that street, four doors along.'

'That's all right, we'll find her easily from that. I'll go and phone the station. You get some breakfast.'

Ian turned back into Janey.

As Annie went out into the hall, she heard Janey say, 'It's all right, you cry as much as you want. It's better to cry than to bottle it up.'

Annie couldn't help the wry smile that crossed her lips. How often she'd told Janey that, and how finally it had helped her to cry all of her pain out.

When Annie went back into Mum's living room, feeling tired to the bones of her, Janey was humming to a sleeping Ian.

Mum wasn't anywhere to be seen, so Annie guessed she'd wheeled herself into her bathroom. She often washed and dressed herself in the mornings and it was night-time that she mostly needed help.

Cissy motioned for Annie to follow her.

Going into Cissy's neat flat, which always seemed so bright and airy with its double doors leading to the garden, Annie sunk into one of the comfy chairs that stood each side of her fireplace. 'Brr, it's cold in here, Cissy.'

'I've me fire all laid. I usually pop in and light it before going to breakfast, but I didn't get the chance today.'

As she spoke she knelt and lit the kindling and the fire jumped into life, giving immediate warmth.

'I need to talk to you about Vera, lass.'

'Mum? Why, is there something wrong?'

'Eeh, there is, Annie. She ain't said nowt, but she's struggling. You see, she can't crouch over the bucket, and most nights, she won't have her drink as she's afraid of needing to go in the night. I don't think she can use the shelter much longer, and I was wondering what we could do . . . And, to tell the truth, I find it hard, but eeh, when you get older, you want to pee more often and rarely sleep right through.'

'Oh, Cissy, I don't know the answer to that one. With not sleeping in the shelter for a long time, I hadn't seen the problem and Janey never said anything.'

'Janey's been grand with how she's helped us both. She's been taking that old jug we keep outside for watering the plants into the shelter and getting Vera to the edge of her bunk and holding the jug while Vera has a pee, but she weren't there last night, and I'm thinking if little Ian stops with us, he ain't going to want to see that, lass.'

'No . . . Let me think about it. Though we haven't got many options . . . Maybe don't go into the shelter until the siren goes. I know you didn't last night, but mostly you do go in readiness. Then if Mum uses her lav just before you go, it might help. You'll be down there less time . . . Anyway, me darlin', I've to go to bed. We'll sort something.'

Hugging Cissy, then popping back into her mum's flat, Annie was glad to see Ian sat at the table eating some porridge. He looked up expectantly. She smiled at him and told him, 'As soon as there's news, you'll be told, luv. Now, I'm off to bed as I've been working all night.'

After a hug from Janey and one from Mum who came in

330

from the bathroom, Annie went to go upstairs. Before she did she turned and looked at her mum properly. The pity of how weary and in pain she looked cut Annie's heart.

When she'd washed, was ready for bed and went into the bedroom, Annie saw the shape of Ian still indented in the bed and in how the blankets were curled up, and all her cares left her as she had a feeling Ian was going to bring joy to their lives. She almost wished his granny wasn't found so that she didn't come and take him away.

Sleep didn't come easily as Annie tossed and turned, her mind replaying horrific scenes from the night before.

Olivia came to her mind. *I miss you, my lovely friend. If only I could find out how you are.* With this thought she drifted off with memories of her time with Olivia giving her much better images than her night in the hell of the Blitz.

Janey woke her.

Stretching out her limbs, she asked, 'What time is it?' Then she shot up. 'Is there anything wrong, Janey?'

'No. You said to wake you at four as you're to meet Lucy at six.'

'Is it really four? Oooh, I could sleep for a year.'

'I know, luv. I feel the same and usually do sleep most of me day off, but with having Ian . . . Anyway, they found Granny Mansel.'

Yawning and stretching once more, Annie, said, 'Oh? That's good, I'm glad.'

'She's on her way. She's taking a cab, so she must have a bit of money.'

'I'll get washed and dressed now then. I won't be long.'

By the time Annie got downstairs a knock came on the door. Ian ran to it and opened it. 'Granny!'

He was in her arms, his little body shaking with sobs. 'Me mum's dead, Granny, and me Jerry and Charlie.'

His granny, a small woman with her grey hair clipped back in a bun, much the same as Annie wore hers most of the time, held her grandson to her. 'I know, luv. Be a brave boy now.'

Janey stepped forward. 'Let yer granny get inside, Ian. It's all been a shock for her too.'

'And not just a shock. I'm full of guilt. I shouldn't have judged Liz, she weren't a bad girl. I did help her till she went and got herself . . . Well, anyway, what's gone can't be changed. But, Ian, your mum weren't a bad person. She did what she had to, that's all.'

Ian looked confused, but then a ten-year-old cannot be expected to understand how feelings change once there's a death.

Once inside and introductions were over, Fran, as they'd learned Granny Mansel was called, seemed a nice lady. She had a much-wrinkled face, but lively blue eyes. These filled with tears once more as she held Ian to her. 'Thank God you're all right, Ian. Though what we're going to do, I don't know.'

'It's all right, Granny, I can stay with Janey and come and see yer like I did before.'

'But this ain't just a walk, Ian, it's quite a way. I've just spent me rent money to get here. Besides, yer should be with me, I'm your granny . . . Only, well, it might be difficult, as me landlord said the next time I miss paying him, he'll have me evicted.'

Annie felt a lump in her throat. Ian adored Fran, which probably meant she was a nice, loving person, even though she hadn't thought so when she'd heard that she'd fallen out with Ian's mum. She looked over at Janey, then was glad to hear that Janey was of the same mind as she said, 'You can come and stay here, Fran. We have a basement flat that's empty. I wouldn't charge yer rent, but it would help yer both until you get on yer feet.'

Fran's mouth dropped open.

'Say yes, Granny. We can be together then. Your 'ouse is cold and damp anyway, so you'll be nice and warm here. Yer always complaining of the cold.'

'I am, ain't I? But I've lived in me 'ouse all me married life; I had your dad in that 'ouse. It'd be like leaving him.'

'I'm sure if your son was alive, he'd want you to move, Fran, if your house is as Ian describes it.'

'I suppose, Annie . . . Look, let me think about it, as I've never been one for charity.'

'Well then, how about you pay me what you can afford, Fran?'

Annie could have hugged Janey as she went on to say, 'This house belongs to me, so I can let you stay for nothing, or let you set your own rent.'

Fran's expression was a picture. It was as if no one had ever been kind to her before.

Cissy put in, 'We're a lovely household an' all, lass. By, you'd be happy here and we can all help take care of Ian.'

'You're from the North, aren't you, luv? Me husband was from up there. He came down to make his fortune and met me, so never did get rich! Though we were rich in love and 'ad our lovely boy. And he gave me Ian, so I've been blessed.'

'That's good to hear. And me and Cissy could do with another domino player as we always know what the other's got. Though when it comes to cards, even though we're both good at the games we play, a third would make a nice change.'

Fran smiled at Mum. 'I'll let yer know in a week, luv – though me landlord might make me mind up for me.'

For all the world, Annie wanted to say that she would give Fran her rent money, but she had to be careful, there was only hers and Janey's money coming in and they had to see to all the expenses of the house as well as the food. Even Cissy was getting low in funds as her allowance hadn't been paid, so they only had half of her rent coming in.

She thought of the money Ricky left for her. What she'd paid out for a doctor for Janey hadn't made too big a hole in it, but she wanted to make sure there was some left. If . . . no, 'when' Ricky came home, they'd need money to set up their own home.

The thought made her long for it to happen.

So, instead of offering money, she said, 'I'll take you home, Fran. So you don't have to take another cab.'

'Ta. I can stay a little while, though, and I like the sound of them dominoes and cards. I used to go to a group, but had to give it up as there was a subscription.'

'Ha, a shark, Cissy. I reckon we should change our minds!'

They all laughed but Ian. Janey told him that Mum was only joking.

Ian laughed, but then asked, 'So, what's happening to me, Granny? Am I coming or staying?'

'Well, if Janey and all these lovely ladies'll 'ave yer, mate, and yer want to stay, that's all right by me. Or yer can come with me to live, but either way, I think yer can come to either of us when yer want to. Anyway, when Granny's got used to the idea, I might be 'ere too.'

Annie had an idea then. 'Janey, why don't you show Fran the flat? That might make her mind up for her.'

'I never thought of that, Annie. Would you like to see it, Fran?'

'I would. Basement, did you say? Is there many stairs?'

'A few.'

'Well, let's take a look. I can manage a few.'

'Or you could just use the outside door, that has a slope. Only problem is there's no inside lav so you have to climb steps to the one in the yard at the side of the house.'

'I've only got an outside lav, so I'm used to that. And I use a tin bath, though I've found that hard going lately.'

'Eeh, you can have a bath in my bath, Fran. I'd even scrub your back.'

This from Cissy had them all laughing. Even Ian gave a spontaneous giggle.

Fran loved the flat. Janey told her why it was empty.

'So, you're away from your little girl then. I wanted Ian's mum to send him and his brothers away, but she hid them. They ain't been to school for years as she was afraid they'd be taken, and the things he's seen . . . Still, we won't speak ill of the dead.'

Annie looked at Ian. None of this seemed to affect him, so he must be used to his granny's point of view, but still, if she did come to live here, Annie thought, there would have to be gentle words about what should be said in front of him.

What Fran was saying now made it seem as if she was changing her mind and Annie was glad to hear it.

'If I do come, I wouldn't want to bring much. Most of what I 'ave is riddled with woodworm, as well as mildew from the damp, so I'd only need to bring me clothes. But I can't believe this is happening. Are yer sure, Janey?'

'I am. You're an East Ender, you know how we all look out for each other, and it's a tragedy what's happened to you and Ian . . . He's a lovely lad, and don't deserve any of this.'

Ian, who hadn't left Janey's side, touched her arm. Janey put it around him.

'He's taken to yer, that's for sure, and yes, it is the way of us East Enders to look out for one another.'

'Well, you let us know.'

'I'll have to take you back now, Fran, as I've to go out to meet someone. Have you got any of Ian's clothes at yours?'

'No, he never stayed with me, Annie.'

'You could call in at the WVS HQ, Annie. They'll have a lot of stuff. You can pick out what you need. Shall we come with you?'

Annie thought quickly. She was going straight from taking Fran to see Lucy, but she couldn't turn up with Janey and Ian in tow in case Lucy had any news for her. Janey had no idea about Olivia's connection to Lucy, and she couldn't let her find out.

Hoping Janey would accept her giving an excuse, Annie told her, 'I'll drop you off on the way, then come for you after I've seen Lucy. I can't stay long with her as I've to get to work.'

'That'd be the best idea as we might need a little time to find the right things for Ian. I'm all right as I'm not working tonight. I'll get my coat and a blanket to wrap around Ian. He froze last night walking home.'

'I ain't a baby, Janey.'

'Ha, I know, but adults know best when it comes to these things, so no backchat, me lad.'

Ian grinned. To Annie, it was so lovely to see the way Janey and he had taken to each other. Ian would be good for Janey, as Annie knew she pined so much for Beth.

Lucy did have news.

'You know about Olivia having been in touch about Karl. Well, she's now very worried as things are not right for Hendrick.' Annie listened with increasing concern to how Hendrick was also using the transmitter and hadn't been party to anything to give them any information.

'Do you think he's under suspicion?'

'Possibly. It's all very strange. We're worried that Olivia may be on air for far too long. However, she is in favour as she is teaching English to soldiers and has a choir and a small band of musicians she teaches. And she's getting ready to put on a concert for the Kommandant. Our fear is that being married to a German and having special privileges, she does have enemies, and many don't trust her. She could be betrayed.'

Annie closed her eyes against the pain of what would be the consequence of this for Olivia.

'I'm sorry to worry you with this, but Olivia is taking too many risks. We wondered if you could somehow stop her. Maybe send a message through us, anything that might make her more cautious. We feel that she is under the impression that she can get away with anything.'

'No, Olivia wouldn't think like that. At all times she has Hendrick's safety in mind. She knows that if she is compromised, he will be . . . Oh, Lucy, I'm scared for her . . . All I can think of is to beg her to stop and not take so many risks, but would she listen?'

'We have tried that.'

'Use Hendrick. Remind her that by taking risks herself she's putting him at risk . . . Oh, why is Hendrick using the transmitter to communicate when he can telephone? He must know that the more Olivia is on air, the greater the risk to her and to him . . . He hasn't . . . No, he'd never do that.'

'Gone over to the other side, you mean, and be doing this deliberately?'

'No. Hendrick would never even think of doing that . . . Oh, I don't know, it's all so mysterious.'

'It is and it isn't. The simplest answer is that there is nothing more to warn us of. We are being attacked on all fronts and dealing with it. We know they won't give up and that we have to beat them back. And we will. We have the skilled men and the best planes to do that. And as far as Olivia goes, she has become overconfident and is not realizing the dangers.'

'Yes, that must be it. Send her a message saying that you've spoken to me. Tell her that I am so worried that I've asked you not to take any messages from her unless they are useful to our war effort . . . Give her a codeword to use before she tells you anything, but that must only be when she has information to give. And tell her that she has no need to listen in to the BBC, as you'll inform her of any changes here. Tell her, I'm begging this of her and that I love her very much.'

'We'll try that, she might listen. Is there anything I couldn't possibly know about that will assure her this is you speaking?'

Annie frantically searched her mind for anything that would convince Olivia. Almost everything that came to mind she could have told Lucy at any time. It had to be something only they shared . . . Then it came to her. The time they'd done a jigsaw together in Guernsey and the last

338

piece was missing. That was something so mundane that she'd have no reason to share it with anyone. 'Tell her I am the last piece of the jigsaw and when we're together, we will have completed it.'

'That's very cryptic. No wonder you're a good police officer with a mind like that . . . I'm intrigued. But I don't want to know, not yet. Maybe when it doesn't matter any more you can tell me.'

'Lucy . . . why did you make the decision that Olivia couldn't send me messages? I would have picked up Morse code and learned how to use a transmitter.'

'For the exact reason we're having problems now. You two may have been lulled into chatting for hours and Olivia would have been caught out.'

Annie knew this was true. She smiled to herself as she thought of how long she and Olivia could chat without wanting to stop. But she also thought of all the things she so longed to share with her best friend. If only there was a way, but not even letters were getting through and if they did, she was sure they would be censored.

'We've got to win this bloody war, Lucy.'

'We will. Though we do need help. Churchill keeps begging for that and has had some success, but we need more.'

They chatted on for a few minutes, but with the time getting on, Annie had to leave. As they said their goodbyes, Lucy caught hold of her hand. 'Take care, Annie. I couldn't bear to lose you . . . and, well, I won't be able to meet you again.'

'Oh, Lucy, why?'

'This is top secret, but I've been recruited for a special operations group. We'll be dropped behind enemy lines and live as locals but be helping resistance groups of occupied countries.'

'My God!'

'I know, it's a bit of a shock to me, but I so want to do it.'

'But you'll be in so much danger!'

'That doesn't worry me. All I can think of is helping to win the war, and this is a chance to make a real difference. You know, you have all the qualities and even the look – you would blend in well with the French, but you have to be able to speak fluent French.'

'I would do it too, but the language would be a big stumbling block. Olivia used to teach me a few words of French and I loved using them. I was always saying, "*Merci, madame*" and "*voilà*". I just love the sound of their words.'

'And your pronunciation is perfect! But you would need such a lot more than that.'

'You seriously think I could do it?'

'I do.'

'Well, that's boosted me up. I never thought meself capable of anything when I was a housemaid. Now, I think I can do whatever I put me mind to.'

'You can. Look at your career and how you almost speak the King's English now apart from the odd "me" instead of "my". You were a broad cockney when I first met you. And you are helping the war effort with your job . . . Oh, changing the subject, Dan's been brought home as he is a recruit too. We've been seeing each other . . . and well . . . Oh, Annie, he loves me. He truly loves me.'

'Oh, mate, you're full of surprises today. I'm really happy for you. And I have news about Ricky, as well.'

When she told Lucy, Lucy burst out laughing. 'It's such wonderful news, but you're making me laugh because having just said you are nearly speaking the King's English, you said all of that in broad cockney!'

Annie laughed with her. 'Well, I am an East Ender through and through, luv.'

They hugged and parted then, both shedding a tear as they didn't know when they would see each other again.

For once there were no bomb warnings all night. Around two in the morning, the sarge sent them all home for a well-earned rest, but if the siren did go off, they were to report back immediately.

If Annie had thought herself tired before, she now knew herself to be drained as she quietly opened the door to her home, having checked the shelter to find that it was empty. This pleased her so much as it meant they'd taken her advice to only go into it if the siren went off. It was so nice to think of them all, especially Mum, having a comfortable sleep in their own beds.

As she quietly closed the door behind her, an envelope on the table next to the telephone caught her eye. Her heart skipped a beat when she saw the Red Cross symbol and that it was addressed to her.

Deciding she wanted to be alone, Annie went back outside to the shelter. Shivering as she undressed, she quickly grabbed her mum's warm pyjamas that lay folded neatly on the bed Mum always used, then climbed into her mum's bunk. It was as if her mum was cuddling her – how she needed her at this moment.

Her hands shook as she opened the envelope, her nerves and excitement mixing with the coldness of her body.

Four small scraps of paper fell out – all pieces of a label from a condensed milk tin, which must have been delivered in a Red Cross parcel. Picking them up, she read the words, on one, written in charcoal:

*Never forget I love you, R x*

'Oh, Ricky. My love. Such a short note, but it means so much to me.'

Holding it close to her heart, Annie thought how Ricky must have managed to get hold of a piece of burned wood from a fire to make his charcoal but been afraid of writing more than a few words at a time in case he was seen.

Though she'd shed many tears, none had emptied her heart. Those she wept now did, as she read the other three notes:

*Always mine x*

*My love never dies x*

*Wait for me, I will return x*

# PART FIVE

One Year of War Ends, Another Begins
and All Is Taken

1940–1941

# Chapter Twenty-Seven

## Olivia

As Olivia drove out to her farmhouse, something she often did, she mused on how everything had settled into a pattern since August.

Hendrick had resumed his telephone calls as well as his messaging through the transmitter. He'd told her through Morse code that he'd felt threatened and had taken all precautions because of it. But now his fears were unfounded, and he felt they could continue as they'd planned in the beginning.

Their chats were the highlight of her week, especially as the Germans had lost interest and left her alone to take Hendrick's calls. But there were still only rare bits of information for the mainland as England continued to deal with home troubles, although her contact at the War Office had recently asked for any information Hendrick could give on the situation in France with the view to dropping agents into that country.

Hendrick had obliged and his messages had become more frequent.

Her contact no longer criticized her having to use the transmitter more often when they had only recently instructed that she should be cautious, and so she assumed the fear Annie's message had given her no longer stood. Though always she knew the loving last sentence of Annie's message did.

Now, she had discarded the warnings altogether and once more listened in to the BBC and, almost as often, to Joseph Goebbels, the Nazi Minister for Propaganda's broadcasts too.

She was taking a risk but had got away with it so far. And this had made her feel secure enough to pass anything on she could to her band and choir about what was happening in the outside world as many had become too scared to listen in.

They'd all felt such sadness at the awful bombing of England and of how many lives had been lost and how much property had been destroyed. But Olivia's contact in the War Office assured her that Annie and her family were safe, as was Karl. How she longed to hold him, to know what he looked like now and how much he'd grown.

Olivia imagined it was the Nazis' success in destroying much of the mainland that had relaxed their vigilance in seeking out anyone listening to the news.

For her, it beggared belief that the Nazis could carry out such atrocities as shooting innocent people like Leonard and still worship God. And yet, since the first concert for the Kommandant, which had been a tense affair, but a very successful one, they'd put on many recitals, and were practising for another with a Christmas theme.

And now she'd been told she could put on a Christmas recital that the islanders could attend.

Having reached the farmhouse and pulled up outside, as always, her heart was gladdened and yet lay heavy in her chest as she got out and leaned on her car and stood gazing at the place of her dreams.

She was relieved to see that nothing had happened to it

and that it still stood, as ever, proudly awaiting her return, and that as yet, there wasn't any sign of it being demolished or touched in any way. But she was heavy-hearted to see the notice nailed across the door warning to keep out!

She wanted so much to just rip it down and let herself inside, but always there could be watching eyes and the last thing she needed was to draw attention to herself.

Her misery didn't last long as tonight was when Hendrick rang and then it was band practice. This she loved more than choir practice for during that she had to contend with Gunter, who she despised.


Arriving back home, Olivia went to the music room to check once more the score they were to practise.

Daphne came in before Olivia had a chance to look through her music. 'Oh, Olivia, I've been petrified. Where have you been?'

'Why? What's happened?'

'Stefan came to see me; he told me that they have been informed that someone picked up on a signal coming from this area – a transmitter!'

It seemed to Olivia that every hair on her body had stood up. 'Oh, God! Did Stefan say who was under suspicion?'

'No. That's all he knew. Though he did say that some sort of detector was being brought into force as otherwise it would be like looking for a needle in a haystack!'

Olivia tried to turn the conversation so as not to make Daphne suspicious.

'Well, I hope they don't catch who it is, but it seems Stefan is more than fond of you to warn you.'

'Yes, and I of him . . . I've fallen in love with him, Olivia, and he feels the same way. He said he was worried and scared that I might know something . . . Oh, Olivia, he didn't say, but I think he was trying to tell me that our apartments are suspected as being the source. I told him that was ridiculous. But . . . well, you did say once that you had to do things but weren't able to tell me about them . . .'

Olivia's heart painfully beat against her chest wall. She could hardly breathe. 'You didn't tell Stefan that?'

'No, I would never betray you, even to the man I love, but . . . It isn't you, is it . . . ? Oh, God, we've got to do something, Olivia.'

Olivia knew the moment had come when she would have to trust Daphne with more than she had so far.

'I have only done what I have had to do. That is all I can tell you, but you must act as if you know nothing. Whatever they say to you, or even if I'm caught, you must stick to the same story: that you never went into my attic office, you weren't allowed to and you didn't know anything about what I have up there. Do you understand?'

Daphne nodded, but the terror she felt was visible on her face. Her eyes were wide and staring. She constantly wrung her hands together.

'Right, just carry on with your normal work for this time of day and act shocked and surprised if the Germans arrive. Don't let Jean suspect anything is on your mind and I'll talk to my father.'

Daphne nodded. 'Please be careful. Oh, Olivia, I never dreamed that what you said you had to do involved anything like this, and even now I don't understand how or why. But just hurry, please hurry, and put it all right.'

Daphne hugged her then, but only briefly. The gesture assured Olivia that she had a true friend to rely on.

* * *

Father's face seemed to freeze and, like Daphne, his eyes opened wide. 'No! Oh, Olivia, who would be able to detect your transmitter? I mean, if it was an islander, then they would be afraid of being caught, so wouldn't say they'd found someone using one . . . How does it even work that they can be detected?'

'I don't know, but think, Daddy, where can I hide it? If they are so sure it is in this area, they could be here at any moment!'

'But surely the cupboard in your office with the false back is a good enough place? You can't tell it's any different to a normal cupboard and you're always careful about not leaving a trace of your messages around, or any part of your equipment. I should relax and act normally in the unlikely event they do come here, my dear.'

This settled Olivia's mind a little, though she still had her doubts. 'What if whoever informed them knew the signal came from me? I mean, why did Stefan come to see Daphne in particular? And she had the idea that he was trying to tell her that this building was suspected. We've heard what they do in these searches – they smash everything!'

'Oh, Olivia, no!'

'I'll go and get it and put it in the car, and then drive to the other side of the island and hide it somewhere – maybe in those old barns that are still on old Mr Jenkins' farm that everyone knows he never uses . . . No one will suspect anything as they just look like cases, and I'm always putting musical instruments in my car that are packed into cases – that's it, my cello case!'

With this, Olivia ran up the stairs to the attic. Hurrying down with the transmitter, she quickly grabbed the cello case, took out the instrument with care, for no matter how much of a hurry she was in she could never treat her musical instruments with anything but respect.

Soon she had the set packed and hurried down the stairs with it. By the time she reached the car, sweat poured from her and she was gasping for breath.

Looking up and down the street, all seemed normal. Stefan must have given plenty of warning. But could he be trusted? He did seem different to the rest, and with loving Daphne, he would want to protect her. Maybe he was able to delay things.

Driving as normally as she could, Olivia kept her eye on her rear-view mirror. Never had she felt so terrified as she did at this moment. But she was sure she had made it to the barn unseen.

Once inside, she unpacked the set, then searched for a hiding place.

Stamping around on the floor revealed a loose board.

With this lifted, Olivia went to put her transmitter inside the cavity, but then realized that she must let her contact know that she would no longer be contactable using the radio transmitter and that she would get in touch whenever she could.

To this end, she knew she would have to sort a code out to tell Hendrick to revert back to code messaging during their telephone calls. It would be tricky to have to drive out here to send messages to the mainland, but no one ever followed her when she used her car.

As quickly as she could, she fitted the crystal, then the aerial and switched the transmitter on. Then hurriedly tapped out her message. Her contact answered immediately, wishing her luck at the end.

This had been so easy to accomplish that she thought to try Hendrick. It would be better to tell him of the new arrangements as quickly as she could.

As soon as she changed the crystal, a message came in – Hendrick!

There was no exchange of greetings, just, 'Been trying to contact. Problems here. Father caught.'

Her gasp hurt her throat.

Tapping wildly, she asked, 'Are you implicated?'

There followed an agonizing wait for a reply. When it came, Olivia knew her already fragile world to splinter.

'Yes. In hiding.'

Breathing heavily and feeling as if a hand was strangling her, Olivia went to reply, but another message came through.

'I have help to escape, but . . . hide, my darling.'

Nothing more, though Olivia tried tapping a message for him to tell her more. At last, she gave up and put her head in her hands.

Despair entered her. There was nowhere for her to hide! And if she didn't go back, then her father might become a suspect. No, she had to behave as if everything was normal.

Tears of fear for her darling Hendrick ran down her cheeks as she removed the crystals and packed her beloved's transmitter away – would they ever come here together and find it in the future? Her heart was breaking.

How she drove back to town, she did not know, only that she prayed and prayed to God to keep her beloved safe.

But when she reached the outskirts of town, she realized that she had to look as if nothing had happened. Pulling up in a gateway, she fumbled for the bag of make-up she always kept in the car, now never needed, but often used in the past when meeting a client and she would want to freshen up.

As she looked at her reflection, she asked herself, *How did it all go so wrong?* Such a short time ago, her father owned a bank. Now it was all gone, and he'd said that he was sure proceedings would have been started to wind up his holdings. She hadn't worried about it, but as she sat here now thinking of all she'd had and how it was all going, she knew that there was still a long way to fall, and it was likely they would end up with nothing.

But that paled into insignificance when she thought of the plight of her darling Hendrick.

She tried desperately to hang on to his saying he had help to escape and this enabled her to gain a calmer exterior.

With unsteady hands Olivia applied her make-up, breathing deeply to bring her racing heart to a slower pace.

When she was ready, she reversed out onto the road and drove home.

The sight that met her tore her fragile facade into shreds. Their building that had once been the pride of St Peter Port and of her and her father was surrounded by armed soldiers.

The moment they spotted her, they crowded around her, shouting to her to get out of the car.

Terrifying horror gripped her. Her hands shot into the air.

Once she was out of the car, the barrel of a gun dug painfully into her back, propelling her forward.

Inside the bank, her father lay on the floor, a gun, held by Gunter, aimed at his head. Just beyond him lay Jean, her still body lying in a pool of blood.

Olivia's mouth stretched wide. Her throat dried. Somehow, she gasped out, 'No! No!'

Gunter looked at her with the same look in his eyes he'd had before killing Leonard.

'Tell us where your transmitter is, or your father dies!'

'No, Olivia. Tell him we don't have one . . .'

Gunter brutally smashed his gun over her father's shoulder.

Olivia screamed, 'In the barn of Mr Jenkins' farm.'

Gunter grinned. 'I know where that is, it is where I take the girls who want to give me a good time.'

Without taking his eyes off her, he pulled the trigger.

Blood splattered Olivia's face and clothes. She sank to her knees. 'No! No! No!'

'Yes, dear Olivia. And this is only part of your punishment. You will be shipped to a camp in Germany where you will watch us shoot your traitor of a husband and his Jew-loving father!'

He turned to the other soldiers looking on. 'Get her out of here!'

A hand grabbed her hair. The tearing of her scalp as he pulled her along the floor didn't register with Olivia. Pain of loss consumed her body, as did fear of what Gunter had said would happen to her darling Hendrick.

They took her to the island's prison, where the Jews, and anyone who had shown any defiance, were held – their fate was to be shipped out when the prison was full to a destiny they could only imagine, something that cut at the heart of all islanders. Would this be her fate too?

Like a rag doll, Olivia was thrown onto the cell floor. She hollered out in pain as she landed with her weak and painful leg underneath her.

Gunter followed her in. In German he ordered the rest of the soldiers out, adding, 'You can watch from out there if you like,' as his hand went to his flies.

Disgust and horror clothed Olivia, but from nowhere, Stefan appeared.

Olivia hadn't given thought to him and hadn't seen him

since this all began, but now hoped that he'd been able to make Daphne safe.

He challenged Gunter. 'No, Gunter. You will be ill advised to take your pleasure with Olivia. You do not know if Hendrick has been captured, or even if he will be found guilty. If he is not, and you have violated his wife, it will be you who is shot!'

Olivia's heart lifted. *Hendrick may still be free!*

'Ha! I have known Hendrick is a dissenter for many years. It was I who reported the conversations we had together when he came to Germany to visit his father. Always he preached that we should not vilify the Jews, that they were people just like us!'

Gunter spat on the ground.

'Because of this, his father, another known dissenter, has been watched and caught red-handed. It was me who alerted the SS to Hendrick's father having a transmitter and that I didn't trust him. That Hendrick had access to many secrets, that if his father would betray us by transporting Jews to save them, then would his son be any better? Hendrick must have got wind of all of this and scarpered! I have no doubt they will find he has the transmitter as searches of his father's house haven't been successful. So, my dear Stefan, how can you think him innocent? Even my theory that he could be messaging this bitch is proving true. In turn, I believe she is messaging the friend we know she has in England!'

In some strange way, Olivia felt relieved that it wasn't an islander who had betrayed her. But then, fresh fear struck her as Gunter once more began to undo the buttons of his fly.

'Well, my dear Stefan, am I to arrest your sweetheart as an accomplice too? Or are you going to let me have what I have wanted since meeting our choirmaster?'

Stefan's eyes were full of his pain when he glanced at Olivia. He uttered the words, 'I am sorry.' Then turned and marched away.

Gunter's laugh echoed around the walls of this cold, damp cell.

Something died in Olivia as Gunter knelt beside her, encouraged on in his quest by those who'd stayed to watch.

Despite her pain, Olivia rolled away from him. 'No! Please don't.'

But Gunter took no notice. Grabbing her, rolling her over and getting on top of her in one brutal action, she could do nothing as he prized her legs open and pulled her knickers aside.

When he entered her, Olivia prayed to die.

A cheer went up and cries of, 'Go on, Gunter. My turn next.'

Olivia tried but couldn't resist. Her bad leg shot with pain every time she tried to get leverage to push him off. In the end she lay exhausted as Gunter pounded her.

Bile came into her throat. She wanted Hendrick, but dare not bring him to mind as this vile act was happening.

At last, Gunter gave a deep-throated moan and fell limply on top of her. Her breath left her body.

He didn't stay long but got onto his knees and in a tone that made her feel like nothing more than a piece of meat, he said, 'Next!'

All fight left Olivia and her mind shut down as one after the other took her. She couldn't even react when the third one beat her as he pounded her, to Gunter saying, 'Jürgen, how is it you are turned on by hurting women?'

As if he hadn't hurt her with his violation of her and allowing this rape of her over and over! But she didn't feel the pain of Jürgen's blows. Her body and mind had shut down.

When Gunter took her for a second time, he was brutal in his few thrusts that hailed the end of her ordeal.

'Right, let's clean her up.'

With this, someone threw a bucket of icy cold water over her as others laughed. That laughter increased as Gunter said, 'I wonder which one of us hit the bullseye. There could be a bastard born with a bit of all of us in it.'

To the sound of the door being slammed and locked, Olivia lay without moving. Never had she felt so wretched.

Her soul cried out for Hendrick, her dear father, for Annie and her beloved Karl.

But then her mind closed down and took her into oblivion.

# Chapter Twenty-Eight

## Annie

Annie woke and stretched her body. They'd had a wonderful and unbelievable Christmas here at Rose's farmhouse, with more food than they'd had to eat for weeks in one meal!

And so many of them all fitting in easily.

Janey and Ian had stayed in the cottage with Loes. Janey had loved every minute of her time with Beth, as had they all with her and Karl too. Both children were thriving, and had a deep love for each other. Loes had done a marvellous job of caring for them. And both children loved Ian and he them, though tiredness and overexcitement had seen a few fallings-out among the little ones. Always, it had been Ian who sorted things out and got them both laughing again. He was proving to be a little smasher and a massive part of their family, as was Fran, his granny.

Fran had held out for a while, but before they left for Rose's she had agreed to move into the basement when they got back. This had relieved Ian, who had been torn between wanting to stay with Janey but wanting to be with his gran. Staying with Janey had won, with regular visits to his granny. He never went empty-handed as Cissy always made a pie or a casserole for him to take with him.

The rest of them fitted into the farmhouse well, with Rose getting one of her farmhands to bring two beds downstairs for Annie and her mum and putting them into what Rose called her snug.

Annie looked over towards where Mum still slept and then around the room, a lovely room furnished in blue that seemed too big for a snug and had fitted their beds in easily, as well as a commode for Mum during the night, though there was a lav for them just outside in the yard.

Fran, Lilly and Cissy each had a room to themselves upstairs and all had been so happy and relaxed over the week they had been there and, joined by Rose, they'd had a proper card school going!

It wasn't all harmony, however, as on one card-playing occasion, Annie had to mediate as they became overenthusiastic on a point of the rules – and that was putting it mildly. For one moment she'd thought Rose would chuck them all out!

She giggled to herself at the incident now, and how Ian had calmed it all down by doing cartwheels and saying they were driving him mad, making them all laugh. Thankfully, they had agreed to disagree and Mum had played the piano instead. What followed had been a good old sing-song, mostly of carols.

And now it was New Year's Day, and they were going home tomorrow. But to what?

Annie began to dread how much destruction might have taken place during the massive raids three days ago when it was said on the news that the Germans had set London on fire. She dared not even think about their home and whether it was still standing.

Flinging the covers back and getting out of bed, Annie

358

grabbed her dressing gown to wrap up against the cold. Stopping to ignite the kindling she'd laid in the grate the night before, she went to the window and peeped through the curtains at the beautiful view of fields, made the more so by the frost clothing everything in white.

It seemed a world away from crippled London.

Tiptoeing out to the kitchen, Annie was met by the comforting warmth of the huge aga which never seemed to go out.

Rose, still in her nightie, sat at the huge, scrubbed table sipping tea.

'Morning, Annie, luv. There's plenty in the pot if yer want a cuppa. I've put milk in all the mugs, so yer just need to pour it.'

Annie crossed the kitchen and put her arms around Rose's shoulders. 'Ta, Rose. And Happy New Year, though it's not had a good start for those left in London!'

'No, and the report this morning is worse than it was yesterday. We've lost, or had badly damaged, some of our most loved buildings: the Old Bailey, though I imagine a few are cheering at that one! But the Guildhall took a hit, and eight churches that had been designed by Christopher Wren, whoever he was.'

Annie thought it was funny how in the peace of the countryside none of the horror really touched you. It was just something on the news you could talk about without the reality of it all impacting on you. These buildings were just bricks and mortar at the end of the day – they could be replaced. The poor souls lost last night couldn't. But she didn't say all of this. This was New Year's Day, a time for hope for a better future. So, she just said, 'Christopher Wren was an architect, and a very famous one.'

'Get you, having knowledge like that, mate!'

'Olivia and my Ricky told me a lot of things as we went around London.'

'Yes, and I've been told a lot of things, but I don't retain them like you do. You've a clever brain, Annie.'

Annie smiled, but then frowned as Rose gave a heavy sigh. 'I'm going to miss you all when you've gone. You've made me first Christmas without Jimmy bearable . . . Yer know, I keep wondering what kind of Christmas he's 'ad and want to go and tear the walls of that place down and drag 'im out. But then, I think of me little Angie, me own granddaughter, and Beth and Janey going through such a lot with 'im, and it 'elps me to know he's in the right place.'

Annie just put her hand over Rose's shoulder once more and told her, 'It's all right for you to miss him, Rose. We all know your pain. He's your son – though he was taken from you the moment that gun went off. So, remember him how he was before that and make that your point of losing him. Don't think of the monster that came back after as being your Jimmy. He was no longer.'

'Ta, Annie. Yer right, girl . . . Maybe it would have been better if Jimmy had died from that gun shot. It truly would have been all over then.'

Annie just patted her arm and was glad when Rose changed the subject as she asked, 'So, what do yer wish for in the new year then, luv?'

'Oh, Rose, I wish for so much, but none of it can happen. But me biggest wish is to have me Ricky back safely . . . I got three little notes from him, though, and they keep me going. I keep them pinned inside me bra so that he's near to me heart.'

'Ah, that's lovely, girl. 'Ere, 'ow big are they? Only I've a Victorian locket left by me gran. I'll go and get it, and we'll see if we can fit them in. That'd preserve them better for yer and keep them by yer heart. Though I'd like yer to make sure that it goes to Beth eventually.'

'Ta, luv. I'll go and get me notes, as I ain't put me bra on yet.'

Mum was awake when Annie went back into the snug.

'Happy New Year, Mum.'

'And the same to you, luv. We'll make the best of it, eh?'

'We will . . . But, Mum, I've been thinking. Well, it was something Rose said about how she's going to miss us all. Why don't I ask her if you could stay here, eh? Things are getting worse in London. I fear for you all.'

Mum surprised her then as she thought she'd resist. 'I wouldn't mind staying a bit longer, luv, though I'd miss you and Janey. But the peace here, it's like there ain't a war. Except for when the aeroplanes go over. Then you have your heart in your mouth till they come back to Biggin Hill.'

'I know. And I'm so glad you agree. I'll miss you so much, Mum, but I can keep telling meself that you're safe and that will make up for not being with you . . . Now, I'll just go back through, and I'll bring you a cuppa in a mo. Will you be all right?'

'I will. I'm so all right that I'll probably go back to sleep after me cuppa.'

This made Annie smile. If only Rose would agree, she knew Cissy would be happy to stay as long as Mum was here, but she couldn't ask about Lilly, Fran or Ian, that would be too much.

* * *

361

The locket was beautiful and real silver. It had an engraved pattern on the front. Annie couldn't believe how big it was. 'It's beautiful, Rose, and I'd be honoured to be the keeper of it and for it to be the keeper of me notes. Ta, luv.'

'I like that, "the keeper". It makes me think that really it's Beth's now and it'll be in safe hands.'

With the notes folded and tucked inside, Annie put the locket on. And then, as no one else had surfaced, Annie decided she would ask Rose about Mum and Cissy staying here for a while longer.

'Oh, Annie, I would love that. And I can get 'elp in for Vera too. We've a woman in the village who delivers all the babies. She ain't a proper nurse but she takes on any jobs that involve nursing and she's good and kind.'

'That's just the sort of person we need for Mum. Does she charge much?'

'No, there's a system round 'ere. We pay for services by giving another. I could give her a box of veg a week and some eggs and that would be more than enough to her, so don't worry about it.'

'So, we're all set if Cissy agrees. Mum won't stay unless she does. And anyway, Cissy can see to such a lot of Mum's needs, and loves doing it. And she'd cook for you all as she loves cooking and you've so many more ingredients here for her.'

'That's settled then, as I 'ave me work cut out around 'ere at times as you've seen, what with feeding the chickens, collecting the eggs, and planting season is on us, which I 'elp out with. Mind, yer not going 'ome empty-'anded. Alfie's already marked out a sack of spuds for yer, and a box of winter veg.'

Alfie came in at that moment, followed by his faithful collie, Ruffles, who Ian loved to take for walks.

A typical farmer, with his huge wellies and corduroy trousers tied with string, red, round face that seemed to always glow and his tattered, brimmed hat allowing strands of spiky hair to show, he took all they told him about his new residents in his stride with his usual grin. His only comment being, 'Flipping 'eck, I've to be the referee then when yer all play yer card games! I think once I see the pack come out, I'll take meself down to the pub!'

Rose laughed that loud that she brought Mum out of the snug, pushing her wheelchair, as she often did, using it as a walking aid.

'What's all the frivolity in here, eh? A girl can't have a decent lie-in around this place!'

They all laughed and together said, 'Happy New Year, Vera!'

Alfie added, 'And welcome to yer new home for as long as yer need it, luv.'

The noise brought everyone crowding into the kitchen, and soon it buzzed with activity until they were all tucking into the treat of every morning, boiled egg and bread cut into fingers.

Cissy was in agreement to stay longer with Mum, and with that settled, the day became a happy day of walks, relaxation and more food than they would ever see on a table in London.

The happiness in the room warmed Annie's heart. Though she couldn't have all she wanted on this New Year's Day, as it ended with their usual sing-song she thought it the next best thing – a room full of love and strong East End women. And now she knew her mum was going to be safe, to Annie, it was the very best of a bad situation.

\* \* \*

Ruffles woke her in the night. It was one sound she hadn't got used to – his barking. As she looked at the clock and saw it was four in the morning, other sounds came to her – those she was used to and had learned to sleep through: the droning of aircraft.

Sighing, she knew they would be Germans on their route home after a bombing raid.

Throwing the covers back, she went to where her coat hung on the back of the door, pushed her feet into her shoes and went to try to soothe Ruffles.

No one else appeared, so she guessed she, being so near to where Ruffles had his kennel, was the only one to hear his distress.

Not turning on the lights for fear of breaking the blackout, she found her way to the door. Though Ruffles had quietened a little, she still wanted to stroke him. He had a calming effect on her. So much so that if things weren't as they were, she'd even think about getting herself a pet dog.

When she reached the kennel, a voice said, 'He's all right now, Annie.'

'Ian! What are you doing up, mate?'

'I've got up a few times this week to be with Ruffles. I just love him so much and wish I didn't have to leave him. I've taken him for walks in the middle of the night too. I know the path like the back of me 'and and don't need lights to find me way.'

'Do you know, I'd love that. A moonlight walk. As I'll not get back to sleep now.'

'No, yer think of what them planes might have done to where we live, and it all gets on yer mind. I can take yer if yer like?'

'I do like, and the Luftwaffe have gone over now.'

They walked along talking away about the farm, the week they'd had and how Ian and his granny had loved it all.

'I ain't never known anything like it, though I 'ave felt sad at times and that's stopped me sleeping. Ruffles 'elps, though. He seems to know and he snuggles into me.'

Annie bent and took his hand. 'You can always come to any of us when you feel that way. We understand as we're all going through similar heartache and loss.'

The words were hardly out of her mouth when a second wave of Luftwaffe could be heard.

'Oh no, Annie, they're coming again!'

Annie didn't have time to answer as massive explosions sent them both flying onto the ground.

If Annie had thought she'd visited hell, she now knew that this was worse as the house and the cottage took a direct hit.

Her screams were matched by Ian's as they lay in a huddle not feeling the icy cold of the grass.

'No! No! Please, no!' Her throat and nostrils filled with smoke. As she coughed violently, it came to her to protect Ian. Standing, she took off her coat and threw it over his and the barking Ruffles' head then tucked her own underneath it.

'Me granny, me granny!'

Annie could do nothing but hold him closely to her, as he went through the names of those most dear to him, who were the dearest to her too.

'Janey . . . not Janey, Annie, and Beth and Karl . . . and Nanny Vera . . . Don't let them be dead, Annie!'

His sobs tore at her heart as she prayed the same prayer over and over. But in her heart of hearts there was despair as she couldn't imagine how anyone could survive the awful explosions.

With the planes having gone, Annie sat up and cradled Ian to her. The light from the house being on fire lit the night as Annie had seen so often. But never with her heart breaking as it was. The cottage was half gone but not on fire. Hope came to her that maybe one of her loved ones was still alive.

'Come on, Ian, we have to be the rescue team, mate.'

By the time they got to the cottage, the heat was unbearable.

Ian tugged at her arm.

'Annie, since I told Loes about me mum getting us under the table, she's been doing that every time she hears the bombers going over. She gets Beth and Karl, even though they're still sleeping, and she takes them under with her. She said that they could always drop them on the wrong target and often do . . . I always come outside as I'm scared, but Janey . . .' – Ian sobbed – '. . . she – she said not to wake her as it was a daft idea and wouldn't be needed 'ere . . . I don't want to lose me Janey, Annie.'

Annie couldn't answer that. She couldn't even give thought to such a horrific thing. She hadn't even thought about the loss of so many of her dear ones engulfed in flames. She just couldn't. Instead, she latched on to this small thread of hope Ian had given her.

'Oh, Ian, I hope she did that as with no fire, it could have saved them.'

She couldn't believe how calm her voice sounded. It was as if she wasn't really in her own skin.

'Let's try to shift some of the rubble, eh, lad? Let's do what we can to try to save them.'

Suddenly, the noise of tractors and car engines and the tramping of feet filled the air.

366

Arms came around Annie, and she saw a man lift Ian.

Others were saying, 'My God, the bastards!' Or, just, 'No, no!'

But one man who'd jumped off a tractor took charge.

'Right, some of you make a human chain to the main house from the well and tackle the fire.'

It was then that Annie noticed most carried buckets with them.

'The rest of you, get stuck in and start to shift some of this rubble – there may be someone alive inside.'

Annie went to help with this, unable to face the fire, but the woman holding her told her, 'Not you, luv. You sit on that tree stump with the lad and 'ave an 'ot drink. Some of us brought flasks with us.'

'No, I must help! Me sister and niece and me mum are in there, as well as me friend's little boy and his nanny – and me mates who are like family, and Rose and Alfie, the owners of the farm!'

'I can 'elp as well.' Ian put in. 'I want to. . . I couldn't 'elp me mum, Annie. Please let me.'

Annie implored of the woman, 'Please, we're better off doing something.'

'All right. 'As the lad been through this once?'

'Yes, only his house caught on fire. He'd only gone out into the yard to the lav.'

'Well, maybe he needs to do this then.' She turned to Ian. 'Get stuck in then, lad, but do as the men tell yer, don't be trying to rush at it.'

As they worked, Annie's heart was heavy as she could now make out that the part of the house that had collapsed was where the bedrooms were. Her prayers were like a mantra in her mind as she frantically pulled at beams with others.

They served to help her and to keep the horror of what was happening behind her out of her mind.

At last they could see into the kitchen. A voice called out. 'I am here, under the table.'

Despite her fears, Annie wanted to cheer.

'Loes, is that you? Who's with you?'

'The little ones.'

'Are you all right, luv?'

'Yes, we're not hurt. I have been singing to them and they have gone back to sleep.'

'Oh, Loes, thank God . . . but . . . Oh, Loes, is Janey not with you?'

Even as she asked the question, she knew the answer. Dropping onto her haunches, Annie fell forward. Her grief took her over and she beat the ground and clawed at the earth as her desperate pleas to God not to have let it happen fell on deaf ears.

Nothing was found of the bodies of Mum, Cissy, Lilly, Fran, Rose or Alfie, but Janey's broken body was recovered by the early hours.

By this time, Annie sat in the front room of the cottage of one of the helpers from the village, huddled with Beth, the only member of her family she had left, and with Karl, so precious and saved for her dear Olivia. And Ian and Loes who were almost like family, and who she loved dearly. Somehow, she found the strength to comfort them and assure them everything was going to be all right. Tears plopped onto Beth's head. It was then that she knew she had to find a way as these beloved children needed her. Somehow, she had to make their world right again.

# Chapter Twenty-Nine

## Olivia

Disorientated when she woke, Olivia didn't know how long she had lain on the floor. Only that she was hurting everywhere and that it was still night as the cell was in darkness – whether it was the same night the horror had happened, she didn't know, nor did she care as she'd closed her mind to it all and given herself up to whatever was her fate.

The only thing that penetrated her thoughts was that her lovely daddy was dead, as was Jean, the woman who had become as dear to her as Cissy was. But she couldn't even cry for them. Her emotions had shut down.

Her thoughts went to Daphne, and she prayed that Stefan had been able to get her to safety as it was possible Gunter would go after her next, looking on her as a collaborator even though she'd known nothing of what was going on.

Taking as deep a breath as her bruised ribs would let her, the thought came to Olivia that she didn't regret any of what she'd done. She was proud of the help she'd given to Britain.

Even when she thought of Hendrick and so wanted him to be safe, she couldn't cry, or beg this of God. It was as if her heart had turned to stone.

Neither could she feel anything about the violation of her body. What she did know was that she never wanted to feel again, as the unbearable pain of it all flooding her body would destroy what threads of her were left. She didn't want that. Neither did she want to die. She wanted to live for her son.

The clanging of the door being opened woke her when she hadn't been aware of falling asleep. Then she heard Stefan's voice commanding, 'Leave me alone with her! I will call you when I need you!'

'Ha, come back for your turn, have you?'

'What is your name, dog?'

The voice that had mocked now whimpered, 'I'm sorry, I . . . I thought . . . I beg your pardon . . .'

'Get out of my sight! But come when I call!'

Olivia felt Stefan kneel beside her. In English, which he had mastered well with her lessons and being with Daphne as much as he could, he said to her, 'Don't be afraid, just do exactly as I say. I am going to make them believe that Daphne has told me you are a Jew. That I have come here to kill you. When I call the guards to carry you out of here and into a hearse, you will appear dead; you will be floppy and non-responsive. The undertaker thinks he is just picking up another body. He won't examine you. I have a boat arranged. We are going to England, God willing, as our journey is fraught with danger. Though as we will be on an English boat, we should be safe once we reach the British coastline.'

Olivia's heart raced and for the first time, she felt some of her emotions awakening as hope filled her. But something troubled her. Through her dried and cracked lips, she managed to say, 'Daphne?'

'Daphne is at the farmhouse. I broke into it and then boarded it again. We are going from there as she told me of you getting an English soldier out by that beach. Daphne has arranged this with . . . is it Bertie?'

Olivia could hardly believe this, but maybe with Joe gone, his father wanted to leave too.

'Now, I have to hurry. I'm going to do something I abhor, Olivia. Forgive me.' In German, he told her he had been training to be a doctor and had studied martial arts as a hobby. 'Once the guard is on his way, I'm going to do a manoeuvre that will render you unconscious, so you won't feel a thing. They will think you dead, but do not worry, I know how to care for you. I will tell the guard that I came here to confront you as Daphne had betrayed you and told me that you are of Jewish descent. I will also say that I took this most drastic of actions as I found you ill after what had happened to you at their hands, and that none of our medical supplies were to be wasted on a Jew. And just so you have no doubts about any of this, Olivia, I have my car waiting around the corner from the mortuary. Once the undertaker pulls up, I will get out, and go to the back of the hearse with him. There, I will do the same to him as I am going to do to you, and then whisk you away. We will have to get straight into the waiting boat as soon as the coast is clear. The undertaker may or may not raise the alarm when he comes round, it depends on how afraid he is of us Germans.'

Olivia found the bit about the Jews painful to hear, as she knew from Hendrick that this would happen for real, though she did wonder if the guard would find this a strange thing for Stefan to do after his actions earlier. But then, maybe they expected this reaction to the Jewish people even from the most principled and gentlest among them.

She jumped when he hollered, 'Guards!' She'd never heard him raise his voice.

Footsteps resounded, as the guards immediately obeyed.

Then a sudden movement by Stefan and she knew no more.

She came to when in the back of the hearse and found it difficult not to cry out from the pain the motion of the vehicle caused her, but she realized she was free, and she would do nothing to jeopardize that.

Soon she was being held by Daphne and feeling her tears join Daphne's as she gently hugged her.

'I've blankets to wrap you in, Olivia. Oh, love, I can't believe what has happened to you.'

Once in the boat with Stefan and Bertie rowing them away from the shore, Olivia lay between Daphne's legs, and she cuddled her from behind.

She could almost touch Daphne's fear as her body trembled, but for herself, she was back in the state where she felt nothing. She couldn't let herself for she knew that the world would collapse onto her and she would never be herself again.

With no rowing to do now, Stefan turned towards them. 'When we arrive, I will hand myself in. I will tell them that I have rescued you at the cost of myself being imprisoned and hope they will be lenient with me.'

Daphne gasped. Olivia realized that she couldn't have thought this far as Olivia hadn't either.

'No! No, Stefan, we'll hide you, won't we, Olivia? . . . Your friend will know where.'

Olivia wanted to say that couldn't happen – how could they hide a man in German uniform? Besides, Annie being a police officer, they couldn't put her in that position. But she just closed her eyes and hoped they would think her asleep.

But then she opened them again as images of her father lying on the floor came to her. A huge moan left her throat as the pain of reality flooded into her.

'No! No, don't let it have happened! Daddy! Daddy!'

Daphne's arms tightened around her. Her own problems forgotten, she told Olivia, 'Cry it out, love. I have. I've cried a million tears for your dad, for Jean, and for you. And for my own mum too as I don't know when I will see her again and now I face losing Stefan.'

After she had calmed, though forcing herself to, Stefan told Daphne, 'Daphne, you won't lose me. The talk is of the English treating their prisoners with respect, especially officers like me, and with my medical training, they may even use me in a medical facility for other prisoners.'

'Well, you never said you were a doctor!'

'No, Daphne, I'm sorry, but I find it painful that I was stopped in my chosen path and forced to do what I hate – become a soldier. It was a relief to me to be stationed on the island as I hated fighting and killing – I didn't expect to see it there too, though it is different and I don't have to do it, only watch the sadists carry out atrocities, which hurts me. But now, I feel hopeful that I may one day be able to pick up my training again. Being a prisoner for the duration of this war will suit me. I will not have to kill for principles I do not believe in.'

Feeling safe now that Stefan would never harm or cause harm to Hendrick, she told them that what Gunter had suspected was true. 'Hendrick did pass secrets on to me that helped the British war effort as he too hates the regime, but it was important to him to help all he could, especially the islanders who he loves.'

Only Bertie expressed surprise at this.

'So, Hendrick is a spy for us? I think I owe you and him an apology, as do most on the island, Olivia.'

'No, I understood. You didn't know and what Hendrick had done did look bad . . . And now, I don't know if he is dead or alive.' Once more the tears threatened, but then Stefan said, 'The last I heard Hendrick hadn't been caught, so I think we can assume he made it to the border. It seems that his transmitter hasn't been found either, so he may be able to contact you. He was in Bad Münstereifel, wasn't he?'

'Yes.'

'Well, it is about eight hours from there to Switzerland by car. But maybe three days' walking.'

Olivia hardly dared to hope. With all that had happened, she knew that if she did anything else, she would break altogether. She just needed to focus on the good things, like seeing her beloved Karl and Annie and Janey and their mum, and her beloved Cissy.

Once she did, she wouldn't leave them again until the end of the war, but even then, she would hope to stay as there was nothing in Guernsey for her any more. And Britain and the Allies *would* win the war. She would never let herself think any different to that.

# Chapter Thirty

## Annie

Broken, but keeping herself together for the others, Annie arrived back home. The past two nights were a blur, but now she felt that she had a world of responsibilities on her shoulders.

Anxious villagers who relied on Rose's sprawling farm had come to see her, looking a little ashamed at having to mention their concerns but worried about their jobs.

One had told her that a 'Ranking and Tottal' were the solicitors' firm in Maidstone who Rose and Alfie had dealt with. He'd seen Mr Tottal visiting with paperwork not long after Rose arrived.

She'd asked them if they could carry on with their jobs as before and she would try to sort everything out.

Wanting to curl up and die when she reached home, the way that Karl, Beth, and Ian clung to her and went everywhere she did, even sitting outside the lav while she was in there, made her make a supreme effort to do all she must do to keep them all going.

Losing all she had felt like something that had happened to someone else, and nothing to do with her.

\* \* \*

Getting out of bed the next morning proved difficult with them all in various positions around her on Janey's double bed, but she made an effort to, and then nearly tripped over something lying at the end of the bed. It was Loes.

'I am sorry, I did not want to be on my own.'

'It's all right, luv. We'll most likely all sleep together in the shelter most nights, but the siren didn't go off, so we've been lucky.'

'You make me feel safe, Annie. You are so very brave.'

Annie couldn't answer this. Instead, she resorted to sorting out the coming day.

'I'm going to contact Potter and Gardener today, Loes, and tell them what has happened. I'm hoping they will help me with everything – this place, the farm, and registering everyone's deaths.'

She plonked back down on the bottom of the bed. 'I just can't take it all in, Loes.'

'I know. It is as if it didn't happen, and yet it did.'

'Yes, it did . . . Oh, how are we to get through it all?'

'I will help you, Annie. I will try to be strong. I can look after the children and see to all the meals.'

'I don't know if it can be here, though, Loes. I can't stand it. It seems alive with them all and yet it will never be so again. I want to cry.'

This pulled Annie up. The times she'd told Janey to cry, but now she knew that if she did, she would never stop. *Oh, Janey, the pain of losing you all is like I'm cut in two.*

Brushing this thought away with actions, she told Loes, 'Come on, let's get dressed and get breakfast for the kids. Despite everything, they're still always hungry. You put some porridge on while I use the bathroom then I'll wake them when I'm ready and while you wash and dress, I'll see that they are.'

Once in the bathroom, Annie leaned over the sink and clung on to it as if it was a life saver. But it wasn't. *Everything in me life has gone! I don't even have Lucy to turn to. Nothing could ever be a life saver to me again, other than me Ricky coming home.*

She ran the cold water and splashed her face and told herself that she still had the kids, and Loes, and one day she would have Ricky, Olivia and Lucy back too. She stopped herself from doubting this as she had to hang on to something.

By mid-afternoon, she had unloaded all her problems onto Mr Potter. He told her he would take all of it in hand and report back to her very soon.

It was three days later that he did. It appeared that when Janey had gone to see him about her divorce, he had advised her to make a will.

If Janey died first, the house was to pass to Annie, and then to Beth with the proviso that Annie adopted Beth. Janey also left it that Annie could do as she wanted. If she no longer wanted to live there, she could sell it. In which case, she was to put half of the money made from it into trust for Beth.

Janey had made provisions for Mum too, saying that she and Cissy must be allowed to live in the house for as long as they wished.

This cut Annie in two. Mr Potter had been so kind and had comforted her. But she hadn't completely broken down.

On the matter of Rose's farm, Mr Potter had contacted the firm of solicitors and it appeared that it would all come to Beth. And that if she was a minor at the time of Rose's death, and Alfie hadn't outlived her, then arrangements were to be made for a farm manager to be put in place with her solicitor being a countersigner on all transactions. This would cease when Beth was twenty-one, and then her wishes would be carried out.

With all this in hand, Annie, though exhausted and torn apart, had one more thing to settle. But doubts as to whether her status would fit the criteria needed had hounded her. Her heart pounded as she told Mr Potter, 'I want to fulfil Janey's wishes and adopt Beth, but what about Ian? . . . I cannot give him up, I need to know he is mine too,' she pleaded from her soul.

She needn't have worried. Mr Potter had told her that he didn't see any problems with that at all and he would see to papers being drawn up for both Beth and Ian to become legally her children.

Not thinking anything could lift her heart again, Annie found that this had. A small part of her knew hope as she went along to the police station.

There, it was difficult for her to contain herself, but she managed it.

When she walked out, she wondered if she would ever go back, for now she had been put on long-term compassionate leave with half pay – a relief to her in all this hardship as at least she knew she could put food on the table.

It was a week later that her sergeant appeared at the door. What he told her shocked her, and lifted her spirits all at the same time.

Olivia was here in England! She and Daphne were in hospital in Southampton suffering with shock and exposure. The Guernsey man with them was all right.

'I believe he's called Bertie.'

'Oh, I know him and Daphne, so they're all safe. Did Bertie save them?'

'No, it was a German officer.'

Nothing could have shocked Annie more. She couldn't imagine a German being with Olivia! 'He's now a prisoner of war, but he's also a hero as he saved Olivia from prison after she was found to be a spy.'

'Oh, God! And Hendrick? Has he been caught?'

'I don't know. The War Office will inform you further.'

'But Olivia is safe?'

'Yes. She is recovering well.'

Annie felt like hugging her sarge. 'Annie, luv, we're all here for you. At any time, you can call on me, me wife, or anyone at the station. We're all so sorry.'

She didn't know how it happened, but she leaned towards him, and his arms came around her. He held her how she imagined her dad would have done if he'd have lived.

Her tears threatened, but she wouldn't give them rein. She dared not.

'Is there anything we can do, Annie, luv?'

'Can you take me to Olivia?'

'I can. I will do it personally, as I have a couple of days' leave. But you need to take clothing for them all, Annie. I can lend something for the gentleman if it will fit him. Is he around my size?'

'Yes, but it's all right, I've got plenty of clothes here from Olivia's apartment. Loes brought what Olivia and her father had left behind when we were moving them into the basement flat.'

Two days later, Annie was in Olivia's arms with Daphne's arm around her shoulder.

'Oh, Annie, Annie, you're safe! Is my little Karl safe too?'

'He is, luv, he's with me at home in Bethnal.'

'But the bombings?'

'He's safe, I promise you, me darlin'.'

Annie had been told that they were all strong enough to be discharged, so she encouraged Olivia that they should get dressed and ready.

Once they were they sat in the corridor, deciding what to do, Daphne told them that they hadn't seen or heard what had happened to Stefan . . . 'You see, he and I are in love, Annie.'

Annie squeezed her hand. She was trying desperately not to break.

The sergeant told them what he knew about Stefan, and that once they were home, he would make enquiries.

Poor Daphne looked downcast, but Annie had no more comfort to give her. Her heart was hurting too much. Her lovely Olivia was a shadow of the girl she'd known. Her eyes were sunk into dark sockets, her skin was bruised, her cheeks blotched and red, and her clothes hung on her.

Not dwelling on this, Annie dealt with the practical things needed as she didn't feel she could ask Olivia what had happened or tell her what she had been through. Not with everyone there.

'There's no need for any of you to worry. You all have a home with me.'

Olivia didn't react, or ask how they would all fit in. She was staring at Bertie. Out of the blue, she said, 'Daddy won't need his clothes any more, Annie.'

The gasp that followed this had Annie clinging on to Olivia and yet feeling confused too. Had something happened to Olivia's father?

With this thought, she knew the time was on her. Both she and Olivia needed to talk. 'Are you strong enough to go for a walk with me, Olivia? I've brought coats for you all.'

Olivia nodded. 'Yes. I so want to talk to you, Annie.'

The sarge latched on to this. 'I'll take Bertie and Daphne for a cup of tea at that cafe we passed, Annie. You go into the grounds with Olivia. I'll pick you up in half an hour, luv.'

Once outside they found a bench. Neither of them seemed to feel the cold but they sat down and held hands.

'What happened to your dad, Olivia, luv?'

With her mouth stretched wide and her eyes tumbling tears, Olivia gasped out, 'They shot him, and Jean, our cook.'

Annie broke.

She clung on to Olivia and sobbed out what had happened to Mum, Janey, Cissy, Rose and Lilly, even mentioning Fran, though Olivia didn't know her. 'Oh, Olivia, I've lost them all.' Between sobs she told how Karl and Beth and Loes had been saved. 'And you will meet Ian, too.'

Their sobs became howls as they sat there in each other's arms.

It was Annie who straightened first.

'But we'll get through it, Olivia. We must for the children and for Ricky and Hendrick, for they will make it home, Olivia. We have to believe that.'

Olivia straightened too.

'As long as I have you by my side, I will get through, Annie, and I'll support you all the way too. Like you say, we have the children, and we're not alone. We have Loes, Daphne and Bertie.'

'And me sarge. He and everyone at the station have been my rocks, they'll all stand by us. We have to do this, Olivia.'

'We can, Annie. We can do everything asked of us. We're strong. No German is going to bring us to our knees.'

Annie managed a smile. 'Just let them try and they'll find themselves up against the Guernsey Girls!'

They stood then and hugged before, arm in arm, they walked towards their unknown future, with one certainty: they would do it together, and together they would face all it threw at them.

# Acknowledgements

To the team at Pan Macmillan for all the attention they give to my books: my commissioning editor, Wayne Brookes, who for ten years oversaw the umpteen processes that my books go through; for his cheerful encouragement and optimism – a joy to work with. And to Lucy Brem, my new editor, who has made the changeover of editors so smooth for me and is now supporting me whenever I need it. My editorial team headed by Lucy Hale, and desk editorial team headed by Rosa Watmough, whose work brings out the very best of my story to make it shine. Victoria Hughes-Williams, who is responsible for the structural edit and makes sure the story flows. And my publicist, Chloe Davies, and her team, who seek out many opportunities for me to showcase my work. The cover designer and the sales team who make sure my book stands out on the shelf. My heartfelt thanks go to you all.

And a special thank you to:

My son, James Wood, who reads so many versions of my work to help and advise me, and who works alongside me on the edits that come in. I love you so very much.

My readers, who encourage me on as they await another book, supporting me every step of the way and who warm my heart with praise in their reviews.

Paul Falla, the Guernsey taxi driver, who helped me so much with my research when I visited the island. Thank you, you made my day perfect.

But no one person stands alone. My family are amazing. They give me an abundance of love and support, and when one of them says they are proud of me, my world is complete. My special thanks to all. You are all my rock and help me to climb my mountain. I love you with all my heart.

# *Letter to Readers*

Dear reader,

Hi. To have reached this point in my book means you have now read of Olivia's and Annie's experiences during the war, and are probably still shedding tears, as I was for several minutes after I wrote the final words. I hope, though, that you have enjoyed my work. Thank you so much for choosing it.

You may have read the first in the series too. If not, and you enjoyed this one, maybe you can now catch up with how the girls became friends and all they went through to get to this point, as well as the joy and happiness they experienced in *The Guernsey Girls*.

There is still one more in the series to come, in December 2024: *The Guernsey Girls Find Peace*. More about this below.

But first, I wanted to tell you about the next step for me, which I am very excited about. And that is that I will be writing stand-alone novels for a time. I am so looking forward to completing my characters' stories in one book. I hope this format will suit you all too, as I am already beavering away writing the first of these.

Once a book does catch your eye, whether it be in the

supermarket, the bookstore or the library, and you then go on to enjoy it, may I ask you to think about the author and how much she/he needs her book to be noticed and to be read?

To help with this process and to show your appreciation, the very best thing you can do is to leave a review – let other people know how the book entertained you, involved you emotionally and took you into another world. Doing so is like hugging an author. My heart soars when I see a review for my work, or when someone takes the time and trouble to contact me.

I love interacting with readers and will always personally reply to emails and messages. You can see my contact details below.

And so to the last of the series, already mentioned: *The Guernsey Girls Find Peace*. I researched this series by visiting Guernsey as part of a cruise around the British Isles. We only had one day in St Peter Port, Guernsey, and so I booked a private taxi online before we left home. This was so that I could be taken to the places I needed to see instead of joining the conventional tour. My guide was taxi driver Paul Falla of Guernsey Taxis, who greatly enhanced my knowledge and took me to un-touristy places I might never have explored. I learnt such a lot about how it was for the people of Guernsey to live under occupation, and then how they adjusted when peacetime came.

This book will follow Olivia as she endures the hardships of the island's invasion; courageously soldiers on with receiving and sending messages; helps her fellow islanders; and then finds herself in extreme danger as her radio is discovered. What she goes through as a consequence will tear you apart, as will what Annie endures back in London as she tries to keep her family, including Olivia's little Karl and his nanny, together; she will have to make sacrifices to ensure their safety during the Blitz. A safety that proves heartbreaking.

But, by the time you get to the end, your heart will be mended, as theirs are, and a conclusion to their journey will be reached as they find the peace they seek. I am excited for publication day. To be sure of your copy, you can pre-order from Amazon.

As mentioned, I would love to hear from you, and am available for talks to any groups, and in your local library. Here are my contact details to chat, or for bookings:

My Facebook page, where you can 'like' and 'follow' me: www.facebook.com/MaryWoodAuthor
My Instagram: www.instagram.com/mary.wood.7796420
My TikTok: www.tiktok.com/@marywood616
My X: www.twitter.com/Authormary

And for news and email contact: my website: www.authormarywood.com/contact

Take care of yourselves and others.
Much love,
Mary xxx

# The Forgotten Daughter

## Book One in
## The Girls Who Went to War series

From a tender age, Flora felt unloved and unwanted by her parents, but she finds safety in the arms of caring Nanny Pru. But when Pru is cast out of the family home, under a shadow of secrets and with a baby boy of her own on the way, it shatters little Flora.

Over the years, however, Flora and Pru meet in secret – unbeknown to Flora's parents. Pru becomes the mother she never had, and Flora grows into a fine young woman. When she signs up as a volunteer with St John Ambulance, she begins to shape her life. But the drum of war beats loudly and her world is turned upside down when she receives a letter asking her to join the Red Cross in Belgium.

With the fate of the country in the balance, it is a time for bravery. Flora's determined to be the strong woman she was destined to be. But with horror, loss and heartache on her horizon, there's a lot for young Flora to learn . . .

The Girls Who Went to War series continues with *The Abandoned Daughter*, *The Wronged Daughter* and *The Brave Daughters*, all available to read now.

# The Orphanage Girls

## Children deserve a family to call their own

Ruth dares to dream of another life – far away from the horrors within the walls of Bethnal Green's infamous orphanage. Luckily she has her friends, Amy and Ellen, but she can't keep them safe, and the suffering is only getting worse. Surely there must be a way out?

But when Ruth breaks free from the shackles of confinement and sets out into East London, hoping to make a new life for herself, she finds that, for a girl with nowhere to turn, life can be just as tough on the outside.

Bett keeps order in this unruly part of the East End and she takes Ruth under her wing alongside fellow orphanage escapee Robbie. But it is Rebekah, a kindly woman, who offers Ruth and Robbie a home – something neither has ever known. Yet even these two stalwart women cannot protect them when the police learn of an orphan on the run. It is then that Ruth must do everything in her power to hide. Her life – and those of the friends she left behind at the orphanage – depend on it.

The Orphanage Girls series continues with *The Orphanage Girls Reunited* and *The Orphanage Girls Come Home*, all available to read now.